REGENCY
Temptation

Christine
Merrill

First Published in Great Britain 2017
By Mills & Boon, an imprint of HarperCollins*Publishers*
1 London Bridge Street, London, SE1 9GF

REGENCY TEMPTATION © 2017 Harlequin Books S.A.

The Greatest of Sins © 2013 Christine Merrill
The Fall of a Saint © 2014 Christine Merrill

ISBN: 978-0-263-92381-0

52-0617

The Greatest of Sins

To James:
who is living in interesting times.

Christine Merrill lives on a farm in Wisconsin, USA, with her husband, two sons and too many pets—all of whom would like her to get off of the computer so they can check their e-mail. She has worked by turns in theatre costuming and as a librarian. Writing historical romance combines her love of good stories and fancy dress with her ability to stare out of the window and make stuff up.

Chapter One

Sam was coming home!

They were such simple words to have such an effect upon her. Evelyn Thorne put a hand over her heart, feeling the frenzied beat of it at the thought of his name. How long had she been waiting for his return? Very nearly six years. He had gone off to Edinburgh when she was still in the schoolroom and she had been planning for this day ever since.

She had been sure that, following his education, he would come back for her. Some day, she would hear his light, running step on the boards of the front hallway. He would shout a welcome to Jenks, the butler, and make a joyful enquiry about her father. There would be an answering welcome call from the office at the head of the stairs, for certainly Father would be as eager to hear what his ward had made of himself as she was.

After the greetings were done with, things would return to the way they had been. They would sit in the parlor together and in the garden. She would force him to accompany her to balls and routs, which would all be less tedious with Sam there to talk to, to dance with and to protect from the marital ambitions of other girls.

At the end of the Season, he would return with them to the country. There, they would walk in the orchard and run down the path to the little pond to watch the birds and animals, lying on the rugs that he would carry, eating a picnic from a basket that she would pack with her own hands, not trusting the cook to reserve the choicest morsels for a man who was not 'truly a Thorne'.

As if to reinforce the thought, Mrs Abbott cleared her throat, from the doorway behind her. 'Lady Evelyn, would you not be more comfortable in the morning room? There is a chill in the hall. If there are guests…'

'It would be more seemly to be found there?' Eve completed with a sigh.

'If his Grace were to come…'

'But he is not the one expected, Abbott, as you know full well.'

The housekeeper gave a slight sniff of disapproval.

Evelyn turned to her, putting aside her girlish excitement. Though only one and twenty, she was mistress of the house and would be obeyed. 'I will hear none of that, from you or any other member of the staff. Doctor Hastings is as much a member of the family as I am. Perhaps more so. Father took him from the foundling home a full three years before I was even born. He has been a part of this house since my first memory and is the only brother I shall ever have.'

Of course, it had been quite some time since she had considered Sam her brother. Without thinking, she touched her lips.

Abbott's eyes narrowed slightly as she noticed the gesture.

For a moment, Eve considered making a diplomatic retreat to a receiving room. Her behaviour would be less obvious to the servants. But what message would it send to Sam if she made him come to her like an ordinary guest?

She bowed her head, as though she had considered the wisdom of Abbott's suggestion and said, 'You are right. There is a draught. If you could but bring me a shawl, I will be fine. And I shall not pace about before the window, for it will be much more comfortable on the bench beneath the stairs.' From there, she could see the front door quite well, yet be invisible to the one who entered. Her appearance would be sudden and a pleasant surprise.

As she passed it, she glanced in the hallway mirror, straightening her hair and gown, smoothing curls and fluffing ruffles. Would Sam find her pretty, now that she had grown? The Duke of St Aldric had proclaimed her the handsomest girl at Almack's and a diamond of the first water. But he was so easy in his compliments that she quite wondered if he was sincere. His manners would have required him to say such, once he had set his sights upon her.

In the same situation, Sam would have offered no false flattery. He might have pronounced her attractive.

If she had begged for more, wishing to be called beautiful, he would have accused her of vanity and named several girls that he found prettier.

Then he would have eased the sting by reminding her that she was fair enough for the average man. He would say that, for a humble man like himself, she was like a vision from heaven. Then he would smile at her, to prove that they understood each other. And his comment would make all other suitors seem unworthy.

But he'd had no chance to make such observations, because he had not come back for her first Season. He had gone straight from university, into the navy. It had been several years since. She had spent it scouring the papers for news of his ship and taking care to become the sort of woman he might hope to find when he returned. She had crossed days off the calendar and told herself each December that, next year, the wait would be over. He would come home and she would be ready for him.

But the only contact from Sam was a terse letter to Father that had outlined his plans to take a position on the *Matilda*.

And he had written not a word to her since the day he had left. She had not even heard of his appointment as a ship's surgeon until after he had set sail. There had been no chance to reason him into a safer plan. He was gone and that was that.

Three years of dragging her feet had kept her in the marriage mart. She could not possibly make a match until she had seen him again. People thought it quite odd that she had not accepted an offer already. If she refused St Aldric, she would be properly on the shelf, too high in the instep for any man. Any save one, of course.

The knock came at the door, sharp and sudden, and she started in her chair. It had not sounded the way she'd imagined it would. Although how much personality could be conveyed with a door knocker, she was not sure. All the same, it startled her.

Instead of rushing forwards to open it for him, she drew back into the little space beneath the curve of the stairs. It was cowardly of her. But the secrecy meant that she would catch the first glimpse of him without his knowing and keep the moment all to herself. She would not need to guard her expression from the servants. She could devour the sight of him, thinking of things that had nothing to do with walks in the garden and picnics by the stream.

Jenks came forwards and opened the door, his tall, straight body hiding the man on the steps. The request for entrance was firm and had a polite warmth, but it was not as impulsive or raucous as she had imagined. She had been thinking of the boy who had left, she reminded herself, not the man he had become. He would still be Sam, of course. But he was changed, just as she was.

The person who appeared in the doorway was a strange combination of novelty and familiarity. He walked with the upright gait of a military man, but was free of the scars and disabilities she had seen in so many returning officers. Of course, he had spent his time well away from the battle proper, below decks, tending to the injuries that resulted from it.

He was still blond, although the reddish highlights in his hair had gone dark, almost brown. The boyish softness had left his cheeks, replaced by a firm jaw line scraped clean of stubble. His eyes were still blue, of course, and as sharp and inquisitive as ever. They took in the hall at a glance, looking at it much the same as she was looking at him, noting changes and similarities. He completed the survey with a brief nod before enquiring if her father was at home to visitors.

The boy she remembered had had a sunny disposition, an easy smile and a hand always reaching out to help or to comfort, but the man who stood before her now, in a navy-blue coat, was sombre. One might call him grave. She supposed it was a necessity of his profession. One did not want a doctor delivering bad news with a smile upon his face. But it was more than that. Though his eyes held great compassion, they were bleak, as though he suffered along with the suffering.

She wanted to ask if his life in the navy had been as horrible as she'd imagined. Had it troubled him to see so many mangled bodies and to do so little for them? Were the successes he had won from death enough to compensate for the brutality of war? Had it really changed him so much? Or did anything remain of the boy who had left her?

Now that he was back, she wanted to ask so many things. Where had he been? What had he done there? And, most importantly, why had he left her? She had thought, as they had grown past the age of playmates, that they were likely to become something much more.

His current disposition, as he passed her hiding place and followed Jenks up the stairs, was a stark contrast to St Aldric, who always seemed to be smiling. Though the duke had many responsibilities, his face was not as careworn, or marked, as Sam's. He greeted obstacles with optimism. But he had a right to do so. There seemed little that he could not accomplish.

In looks, she could see many similarities between the two men. Both were fair and blue eyed. But St Aldric was the taller of the two and the handsomer as well. In all things physical, he was the superior. He had more power, more money, rank and title.

And yet he was not Sam. She sighed. No amount of common sense would sway her heart from its choice. If she accepted the inevitable offer, she would be quite happy with St Aldric, but she would never love him.

But if the person one truly loved above all others was not interested, what was one to do?

Just now, he had gone straight to her father, without enquiring of Lady Evelyn's location. Perhaps he did not care. In his silent absence, Samuel Hastings seemed to be saying that he did not remember her in the same way she did him. Perhaps he still thought of her as a childhood friend and not a young lady of marriageable age who might have formed an attachment to him.

Did he not remember the kiss? When it had happened, she had been sure of her feelings.

Apparently, he had not. After, he'd grown cold and

distant. She could not believe that he was the sort of youth who would steal a kiss just to prove that he could. Had she done something to offend? Perhaps she had been too eager. Or not enthusiastic enough. But how could he have expected her to know what to do? It had been her first kiss.

It had changed everything between them. Overnight, his smile had disappeared. And, shortly thereafter, he had been gone in body as well as spirit.

Even if she had misunderstood, she would have thought that he might have written a note of farewell. Or he could have answered at least one of the letters she'd sent to him, dutifully, every week. Perhaps he had not received them. On one of his brief visits home from school, she had enquired of them. He had admitted, with a curt nod and a frozen smile, that he had read them. But he'd added nothing to indicate that the messages provided any comfort or pleasure.

It was a moot point now, of course. When one had captured the attention of a duke, who was not only powerful and rich, but handsome, polite and charming, one should not lament over a snub from a physician of no real birth.

She sighed again. All the same, it had been much on her mind of late. Even if he did not love her, Sam had been her friend. Her dearest, closest companion. She wanted his opinion of St Aldric: of the man, and of her decision. If there was any reason that he disapproved…

Of course, there could not be. He would bring no last-minute reprieve with an offer of his own. And she must remind herself that it was not exactly a march to the gallows, becoming Her Grace, the Duchess of St Aldric.

But if he did not want her, the least Dr Samuel Hastings could do was give his congratulations. And that might make it possible for her to move forwards.

'A ship's surgeon.' Lord Thorne's tone was flat with disapproval. 'Is that not a job that can be done by a carpenter? Surely a university-trained physician could have done better.'

Sam Hastings faced his benefactor's dark look with military posture and an emotionless stare. He could remember a time when his actions had met with nothing but approval from this man. In response, Sam had been eager to please and desperately afraid of disappointing him. But it seemed that his best efforts to abide by Thorne's final instructions to 'make something of yourself' were to be met with argument and doubt.

So be it. His need to prove himself had cooled when Thorne's affection had. 'On the contrary, sir. On most ships, they are forced by a scarcity of skill to make do with any willing man. While they often employ the carpenter's mate for the job, no one wants to be the man's first patient. I am sure both captain and crew appreciated my help. I saved more limbs than I took. I gained experience with many diseases that I might never have seen had I remained ashore. There were some tropical fevers that were quite challenging. The time not spent in action was spent in study. There are many hours in the normal running of the ship that can be devoted to education.'

'Hmmmpf.' His guardian's foul mood turned to resignation, when presented with reasonable opposition. 'If you could find no other way to get sufficient experience, then I suppose it had to do.'

'And it was quite far away,' Sam added, subtly colouring the words. 'When I left, you encouraged me to travel.'

'That is true.' Now Thorne was circumspect, which might be as close as Sam could get to approval. 'And you have made no plans towards marriage? I encouraged you to that as well.'

'Not as yet, sir. There was little opportunity, when so totally in the company of men. But I have ample prize money in the bank and a plan to set up practice.'

'In London?' Thorne said, brows furrowing.

'In the north,' Sam assured him. 'I can certainly afford wife and family. I am sure there will be some woman not averse…' He left the ending open, not wanting to lie outright. Let Thorne think what he liked. There would be no marriage, no children, no future of that sort at all.

'Evelyn, of course, is on the cusp of a great match,' Thorne said, as though relieved to change the subject. He smiled with obvious pride of his only daughter. For Sam's sake, the words were delivered with an air of finality.

Sam nodded. 'So I was given to understand by your letters. She is to marry a duke?'

Now, Thorne was beaming with satisfaction. 'Despite his rank, St Aldric is the most magnanimous of gentlemen. He is so full of good humour and generosity that his friends have shortened the title to Saint.'

Evie had won herself a saint, had she? It was no less than she deserved. Sam had best keep as far away from her as possible. His own nature proved him to be as far from that lofty state as it was possible to be. 'Evelyn is the most fortunate of young ladies to gain such a husband.'

'It is a shame that you cannot stay to meet him. He is expected this afternoon.' It was as blunt as shutting the door in his face. Being 'like a member of the family' was not the same as recognised kinship. Now that he was raised and settled in a trade, Thorne felt no responsibility to him at all.

'A pity, indeed. But, of course, I cannot stay,' Sam agreed. It was just as well. He had no real desire to meet this Saint who would marry his Evie, or remain under the Thorne roof a moment more than was necessary. 'You will give my regards to Lady Evelyn, of course.' He added her title carefully, to avoid any sign of familiarity.

'Of course,' her father said. 'And now, I do not wish to keep you.'

'Of course not.' Sam managed a smile and rose, as though this brief visit had been his intent all along, and his departure had nothing to do with the abrupt dismissal. 'I only wished to thank you, sir, and to remind you of the difference your patronage has meant to my life. A letter hardly seemed appropriate.' Sam offered a stiff bow to the man who had claimed to be his benefactor.

Thorne got up from his desk and clapped him by the shoulder, smiling as he had of old. That such approval could only come by his leaving was another bitter reminder of how things had changed. 'I am touched, my boy. And it is good to know that you are doing well. Will we see you, again, while you are in London? For the wedding, perhaps?' When it was too late for him to do any harm.

'I do not know. My plans are not yet set.' If he could find a ship in need of his services, he would be gone with the tide. And if not? Perhaps there was some distant spot in Scotland or Ireland that had need of a physician.

'You are welcome, of course. We will have much to celebrate. Little Eve is not so little any more. St Aldric has been quite set on the match, since the beginning of the Season, but she has yet to answer him. I have told her that it does not do to play with the affections of a duke. She will not listen.' Thorne still smiled, as though even her disobedience was a treasure, which of course, to him, it was.

If he had continued to indulge her every whim, she had likely grown into a wilful hoyden. She would run wild without a strong man to partner her. Himself, for instance... Sam put the thought from his head. 'She will come round in time, I am sure, sir.' With luck, he would be gone without seeing it happen. If she had not decided, it would be disaster to hang about here and run the risk of muddying her mind with his presence.

He and Thorne went through the motions of an amicable parting as he walked towards the door of the room, but it went no further than that. They might as well have been strangers, for all the emotion expressed. There had been a time when Sam had longed for a deeper bond of affection. But now that he knew the truth of their relationship, he would as soon have never met the man. It took only a few more empty promises to keep in contact, before the interview was at an end and he was out of the office and retreating down the main stairs of the house he had once thought his home.

Only a few more feet and he would be out the front door and away. But a departure without incident was unlikely, since, as he had climbed the stairs to Thorne's office, he had known that *she* waited, scant feet away.

When he had passed through on the hallway, he had taken great care not to look too closely at the place she must be concealed. He did not want to see her. It would make leaving all the more difficult.

But as he'd approached the house, a part of him had feared that she would not be there to greet him. That poor fool had wanted to search the corners for her, to hold out his arms and call out her name. He would be equally foolish to suffer if she did not come to him, or if she had already gone into the arms and the house of another. One could not bring back the past, especially when one found that the happiness there had been based on ignorance and illusion.

The door had opened and he had not seen her. Torn between fear and relief, he had been afraid to enquire after her. But then, as he had passed her hiding place, he had smelled her perfume.

That was not wholly accurate. He could smell a woman's scent in the air of the hall, fresh and growing stronger as he neared the alcove at the curve of the stairs. He could not be sure it was her. The girl he had left had smelled of lemon soap and the mildest lavender eau de toilette. This new perfume was redolent of India, mysterious, sharp and sophisticated.

He should have simply turned and acknowledged her. He'd have caught her hiding at the base of the stairs, for he was sure that was what she had been doing, just as she had done when they were children. He could have pretended that nothing was amiss and greeted her easily, as an old friend ought. They could have exchanged pleasantries. Then he could have wished her well and they'd have parted again after a few words.

But the fragrance had been an intoxicant to him and he would have needed all his wits for even a few words of greeting. If he could not master himself, there was no telling what his first words would have been. So he had taken the coward's way, pretending that he was unaware of her presence and hoping that she would have given up in the hour of the interview and gone back to the morning room, or wherever it was that she spent her days.

He could not imagine his Evie, sitting like a lady on a divan or at a writing desk, prepared to offer a gracious but chilly welcome and banal conversation. He had spent too many years brooding on the memory of how she had been, not wanting her to change. He could picture her in the garden, running, climbing and sitting on the low tree branches he had helped her to, when no one had been there to stop them.

Yet she would have put that behaviour aside, just as she had the eau de toilet. She had grown up. She was to be a duchess. The girl he remembered was gone, replaced by a *ton*-weary flirt with poise enough to keep a duke dangling. Once he had met that stranger, perhaps he could finally be free of her and have some peace.

Then, as he reached the bottom step, she pelted out from hiding and into him, body to body, her arms around his neck, and called, 'Tag.' Her lips were on his cheeks, first one, then the other, in a pair of sisterly but forceful kisses.

He froze, body and mind stunned to immobility. With preparation, he had controlled his first reaction to her nearness. But this sudden and complete contact was simply too much. His arms had come halfway up to hug her before he'd managed to stop them and now they poked stiffly out at the elbows, afraid to touch her, unable to show any answering response. 'Evie,' he managed in a tone as stiff as his posture. 'Have you learned no decorum at all in six years?'

'Not a whit, Sam,' she said, with a laugh. 'You did not think to escape me so easily, did you?'

'Of course not.' Hadn't he tried, going nearly to the ends of the earth to do so? If that had been a failure, what was he to do now? 'I'd have greeted you properly, had you given me the chance,' he lied. He reached up and pried her arms from his neck, stepping away from her.

She gave him a dour frown, meant to be an imitation of his own expression, he was sure. Then she laughed again. 'Because we must always be proper, mustn't we, Dr Hastings?'

He took another step back to dodge the second embrace that he knew was coming, taking her hands to avoid the feeling of her body wriggling eagerly against his. 'We are no longer children, Evelyn.'

'I should hope not.' She gave him a look that proved she was quite aware that she, at least, had grown into a desirable young woman. 'I have been out for three Seasons.'

'And kept half the men in London dangling from your reticule strings, I don't doubt.' Lud, but she was pretty enough to do it. Hair as straight and smooth as spun gold, eyes as blue as the first flowers of spring and lips that made his mouth water to taste them. And he might have known the contours of her body, had he taken the opportunity to touch it as she'd kissed him.

The thought nearly brought him to his knees.

She shrugged as if it did not matter to her what other men thought and gave him the sort of look, with lowered lashes and slanted eyes, that told a man that the woman before him cared only about him. 'And what is your diagnosis, Doctor, now that you have had a chance to examine me?'

'You look well,' he said, cursing the inadequacy of the words.

She pouted and the temptress dissolved into his old friend, swinging her arms as though inviting him to play. 'If that is all I shall have out of you, I am most disappointed, sir. I have been told by other men that I am quite the prettiest girl of the Season.'

'And that is why St Aldric has offered for you,' he said, reminding them both of how much had changed.

She frowned, but did not let go of his hands. 'As yet, I have not accepted any offers.'

'Your father told me that, just now. He said you are keeping the poor fellow on tenterhooks waiting for an answer. It is most unfair of you, Evelyn.'

'It is most unfair of Father to pressure me on the subject,' she replied, avoiding the issue. 'And even worse, it is unscientific of you to express an opinion based on so little evidence.' She smiled again. 'I would much rather you tell me what you think of my marrying, after we have had some time together.'

'I stand by my earlier conclusion,' he said. It made him sound like one of those pompous asses who would rather stick to a bad diagnosis than admit the possibility of error. 'Congratulations are in order. Your father says St Aldric is a fine man and I have no reason to doubt it.'

She gave him a dark, rather vague look, and then smiled. 'How nice to know that you and my father are in agreement on the subject of my future happiness. Since you are dead set in seeing me married, I assume you have come prepared?'

He had fallen into a trap of some kind, he was sure. And here was one more proof that this was not the transparent child he had left, who could not keep a secret. Before him was a woman, clearly angry at his misstep, but unwilling to tell him what he had said, or how he was to make amends. 'Prepared?' he said, cautiously, looking for some hint in her reaction.

'To celebrate my imminent engagement,' she finished, still waiting. She then gave an exasperated sigh to show him that he was hopeless. 'By giving me some token to commemorate the event.'

'A gift?' Her audacity startled a smile from him and a momentary loss of control.

'My gift,' she said, firmly. 'You cannot have been away so long, missed birthdays and Christmases and a possible engagement, and brought me nothing. Must I search your pockets to find it?'

He thought of her hands, moving familiarly over his body, and said hurriedly, 'Of course not. I have it here, of course.'

He had nothing. There had been the gold chain that he'd bought for her in Minorca and then could not raise the nerve to send. He had carried it about in his pocket for a year, imagining the way it would look against the skin of her throat. Then he'd realised that it was only making the memories more vivid, more graphic, and had thrown it into the bay.

'Well?' She had noticed his moment of confusion and was tugging upon his lapel, an eager child again.

He thrust a hand into his pocket and brought out

the first thing he found, an inlaid wood case that held a small brass spyglass. 'This. I had it with me, very nearly the whole time. At sea they are dead useful. I thought, perhaps, you could use it in the country. Watching birds.'

Any other woman in London would have thrust the thing back at him in disgust, pointing out that he had not even taken the time to polish the barrel.

But not his Evie. When she opened the box, her face lit as though he had handed her a casket of jewels. Then she pulled out the glass, gave it a hurried wipe against her skirt to shine it and extended it and put it to her eye. 'Oh, Sam. It is wonderful.' She pulled him to the nearest window and peered out through it, looking as she always had, into the distance, as though she could see the future. 'The people on the other side of the square are as clear as if I was standing beside them.' She took it away from her face and grinned at him. The expression was so like the way he remembered her that his heart hurt. She was standing beside him again, so close that an accidental touch was inevitable. He withdrew quickly, ignoring the flood of memories that her nearness brought.

She seemed unmoved by his discomfort, sighing in pleasure at her improved vision. 'I will take it to the country, of course. And to Hyde Park and the opera.'

He laughed. 'If you actually need a glass in town, I will buy you a lorgnette. With such a monstrous thing pressed to your eye, you will look like a privateer.'

She let out a derisive puff of air. 'What do I care

what people think? It will be so much easier to see the stage.' She gave a sly grin. 'And I will be able to spy on the other members of the audience. That is the real reason we all go to the theatre. Nothing in London shall escape me. I share the gossip the next day and show them my telescope. In a week, all the smart girls will have them.'

'Wicked creature.' Without thinking, he reached up and tugged on one honey-coloured lock. She had not changed a bit in his absence, still fresh faced, curious and so alive that he could feel her vitality coursing in the air around them.

'Let us go and watch something.' She took his hand, her fingers twining with his, pulling him back into the house and towards the doors that led to the garden that had been their haven.

And he was lost.

Chapter Two

He ought to have known better. Before coming, Sam had steeled himself against temptation with prayer. His plan had been to resist all contact with her. Just moments before, he had assured her father that he would be gone. And yet, at the first touch of her hand, he had forgotten it all and followed her through the house like a puppy on a lead.

Now he sat at her side on a little stone bench under the elm as she experimented with her new toy. It was just like hundreds of other happy afternoons spent here and it reminded him of how much he missed home, and how much a part of that home she was.

Evie held the spyglass firmly pointed into the nearest tree. 'There is a nest. And three young ones all open mouthed and waiting to be fed. Oh, Sam, it is wonderful.'

It was indeed. He could see the flush of pleasure on her cheek and the way it curved down into the familiar dimple of her smile. So excited, and over such a small thing as a nest of birds. But had she not always been just so? Joy personified and a tonic to a weary soul.

'You can adjust it, just by turning here.' He reached out and, for a moment, his hand covered hers. The shock of connection was as strong as ever. It made him wonder—did she still feel it as well? If so, she was as good at dissembling as he, for she gave no response.

'That is ever so much better. I can make out individual feathers.' She looked away from the birds, smiling at him, full of mischief. 'I clearly made the best bargain out of your empty pockets today, sir.'

'I beg your pardon?'

'If you had reached in and pulled out a snuff box, I'd have had a hard time developing the habit of taking it. But a telescope is very much to my liking.'

'Was it so obvious that I did not bring you anything?' he asked, sighing.

'The look of alarm on your face was profound,' she admitted and snapped the little cylinder shut to put it back into its case. 'But do not think that you can get this away from me by distracting me with a necklace. It is mine now and I shan't return it.'

'Nor would I expect you to.' He smiled back at her and felt the easy familiarity washing over him in a comfortable silence. With six years, thousands of miles travelled and both of them grown, none of the important things had changed between them. She was still his soul's mate. At least he could claim it was more than lust that he felt for her.

She broke the silence. 'Tell me about your travels.'

'There is not enough time to tell you all the things I have seen,' he said. But now that she had asked, the temptation to try was great and the words rushed out of him. 'Birds and plants that are nothing like you find in England. And the look of the ocean, wild or becalmed, or the sky before a storm, when there is no land in sight? The best word I can find for it is majesty. Sea and heaven stretching as far as the eye can see in all directions and us just a spot in the middle.'

'I should very much like to see that,' she said wistfully.

He imagined her, at his side, lying on the deck to look at the stars. And then he put the dream carefully away. 'Wonderful though some times were, I would not have wished them on you if it meant you saw the rest. A ship of the line is no place for a woman.'

'Was naval life really so harsh?'

'During battle, there was much for me to do,' he admitted evasively, not wanting to share the worst of it.

'But you helped the men,' she said, her face shining when she said it, as though there was something heroic about simply doing his job. 'And that was what you always wanted to do. I am sure it was most gratifying.'

'True,' he agreed. He had felt useful. And it had been a relief to find a place where he seemed to fit, after so much doubt.

'If it made you happy, then I should like to have seen that as well,' she said firmly.

'Most certainly not!' He did not want to think of her, mixed in with the blood and death. Nor did he want to lose her admiration, when she saw him helpless in the face of things that had no cure.

She gave him a pained look. 'Have you forgotten so much? Was it not I who encouraged you in your medical studies? I watched you tend every injured animal you found and dissect the failures. I swear, you did not so much eat in those days as study the anatomy of the chops.'

'I could just as easily have become butcher, for all I learned there,' he admitted. 'But working over a person is quite a different thing.' Sometimes, it was its own form of butchery.

'You learned human anatomy in Edinburgh,' she said. 'Through dissection.'

He suppressed a smile and nodded. Evie was as fearless as she had always been, and no less grisly, despite her refined appearance.

'You did many other things as well, I'm sure.'

'I observed,' he corrected. 'It was not until I left school that I could put the skills to use. Now I am thinking of returning to Scotland,' he said, to remind them both that he could not stay. 'I still have many friends at the university. Perhaps I might lecture.'

She shook her head. 'That is too far away.'

That was why he had suggested it. She was clinging to his sleeve again, as though she could not bear to have him taken from her. He considered detaching her fingers, but it was very near to having her touch his hand, so he left them remain as they were. 'You will be far too busy with your new life to waste time upon me. I doubt you will miss me at all.'

'You know that is not true. Did I not write you often in the last years? Nearly every week, yet you never answered.' Her voice grew quiet and, in it, he could hear the hurt he had caused her.

'Probably because I did not receive your letters,' he said, as though it had not mattered to him. 'The mail is a precarious thing, when one is at sea.' He had received it often enough. And he had cherished it. In the years they'd been apart, her correspondence had grown from a neat ribbon-bound stack to a small chest, packed tightly with well-thumbed missives, so familiar to him that he could recite their contents from memory.

'You had no such excuse at university,' she reminded him. 'I wrote then as well. But you did not answer those letters, either. It rather appeared to me that you had forgotten me.'

'Never,' he said fervently. That, at least, was the truth.

'Well, I will not allow it to happen again. Edinburgh is too far. You must stay close. And if you must teach, then teach me.'

He laughed, to cover the shock. It was not possible, for so many reasons. While he was not totally unwilling to share the information, he did not dare. She was a grown woman and not some curious girl. Discussing the intimate details of the human body would be difficult with any female. But with Evie, it would be impossible.

And if she was to marry, their circles would be so different that even casual conversation would be infrequent. Next to a duke, he would be little better than a tradesman.

'You know that is not proper,' he said at last. 'Your father would not allow it. Nor would your husband.' They both must remember that there would be another man standing between them.

And more than that.

He was forgetting himself again—and forgetting the reason he had to stay away. They could not be friends any more than they could be lovers. He had spent years away from her, known other women and prayed for a return to common sense. Nothing had dulled his feelings for her. The desire was just as strong and the almost palpable need to rush to her, catch her in his arms and hold her until the world steadied again. If she married, it would be no different. He would still want her. He would simply add the sin of adultery to an already formidable list.

He patted her hand in a way that showed a proper, brotherly affection. 'No, Evie. I cannot allow you to spin wild plans, as you did when we were children. I must go back to my life and you to yours.'

'But you are staying in London for a time, aren't you?' she said, looking up at him with the bluest of eyes, full of a melting hope.

'I had not planned to.' Why could he not manage a firmer tone? He'd made it seem like he might be open to persuasion.

'You must stay for the engagement ball. And the ceremony.'

As if that would not be the most exquisite torture. 'I do not know if that is possible.'

Her hand twisted, so that her fingers tightened on his. 'I will not allow you to go. Even if I must restrain you by force.' She should know that she had not the strength to do so. But she had tried it often enough, when they were young, tackling him and trying to wrestle him to the ground in a most unladylike fashion.

The idea that she might attempt it again sounded in his mind like an alarm bell.

'Very well,' he said with a sigh, if only to make her release his hand. 'But I expect I will leave soon after. Perhaps, instead of Scotland, I shall return to sea.'

'You mustn't,' she said, gripping him even more tightly before remembering herself and relaxing her hold. 'It takes you too far away from me for too long. And although you did not speak of it, I am sure it must have been very dangerous. I would not have you put yourself at risk, again.'

It had been quite dangerous. He was sure that he could tell her stories for hours that would have her in awe. Instead, he said, 'Not really. It was a job. Nothing more than that. Unlike St Aldric, I must have employment if I am to live.' The words made him sound petulant. He should not be envious of a man that had been born to a rank he could never achieve.

She ignored the censure of the duke, which had been

childish of him. 'You must have a practice on land. I will speak to father about it. Or St Aldric.'

'Certainly not! I am quite capable of finding my own position, thank you.' In any other life, an offer of patronage from a future duchess would have been just the thing he needed. But not this woman. Never her.

'You value your independence more than our friendship,' she said, and released his hand. 'Very well, then. If there is nothing I can say that will change your mind, I will bother you no further on the subject of your career.'

There was one thing, of course. Three words from her would have him on his knees, ready to do anything she might ask.

And since they were the three words neither of them must ever speak, he would go to Edinburgh or the ends of the earth, so that he might never hear them.

Chapter Three

There was really nothing more to say. She had all but dismissed him, with her promise not to meddle in his affairs. Yet Sam was loathe to take leave of her. When would he get another such chance just to sit at her side, as they always used to? She was examining the box that held the spyglass, as though it were the answer to some mystery.

And he was watching her hands caress it. Had they been so graceful when last he'd seen them? He could remember stubby fingers and ragged nails from too much time running wild with him. Today, she had not bothered with gloves and he could see the elegant taper of each digit that rested on the wood. He could sit there happily, staring at those hands for the rest of his life.

'This is where I find you? In the garden, flirting with another. I swear, Evelyn, you are harder to catch than a wild hare. I cannot leave you alone for a moment or you shall get away from me.'

The words came from behind them and Sam flinched

as he guessed the identity of the intruder. The voice marked the end of any privacy they might have this afternoon. Or possibly for ever, assuming the duke had any brains. If Sam had been Evie's intended, he would never have allowed another man near her. He rose and turned to greet his newfound enemy face to face.

If Sam had been called to give a professional opinion on the man approaching them, he'd have proclaimed him one of the healthiest he had ever seen. Under his expensive clothing, St Aldric's form was symmetrical. There was not an ounce of fat and no sign that the perfection was achieved with padding or cinching. His limbs and spine were straight, his muscles well developed—skin, eyes, teeth and hair all clean, clear and shining with vigor. Likewise there were no wrinkles on his brow, of age or care, and no evidence in expression of anything but good humour. His gaze was benevolent intelligence, his step firm and confident. If Sam had been forced to express an opinion of another man's looks, he'd have called this one exceptionally handsome. From the toe of his boot to the top of his head, the fellow was the perfection of English manhood.

It made Sam even more conscious of how he must look in comparison. Lord Thorne might think him a threat to Evie's happiness. But with his worn blue coat, thin purse and modest future, a duke would hardly notice him. Unless Evelyn had grown to be as foolish as she was beautiful, she would have no trouble choosing the better man.

As if to prove his point, Evie rose as well and held

out her hands to the duke. She smiled warmly and greeted him with genuine affection. 'St Aldric.'

'My dear.' He took her hands and held them for a moment, and Sam felt the uncomfortable pricking of jealousy and the punishment of being forgotten. She was pulling the other man forwards by the hand, just as she had lured Sam to the garden to sit beside her. It was yet another proof that the communion he had felt between them was nothing more than the warmth she showed all living things.

Now she was smiling back at him with proper, sisterly pride. 'I have waited long to introduce the two of you and now I have my opportunity. Your Grace, may I present Dr Samuel Hastings.'

'The one of whom you speak so fondly. And so often.' There was a fractional pause between the two sentences, as if to indicate jealousy, or perhaps envy of the attention she paid to him.

'Your Grace?' Sam bowed, giving a peer the required respect.

The duke was watching him in silence and Sam was sure, if they had shared something as egalitarian as a handshake, it would have become a test of strength. In it, St Aldric would have felt the roughness of the calluses on his hands made by a firm grip on a bone saw, then he would have been dismissed as not quite a gentleman.

'Doctor Hastings.' But it had not taken something so common as physical contact to do that. The less-than-noble honorific had been enough. The duke's frosty demeanour thawed into a handsome smile, now that he had assured himself of Sam's inferiority. Then St Aldric gave Evie another fond smile. 'I have been quite looking forwards to meeting this paragon you have been describing to me. I swear your face fairly lights up when you speak of him.'

'Because he is my oldest and dearest friend,' Evie said dutifully. 'We were raised together.'

As brother and sister. Why would she never say it? It would make life so much easier if she would understand the significance of that.

'We spent very little time apart until he went to university,' she added.

'To be a leech,' the duke replied blandly. It made Sam feel like a parasite.

'A physician,' Evie corrected, protective of his dignity. 'He was ever so clever when we took lessons together. Good at maths and languages, and fascinated by the workings of the body and all things natural. Sam is a born philosopher. I am sure he is most wonderful at his job.'

'And you have not seen him in all these years,' the duke reminded her. 'I shall try not to be too jealous of your obvious affection for him.' Then he stated the obvious, so that there might be no confusion. 'If Dr Hastings has not come back to sweep you up before now, the man has quite missed his chance.'

'I suppose he has,' Evie answered. She sounded unconcerned, but Sam suspected the words were a goad to action.

'Suppose?' St Aldric laughed again, willing to pretend that she had been joking. 'That is not nearly as confident as I wish you to be. Do you expect us to duel for you? I will call him out and we will see who is the better.' This too was more joke than threat.

'Do not talk nonsense,' Evie said hurriedly. 'I would think you both very foolish if you fought over me.'

'If it displeases you, then I shall not attempt it. He is a military man, after all. It would be even worse should Dr Hastings prove skilled enough to defeat me with a pistol.' The duke smiled at Sam, as though inviting him to join in the fun and prove that he had no feelings for her. 'With my luck, I would end with a ball in my shoulder that would have to be removed by the man who put it there. He would be doubly the hero and I would lose you twice as fast.'

'You have nothing to fear,' Evie repeated.

'Nor do you,' St Aldric reminded her softly and kissed her on the forehead.

There was no passion in it. It was delivered almost as a benediction. But Sam saw it for what it was. Even if there had been no public announcement, the woman between them was spoken for. In response, Sam gave St Aldric the slightest nod to prove that the message was understood.

Evelyn paid no more attention to the kiss than she would have to any other salute. But she was staring at the duke with the same teasing affection that she had shown to Sam only moments before. 'I see you have arrived empty handed again.'

Rather than chide her for her greediness, St Aldric laughed as though this was another old joke between them. 'I know you better than that, my dear. You would send me packing if I came without some sort of gift.'

Once again, Sam cursed himself for not being able to say those words to her himself. But it might ease his jealousy if St Aldric proved to be as shallow as Sam hoped, and gave her something that did not suit her.

It appeared that was not to be the case. The bulging pocket of his coat trembled slightly, though the duke did not move.

'What is it?' Evie said, eyeing the lump with curiosity. 'Give it to me this instant. It does not appear to be very happy where it is.'

'And that is why I brought it to you. I am sure it will be much happier, in your care.' He reached two fingers into the coat and withdrew a sniffling ginger kitten, placing it gently in Evie's lap.

'Oh, Michael.' Instantly captivated, she set Sam's spyglass aside and scooped the little thing up so that she could look at it, eye to eye. It blinked back at her, before letting out a nervous mew and settling down into the hollow of her hand. She stroked its head and nuzzled it to her cheek, smiling. 'It is too perfect.'

And Sam had to admit it was. Like the telescope, it held her attention in a way that a necklace never could. But unlike Sam's desperate good luck in finding something suitable already in his pocket, St Aldric had learned her preferences and planned in advance for this surprise.

She rewarded him with a smile so warm that Sam could swear he saw the duke colour with humble pleasure. It was sickening. Could not this interloper have behaved like the peer he was, pompous and demanding, blustering into this sacred space and defiling it so that Sam might hate him in good conscience? Could he have been a slightly less imposing physical specimen, with the beginnings of a paunch, or some spot or blemish?

Instead, he continued to be perfect. And he was looking down at Evie and the kitten as though he had never seen a lovelier sight.

'What shall I call you, little one?' She held it up again, staring into the grave green eyes. 'Something to suit your nature, for I am sure you shall be a great hunter, when you are old enough. Orion, perhaps.'

St Aldric cleared his throat. 'I should rather think Diana would be more appropriate.'

He was educated as well? A cursory knowledge of mythology and feline anatomy was not an indication of genius. But at least it proved that he was not some inbred dolt.

Evie turned the kitten in her hands and gave the underside a second look. 'I think you are right.' Then she turned it right way up and kissed it upon the head by way of a christening. 'Diana it is. And you shall have the run of the garden, a bowl of cream and, when you have lost your milk teeth, you shall have all the mice you can eat.'

'You will spoil it horribly,' Sam said, trying to be the gruff and grumbling older brother.

Evie gave him a disgusted look. 'It is not possible to spoil a thing by giving it too much affection. If I coddle her a bit, I am sure she will only become more devoted and do her job better. You could learn by that and not neglect your family for years at a time.' Then she smiled again at the kitten and the man who had given it to her.

It was like watching her hold out a gift of her own and then turn and give it to someone else. She was punishing him, deliberately favouring the duke. And though he was filled with the jealousy she wished for, he could do nothing to show it. He should not have come here. If her smiles were all for St Aldric, that was as it should be. There was no place for him any more.

And much as Sam might have wished to find fault with his rival, he could not. He was worthy of Evie. Evie was obviously fond of him. He had but to step out of the way and let nature take its course. These two would be married by summer's end.

All the more reason not to be trapped in the garden with the happy couple and sick to his stomach at the sight of love in bloom. He prayed for an excuse that might allow him to escape.

'Evelyn!' Lord Thorne called from the house, hurrying out to be with them. At any other time, Sam would have thought an interruption of his foster father as a sign that the situation had gone from bad to worse. But today it was a welcome relief.

'You have found her, then, your Grace?' Thorne gave a self-deprecating laugh and answered his own question. 'Of course you have. She was not lost, after all. And Sam?' His eyes widened with surprise that was actually annoyance. 'You are still with us? As I recall, you said you would be leaving.'

'I had other plans for him,' Evelyn said triumphantly. 'He tried to get away without so much as a hello. But I stopped him.'

'I am sure he could have escaped you, had he but tried.' Another warning from Thorne to mind his place. Sam could feel his normally placid temper stretch to a breaking point. He had a mind to tell the man aloud that he would leave immediately, if only to put an end to these continual reminders of his obvious inferiority.

'And he is staying at an inn, and not with us, as he should. It is truly horrible of him. I will not stand for it,' Evie added, in the same playful scolding tone she had been using on St Aldric.

'If the good doctor wishes to stay at an inn, it is not our place to correct him,' Thorne answered, putting the blame on Sam.

'Of course it is,' Evie said, unbothered. 'We are his family. I will allow nothing less than his sending for his baggage and moving back to his old room for the duration of his stay in London. I will have the space aired and made up for him immediately.' She rose and set the kitten on the bench, twining her arm with her father's. Though she might be his affectionate and loving daughter, she had a will of iron and was used to getting her way. If Sam did not go soon, she would work on Thorne without mercy until he gave her what she wanted. 'Come along, Papa, and add your voice to mine. I am sure Mrs Abbott will be quite cross with me for the sudden change in plans.' She was fairly dragging her father by the arm and back towards the house, lecturing him on hospitality while she was neglecting both her guests.

She tossed a smile in their direction, as though that would be more than enough to keep them, until she returned. 'If you gentlemen would spare our company? You must know each other better.'

'Of course,' St Aldric said, speaking for both of them. 'I am sure that Dr Hastings can entertain me in your absence.'

'I will leave Diana with you as well,' Evie said, as though she was not sure that Sam's company would suffice on its own. Then she fixed him with a cool stare. 'And do not move from this spot, Samuel Hastings, without taking leave of me. I still have not forgiven you for the last time you did.'

Nor had he forgiven himself. This time, he owed her a goodbye, if nothing else. He gave a grudging nod of agreement and she returned to take her father's arm. 'Do not fear. I will not be long.'

Chapter Four

'What is the meaning of this rudeness, Evelyn? You left St Aldric alone, when he came specifically to see you.' At her side, Evelyn could feel her father puffing in indignation like a tropical fish.

She smiled at him and added a loving hug and a doting look, ashamed of herself for this blatant manipulation. She had been taught by Aunt Jordan that a lady must use honey to catch flies. But sometimes she could not help but envy men their ability to catch flies with a reasonable argument. 'I did not leave St Aldric alone, Father. Sam was there.'

'That hardly signifies.' His grumbling was a last desperate attempt to rein her in. But since he had not been successful in twenty-one years, she had no real fear of punishment.

'I believe it does,' she said, quietly, still smiling, but renewing her grip on his arm and leading him down the hall to the library, shutting the door behind them so that there was no chance for a servant to hear what she wished to say. Then she checked the window that looked out on the garden to be sure that it was closed. No word of their conversation must reach the men talking there until she had confirmed her suspicions.

'A physician and a duke?' Father was shaking his head like a dog worrying a bone. 'The only reason that the two of them should speak is if the peer is ill, and you know for a fact that he is not. Unless... You have no fears, have you?' As usual, her father was thinking ahead to a future that she had not yet agreed to.

'Are you worried about my widowhood before I am even a bride?' she said with a raised eyebrow. 'It is nothing like that. St Aldric is perfectly healthy, as is obvious to all who see him. But Sam is a member of the family. I think it is important that the two get to know each other. Don't you?' She looked expectantly at her father, hoping that he would not force her to badger the truth from him.

'If you assume that Hastings will play a part in your future, you harbour a misapprehension. We have discussed it and he is leaving London shortly. I doubt you will see him again.'

The finality of this statement was in direct opposition to her desires, so she ignored it. 'Hastings?' she chided. 'Really, Father. Now you are the one who is being rude. When did you cease to think of him as Sam? And for what reason? If there is some breach between the two of you, then I beg you to heal it, for my sake.'

'There is no breach,' her father insisted, probably

afraid that she would resort to tears. 'But we have an understanding, he and I. And what has been done is all for your sake, I assure you.'

As if she needed protection from Sam. The idea was quite ridiculous and not worth mentioning. 'I am more concerned with Sam and his future, Father. So should you be.'

'He is seeing to that well enough, without my help,' her father said. Perhaps he was simply hurt that the boy he had raised could manage to prosper without him.

'His success is a credit to your early tutelage, I am sure.' She must turn the topic, for she wished to close the breach and not widen it. Her father appeared somewhat mollified at the thought that he had contributed to Sam's obvious success. 'And I see no reason that he cannot stay here with us, while he is in London.'

'He does not wish to,' her father said, firmly.

'I am happy to see that you have no objection,' she said with another smile. One thing did not imply the other. But it was better to let him think her illogical than to allow argument. Then she added, as though in afterthought, 'Once he is here, it will give you a chance to tell him what you know of his true parentage.'

'I?' That had caught him unawares, she was sure. He was flustered out of countenance and almost beyond speech. It took several seconds for him to manage a proper denial. 'I know nothing. And whatever Samuel Hastings has told you on the subject is clearly a lie.'

'He...told me?' She gave a bat of her lashes to reinforce the innocence of her discovery. 'He did not tell me anything. But I needed no great wit to draw my conclusion. I have my own eyes, if I wish to see the truth. You had best give him the whole story, if you have not already.'

'I have no idea what you mean,' said her father, in the slow and deliberate way that people sometimes used to deny the obvious.

Eve sighed and gave up on honey, preferring to catch this particular fly with a swatter. 'Then I will explain it to you. I have had suspicions for quite some time. But it was only until just now, in the garden, that I was sure. When they are seen together by others, someone will remark on the resemblance between them. From there it is only a short step to seeing that the Duke of St Aldric and Dr Samuel Hastings are as alike as brothers.'

'Evie, you mustn't meddle in this.' It was the same weak prohibition that he tried whenever she stepped out of bounds.

Since she knew there were no consequences to disagreeing, it would meet with the same lack of success. She continued. 'You were a good friend of the old duke when he was alive, were you not?'

'Of course, but…'

'And mightn't he have asked you a favour, at one point in your life, when you and mother feared that you would be childless?' In case she had been too direct, she larded the question with more feminine sweetness. 'I only ask because I know there will be gossip.'

'There will be none if Hastings leaves, as he is promised to,' her father said stubbornly. He had not affirmed or denied her theory. But evasiveness was an answer.

'It is hardly fair to Sam, if you make him leave London just because of the duke.' Nor was it fair to her. She would not lose him again, over something that should not matter to anyone. 'If the estrangement between you is nothing more than a fear of making this revelation, you had best get it over with. Since I love both men, I mean to keep them close to me for as long as I am able.' She smiled again and offered a bait that she doubted her father could resist. 'I am sure that St Aldric would welcome the news. He has spoken frequently of the burden of being the only remaining member of his family. You would gain much favour by telling him what he longs to hear.'

'Revelation of a natural son...' her father stopped himself before revealing the truth '...if there were such, would do nothing to change his status as the last of the line.'

'It would change the contents of his heart,' Eve argued. 'I know his spirit; it is generous to a fault. He would want to share his wealth with his father's son. And it would at least make him cease his jokes about duels between them. Imagine his reaction, should they fight for some reason, and not learn the truth until after one of them had been injured.'

'For some reason?' She had pushed too far. Her father had spotted the hole in her argument and made his escape. 'Really, Evelyn. Do not play the naïf. You know perfectly well that they would be fighting over your attentions. If an accident occurs, it will be your fault and not mine. You must send Hastings away. I have assured myself that the man is too sensible to harbour false hope on a match between you. And neither should you.'

'I am not offering false hope.' There was nothing false about it. After the time spent in the garden, the hope she felt was quite real. As was her conviction about the identity of Sam's father. 'I am simply attempting to right a wrong, before it goes further. It pains both men and does no credit to you.'

'You are meddling in things you cannot understand,' he said, patting her on the hand and treating her like the child he still believed she was. 'If this is the reason you were impolite to St Aldric, then I am sorry to disappoint you. I have nothing to say on the matter, because there is nothing to say.'

Had she failed to persuade him? This happened so rarely that, for a moment, she suspected she might have been wrong. Perhaps there was no secret to reveal. 'Father...'

'Go!' He pointed a finger back towards the garden, once again secure in his control of the situation. 'Send Dr Hastings on his way before the duke tires of his company. Visit with St Aldric, as he desires. I have no intention of helping you out of the muddle you are making. This discussion is at an end and will not be repeated. Now, go.' Her father's lips were set in a firm line, as if to show her that no more words would pass between them until she had fulfilled her obligation to him, to society and to the duke.

But he was giving no thought to Sam's needs. If he would not, then someone must, or he would be back on a boat and out of her life for ever. 'Very well, then. I will talk to St Aldric. But you are wrong about the rest, Father. We will speak of this again and, next time, you will tell the truth.' She would worry him with it night and day, if necessary. But she would have her way, and Sam would know his brother.

In Evelyn's absence, an awkward silence had fallen between the two men. It was hardly surprising. Sam seldom had cause to speak to a man of such great rank and no right to initiate conversation. The duke had no reason to speak to him. It left the pair of them staring morosely at the kitten on the bench until the thing stumbled to the edge and off, wandering into the grass to stalk and pounce on crickets.

Now there was not even an excuse for the silence. It seemed that St Aldric was not content with this, for he was searching about him as though expecting to see an opening to a conversation. At last he offered, 'Evelyn says you were educated in Scotland, and after you took to the sea.'

'Indeed, your Grace.' Sam shifted uneasily, clasping his hands behind his back.

'The navy is an unusual choice for such a well-educated man. But I cannot fault your adventurous spirit.'

Sam was tempted to announce that he had not requested an opinion, but he had only one reason to dislike this man and no reason at all to be rude to him. Excessive fondness for Evie was no excuse for a lack of respect to the peerage. 'The navy is an economical way to see the world,' Sam admitted. 'The prize money from ships taken was sufficient to make up for the lack of a medical practice.' It would be nothing to the holdings of a duke, but it had been more than satisfactory for Sam.

The duke nodded approval. 'The captain of the *Matilda* was ambitious.'

It was the truth, but St Aldric had stated it as though he already knew. Had he made an effort to discover this, or had Evie revealed it to him? 'A very ambitious captain indeed, your Grace.' He'd made enough to retire and return to land, and to have a house and family, should he wish for one.

'Your record is admirable,' the duke continued. 'Other than a brief flirtation with the church of Rome, while you were in Spain.'

So he had read the record, then. And the warning put there by the captain, for the time he had spent conversing with priests. 'It was curiosity. Nothing more.' And a desire to find a cure for his spiritual affliction, or at least absolution, from a clergy that was bound to secrecy. In the end, the priest had looked at him with pity and disgust, and given him beads and prayer, almost as Sam might have prescribed a pill.

It had done no good.

'It is strange that you have taken such an interest in

my interest.' Sam allowed himself the candid observation. The meddling in his affairs by this stranger annoyed him. 'I do not mean to bother Evelyn with it, if that is what you fear.'

'Not at all, sir,' the duke said hastily. 'I merely wished to take your measure.'

'Then consider it done. I am what you see before you. No more, no less. In the future, if you have a question, you might ask me directly and I will answer it honestly and to the best of my ability. For Evelyn's sake, if for no other reason.' Did invoking her name make the words sound any less rude?

'I see,' the duke said.

'I wonder if you do?' Sam said, too tired of the games they were playing to dissemble. 'I might as well have sworn to you on all that is holy. Such an oath would have had no more strength than my wish for Eve's continued well-being. No matter what you might suspect, I want what is best for her.' And then he admitted grudgingly, 'If what I am hearing is true, she is on the verge of a fortunate match.'

Rather than answer this, the duke merely shrugged. It was a strange, rather boyish response from one so confident. 'I have hopes. But it is up to the lady, is it not?'

'I wish her well,' Sam added. 'She deserves the best that life offers. I have no reason to think she is not about to receive it.'

The duke gave him a long, slow look in response to this, as though trying to decide if he believed it.

At last, he answered, 'I am happy to hear you say so. Should I be the future you predict, I shall do my best to be worthy of her.'

This made Sam respond with an equally probing look. He could have understood a warning to stay away. But this behaviour seemed to indicate that the duke sought this approval. It was not necessary.

The silence fell between them again. It was even heavier this time, like the exhausted rest of men who had fought each other and were waiting between rounds to regain their breath.

Into the tense pause came Eve. As though she had not been between them the whole time, thought Sam with an ironic smile.

She was smiling as well, totally unaware of the direction their conversation must have gone. 'I have returned to you,' she announced. 'I hope that my absence has given the pair of you a chance to become acquainted.'

'You were gone barely ten minutes, Evelyn,' the duke responded. 'It was hardly enough time to establish a lasting friendship.'

'But you spoke,' she said as though prodding a wayward child through his lessons. 'And you found him to be all that I have said?'

It made Sam wonder just what Eve had said of him.

'I did not doubt your description,' St Aldric answered. 'But, yes.'

'Then did you tell him what we discussed?'

'I was a topic of discussion?' Sam interrupted. He

did not like being talked about. It was almost as annoying as being the subject of an enquiry.

'I simply made clear to St Aldric how your career worried me,' Evie replied, sitting between them in the space the kitten had occupied. She reached out and clasped his hand. 'You were gone so long, Sam. I missed you. And do not tell me the navy is not dangerous. Even with Napoleon defeated, it must be. There are storms and pirates, and all manner of accidents that might befall you. Suppose you took ill? Who would treat the physician?'

'Evie.' Now she was coddling him and doing it in front of the duke. He added embarrassment to the host of other discomforts she caused.

'I wondered if something might be done to persuade you to stay ashore.'

'Do you not think that I am best able to decide for myself?' Sam said, as gently as possible.

'I told her as much,' St Aldric said with a sigh. 'But she did not wish to hear it.' For a moment, they were brothers in arms against a foe as tenacious as Bonaparte. But having fought both, Sam credited Evie as more stubborn than the whole French army.

'I am tired of people ignoring my letters and dismissing my fears,' Eve said, eyes narrowed and jaw set. 'Samuel Hastings, you are risking your life at sea and there is no reason for it. I have been quite beside myself, praying for your return. A practice on land will be safer. Something must be arranged for you.'

Sam took a breath before speaking, trying to keep

his temper for her sake. 'As I told you before, I prefer to make my own way. My early life was spent beholden to your father and it was difficult.' More difficult than she could possibly imagine. 'The debts of gratitude I incurred are something that can never be repaid.'

'You need not be grateful for a job,' she snapped back. 'I am sure you are skilled enough to merit this position. It is an opportunity, nothing more. You will prove your worth by your service. I have spoken to St Aldric and he is agreed.' She gave the duke a warning look that said this had best be the truth, if he knew what was good for him. And then her expression changed to sort of smile that no man could resist and she took the duke's hand, giving it the same warm squeeze that she had given Sam. 'It is all settled. You will come to Aldricshire with us and act as Michael's personal physician.'

For a moment, the anger was stunned out of him. Any doctor in England would be overjoyed with such a post. St Aldric was young and strong, and of an amiable nature that bespoke a long and pleasant career in his service. It would mean a life of comfort and a chance to keep a wife and children in luxury.

As long as he was willing to keep Evelyn's husband fit and healthy. Perhaps he would be required to watch over her, as she grew big with another man's child, and stand by in approval as their brood increased. And now she was holding both their hands and looking from one to the other as though it would be possible to make the three of them into one happy family.

'No.' He made no effort to hide his disgust as he pulled his hand out of her grasp and stood, turning and backing away from the pair on the bench. 'You ask too much of me, Evie.' He looked to the man beside her, trying to maintain a frigid courtesy. This idea was no fault of the duke's, but it explained his rude questioning of moments before. He probably feared that Sam was the sort of man who would use Evie's fondness to his own betterment. 'I apologise, your Grace, but I must respectfully refuse the offer.' Perhaps St Aldric could explain it to her. The man must have guessed his feelings, if Thorne had not already explained the situation.

He looked at Evie, whose beautiful eyes were beginning to fill with tears, and then he backed away from her, towards the house. 'And I should take my leave as well. It is long past the time I meant to go. You persuaded me to tarry. But I should not have listened.'

Lead us not into temptation... The words of the prayer echoed in his mind.

But they offered no protection from the stricken look on her face. 'Sam, wait...'

If she spoke another word, he would weaken. He would wipe those tears and agree to anything that might make her smile again. She would have him moved into the house by evening, sleeping scant feet from her bedroom door.

'I cannot.' *Must not.* 'Not another moment. Good day to you, Lady Evelyn. And you as well, your Grace. And goodbye.'

Chapter Five

Evie watched the London streets passing by outside the carriage window and tapped her foot impatiently on the boards beneath the seat. It was really too much to bear.

Before making her come out, it had been drummed into her by Aunt Jordan that her future depended on her ability to be pleasant. It was almost as important as looks and much more important than intelligence. Men might marry a beautiful ninnyhammer, as long as she hung on their words and did not correct them. But a shrew would be a shrew, long after looks faded.

So Eve had done her best to be good company. And though she could not keep herself from arguing, she always did it with a smile on her face. Perhaps that was why the men in her life were treating her like a child, alternately scolding and humouring her, thinking that they could render her agreeable to what they wanted. Because she did not look angry, they did not believe she was serious.

Father was clearly lying about what he knew of Sam. Sam was equally evasive when it came to the truth of his feelings for her, changing from hot to cold and back again so suddenly that she could hardly understand him.

And St Aldric? She smiled in spite of herself. He would appoint the devil himself as a personal physician if he thought it would bring her any closer to accepting his offer. At least the man was consistent. But since she did not love him, his opinion hardly signified.

The carriage pulled to a stop outside the inn where Sam was staying. It was another piece of nonsense that he had refused his old room, remaining aloof in a place that could not be half as nice as home. Even worse, she had been forced to worm the location of it from the coachman who had taken him away. Sam had left no direction for her and her father had announced that he had no idea where to find the man, nor was he bothered by his ignorance.

Now that she was here, she told her Banbury tale to the hostler and was shown to the room where Sam had gone to ground. She knocked smartly on the door and heard the answering 'come' from the other side. Perhaps he was expecting a maid with his dinner.

She smiled to herself. He was certainly not expecting her. But he must learn to like surprises. She opened the door and swept into the room, her smart day dress swirling around her. 'Good afternoon, Dr Hastings. I have come to continue our discussion in private.'

'Evie.' He rose from the desk where he had been

seated and a prayer book tumbled to the floor, brushed from the table in front of him.

She had not known him to be particularly religious, but people altered with time. He probably did not think of her as a sophisticated débutante. When he'd left, she had been a scapegrace companion with manners no better than his. But the change in her should not have shocked him this much. He was backing away from the door as though he meant to brace his shoulders against the wall. He had the look of a startled animal.

But a thoroughly masculine animal, if she was to be honest. He was out of his coat, with his shirt sleeves rolled up to keep the grime from his cuffs. She could see muscles in those arms, and shoulders more broad and strong than she'd imagined. She swallowed and remembered, for just a moment, why one did not court impropriety by forcing one's way into a gentleman's room for a private interview.

But the gentleman was Sam. And no matter what might happened between them, she did not fear it.

'What are you doing here?' he asked, wary. 'And why were you even allowed above stairs? The innkeeper will think you a common trollop for behaving so.'

'Nonsense,' she said and gave him a wink, trying to coax a smile from him. 'I told him that we were family. Is it not natural for a sister to visit a brother?'

He made a strange, strangled noise, as though he could not quite master his speech, and then said weakly, 'It was still very wrong of you.'

'But I could not allow you to leave me in anger. I do not want to part this way. I do not want to part at all.' She glanced at the sea chest on the floor. It was clear that he was packing again. 'And I certainly do not want you to go as you did before, without a word.'

For a moment, her voice sounded strange as well. If she was not careful, she would break down in front of him and beg him to stay. Excess emotion was effective against Father. But Sam would likely think she was shamming and put her out of the room.

She conquered the tears, before they could escape. Running down the back of her throat, they tasted very like the ones she had shed when he'd first left her. She did not cry any more. Gentleman might be moved by a weeping woman, but they did not like her nearly as well as a smiling one. She dropped her head a bit so that she might appear demure and properly sorry for getting above herself. 'I will talk no more of finding you a position. I will not meddle at all. But you promised you would stay for the wedding. Remember? You promised. You cannot break your word to me, just because of a silly misunderstanding. Forgive me.' She looked up through her lashes and held out a hand to him. Contrition, helplessness, and a hint of flirtation should bring him round.

He ignored the hand, back still firmly against the wall. 'There is nothing to forgive. What you did was out of concern for me and I thank you for attempting to help, even if I must refuse. I will do as you ask and stay for the wedding. I will even buy a new coat and have my neckcloth properly tied for it, so that I do not shame you before St Aldric.'

His expression was frozen and his tone wooden. He looked and sounded as false as she felt, trying to snare him with her feminine wiles. He paused, wetting his lips before speaking again, as though it had been necessary to prepare himself for the answer. 'Now when is this wedding you are so eager for me to attend?'

She smiled in triumph. 'I really have no idea. I have not said yes, you remember. But if you mean to leave as soon as I am wed, I suspect it shall take me some time to decide.'

He lurched forwards as though about to give her a good shaking for her impudence, then regained control and ran his fingers through his hair. 'Evelyn, I swear, your behaviour is enough to drive a sane man to madness.'

'So I have been told,' she said with another smile. 'It is good to see that you are not unaffected by it.' She took a step closer to him, pressing her advantage. 'We were quite close at one time, though you work very hard to deny it.'

'Like siblings,' he said firmly.

She shook her head. He must have known how she'd felt about him. She had made no effort to hide her love. But he had given her no chance to elicit some promise from him, before he went off to school, so that she would know to wait for his return. Now that they were alone, there would be no better time. 'You were always more than a brother to me, Sam.'

'But you were always my dear little sister,' he said, stubbornly. 'And I am very proud to think that I will soon have to call you "Your Grace". Or I will once you stop stringing poor St Aldric along.'

'I cannot accept him while there is still a question as to where my heart might lie,' she said.

He flinched. 'Surely such questions were answered long ago, Evelyn.'

'When you left me with no explanation?' she supplied.

'You knew I was to go away to school.'

'But I did not expect you to run the whole way. Nor did I expect you to run again today, in the middle of a simple conversation about your future.'

'A future you wished to choose for me,' he reminded her.

'And you are seeking a different one?' Perhaps it was with some other girl that felt the same way as she did. If it was another woman, why could he not just tell her? If it was to spare her pain, he had misjudged the situation. A simple answer for this rejection was bound to be better than not knowing.

And if there was another, the key to his absence was right here in the room with him. The other woman, if she was smart, would not have wanted him to forget that someone waited for his return. There must be a lock of hair, a miniature or some other token of her affection. Eve had but to find it and understand. And there before her was the sea chest and doctor's bag, waiting to be explored.

She trailed her fingers along the edge of the open chest and then turned to it suddenly, dropping to her knees to examine the contents.

There was no sign of another woman here. The box in front of her contained nothing but the tools of his profession.

It was novel enough that he had a trade, for most gentlemen did not. Eve tended the folks around their country home quite efficiently without a doctor's help, but she did it with little more than instinct, herbs and a needle and thread from her sewing box. It was charity and not real work at all.

But here before her were all the things that a trained physician might have at his disposal. To Eve, it was a revelation. She had read about the uses of such instruments in the books on medicine that she had got, but she had never seen them.

These were arrayed neatly, carefully, immaculate in their cleanliness and as ordered as idols in a temple. Lancets with smooth tortoiseshell handles, the gleaming steel of bone saws and drills, the terrifying razor edge of scalpels and the curved needles threaded with silk and gut. Beneath them, in neat rows, were cobalt-blue medicine bottles and the weird globes of the leech jars.

The third layer was a collection of more esoteric items, harder to pack, but obviously well used. A syringe made of hollow bone, ivory-and-silver medicine spoons and forceps. She examined each one in turn.

'Are you searching for something, Evelyn?' Sam

had been so silent that she had almost forgotten him as she explored. But it seemed that her curiosity had relaxed him. He was no longer pinned to the wall, but standing just behind her. His voice had changed as well. The strangled desperation had changed to a familiar combination of disapproval, amusement, resignation and affection.

She wanted to turn and answer honestly. *Yes, I am searching for the key to understanding you.* Instead, she was almost as truthful. 'I am curious about your profession.' She turned to face him and sat on the floor, her legs tucked under.

'And once again, you prove that the years have not changed you. You always were a horrible little snoop.' He relaxed enough to sit down on the end of the bed. 'Is there anything you wish me to explain?'

'I know most of them,' she admitted.

'You do?' This seemed to surprise him.

'I have studied,' she admitted. 'I ordered the same texts you used in Edinburgh and read them cover to cover.'

Another man might have questioned her ability to understand them. But all that Sam said was, 'Does your father know?'

It was difficult to meet his gaze and admit the truth. Eve had not thought of herself as a deceptive person, when he had left her. Although she often disagreed with her father, she never set out to disobey him. But she had suspected in this it would be necessary and had kept the extent of her knowledge a secret from him. 'You know he does not. He would never have approved of it. He thinks I tend to the sick in the same way other women do, by bringing broth and good wishes, and the sort of herbal tinctures that Mother would have used had she survived. But I prefer to be more scientific about it.' Then a thought occurred to her. 'You will not tell him, will you?'

Sam laughed. 'Of course not.' And then he grew serious. 'Nor will I tell St Aldric. I doubt he is expecting a wife with such *outré* hobbies.'

If Sam loved her as she hoped, he could use the information to his advantage and spoil her chances with the duke. Instead, he was being noble. She sighed. 'The ways of men are very confusing. They have no care if we women meddle with illnesses, as long as we do it in ignorance. Do they not want people to recover?' She tipped her head to the side and watched Sam for an honest reaction as she asked the next question. 'What do you think of my dabbling? Am I wrong to want to practise what I can read clear on the page?'

He thought for a moment. 'I do not think I approve. There are many things I have seen in the service of medicine that I would not wish upon you. But I also know how difficult it is to dissuade you when you take an idea into your head. You have your own mind, Evie. No amount of disapproval on my part is likely to change it.' But the fact of the matter did not seem to frustrate or anger him. He was looking at her with the calm acceptance that she had hoped to see.

'Do you think I might make a decent physician?'

'The colleges will not train you, of course,' he said. 'But if they would, you are quick witted enough. You say you know the contents of my bag?'

She nodded. 'Of course.' She held up a tool. 'Forceps, to deliver babies. They are unnecessary, you know. The majority of births can be sorted out in other ways, if one is patient and has small hands.'

His eyes widened. 'You speak from experience?'

'Do you not remember our old country home? Thorne Hall is quite remote. The nearest doctor is miles away and we have learned to manage without a physician. I have grown to be quite a capable midwife, Dr Hastings.'

'And you limit yourself to that?' She had feared censure from him. But the question was asked with good-natured resignation, as though he already knew the answer.

'Perhaps I am more deeply involved in care than some people would wish,' she admitted. 'And perhaps I go more frequently to sick beds and birthing rooms than propriety requires. It is not as if I take money for the things I do.'

'Well, then…' he said, with an ironic smile. 'As long as you are no threat to my business.'

'No threat at all. And I suspect you have little practice with childbirth, if you have been on a ship full of men.' She set the forceps aside. 'Especially if you rely on these things. There is a place for them, of course. But most times I can do without them.'

He bowed his head to hide his smile. 'Then I yield

to your superior experience in that part of the field. What else do you think to teach me?'

She pointed to the drill. 'This is for the trepanning of the skull. And here are the implements that scrape away the scalp and lift the bones from the wound.' She picked it up and gave the handle a turn. The thought of saving a person by drilling holes into their head was really quite amazing. 'Did you ever have to do such a thing?'

He laughed again. 'You have not changed at all, Evie. Your curiosity is as gruesome as ever. Yes, I have used it. Once successfully. Once not.' As though he wished to change the subject he advanced to the chest and pulled out an ebony tube. 'But I am sure you will not recognise this.'

She turned it over in her hands, looking for some clue to indicate its purpose. 'I have no idea.'

'That is not surprising. I suspect I have one of the few in England. I got it off a French surgeon on a prize ship we took. It takes the place of the percussion hammer, when sounding the lungs and listening to the heart.'

'How wondrous. You must show me.' She leaned forwards on her knees and held it out to him.

Something about this alarmed him. He stared at it for a moment and then at her. Then he took a breath, swallowed and placed one end against the bare skin above her bodice, then gingerly put his ear to the other. He moved the tube to several locations on her chest, requested that she breathe deeply each time and, with a scholarly nod, pronounced her sound. He withdrew with obvious relief.

So the nearness of her frightened him, did it? He had put on his best professional demeanour before attempting to examine her. But she had been well schooled in breaking down a man's objections. Those lessons would do for a drawing room, but with Sam she could be more direct. She smiled, sweetly. 'Now I must do you.' She took the tube away from him without waiting for permission. Then she undid several of the buttons on his waistcoat and spread the opening of his shirt hiding under the cravat.

'Evelyn!' He tried to back away from her and bumped into the headboard of the bed behind him.

She laughed. 'Oh, Sam. Do not be such a girl.' And then she leaned forwards to listen.

The sounds were strange and hollow, compared to simply putting one's head to the chest of the patient, but the clarity was uncanny. As she listened, she heard the slight hitch in respiration, as though he could not manage to breathe normally. His heartbeat, compared to what she considered normal, was hard and rapid. For a moment, it worried her. Perhaps he was ill. Had his absence concealed some physical problem?

Or the rapid beat might be the sign she had hoped for. She put her hand on the bare skin of his chest to steady the tube and felt his breathing stop all together, even though his heart was racing.

It was her. He might pretend otherwise, but to have her near affected him in ways he could not control.

To test the theory, she moved her hand again and felt his heart jump. Then she looked up at him with a long slow smile.

He looked back with an expression she might have described as shattered.

'Why, Dr Hastings…' she removed the tube, but left her hand flat against the warm bare skin of his chest '…you are most excitable today.'

'Evie.' It was the warning tone of someone afraid of getting caught in an indiscretion.

She ignored it. 'Samuel?' She scratched her nails lightly against the skin of his chest, amazed at her own boldness, and waited for his reserve to crack.

Instead, he gripped her hand and removed it from his person, arranging his clothes to hide the place she had touched. 'Do not behave nonsensically. If someone were to discover you touching a man that way, it would do no good to claim it began as an interest in medicine. You would be quite ruined.'

'I am not touching any man,' she explained patiently, kneeling at his feet. 'It is just you.'

'Just me.' He let out a resigned sigh. 'You must remember we are grown now, Evelyn. The games that might have seemed quite natural twenty years ago are no longer proper.'

'Are there other games that might be more appropriate?' It was a daring question and she wondered how he might answer it.

'No.' He wet his lips and swallowed, as though it was an effort to talk to her.

'Just what is it that makes you so afraid of me, Sam?'

'Afraid?' He was parroting back her words, stalling for time, but it was clear from his expression that she had been right. He was terrified.

She leaned closer and put her hands on his knees, to look up into his face. If it was rejection he feared, he would not receive it. 'Have I changed so much, Sam? Because I never used to frighten you. You even kissed me once,' she reminded him.

'Did I?' He looked away from her, at the sea chest on the floor. 'I hardly remember it.'

'I remember it all too well. It was a week before you went away. We were in the garden. It was a morning, in summer. We were playing at games. I hid. When you caught me, you held me by the waist. Your eyes went very serious for a moment, then you pulled me close and kissed me on the mouth.'

'Ah, yes.' If possible he looked even more uncomfortable.

'And shortly after that, you left me to go to school.'

'It was but a bit of foolishness on my part. We were both very young, were we not?'

'I was fifteen,' she reminded him. 'Some girls are already married by then.'

'And now you are twenty-one. And likely to make a much better marriage than you might have, had you rushed into it at such a young age.' He said it as though he was trying to convince himself.

'I might be married to a physician now, had he asked me.'

'Evie.' Was that all he could manage to say to her? This time her name sounded just as sad, but full of longing as well.

'Since you will not speak plainly, I must,' she said, 'so that you cannot pretend to misunderstand me. If you offer, I will accept. If you wish it, I will go with you to Gretna tonight.'

'St Aldric...' he said, almost choking on the name.

'Is nothing to me,' she said, laying a hand against his cheek. 'Not compared to you.'

Finally his strength failed. He laid his own hand over hers, pressing her palm to his mouth. His lips were hot against her skin. Even hotter as they met hers when he released her hand and pulled her forwards to take her lips.

And if she had thought this kiss would be like the one that they had already shared, she was proved wrong. He opened her mouth with a steady pressure and his tongue touched hers, advancing and retreating. At first it was a gentle tide, but it grew to a storm and she gave herself to it, trembling. She clung to his body and he held her there, between his legs so that she could feel his manhood growing against her belly. The thought of it pressing into her made her moan into his mouth.

He was aroused. She had but to give in to him and soon he would be beyond control. There would be no hesitation on her part. When the moment came, she would succumb. Once they had lain together, he would never leave her again.

She pressed his hand against her breast, urging him to stroke it through her gown. At the merest touch, he grew harder. He raised his other hand, kneading both, as if to prove that every inch of her body belonged to him. His kisses took on a desperate quality, as though he was trying to reach into her soul with each thrust of his tongue so that he might claim that as well.

She had imagined giving herself in passive submission, but suddenly she needed more than that. She wanted his hands on her bare skin and his body filling the wet empty place between her legs. As she knelt before him, he trapped her body between his thighs. So she ran her hands over them, back and forth, each time growing closer to their apex.

Her palms itched to caress him. It would not take much more than a touch, she was sure, and he would be irrevocably hers. Her fingertips grazed him, once, twice, three times through the cloth, and then they settled on the buttons of his breeches.

He pushed her away suddenly, scrambling back on the bed as though he could not put enough distance between them. His expression was wild, eyes fixed and staring, lips drawn back, as his head shook once in an emphatic 'no'. Then he wiped his mouth with the back of his hand. It was as gesture of revulsion.

He pointed towards the door.

'I don't understand,' she whispered. She was near tears again. She swallowed hard to stop them. Crying was the lowest type of female trick. She would not give in to it with Sam, no matter how much she hurt. 'If you love me...'

'It is not love,' he said with finality, cold and professional again. 'I doubt I am even capable of the feeling. But if you value me, as you say you do, get up off your knees and get out of this room.'

'Leave you?' Now that she had finally found him, he wanted her to go?

'Marry St Aldric. Be safe and happy. But for God's sake, woman, go away and leave me in peace.' He stood and grabbed her again, but it was not for another kiss. Instead, he hauled her up off the floor and spun her away from him. Then he opened the door and pushed her through it and out in the hall.

The oak panel slammed behind her, cutting off her words of apology.

You must understand, my boy, it is quite impossible...

Sam looked wildly around the room, searching for the bottle that he had already packed. Rum. Stinging, harsh and nothing like her kiss. He pulled the cork and took a mouthful, swished it and spit it into the basin, expelling the memory of her taste.

Nothing he had seen in his studies at land or at sea could explain the feelings coursing through him now. He understood the pumping of the blood, the mechanical and chemical processes and increases in humour that led to arousal and release.

But none of it explained the demon that possessed

him, the maggot in his brain that made him want the one woman he could not have.

It is my fault really. I should not have raised you together, as I did. At the very least, I should have made clear the relationship between you, to prevent this misunderstanding...

Lord Thorne's words were as fresh in his mind now as they had been on the day he had heard them. And they offered no more comfort now than they had then.

Your birth was the mistake of a youthful man. My wife was understanding, of course. She agreed that we should take you in. A natural son might ease her loneliness. We had no child of our own. And when, finally, we were blessed, she did not survive long enough to know our Evelyn.

Why could they not have left him where he was? If duty needed to be done, it could have been done at a distance, with a series of discreet and anonymous payments to guardians and schools.

And then he might never have met Evelyn Thorne. A life with no Evie in it was his greatest desire, and his worst nightmare, hopelessly mixed.

I could have acknowledged you. Perhaps I should have...

Before puberty, perhaps. Sam laughed bitterly at the thought, and took another swig of the rum to wash the bitterness away. If he had understood what Evie was to him, then he would never have fallen in love with her.

And as he had done so many nights before, he went

to the desk and took up his beads and a Bible so worn from use that it fell open automatically to Leviticus.

The nakedness of thy sister, the daughter of thy father, or the daughter of thy mother, whether born at home, or born abroad even their nakedness thou shalt not uncover.

He prayed, as he always did, for strength and for forgiveness.

Chapter Six

'Evelyn! Stop tormenting that poor kitten and see to your hem. I swear, girl, you cannot keep the stitches straight if you allow a beast to swipe at the edge of the linen.'

'I am sorry, Aunt Jordan.' Evie glanced at the work in her lap and tried to raise any interest in it. These sessions of needlework were another concession to her father's wish that she behave like a young lady. On the few evenings when she had no other engagement, she was forced to endure them, along with critiques of her deportment. As usual, they were a trial both to her and the poor aunt charged with teaching her.

She set the shirt aside and lifted the kitten into her lap, offering it the end of the string to chase. 'It is hardly fair to blame Diana for my indifferent needle-work. I was equally bad at it before she arrived.'

'Your manners have improved much in the last years,' her aunt reminded her. 'And you are on the cusp of success with St Aldric. Snaring a peer is much more challenging than plain sewing. Your stitching would improve as well, if you would but make an effort at it.'

If it was put to some other purpose than making shirts, then perhaps she would try harder. She remembered the pages in Sam's text books that explained suturing and wondered if large wounds were more difficult than the cuts she had closed. The stitches would need to be bigger, of course, and more numerous. As she poked at the linen, she imagined the resistance of skin, and the difficulties created when the subject flinched...

'Evelyn!'

The needle slipped and she pricked her finger instead of the cloth. She waved her hand in the air for a moment, trying to shake the pain away, then held it high to keep the drop of blood that formed from falling on the work. This sent her mind to the various methods to staunch bleeding, and the efficacy of causing it when one had an excess of certain humours.

Not that she would need any of this information as the wife to a duke. But that had never been her plan, not even from the first. She had studied and prepared so that, on the day that Sam finally realised his mistake and came home to her, she might prove herself a useful helpmeet to him. If she understood his work, then they would always have something to talk about.

But he had barely given her time to display any of her hardwon knowledge to him. While in his rooms, she had allowed the physical side of the conversation to come to the fore, proving to him in a most unlady-like way that she understood biology.

Perhaps she would have fared better if she had put the stethoscope back into the chest and turned the conversation to the use of leeches and cupping as the old Evie would have. Or behaved as the charming and witty young lady Aunt Jordan had taught her to be. Instead, she had tried to combine the two and it had been a disaster.

She had offered herself to the man she loved—and he had rejected her. Though she might deny it to herself, it was what she had feared might happen. Sometimes, six years of silence meant exactly what they appeared to. Girlish sureties might owe more to fairy tales and fantasy than they did to truth. There had always been a chance that the kiss she remembered as loving and passionate was nothing more than a peck on the cheek. She had been prepared for that.

But not for what had occurred. If anything, she had remembered the past too innocently. Or had his passion grown to conflagration during their separation?

And yet he denied it. He did not seem to know love from lust. She was sure, after all they had been through together, that she did. Why else had she waited so many years for him to come back to her? She was still a maid, in heart and mind. While she was sure that physical attraction played a part in her feelings for Sam, it was not the only reason she wanted him.

She thought of the kiss.

She must admit that, after the recent interlude in his

arms, lust played a stronger role than it had a few days ago. So that was what poets wrote about, and why men had fought for Helen at Troy. It was a quite different feeling than she'd had last week. Much more urgent. The feelings were as clear in her mind now as when he had been kissing her. She had but to think for a moment about them to feel the desire renew itself.

It made her feelings for St Aldric all the more unworthy. She had hoped that it would be easier to make the decision between them, once she had talked to Sam. And it certainly was. There would never be anyone in her heart of hearts but Sam Hastings. What she felt for Michael was but a pale imitation.

Why could Sam not understand that?

Aunt Jordan gave up a small yawn and Eve encouraged it with a yawn of her own and a stretch of her arms. She held out the poorly finished shirt for approval. The older woman inspected it and sighed, still disappointed in the work. 'We will try again, next week,' she said. 'And I will be attending the ball at the Merridews tomorrow, as your chaperon.'

'Yes, Aunt Jordan.'

'The duke will be there as well.' Her aunt gave her a significant look. 'It will give you another chance to demonstrate graces that do not come so difficult to you.'

It meant that the time for indecision was nearing an end. He might offer again. If he did, what reason did she have to refuse him? After this afternoon, it was likely that Sam would leave her again before he could learn the truth of his birth. She owed him that, at least.

When her aunt was safely stowed in a carriage and on her way back to her own town house, Eve turned from the door to search out her father. He might have claimed to be intractable this afternoon. But in her experience, even those edicts set in stone could be worn down by begging, pleading and promises to be the best possible daughter, and to never bother him again.

She found him in the study and, as he always did, he looked up from the book he had been reading and smiled as though her interruption was welcome.

'Father?' She smiled to show that the conversation would be a pleasant one and no real disruption. She bent to kiss him on the cheek.

'My dear.' He gave a curious cock of his head, as though already suspecting her intentions. 'Did you have a pleasant evening with your aunt?'

'Of course, Father. She is just gone home,' she said.

'But no visit from the duke this evening,' her father said with a slight frown.

'He was here earlier,' she said, with a little sigh of impatience. She did not wish to discuss Michael. Those conversations always ended with her father hopeful and her searching for a way to postpone capitulation. 'I will see him tomorrow at the Merridews. He cannot spend all his time with me, you know.'

'As long as he was not put off by the presence of

another man in the garden with you this morning,' her father said.

'You are speaking of Sam?' She managed an incredulous smile. But she could not very well argue that he was not 'a man'. He had removed any doubts on the subject as he kissed her. 'He is family, Father. And surely it was good to see him after all this time.'

To this, her father responded with a blank look, as though the matter was practically forgotten. 'He has not performed as well as I had hoped. Despite what he says, he hardly needed a university education in the navy.'

'Perhaps he felt the navy needed him,' she suggested. 'He was always an altruist at heart. And I am sure it is better, in the aftermath of a battle, to have a skilled man dealing with the injuries.'

'If that is what makes him happy, then I wish him well.' Her father gave a tired sigh, as though he hoped this concession was sufficient to end the discussion.

'Happy?' she responded with a worried frown. 'Content, perhaps. But to me, he seemed rather unsettled.'

'Because he is no longer comfortable in this house,' her father said. 'He had planned to leave immediately after speaking to me.' He frowned back at her. 'I was surprised to find him still with us when the duke arrived.'

'Because I would not let him go,' Eve said. 'It is ridiculous for him to stay at an inn when his old room is here and prepared for his return.' She was very close to pouting, which always felt silly, but it had been effective in the past.

'If he showed discontent, perhaps it was your fault for keeping him here.' Her father gave her a candid look. 'There comes a time when one must recognise one's place in society and know when one is intruding.'

'But he was not an intrusion. He belongs here.' Perfectly true, but too insistent. She moderated her tone and held out a supplicating hand. 'He was like a son to you.'

'Like a son is quite different from being a son,' her father reminded her. 'He was my ward. But Sam Hastings is no one's child.'

'Of course he is,' she said. 'Unless you would have me believe that he was hatched from an egg, or some other such fantasy. He came into the world in the usual way, from a union between man and woman.'

'Evelyn! Do not speak of such things. They are unseemly topics for a young lady.'

'I would not have to, if you would be forthcoming with what you know.' She was giving him a full-on pout now, she was sure. She would follow it with tears, if she had to. It was the height of foolishness. But if topics were continually being put off limits to her because of her gender, a reasonable argument would not be possible. And she must have her way.

'Are you going on about that again?' her father said with a sigh. 'Really, Evelyn, you must realize that this is no business of yours.'

'It is my business,' she said and allowed her lip to tremble. Then she pinched the needle prick on her finger, which gave a fresh throb of pain and made her eyes water. 'Because I love and care about…' she paused to gulp back a sob '…both of the men involved.' Let her father think it was not just Sam that she sought to help. She gave him a hopeful smile through the tears. 'St Aldric would be most grateful, I am sure. He has told me often, in candid moments, how sad it is to know that nothing else of his father has survived. He would welcome any family that he might find.'

'It is not up to me to make such decisions,' her father said a little less confidently. 'I promised, when the boy was merely a baby…'

There. The tears were doing the tick. He was almost ready to admit the truth. 'Any oaths spoken to the old duke can no longer be binding now that both he and his duchess are dead. It is only Michael now. And he is so very alone. If his father had known that telling him would be a mercy, I'm sure he would relieve you from your oath.'

This approach, which did not seem so focused on Sam's happiness, was having its effect. She could see her father's resolve fighting with his desire to impress the duke. 'There are other things that would make St Aldric happy, you know. He will not be alone with a wife and children.'

'He will have those,' she said dismissively.

'When?' her father said, bringing the conversation to a halt. 'You know what he wants, Evie. And what I expect from you. He has waited for months, yet you will not give him an answer.'

'I will, soon,' she said. But perhaps she would not

have to. Sam clearly thought himself unworthy. If it was because he lacked money or status, surely it was better to be half-brother to a duke then a barely acknowledged ward.

'Soon, you say? Then I will tell the duke about his brother, at that time.'

'So! You admit the truth, then?' It was hardly a victory if he admitted it to her, but would not tell Sam.

'Yes,' her father said, with another sigh. 'I fulfilled my part of the bargain by seeing to it that the child was educated and launched in a profession. And by keeping my mouth closed, until you came to me, to pry it open.'

'I knew it. I had but to look at them together to be sure.' For a moment, her own triumph overcame all else.

'And now, I suppose, you think you can blurt the story to them at the first opportunity,' her father said, with a disapproving shake of his head.

'I will, if you will not,' she said, stamping her foot like a child.

'And you will hurt them both. If they must be told, as you think they must, it should be done quietly, privately, and by me. It will be shock to both men, even if it is a favourable one. I have documents to show that this is no idle claim and there can be no doubt in the minds of the parties involved.'

He was right. Random assertions by her would mean nothing. She must allow her father to do it in his own time. 'As long as it is done soon,' she said.

'I will do it when you agree to end this nonsense of

indecision.' He was looking at her directly, obviously unmoved by her histrionics. 'I have been far too lax with you, Evelyn, and have only myself to blame for this. You are behaving like a spoiled and wilful girl. In all other things I might demur. But in this, I will remain adamant. You are my only child and all that remains of my beloved Sarah. You are my heart and my life. I cannot sleep easy until you are settled. And for you, nothing less than a duke will do.'

So this was the impasse. She had known there would be a day when all the girlish wheedling she could manage would not be enough. And it had finally come. Father would release the truth, if she surrendered her hopes.

She weighed the situation as rationally as she was able. Both St Aldric and Sam would know their connection. They deserved it. On their last meeting, Sam had made it quite clear that she could wait for ever and never have him. He expected her to marry the duke.

But he had also kissed her, which negated his other behaviour.

She would accept the duke, as her father wished. Betrothed was quite a different thing from married. Many things might happen before they got to the altar.

Then she would write to Sam, tell him of her intentions, and give him one last chance to stop the engagement. If he did nothing, she would go forwards, just as Father wished her to. There were many things right with having Michael as a husband, but only one thing wrong. The fact that she did not love him was hardly an obstacle. She would love only one man in her life. If she could not have him, better to choose someone that she liked.

But everything must be accomplished soon, before Sam took it into his head to leave London for Scotland or the sea. She took a breath, held it for a moment and committed to a plan.

'If you promise that you will tell them both, I will accept St Aldric the very next time he suggests it, which is likely to be tomorrow evening.' Now that she had agreed, it was simply a matter of scheduling and giving Sam a strict timetable in which to change his mind. She glanced at the calendar on the writing desk. 'We shall have an engagement ball next week. The banns will be read starting next Sunday. The ceremony shall follow shortly thereafter. The whole business shall be settled by next month, if that is to your liking. As long as you swear to tell them.'

Her father was looking at her in amazement, as though trying to decide whether to upbraid her for setting standards or show the happiness he felt at getting his way.

'It is all I want for a wedding present from you,' she coaxed. 'And I doubt I would keep the secret for long, now that I have wormed it out of you. I am but a woman, you know.'

He smiled in response to her joke, though she was not being the least bit funny. 'You are probably right. You are a fickle creature, my dear, and I cannot expect you to keep mum. Accept the duke and set a date for the engagement ball. Invite Hastings to it and we shall settle it all on the same night.'

Chapter Seven

'I do not wish to alarm you, Lady Evelyn, but there is an enormous spider crawling on your shoulder.'

Without thinking, Eve reached to brush it off, realised that she felt no such thing and stopped to stare impolitely at her dance partner.

St Aldric smiled affectionately back at her. 'I have managed to gain your attention at last, have I? A point for me, then. And minus one for you. When faced with such a horror, a young lady is expected to shriek and throw herself into the arms of the nearest gentleman. She is not supposed to settle the matter for herself.'

'I...am sorry.' She tried to remember where they were in the pattern of the dance, so that they could continue without a misstep. She had managed to march through it so far without thinking. But clearly the duke had noticed that he did not have her full attention.

'Is there anything the matter?' he asked.

Yes. Everything. 'No.' She shook her head. 'I am merely distracted.'

'As always, you know to call on me, if there is some-thing I might do to aid you.' He was giving her a sur-prisingly direct look. Though it was still masked in his characteristic smile, she was sure that he was ac-tively concerned with her and would truly do anything, should she ask.

Let me go. And make Sam love me again. Now there was a request that one did not make of one's future fi-ancé. Besides, she was not even sure the second half of it was possible.

'Was your visit with your old friend a disappoint-ment?' St Aldric asked, cutting right to the heart of the matter. 'You seem changed since he has come. More sombre.'

'I am sorry,' she repeated, forcing a smile. 'I will try to be more cheerful.'

'Do not change for my sake,' he said. His hand, when next it took hers in the dance, gave hers an encouraging squeeze. 'You cannot help what you feel. But I take it that your Dr Hastings was much altered since you saw him last. That is bound to be disappointing.'

'Yes,' she admitted. Confusing would have been a more accurate way to describe it. There had been noth-ing disappointing about his kiss.

She glanced at St Aldric, who epitomised disap-pointment in that particular area. She was being un-fair to him. His kisses were as polished and correct as everything else about him. Perhaps it was some flaw in her own character that left her untouched by them.

He continued to smile at her.

She smiled back and felt a wave of the kind of sisterly affection that Sam had tried to thrust upon her, until she had broken his will. This was what it was like, to feel nothing for a man, but to like him well enough not to wish him pain.

'And now that you have seen him, is your mind altered on the subject of our marriage?'

'I...don't understand what you mean.' She tensed and missed a beat, though he corrected easily to compensate for it. The duke had caught her flat footed, again, both in mind and body. She had not expected his next proposal to include any mention of Sam.

His smile was more sympathetic than jolly. 'I am not so dense as all that, Evelyn. You had a *tendre* for the man. I expect you lost your heart to him at a very young age. And that is not an easy thing to forget.'

'You are too perceptive,' she said. 'It is your only fault.' That was not true. He did not miss a beat when they danced. He was never nonplussed or flustered. If perfection was a flaw, he had it in spades.

'I will work to rectify it, once we are married,' he said. 'If you agree to wed me, I shall be as dense as you wish me to be.'

Was he giving her permission to be unfaithful to him? Surely not. But she could not help but think that, when one's heart lay elsewhere, there might be certain advantages to a husband who had announced his willingness to turn a blind eye.

If she had wanted that sort of a marriage, she should be satisfied with the response. But it was likely to destroy the respect she had for him, knowing that he did not care enough for her to be hurt by infidelity.

She thought again of the interlude in Sam's room and tried to focus on the end of it, when he had claimed it nothing more than unworthy lust. On his part, perhaps it had been. But she would have happily died in his arms to give him the peace he requested.

As long as it had occurred after a consummation.

'Will there be any response to my comment? Or are you to keep me guessing?'

'Comment?' She dragged her mind away from Sam and glanced back at the duke again.

'On my willingness to conform to any demands you might set, should you marry me.'

He had made the offer that she had promised to accept and she had been so preoccupied on thoughts of another that she had not heard him. This did not bode well for the future.

'I will offer in another way, if you seek something less businesslike. There could be moonlight, candles and your pick of the jewels in my lock room. I could purchase something new for you, if you do not fancy them. I will get down on one knee. Although I have no experience in it, I will serenade you. Write poetry. I will do anything to see you smile. But you know my feelings on the subject of matrimony. I am eager to hear yours.'

Father was right. She had kept him waiting long enough. If she truly wished to have Sam's approval, it had been given, repeatedly. He proclaimed St Aldric an excellent match. He had also told her, emphatically, that there would be no marriage between the two of them.

Then he had kissed her. Her mind kept coming back to that. She suspected it would, for the rest of her life. Just as she had spent six years thinking of the last kiss, she might spend sixty on this one.

Would the memory of that be enough to sustain her, or would it become a bitter reminder of how a marriage might feel, if it was to the right man?

It did not really matter. Sam had thrust her from the room and was probably still planning to leave the country. And all because she had forced him. If she continued to do so, she would lose his friendship along with his love.

She turned to St Aldric, this time with her full attention, or very near to it. 'I am sorry. I never meant to be cruel to you, or to keep you waiting so long. You are right. It is time that I answered.'

To her surprise, the man at her side looked eager to hear her response. And there was a flicker of doubt in it, as though he was not sure what it might be. She had been so focused on herself and her own wishes that she had been tormenting him with her indifference.

He deserved better.

'Of course I will marry you. At the time of your choosing.'

'A special licence is the thing, I understand,' he said. 'Brides all want them, to show that the groom is ardent and has some pull with court. I will procure one.

But the actual ceremony need not be hurried. We must allow enough time to celebrate the event...'

He continued to plan, as eager as a bride, while Eve retreated to a place where life was simpler, endings happier and kisses as passionate as she knew they could be.

Sam roused to the sound of a knocking at the door. Or perhaps the hammering was in his skull. It was no less than he deserved. Life at sea had inured him to strong drink. But the quantity he had taken in the last day and a half was enough to send a sailor's brain to pounding.

'Doctor Hastings.'

Without another thought he was out of the bed, his hand on his case of medicines. 'What is it? Am I needed?' He shook his head to clear it, ready to face whatever emergency awaited him.

'Nothing so dire, I'm sure. There is a letter for you, sir.' The innkeeper waited nervously in the hall, a liveried footman from Thorne Hall beside him.

Probably a cheerful missive from Evie, expecting him to dance attendance on her, as though nothing had happened between them. But he would not forget the sight of her, kneeling between his thighs.

He shook his head again, harder, and let the pain it caused be a distraction. The girl was far too headstrong for her own good. And naïve as well. The best way to protect that innocence was to stay far away from it. Sam rubbed a hand over his dry eyes. 'Whatever it is, tell him he can take it to the devil.'

The footman looked alarmed, but did not budge. 'I am to put it into your hand directly and wait for an answer, Dr Hastings.' Tom had been an underfootman when Sam had left the Thornes. He had been younger than Evelyn, no more than a child and already in service.

Had she chosen him for this, sure that Sam would remember the boy with sympathy and not wish to give him trouble? She was a demon to torment him with tricks like that. But it was another proof that she knew him as well as he knew himself. He sighed. 'Very well, then.' He held out his hand for the letter. 'Wait.' Then he closed the door on the pair of them and broke the seal.

He could recognise the hand in an instant, for he had seen it often enough, coming to both love and dread her regular letters. It appeared this one could not be avoided. He could not very well climb out a second-storey window in an attempt to get away from it, and by sending Tom she had made it impossible to deny its receipt.

Sam.

He held his breath. The start was innocent enough. But there was not a thing he could stand to hear from the girl, after the shame of what had happened between them.

Firstly, let me apologise for coming to your rooms and upsetting you as I did. I had no right and no invitation.

And no reason to apologise, since the fault and the sin had been totally his.

I must offer a second apology for trying to control the course of your life and choose your future to suit myself. I have no doubt that you are quite capable of surviving without me. It is pure selfishness on my part to try to manage you.

But I beg you, with all my heart, not to return to the sea. Above all, do not go there on my account. I swear, I will do what is necessary to keep you safe, even if that requires me to cease communication with you.

Dear Evie. She was frightened for him and willing to do anything to preserve his unworthy life. He felt the tightness in his chest, half-joy, half-regret, that came with any thought of her. He smoothed the letter in his hands and read more.

On your recommendation, and that of my father, along with the continued requests from the duke himself, I have agreed to St Aldric's offer of marriage. To celebrate the engagement, Father is giving a ball this coming Wednesday. I must remind you, you promised to attend. And despite all that happened after, I hold you to that promise.

Damn the girl. He had promised. And despite what reason demanded, he did not want to go so soon.

If it is truly your wish that I marry, I need your strength to help me carry it through. And if, for any reason, it is not, then you must tell me before that time.

I await your answer...

Et cetera.

For the first time in her life, Evelyn Thorne had done exactly as he'd told her to. It was a trap, of course. She'd finished the letter with a reminder that he might stop the proceedings at any time. He had but to ask and she would cry off.

And in that, she had created the perfect hell for him. It was no less than he deserved, he supposed. He had revealed all to her, or as much as he ever would. Now that she knew he had feelings for her, she sought to inflame them with jealousy. He had given her reason to hope, even as he had pushed her away.

But before that, he had approved her match and promised to attend her wedding. As her older brother, he owed her as much. If he did not want her to think of him, ever again, as anything more than that, he had best learn to play that part.

He went to the table, took up his pen and wrote.

Evie,

You have nothing to apologise for. It is I who am at fault. As to what happened yesterday, it is best that we never speak of it again. I will forget if you shall.

As to my going to sea again? It is clear that this distresses you. My plans are not set. If it is so important to you, I will forgo the navy and practise on land.

But be damned if he would go to work for St Aldric. That was too much to expect of him.

As to your wedding, I am supremely happy for you, and send my congratulations to his Grace as well. I will remain in London and attend your engagement ball and wedding, just as I said. You have my word. Eagerly awaiting the day that I might call you her Grace, instead of my dear little Evie...

He scribbled a signature at the bottom, then blotted and sealed it before opening his door and calling to the footman, who was still waiting in the hall.

There. It was done and the letter was on its way. It might as well have been written on black-bordered mourning stationery, for all the satisfaction he felt. Even though the situation had been hopeless from the first, he could not help feeling a fresh sadness at losing her, any more than he could keep from wanting her.

But in medicine he had found that it was sometimes necessary to give the patient poison to counteract a more serious malady. Attending her wedding would be so to him. Swallowing this bitter pill would be the first step towards a cure for his affliction.

Chapter Eight

Evie was beautiful. Sam had known that already, of course. He had never seen her decked in finery. He had thought her lovely in a simple day frock, but tonight she was magnificent. The silk of her ball gown was as blue as her eyes, and as smooth as her hair. A necklace of gold and diamonds lay, like a collar of stars, about her lovely white throat.

Perhaps Thorne had been right all along. Even without the complication of blood, the creature that stood before him could not have been his. The necklace alone was worth a year's salary. He could never have afforded to put it there. And to her, it was nothing more than her mother's necklace that she had never been old enough to wear. With St Aldric, she would have this and better. A different jewel for every month of the year and a room full of ball gowns to wear them with.

With the duke at her side, the picture was complete. He was tall, handsome and nearly as golden as she. He smiled at her as though it was an honour for him to have won her. They were like two pieces of statuary, designed to complement each other. As a duchess, she would glitter, as she did tonight, from without and within. She was already so bright that it hurt to look upon her.

Yet he could not seem to stop. Once he had fulfilled his promise to her, he would be gone for good. If memories were all he had for sustenance, he would burn each detail into his brain so that he might never forget. As he waited to be presented to the happy couple, he did his best to mask the hunger he felt for her and arrange his face in an expression of brotherly pride.

'Sam.' She reached out and took his hands in hers.

'Evelyn.' She leaned in, presenting her cheek to be kissed. He could not very well avoid it without looking silly. He leaned forwards as well, kissing the air a scant inch from her skin. Even then, his lips tingled as if a spark sizzled between them, bridging the gap.

'It is so good to see you here. I feared you would not come.' She whispered it in his ear as he leaned close to her. When he leaned back, she searched his face with worried eyes. 'It has been almost a week.'

Since he had very nearly ravished her in his rooms. He still woke each night from a dream where the ending to that interlude had been different and he had felt her gasping in passion beneath him. 'I promised I would be here, to celebrate your happiness.'

'That is most kind of you,' St Aldric said. He was still at her side, quietly possessive.

'My felicitations to you as well, your Grace.' He bowed, feeling stiff and awkward.

'Thank you, Doctor.' St Aldric was better at managing a gracious response.

Evie was staring at the pair of them, as though hoping that there could be anything more than cordial dislike between them.

'And now, if you will excuse me?' Sam raised a genuine smile at the thought of escaping. 'I must not keep you from the other guests.'

There. He was through with the first challenge. Now he must manage a few hours of courtesy and then he could be on his way again. But when Evie was involved, nothing was ever that easy. Was it just because she was the hostess that she seemed to be everywhere he turned? Or was she actually following him through the gathering, showing up where he least expected her, to flash a smile or blow a kiss?

Each time, he turned away, pretending that he did not notice, or had not seen, or was too busy in conversation with another to speak to her. At last she caught him standing alone by the dance floor, with no excuse to avoid her.

'Dance with me.' She was holding out a hand to him, sure he would come to her, as he always had, and swing her easily in his arms.

'I do not think that is wise,' he replied. Just the thought of touching her made his palms begin to sweat.

'Dancing, not wise?' She laughed. 'Is that your professional opinion? I assumed that such harmless exercise would be recommended by a physician.'

'You know that is not what I mean,' he said in a harsh whisper, glancing around to be sure that no one else could hear.

She gave him a coquettish flutter of her fan. 'I really have no idea. If you mean something specific by the refusal, you had best tell me directly.'

'If you truly mean to marry St Aldric, I think it is unwise for the two of us to dance,' he said through gritted teeth.

'My commitment to him has not stopped me from standing up with every other man in this room. Save yourself, of course. You have been avoiding me.'

'I have not,' he said, wishing that it was not such an obvious lie.

'I am sure that St Aldric has no objection to it.'

'What he wishes does not concern me.' And now he sounded like a jealous fool.

'If not him, then whom? What reason could you possibly have that would prevent you? If people notice you avoiding me, they will wonder. And they will talk.'

Now she had trapped him. She was probably right. Someone would remark at how strangely he behaved around her. Above all else, there must be no talk.

She continued to pressure him, sure that he could not refuse. 'I am open for the next waltz. Stand up with me and stop being silly about it.' She gave him a sly smile. 'It will be over before you realise and, I swear, no harm shall come to you.'

'No! Not a waltz.' He'd said it too loudly and a matron a few feet away gave him a sharp, disapproving look. But the idea was simply too much to bear. 'I will stand up with you, if you insist. But let it be some other dance.'

'All right,' she said, giving him a disgusted sigh. 'La Belle Assembly. It is starting now. And we will stand up with St Aldric and another, so you need have no fear of upsetting him.'

Sam's eyes narrowed. 'It is not from fear of him that I refuse you.'

'Fear of me, then?' She gave a toss of her head. 'That does little to improve my opinion of you.'

The letter had been a lie. She did not need moral support to make this decision. She merely wished another opportunity to torment him. He seized her hand with no real gentleness, as he had done when they were children, and dragged her towards the centre of the room. 'Come on, then, brat. The sooner it is begun, the sooner it will be done. Then you must leave me in peace for the rest of the night.'

He had been right. This had been a mistake.

She had thought that a public temptation might force a commitment out of him. At the very least, it would give her one last chance to be with him. But this was not the memory she wished for. It was too painful.

They shared the set with St Aldric and his partner, a lady of great beauty and little wit, but she was a skilled dancer and little more was required of her now. They traded bows and curtsies, and the dance began.

Sam swung her to a place opposite him and circled. And though he followed the steps to the letter, it felt as though she was being stalked by a wolf. In comparison, St Aldric's pass was easy, relaxed and confident. He smiled at her, enjoying the dance, enjoying her company.

She turned back to Sam, who was watching her too intently, a frown upon his face. His eyes bored into hers, taking in her every movement to the point where it became alarming. And past the frown and the beetled brow, she saw the truth.

Jealousy. Frustration. Rage. It was not distaste that kept him away. He wanted her as much as he had on the day that they had kissed.

And now she danced with St Aldric again. In his eyes, she saw nothing of importance. He possessed her already, or very nearly did, and thus he was thinking of something else.

But each time Sam took her hand, it was as if he never meant to let it go. The release was stiff and graceless, as though he'd forced his fingers open to let her escape. He was gritting his teeth in concentration. He did not need to count the steps, for he seemed to have no trouble keeping track. His posture was rigid, as though he suffered pain at each touch of her fingers.

Yet he could not seem to get enough of it.

When they finished, she allowed him to escort her

back to the place they had been standing. Then he walked away without a word.

She stood for a moment, in indecision, then she followed, out of the ballroom and through the halls of the house, to the place she knew he must go.

It was dark in the garden, smelling of night-blooming flowers and the beginnings of the still heat that would drive the *ton* to Bath or the country. They had not bothered to light the yard, so no one had strayed from the house. But someone who was familiar with it would need no light to find the garden bench under the elm. He was there, of course, a dim outline against the darker bark of the tree.

She sat down beside him. He did not acknowledge her presence, so they sat in silence for a time, not wanting to spoil the moment. Then he said, 'You promised, Evie. You promised that it would not come to this if I stayed.'

'You were right, before, when you said we could not waltz.' If they had, she'd have made a fool of herself, clinging to him on the dance floor. If she was in his arms, how could she do else?

He sighed. 'You feel it as well, then? I hoped perhaps you had been spared and that the other day, in my rooms, had been an aberration.'

She nodded, wondering if he could see. 'If it is not possible to master the feeling, then perhaps we should not try.'

He did not move to look at her, sitting as still as he

had when she'd joined him. 'You do not understand. Not truly.'

'I understand that there are scant minutes left, before my choice is irrevocable. If there is any reason to change my mind, I will take it.' She reached for his hand and squeezed it, hoping that he would feel the urgency.

'You must trust me to know what is best for you,' he said with his best physician's tone, 'And I tell you that there is no reason for you not to marry St Aldric. In fact, I insist that you do.'

'Why must you keep playing the tiresome older brother?' she said with an amazed shake of the head.

'I have not done it enough in recent years.' he replied. 'You need someone to talk some sense into you, since your father cannot seem to manage it.'

'Sometimes, I wonder if you are just thick, despite all your fancy education, or if you are joking with me. You know that brotherly wisdom is not what I want from you.'

'What else can I offer?' He sounded so hopeless, she wavered between pity and annoyance. It seemed that if she wanted words of love, she would have to speak them herself.

'Let me put it plainly, since you refuse to. I love you, Sam. I always will. I wish you to offer for me. But you are pretending that you do not understand. Please, Sam. Please. Declare yourself. I will speak to Michael, and to Father.' She gave his hand another urgent squeeze.

She shifted her body, ever so slightly, towards his

and turned so that their faces were only inches apart—and suddenly they were kissing in a moonlit garden. In an instant, it was as it had been in his rooms.

She tried to remember where she was. And when. There were people waiting for her in the ballroom. And a man who wanted nothing more than to make her his bride.

But she could not stop wanting the man who would make no promises. There were so many things wrong with the moment that she could hardly enumerate them.

So she thought of none of them and opened her mouth.

She could hear the rustle of her own satin gown as he crushed her body to his and feel the rapid flutter of her tongue in his mouth. His circled to still it, filling her mouth with the taste of him.

His hand was at the back of her neck and he hesitated, stroking once, carefully, so as not to disarrange the curls. Then he smoothed over her neck, her shoulders, her throat, and very carefully slipped inside the bodice of her gown.

The man she loved was touching her breast. She caught her breath and held it, giving him more room to touch her as he kissed. His hand was gentle, even as his mouth was not, warm on her skin, his fingertips barely touching the puckering tip as his teeth grazed her lips and his tongue pushed deep, retreated and returned.

If this was what he wanted from her, she would gladly give it. Her legs trembled and her centre was wet, as she knew it would be when the time was right to join with a man. If she had the nerve to touch him, as she had in his room, she was sure that he would be hard for her and just as eager as she felt.

Her hands were beneath his coat, on his waist. It was improper, but wonderful. She slipped them under the bottom of his waistcoat and could almost feel his ribs through the linen of his shirt.

In response, his fingers closed on her nipple and tugged. She gasped, biting at his lower lip, wanting more. He must give it to her. He simply must. She needed his tongue on her breast, and his body in hers, so that they might be one in flesh, as they had always been in spirit.

Her hands dropped lower, clutching him firmly by the backside. And she pulled herself upwards, forwards, into his lap. And for just a moment, she felt the bulge of him pressing against her through her gown. The trembling seemed to come from inside her now, like the expectant rumbling at the beginning of a storm.

He pulled himself away from the kiss and whispered into her ear. 'Is this what you want from me?' He thrust his hips against her.

She nodded eagerly, digging her fingers into the muscles of his body and pressing herself against the hardness, praying that this was the answer he wanted, the one that would make him continue.

'Because it is what I want from you,' he said. The hand that caressed her breasts squeezed to the point of pain. 'It is what I have wanted from you since my first desire. To taste your body with my mouth. To push myself into you. To spill my seed.'

'Yes,' she whispered, closing her eyes. 'Yes. Yes.' She could imagine him there and the moment of helpless surrender when she became his.

'This is what I want,' he whispered, his breath in her ear even hotter than his kiss. 'And it has nothing to do with a romantic declaration, or a marriage. I want to have you, right now, here in the garden, naked like Eve. I want to use you for my pleasure, without a thought to what is right or good.'

He was making something that would be wonderful sound sordid. But she wanted it all the same.

The hand that had been at her waist pressed her head to his mouth so that he might continue to whisper, 'I want your body, Evie. That is all. I want to ruin you. I want what I want. I do not care if it destroys us both. That is why I left you six years ago. And that is why I must leave now.'

And then he pushed her away, out of his lap and on to her side of the bench. The night air had grown cold. She could feel it against her exposed breasts and the constriction of the bodice pulled low under them.

'Compose yourself. And then go back into the house and find your betrothed.' His voice was as cold as the air, passionless. 'As I have told you before, I am not the man for you. Marry St Aldric, Evie. Please. He will care for you. I cannot. But you must stop this pointless hoping that there will ever be another choice.' He stood then and walked away. Deeper into the garden or back into the house? She was not sure.

She tugged the bodice back into place and laid a hand against her cheek, waiting for the blush to subside. If she sat here a while longer, she would be as cold as he was, but not as emotionless. She was angry.

Sam Hastings was all she had ever wanted. She had tricked him into coming here and followed him like a fool, only to be refused again. He had brought her to the brink of fulfilment. And then he'd delivered nothing more than threats and speeches, like some Drury Lane villain.

Did he not realise that she might have taken some pleasure in the act that he found so base and unworthy? Her body still seethed with desire. It was as if she was waiting for some gift that only Sam could give her. He had shown it to her, held it close and then snatched it away at the last minute. Then he behaved as though she was the one who was cruel.

Well, it would not happen again. Tonight, she would make her choice once and for all. She would go to another man and would never turn back. At least St Aldric would not reject her without even trying to love her.

She would tell herself that what she felt for Sam had been a childish infatuation. And now, as he claimed, it was nothing more than lust. Neither of those things had a place in her future. She would leave the memories of the good Dr Hastings in the nursery where they belonged.

And some day she would revisit the memory of this

night and find it as brittle and faded as a dried flower. She would look at her children, hers and Michael's. And she would wonder why she had ever been so silly as to want another man.

But not today. Today it would be difficult. She thought of St Aldric and his many good qualities. And, slowly, she felt the ardour subside. Michael was handsome. He was kind. He had an excellent sense of humour. When he saw her, he would walk towards her, not away. And there would be a smile on his face that showed promise and a joyful anticipation of their future together.

She stood and took a breath. The air was clean and cool, and if it smelled of a man's cologne, it was probably just her imagination. Then she straightened her dress and went back to the house.

Chapter Nine

'Lady Evelyn has made me the happiest man in London.'

Sam had returned to the ballroom in time to see the announcement. St Aldric was grinning like an idiot, oblivious to the fact that the woman beside him was still flushed from the kisses Sam had given her.

As he had for so much of his life, he stood by mute, struggling with his own base desires, and allowed it to happen. He had stood in the garden for a time, waiting to see that Evie got back to the house without help. There were no tears from her, no passionate cries that he return. A profound silence seemed to emanate from the spot they had been. A few minutes later, she had got up and walked away from him.

It felt like the day he had first put out to sea and watched England retreating until it was a dot on the horizon. He had seen the water as nothing more than distance between him and the woman he could not help but love. It was the same now. The ballroom seemed to stretch before him as couples filled the dance floor for a waltz. And Sam was on the only solid spot, losing her all over again.

He took a sip of his drink, wishing that it was something stronger. Another hour, perhaps, and he could make his excuses and depart. But he did not have to stand here, watching her be happy without him.

It had been so easy in the garden, when all innocent, brotherly thoughts had fled like animals before an advancing fire. She wanted him. He must have her, or he would go mad. He felt the pressure building, the desperation to drag her to the ground, throw up her skirts and lose himself in the softness of her body.

He imagined entering, in one quick thrust, the tightness of her, the rush. Her cry of shock at the loss of her maidenhead.

And discovery. Thorne's shout of outrage. The discovery of the truth.

Disgusting. Obscene. Profane.

He'd pushed her away, horrified at what he had done, but secretly, sinfully triumphant. She was his in all ways that mattered. She would marry the duke. But each time he touched her, she would be thinking of this moment and how much she had wanted another.

It must never happen again. He would go to the Americas this time. Or Jamaica. With luck he would succumb to a fever and his suffering would end.

He turned away from the crowd, hoping to find diversion, in cards, brandy or perhaps a pretty face that might distract him from the only woman he really cared to look at.

Instead, he found their father.

'Doctor Hendricks.' Lord Thorne had tracked him in the crowd of well-wishers and Sam checked the height of his raised glass, the fullness of his smile, searching for any telltale signs in his person or behaviour that might show him to be less than enthusiastic for the match.

'Sam.' Now Thorne's tone was as it had been, when he had still been a favoured son. Before he had made his stammering offer for Evie.

'My lord,' he said, with a half-smile that he hoped was not too strained.

'St Aldric and Evelyn have nearly finished their dance. There is no reason to wait longer.'

For what? he wondered. Was he expected to depart already?

But it seemed Thorne was speaking more to himself, than to Sam, as though there was some duty that he had been delaying. 'I...we...wish to speak to you, in my study.' If anything, Thorne looked as uncomfortable as Sam felt. It was odd that he could not match his mood to the festivities. Surely, this must be a moment of triumph.

'Of course, my lord.' Sam glanced at the clock. 'On the half-hour, perhaps? That should give enough time for the crowd to settle.'

'Twenty minutes.' Thorne seemed to see this as some sort of reprieve. 'An excellent idea. Until then.' He moved off through the crowd again and Sam watched him absently accepting congratulations for his daughter's successful match.

It was damned odd.

And there in the centre of the dance floor was Evie. Dear, sweet Evie, looking almost as overwhelmed as Thorne. As she spun past him, in the arms of the duke, her eye caught his, if only for a moment. She gave him a smile of triumph, her eyes shining not with tears but with an almost evil glee. She had done what he'd requested. She hoped he was satisfied.

If he must lose her—not that she had ever been his— it was better that it be this way. She was angry with him and would be so for some time. If she had doubts about this decision, he would be gone before she expressed them.

But all there proclaimed St Aldric an exemplary man, truly a golden child, who had not allowed the ease of his success to taint his innate goodness. He was worthy of Evie. And he obviously adored her. He would treat her as she deserved to be treated. Sam doubted he could ever bring himself to like the duke. But he would have no cause to see the man again, so it did not matter.

The dance ended. And the precious St Aldric was not at her side, damn him. He had won. The least he could do was enjoy his prize. But Sam had seen Thorne part the couple as soon as the music stopped, whispering something to the duke.

Evelyn had watched. And though she would not have been able to hear what was said, she nodded. There was the strangest look upon her lovely face, as though she was remembering some troublesome detail that rendered the moment less than sweet. Then she had turned back to the crowd, perfection again.

Something was afoot. But damned if Sam could imagine what it might be. The clock ticked out the minutes until his appointment.

When the requisite time has passed, he made his way up the stairs to find Thorne.

And here was St Aldric as well, waiting in the office of his mentor, looking almost like an errant schoolboy, although he had no reason to. The self-deprecation was all the more annoying in its effectiveness. Had he been any other man, Sam would have been instantly in sympathy with him.

But he was not just any man. And Sam could manage nothing more than the expected courtesies. He smiled and bowed to the peer, and to Thorne. 'My lord. Your Grace.'

'Sam.' And there was the old familiarity from Thorne again. Sam greeted it with a cynical smile. Now that Evelyn's fate was sealed, he was to be a favoured son again? Not bloody likely.

'I suppose you are wondering…you are both wondering…why I have asked you here,' Thorne said, unsure which man to look at first. 'It is at Evelyn's behest,' he said.

There was another awkward pause. 'She realised the truth, you see. And has convinced me that, if it was obvious to her, it might be to others. She thinks that perhaps it would be kinder to settle the matter, before there was any speculation. And since you would be here, tonight...'

Then he paused again, as though the previous statements might mean something and need no addition.

St Aldric was looking back with a crooked grin, as though he could not quite contain his amusement. 'As it stands, Thorne, the only speculation occurring is between the two of us. It is clear that you wish to share some information and that it is coming difficult for you. Please, speak. Doctor Hastings and I are quite in the dark.'

Thorne looked back and forth between the two of them now, like a rabbit caught between two foxes. 'I must first say that I mean no disrespect to you, your Grace, or to your father, who was a dear friend of mine. Nor was it ever my wish to betray his confidence.'

'Since he has been dead nearly ten years, he is unlikely to call you out on it,' St Aldric said, with an encouraging smile. 'But I take it that he swore you to some secret or other and that it is weighing heavily on you, now?'

'It is nothing so very serious,' Thorne said, encouragingly. 'Nothing that many other men have not done. There was no real disgrace in it. And you must know that your father was always the worthiest of men.'

'It pleases me to think so,' St Aldric said with a nod.

'It is only because the truth is likely to come forth

with or without my help, that I am speaking now,'
Thorne said.

'Then out with it, man,' St Aldric said, with another
smile. 'The good doctor can attest that, when pulling
a splinter, there is no point in drawing slowly. It only
prolongs the pain, as this prolongs suspense. What is
this not-so-terribly-dark truth that you have been con-
cealing from the world?'

'This happened when you were just an infant, obviously. And your mother still quite fragile. There was...'
another dramatic pause '...an indiscretion.'

Sam's attention had begun to wander. It was clear
that, whatever the problem might be, it was St Aldric's
concern and not his. Perhaps he was here in case the
shock proved too great and a physician was needed. If
that was the case, he would have done better to bring
his bag.

But there was nothing about the duke that made him
think the man would be prone to fits at receiving bad
news. His colour was high, of course. But considering
the reason for the evening, it was only natural.

'Since both my mother and father are gone from this
planet, I see no reason that such information should
be concealed any longer. Speak with my blessing. Immediately, in fact.' Even a saint had limited patience.
It appeared that St Aldric had reached the end of his.

'There was issue, from this indiscretion,' Throne
said hurriedly. 'The child survived. A boy.'

'But that would mean...' St Aldric gave a surprised
shake of his head. 'I have a brother?'

'A half-brother,' Thorne said hurriedly.

St Aldric was forwards in an instant, gripping the man's arm. And for the first time since meeting him, Sam saw what he must look like when angry. 'You knew of this? And did not tell me? Damn it, man, I must know all.' He calmed himself just as quickly. But it was clear that he was eager for more news. 'Did my father reveal anything about him? For I would like to know him. No. I must.'

'It will not affect the succession,' Thorne said hurriedly. 'You are the elder. And he is a bastard.'

'I do not care,' St Aldric insisted. 'He is my blood, whoever he is. He is both kin and responsibility to me. He will not want. I shall be sure if it. I have a brother.' His face split into a grin of amazement.

As usual, St Aldric was proving himself to be the most admirable of men, showing not an ounce of jealousy or outrage at this sudden revelation. There was no sign that he viewed it as an embarrassment. To be gifted with a bastard brother was not an inconvenience to him. On the contrary, he seemed to think it a marvel. Despite his charmed life, the duke had lacked but one thing: a family. And, of course, God had granted him that. Now he was complete.

It was just one more depressing sign that he was the perfect mate for Evie. The man was as kind and generous in private as he was in public. Sam supposed that it was just another sign of his debased character that he still wanted to choke the life from the fellow.

'He has not wanted. Not for a moment,' Thorne said

hurriedly. 'Your father put him in my care from the first and swore me to secrecy.' Now he looked past the duke, to Sam. 'I raised him as my own. I told him nothing of his actual parentage. I misled him…'

And now both men in the room were looking at Sam, Thorne giving a shrug of apology.

'I do not understand.' But, of course, he did. This meeting had been about him, all along.

'I did not get you from a foundling home,' Thorne said. 'Your mother was a seamstress named Polly Hastings, who lived in the village of St Aldric. She was struck with childbed fever and could not care for you. I took you away, shortly before she died.'

'My mother.' He'd known he had one, of course. But he had not thought of her in years. And his father…

'You told me…' He could not manage to finish the sentence, for the implications of it, though they had been horrible before, were becoming all too clear.

'What I told you before does not matter,' Thorne said in warning, as though he would be likely to blurt out the story he had been told, in all its repellent detail. 'This is the truth: the old duke was your father.'

And that changed everything. In one sentence, he had gone from monster to man. His desires were neither base nor sinful. They were a perfectly natural affection towards the most beautiful of women. There was no impediment to realising them.

The room was spinning. Or perhaps he was. The sudden lightness of spirit might have set him turning like a windmill. It had certainly unsettled his brain. His tongue was stuck to the roof of his mouth. He could not seem to call for the brandy he so desperately needed. Or the air, which he could not manage to take into his lungs.

When Sam opened his eyes again, he was staring at the ceiling. Thank God, Evie had not been in the room to witness this or she'd have teased him 'til his dying day. It was bad enough to have fainted in the presence of St Aldric and Thorne. There was no point in arguing that he had weathered battle without incident. He had been ankle deep in blood and severed limbs, the screams of the wounded and the smell of death close about him, and had never had such a reaction as this. They must think him weak, easily overwrought, sensitive and emotional.

But it was worse to think of Evie standing over him, laughing at his discomfiture, while the man who was his half-brother weathered this news with good humour and *sang-froid*.

'Are you all right?' St Aldric was looking down at him with a bemused expression that split into another grin. An oddly familiar expression, for it was rather like the one that Sam saw when shaving. Now that he was encouraged to see the similarities, it was plain that they were brothers. Colouring, eyes, the height of the forehead and position of the ears—all were similar to his. There could be no doubting it.

The Duke held out a hand, ignoring his silence. 'I suppose this comes as rather a shock.'

'You have no idea.' It had been the rush of knowledge that had done for him, just now, the new facts pushing the old certainties from his head. And the knowledge that he had been wrong, so very wrong, about the one thing he had been most sure of.

Evie could never be his. She was his sister. His feelings for her, no matter how powerful, were vile and fetid. All his adult life, he had known himself for a sick dog, or a base sinner, unworthy of the company of the one he most wanted. No amount of distance, violence or Bible thumbing had offered relief.

Then, in an instant, he had been washed clean. The well-manicured hand still hovered before him, blurring slightly as the last of the swoon cleared itself and his pulse returned to normal. Sam gripped it and allowed himself to be pulled upright.

'It was a great shock to me as well,' St Aldric supplied, trying to put him at ease. 'I had grown quite used to the fact that I was the last leaf on a dead family tree.'

'I am a natural son,' Sam said, still confused by the man's joy at this news. 'I hardly think that counts me as part of your tree. A weed beside it, perhaps.'

'Better that than blasted, bare ground.' St Aldric was staring at him with a strange hunger, then pulled him forwards into a brotherly hug.

Sam felt the hand that had lifted him clapping him firmly on the back, then the duke gripped him by the shoulders and held him apart, staring into his face as Sam had to the other, a moment ago. St Aldric was memorising the features, cataloguing, comparing, finding the agreements just as Sam had done and nodding in revelation. 'You have no idea what a relief it is to find kin of any kind, when one has resigned oneself to being alone.'

There was no response Sam could offer to this but a blank stare. He had never felt the need of a brother and certainly did not want the father and sister that he'd thought he had. It was better, so much better, to think oneself alone than to have those. Now, he had been thrown into yet another family that he did not wish for.

His feelings must have shown on his face, for St Aldric looked away in embarrassment. 'I am sorry. I did not think. You know all too well what it is like to be alone. But that has changed for both of us. I will acknowledge you, of course. And I will help you in any way I can. I'd have done it for Evelyn's sake, of course. But there is so much more reason now.'

Evie.

He had forgotten the events of the past hour. Lady Evelyn Thorne was now engaged to the Duke of St Aldric, who was, apparently, his brother. It was like losing her, only to think he had won her, and then lose her again. Everything had been settled between the three of them. It would be most unworthy of Sam to spoil the happiness of his brother and steal Evie's best chance at a match.

The decision took little more than an instant to make. It might be unworthy, but he would do it in a heartbeat. Evie loved him. Her words and actions had proved it, just an hour ago. Sam owed nothing to this interloper. Despite what St Aldric might think, they were still enemies. All the good will and kittens in the world did not change the fact.

'As I said when we first met in the garden, your help will not be required,' Sam said, softly.

St Aldric's eyes widened in surprise, as though he had never considered the possibility that someone might refuse him. 'What reason would you have to deny me? Surely I can open doors for you that you could not open yourself.'

'I have been content with making my own way thus far,' Sam reminded him.

'Sam.' Thorne's voice held a fatherly warning to mind his manners and accept the charity of his betters. It gave him an hysterical desire to laugh in the man's face. There was no earthly reason he need follow the advice. Thorne might have raised him, but the pretences were so false as to render the relationship without value.

'And now you might be more than content,' St Aldric said. 'You must be my personal physician, as Evelyn suggested. It would be little more than an honorary position for many years, I assure you. I am young and healthy. But there would be a stipend attached to it. And the honour of association. You are still unmarried. I suspect that there would be many women who would actively seek you out.'

'Evie.' He was struck dumb yet again, and, if he was not careful, he would faint for the second time in his life, right here on the office carpet.

'And you said she knows of this already?' St Aldric

looked to Thorne for confirmation. 'It makes her actions so much clearer. The eagerness that we meet. The suggestion that I take you on.' St Aldric was grinning at him again. 'For a time, I quite thought that there was something else to it. But now it is clear. You will be as a double brother to her. And dear to both of us.'

If St Aldric had his way, Sam would be just as separate as he had always been from the one woman he wanted and forced for ever into her company. 'You presume far too much, your Grace.' He pulled away from the man who held him and shook the wrinkles from his coat as a distraction from the thoughts racing in his head.

'You are an ungrateful brat, Sam.' After what he had done, Thorne seemed to think he had a right to an opinion.

Sam turned his anger on the more deserving target. 'You have no right to lecture me on it, now that the truth is out. What are you to me, sir, after all this time?'

'Only the man who raised you,' Thorne said.

'And fed me on lies like they were mother's milk,' Sam snapped back. 'For Evie's sake, we will not discuss the extent of your perfidy. But do not think I forgive you for it.'

Thorne's eyes widened. 'She is my only child. I did what was best for her and for you as well.'

From the other side of the room, Sam heard a soft clearing of a throat and remembered that they were not alone with the argument. He turned back towards the duke and stared at the man in silence. Did St Aldric really think it was an honour to be so abandoned by one's father that one had no identity at all? Then Sam had been wrong about him. The man was a fool.

'I can see that it will take some time for us to get used to the knowledge that has been imparted, and to digest the change and decide what best to do about it,' St Aldric said, still the soul of diplomacy. It was clear that he did not think himself in need of delay, but he meant to hold his tongue and bide his time for the sake of his brother. He reached out a hand and patted Thorne upon the back. 'Thank you, for my father and myself, for the service you have done my family and for revealing it to us now.' They were the right words for the circumstance and it made Sam feel all the smaller for his petulance, no matter how justified it might have been. 'And now, if you gentlemen will excuse me?' He gave a gracious nod as though he had already heard the affirmative response and excused himself from the room.

Thorne stared at Sam and let out a hiss of disapproval. 'You might be the son of a duke, Hastings, but it is clear that you have inherited none of that family's grace. Evelyn was right to choose St Aldric over you, for you are behaving just as I assumed you would.'

'Thank you for confirming that,' Sam said.

'Her happiness has been all that mattered, to me, from the first. And you were never meant to be a part of that.' Thorne was smiling in triumph, like a priest in the throes of religious mania. 'Go ahead. Run to her. Tell her everything. Try to turn her against me. See if she thanks you for it.'

Evie looked at her father with the adoration of an only daughter. In her eyes, he could do no wrong. To hear otherwise would crush her. Sam shook his head. 'No, Thorne. I do not think so. I would have to be willing to break Evie's heart and claim it is for her own good. The day I do that is the day I prove I am truly your son.'

Chapter Ten

After leaving Thorne, Sam still wanted a drink. In a case like this, Dr Hastings would prescribe a brandy for shock. That and a chance to sit down and sort this through without people prying through the contents of his head. 'Physician, heal thyself,' he muttered and headed towards the decanter in the library.

When his nerves were settled, he would find Evie. He must apologise for his words in the garden. As soon as they had cleared the air of that, he could persuade her to cry off on the engagement and come away with him. She had offered once to run to Gretna with him. It would have to do. There was no time for a proper courtship and banns.

He must get her out of London before the scandal broke. And, even more important, he must get her away from this house. He had been able to manage a chilly respect when he'd believed Thorne was his father. But he owed that man nothing at all now. He had not been taken in out of love or charity, or for any bond of family. His presence here had been to curry favour with old St Aldric. It was nothing more than that. It was only a matter of time before he shouted those words in Thorne's face, along with the ugliness that Sam had believed to be the truth.

Evie must never know of that. Thorne had been trying, in his own sick way, to protect her. If Sam was to be her husband, that task would fall to him. And he would make a better job of it.

'Hastings!'

Sam flinched. His newfound brother had been waiting for him in the hall, eager to continue the conversation. He turned stiffly. 'Your Grace.'

St Aldric looked faintly amused. 'You cannot avoid me for the rest of your life, you know. Not if I mean to claim you as family.'

Perhaps not. But he was tempted to try. 'I am not avoiding you,' he said cautiously. 'I thought you meant to let things settle, before talking again.'

'How long is that likely to take?' St Aldric asked. Apparently, he thought a few moments were long enough to re-order one's whole understanding of life.

'It was a considerable shock to me, to learn the truth after all this time.'

St Aldric nodded. 'I suppose I cannot really imagine, any more than you could imagine my life.'

'My presence or absence could not really matter so much to it,' Sam said, drily.

The duke seemed surprised. 'On the contrary. Although I can afford almost any luxury, this was one thing that I knew to be ever out of my reach. One cannot purchase a brother.'

Any more than one could cease to have a sister. But it had just happened to Sam. He looked at the duke again, trying to raise some of the filial emotion that the man hoped for. He felt only jealousy. 'It takes more than blood to create such a link.'

'Perhaps,' the duke allowed. 'But I see no reason why the two of us might not at least become friends.'

If he saw no reason, he was deliberately being obtuse. But then, when they had met, the duke had assumed a bond existed between Sam and Evie. Sam had denied it and relinquished all claim on her. He could not suddenly reverse the position without explaining his reasons.

He did not want to become like Thorne, willing to say anything to achieve his ends. The shame of his earlier beliefs would die quietly, assuming he did not speak of them to all and sundry. Newfound kinship did not entitle St Aldric to every sordid detail of Sam's past.

In his mind, he transferred the cordial indifference he had shared with Thorne to his new family and gave a respectful nod. 'I am sorry. You are correct. I am being unreasonable about the situation.'

'As you said, it was a shock,' the duke reminded him. 'You can hardly be expected to take it calmly. Your temper does not offend me in the least. Certain latitudes of personality are permitted. In families.' The words made him grin again, showing that he felt no reservations at all in the discovery. It was yet another example of the man's superior nature.

And it was tiresome in the extreme. 'All the same, I apologise,' Sam said, grudgingly.

'Apology accepted,' said the duke. There was no corresponding apology, of course, because the man never did anything to need one. He was, as he had been from the first, perfect.

But now he was engaged to Evelyn.

'Now that we have settled that, you must excuse me,' Sam said, suddenly sure that if he had to look into the handsome face and listen to one more sensible word he would fall on the duke like an animal and beat him senseless.

'A moment.' St Aldric held up a single finger, as though such a small gesture was all he needed to subdue Sam. 'This still does not answer my question. I do not see any reason why we cannot become friends. Do you?'

It was an opportunity to be honest, for once. To explain the situation and how impossible a friendship between them would be.

Instead, he lied through his teeth. 'Of course not.'

'Then it is settled.' The duke was smiling at him as though a few words had cemented their relationship. 'If you wish, I will put you forth as a member of my club.'

Where they could keep running into each other, he supposed. Did the man intend to be omnipresent in his life?

St Aldric saw his hesitation. 'It will give you a

chance to meet other gentlemen and advance to the position of your choosing. You might not wish to be my personal physician. But there are any number of gouty old lords in need of your services. Perhaps one of them would suit you.'

When put this way, it was actually tempting. And he'd have been on it like a shot had the offer come from any other person. Sam felt a moment's wistfulness for the family he might have had, had things been different. He'd not thought he needed an actual father. At least not for affection. But a hand on his shoulder to steady him, educate him and introduce him in the correct circles would have been damned helpful.

He'd had it once from Thorne. That man had proved false in the end. Then he remembered the reason for Thorne's change of heart. It was the same reason he could not accept the help of the man in front of him. Evelyn.

Sam gave a respectful nod of his head, trying to keep the sarcasm from his voice. 'Thank you for your offer, your Grace. But, regretfully, I decline. I doubt I would have much use for a club membership, for I have no intention of remaining in the city.' Nor would he be particularly welcome there, should his plans come to fruition. He would either leave alone a broken man, or scuttle the romantic hopes of the very man who sought to help him.

'Very well, then. As you wish.' By the look on his face St Aldric could not decide whether to be angry or disappointed by this latest rejection, probably because he was not used to hearing the word no. 'But you must dine with me tomorrow night. I insist upon it.'

Insisted, did he? And what did that have to do with Sam's own desires? He searched for the first available lie. 'Unfortunately, that will not be possible. I am otherwise engaged. Now, if you will please excuse me?' Then he made his retreat to find the only person he really wanted to see.

'Evelyn. We must speak.' Sam was striding towards her with a grim smile on his face and all the purpose and conviction of the British navy.

Eve felt a flutter of apprehension. It seemed she had been holding her breath for the better part of an hour, waiting for some word from the office. Perhaps she would see the two of them, side by side, shaking hands and revelling in their good fortune. It would be awkward, for a while. But maybe some good would come of the evening and she would feel less guilty for her lapse in the garden.

But the duke was nowhere to be seen. And Sam was using her full name, as he only did when he was angry, or maintaining the same artificial formality that he had been.

'Sam.' She turned to him, reminding herself that she must not reach for his hands, or give any of the other familiar gestures that seemed to inflame his passion for her.

He ignored her coldness and held her by the shoulders. Unlike the gentle touches in the garden, his grip was tight, as though he feared she would run from him if he released her. 'How long have you known?'

There could be no question of what he meant. And it did not seem that the truth had set him free, as the Bible said. He looked more guarded than ever. She looked away, afraid to meet his eyes. Must she feel guilty for this as well? It was the one thing she had been sure of.

Other than her love for Sam, of course. And that had been wrong. Now, she was losing confidence in this decision as well. 'I have suspected for some time. When St Aldric began spending time with me at the beginning of the Season, he seemed so familiar to me, like an old friend, though I knew I had not met him before. But it was only a suspicion. And then you returned and I knew.'

'Why did you not come to me with this information? Or did you tell him?' His voice was as rough as his hands and the words were punctuated by a shake.

'Sam!' She pulled away from him. 'Do not think that our old friendship allows you to treat me so. I did not tell you because I had no proof. You would have thought the idea ridiculous and dismissed it. As for telling St Aldric...'

Now it was his turn to look away. Was he still jealous? Why did he bother to show it now, when it was too late? 'It was unworthy of me to accuse you. Just now, he was as surprised as I.'

'I did not mean to keep a secret from either of you. It was only recently that I took my suspicions to Father and more recently still that I convinced him to admit the truth and share the news with you and Michael.'

'Your fiancé,' Sam said, looking seriously at her.

'Your brother,' she added, wishing that he could be happy about the news.

'And was the decision to marry in any way tied to this revelation? The timing seems most convenient.'

'Father agreed to share the information, now that Michael is to be my husband,' she said. And what difference could that make to anything?

'Then this marriage—' Sam gave a broad sweep of his hand '—has nothing to do with the depth of your affection for St Aldric.'

Why did he wait until now to care about how she felt about St Aldric? He had not troubled to ask her of this before. Then, he had been set on her accepting the man, ordering her about, as if he had right to. 'He is as good a man as one could hope for. You told me so yourself. When you know him better, you will like him, as I do.'

'That is quite impossible, Evie. And you should know the reason why.'

Her patience was at an end. 'Do not blame me for a separation between the two of you. You made it quite clear that you did not want to marry me. You spoke highly of him. You insisted that I must accept him. I did as you asked. Put aside your petty jealousy and make peace with the results. Now that I have made my decision, the rivalry is over between you.'

'That's what you think, is it?' He was looking at her with a crooked, rather cold smile, as though he was a frustrated schoolmaster with a particularly dense student. 'Enough of him, then. We will talk no more about it. Tell me more about your feelings for me.' He had been practically trembling with his, just a few hours before. But the news had changed him. Now he was resolute, guarded and very much in control.

'My feelings?' She was not even sure what to call them. How was she to tell him?

His hands turned gentle, settling on the exposed skin between gown and gloves. 'You said you loved me, tonight, before the announcement.'

'Before the announcement,' she repeated. That was more important than the words that came before. 'What I said then no longer matters,' she said, pulling free of his hands again.

'It does to me. Tell me again.' His voice was low, coaxing and unlike any tone he had used before. She felt it under her skin, burning into her very heart. It was the voice she had longed to hear, from the first moment he had returned. The boy who'd left had finally come back to claim her.

She had to fight to remember why she must not listen to him. 'I am engaged to St Aldric now.'

'And you love him?' Sam tipped his head to the side and gave her the kind of expectant look she was used to, when he wished to wheedle some truth out of her. It made her feel like a little girl again.

Now, of all times, after she had chosen to do the adult thing and put nonsense aside, it was infuriating to be treated as a child. 'What I feel for St Aldric is none of your business.'

'But what you feel for me is.' His fingers tightened on her arm again and she felt herself melt.

'Let me go.' The words did not sound very convincing, even to her.

'I tried,' he said, in a tired voice. 'And I was wrong to do so. I find it is not possible.'

'And yet you agreed to do it, not once, but many times over the last week.' How many chances had she been expected to give him to declare his feelings? And he had denied them every time.

'I lied. But you must have known that, for you kept badgering me to change my mind.' He was smiling now, as though secure in his ability to break her down. He was pulling her closer.

She pulled away, trying to resist him. Did he not understand the sacrifice she had made? And all because he would not admit to his feelings when he'd had the chance. Then she reminded herself that accepting St Aldric was not a sacrifice. It was a triumph. 'If you think you can have me now, after a few romantic speeches, you are sorely mistaken, Sam Hastings.'

'Am I?' His smile had changed, full of a knowing confidence that both frightened and excited her. 'Let us see, shall we?' And with one last tug she was in his arms.

This kiss was different than the others had been and, as she surrendered to it, she wondered if he had an infinite variety of tricks to use on her. Perhaps he did. Everything about this kiss shouted, *I know you. I know what you want.*

How was that possible, when she was not even sure of it herself? He opened her mouth with his tongue and explored with an innate confidence, claiming each inch of it for himself. When he'd finished, she was breath-less, as though her heart had forgotten to beat while she was in his arms.

'Very well,' he said, with another confident smile. 'I will not concern myself with your feelings for any other man. I think we have proved them to be insignifi-cant.' His finger was tracing along the cord of her neck.

She batted it away. 'It is too late for this.'

But he paused for only a moment before returning to his teasing. 'The moon is full, and we are alone,' he reminded her. 'And in love. I cannot think of a bet-ter time.'

The correct response would be *I do not love you. Leave me alone.* But it would have been a lie so great that she could not get her lips to form the words. In-stead, she repeated, 'You are a day too late.'

'As long as we both breathe, there is time,' he said, pulling her into his arms again. His hands were on her waist, possessively smoothing over the ribs, and he was kissing her again, his lips travelling from her mouth to her shoulder. There was no anger in him, as there had been when he had complained of his inabil-ity to master himself. It was no selfish attempt to use her. This was a calculated attempt to arouse her. 'Come with me, Evie,' he whispered. 'To the garden. I want to show you something.'

This was the Sam that she remembered, always daring her to be reckless.

But the girl he'd left was gone. She had banished her tonight and vowed to be different. There would be no more visits to the garden, no dabbling in medicine, no more nonsense and foolishness.

Evie Thorne might have allowed these kisses and encouraged this man to pull her down into the grass and do what he would with her. But the future Duchess of St Aldric must not.

She yanked her arm out of Sam's grip, pulled back and let fly with a slap that was worthy of any she'd dealt him as a child, the sort that had sent him to Father over the unfairness of a gender that would taunt him unmercifully while knowing he could not strike back.

He pulled away from her, hand on his cheek, shocked and angry.

'I said *no*.' She hardly recognised her own voice. It sounded low, powerful and humourless. It was the voice of a woman, not a girl. It was a voice to be obeyed. She stared him down, unflinching, and watched the anger change to wariness.

'Evie?' he said, with a wry smile.

'I think it best that you refer to me as Lady Evelyn,' she said. 'As you have been doing since your return. You will take no more liberties with me, in public or in private. In turn, I will be polite and respectful, for Michael's sake. But if you cannot abide these terms, our previous connection will not matter, nor your kinship with the duke. You will not be welcome in my home and in public I shall cut you dead.' Aunt Jordan would have been proud of the speech. It was just as it should have been, when one had given offence to this degree.

But the look on Sam's face was heartbreaking. At least she would have the satisfaction of knowing that she had been right in bringing forth the truth. The care-worn look that had troubled her was gone from his face, but now he was staring at her as though he could not quite believe what he was hearing. He rubbed his jaw, feeling the tenderness where she had slapped him. 'Why, Lady Evelyn, I do believe that you are serious.'

'Of course I am serious, you cloth-headed dolt.' It was a weak epithet that harkened back to the time when they were children. The words that suited him now—rake, seducer, villain—were ones she could not manage to say, even if they were true. 'Unless you can manage to treat me with respect, there can be no more contact between us.'

'Because you are betrothed to St Aldric.' And now he looked as though he wanted to laugh.

'Yes,' she said, in frustration. Had she been wrong about him all along? Was her oldest friend and first love really so cruel as to mock her for behaving exactly as she should have from the first?

'Very well, then.' He was agreeing, but he continued to smile as though caught in some enormous joke. 'I will treat you as I ought, with respect. But not because of your precious Michael. I will do it so that you may see how empty simple courtesy is, compared to our true feelings for each other.' He reached out a single finger and touched her cheek.

And she swore she could feel every touch he had given her in the garden and taste his kiss on her lips.

'In a week, you will be begging me to take you away from him. And I will have mercy on you and do it. I have fought battles to resist you that render your engagement to the duke insignificant. And I have lost every one of them. We belong together, Evie. For better or worse.'

Chapter Eleven

Sam entered the duke's London home with the sort of grim resignation he saved for delivering bad news to patients. He had received the invitation with indifference and refused it out of hand. But after his talk with Evie, he reconsidered. She would likely be attending as well. Since she did not intend to see him alone, he had best take any opportunity offered to be in the same room with her.

And perhaps a small show of co-operation on his part would sate St Aldric's desire to know him better. He had stopped Sam again, before his exit from the Thorne home, to renew his offers of aid, advancement or at the very least a good meal. It appeared that the duke meant to badger him non-stop until he had made a brother of him.

Sam could halt such efforts in their tracks by announcing that his plans to seduce the man's fiancée would make friendship difficult, but such honesty was more likely to reduce his contact with Evie than increase it. He had always thought himself a moral man, other than the repellent desire to bed his own sister, which put him square on the road to damnation. But now that his love was proved innocent, it appeared that he was capable of covetousness, duplicity and any number of other vices, if it helped him gain her back.

He would not hurt her, of course. But he would not have to. It would take only the smallest of nudges and she would drop the plan to marry another, and come running back into his arms. Then things would finally be as they had been meant to be, from the first.

Tonight, she was playing right into his hands. The duke must have informed Evie of Sam's reticence. This morning, he'd another visit from Tom the footman and a terse note from Evie, reminding him of his promise to help her with this match. Unless Sam wanted to make the breach between them plain to St Aldric and answer the questions that would follow, he must put on a smile, come to dinner and prove that he had accepted the new boundaries of their friendship.

He had jotted down a hurried answer. The fact that she had set boundaries did not mean that he must be contained by them. When he had encouraged her to marry, he had not been in full possession of the facts.

When he had realised that he could offer no other explanation than that, he had ripped the paper to bits. Some things must wait until they were alone and face to face. Perhaps, by then, he would have come up with a better answer than this, for it sounded weak, even to him.

Instead, he had written a single line of assent to her and another to St Aldric. He would go to dinner and make nice, as long as it suited him to do so. If an opportunity presented itself to further his plans for Evie, he would take it and boundaries be damned.

But now, he was rethinking his plan. His first impression on arrival at St Aldric's home, was that his rival had him hopelessly outgunned. The house where their father had lived was magnificent. Everything about it was larger, more ornate and superior to the Thorne town house. The ceilings were higher, the carpets deeper and the furniture glowed with a patina of age and privilege. There were likely several other properties even larger, scattered about the country.

Sam thought back for a moment to the little cabin in the bulkhead of the *Matilda*, with its brass fittings and worn wood desk. He had been quite proud of it. It was a symbol of that most cherished thing aboard ships, privacy. To have one's own space was a luxury.

But this house was full: of people, of servants, of responsibility. Was the duke ever truly alone? If not, then Sam would not envy him. Nor would Sam envy him for Evie, who, despite what *The Times* might say, would never truly belong to St Aldric. She loved Sam. And he had no reason not to love her back.

Nearly four-and-twenty hours later, that fact still took him unawares and brought a smile to his face. The identity of his father and his connection to this great house were incidental, compared to the broken link to

Lord Thorne. He was free to love Evie. There was justice in the world, after all.

'Welcome.' St Aldric was striding out into the hall to meet him, as though he did not trust the butler to deliver Sam the last few feet to the place where guests were gathering for the meal. 'I am pleased that you managed to break your other engagement and attend. I hope it did not cause difficulty.'

'Not at all,' Sam said. They both knew he had lied. But if the duke wished to pretend it had been true, then so would he.

Now the great man sat at the head of the table, and a fine table it was. The silver was heavy and the knives so sharp he might have performed surgery with them. The crystal was delicate and the wines superb. The linen under it all was whiter than Sam had ever seen, and monogrammed at the corner with the family crest.

His family crest, Sam thought distantly. *And mine.* If St Aldric still wanted to claim him, when all was said and done, there might be advantages to allying himself with his true father's house. They would not outweigh his love for Evelyn, of course. Until she cried off, he and St Aldric were at war.

But if they battled tonight, at least it would be in good company. Along with Evie and her father, there was a bishop, a cabinet minister and his wife, and several young ladies and gentlemen of excellent breeding and manners.

Seated next to him was Lady Caroline…something or other. It did him no credit that he was thinking of

Evie during the introduction and now could not remember the woman's name. St Aldric had given him a significant look, as though assuring him that this was an excellent match, should he pursue it.

As if the girl would want anything to do with him. Or he her. He could choose his own wife. In fact, he had made his choice already, though he doubted that St Aldric would approve of it.

Evie was giving no outward sign that she remembered their last meeting. She was too smart to think that he would give her up without a fight, but apparently she awaited his next move. She treated him with courtesy and charm, just as she did the other guests. She was as glittering as the ring on her hand and as gracious as a duchess, listening attentively to the conversation around her, contributing intelligently and hanging on every word that the duke spoke.

And damn the man if he was not worth listening to. He was polite, witty and intelligent. He responded to debate with a cool rationality that won the point more often than it lost. He did not allow his head to be clouded by his own rank and people's instinctive deference to it.

Worst of all, he had announced to the others at the gathering that there was a connection between them. He told all who would listen that Sam was a 'distinguished physician' and that they 'shared a father.' He acted as though the sudden appearance of a bastard brother was the best imaginable news.

It was maddening. What could Sam possibly say that

could distinguish himself to Evie? And now St Aldric was questioning him about his profession, making an effort to draw him into the conversation and phrasing questions so that Sam could display his skill without seeming boastful.

It was artfully done. He'd have been most grateful if he hadn't already hated the man. There was no way to bring him down a notch, nor could Sam think of a way to raise himself in the eyes of his beloved. And then, as did all conversations that touched on medicine and care, someone enquired about poor Princess Charlotte.

Inwardly, he flinched. It was a doctor's worst nightmare to be put in care of a beloved member of the royal family, only to manage the birth so badly as to lose both the patient and the unborn child. His usual plan was to have as little opinion as possible, so as not to offend. But then, in a flash of insight, he saw the direction the conversation would likely go, if he but let it alone. 'I would not dare to make a judgement without being in the room for the birth. There can frequently be complications that are not apparent until labor has begun. But I think the subsequent suicide of the attending physician speaks for how deeply he felt.'

'He should not have been involved at all,' Evelyn said, with no attempt at diplomacy.

Sam was eager to see what would happen next. It had been so long since he'd shared one, he'd forgotten that a dinner with Evie was often more diverting than a night at the theatre. It had been less than twenty-four hours since the engagement. And at less than a day, her plan to be a suitable wife to St Aldric had lasted longer than he'd have wagered.

Her blunt statement caused the rest of the table to fall silent in shock. While ladies no doubt had an opinion about such things, they certainly did not voice them with such candour in mixed company. But Evie was not just any lady, thought Sam, and did his best to hide his smile. She had a smattering of medical training and strong feelings on the subject of obstetrics.

'And who would you recommend be at her side at such a time,' St Aldric asked, 'if not a trusted family physician?' The smile he gave her was more indulgent than critical and more patient than many men would be.

But Evie would see nothing but the criticism. 'I suspect a midwife would have done just as well,' she said, chin up in a posture that Sam recognised as a warning sign that she was prepared to fight all who might disagree.

St Aldric continued to smile at her, but glanced at Sam as though expecting an ally. 'It appears that my betrothed does not think much of your profession.'

Evie saved Sam the trouble of choosing a side by answering for herself. 'It is not that I think less of Dr Hastings, or doctors in general. It is simply that I disagree with any man's ability to fully understand birth and labor.'

'They train at university, study texts and the work of experienced physicians,' argued St Aldric. 'I am sure they must learn sufficiently.'

'Most texts are written by men. I doubt their competence in a process that they themselves cannot experience,' Evie said solemnly.

Her future husband could not help himself. He laughed out loud.

For a moment, Sam felt sympathy with his newfound brother. The poor fellow could not have picked a better way to get on his beloved's wrong side.

'Furthermore,' she announced over the sound of the duke's mirth, 'we would still have our dear princess, if the doctors had not been so ham-handed in their treatment of her.'

It was quite possible that this was the case. It was not Sam's place to question the practice of other doctors. He'd have come to the defence of his profession had it been any other evening. Tonight, he did not wish to cross Evie by disagreeing. The high road was diplomatic silence.

But St Aldric was not aware of that. 'What can you possibly know of such things, Evelyn? You are but a maid, after all.' It was an honest question, but it sounded almost like he was questioning her virtue.

It was like watching a man dig his own grave.

Sam saw the increasingly mutinous glint in her eyes as she readied her argument. 'I have been present at any number of deliveries when we are in the country,' she announced. 'I have also read the texts that they use at university. In comparison, I studied the techniques of the village midwives and aided them in their work. They now deem me so proficient that I can manage all but the most difficult deliveries before calling for a doctor.'

Around the table there were giggles and gasps. The good Lady Caroline blushed and the bishop on her other side blanched white.

Just as he remembered her, Evie was unaffected by approval or disapproval. When she was truly set in a course, she would not be moved. Her animosity forgotten, she looked to Sam as though conferring with a colleague. 'I would not attempt a Caesarean, of course. But neither would you, I wager, unless you were sure that there was little to no hope that the mother would be alive to see the birth.'

'They seldom survive the operation,' he agreed. 'But perhaps at table is not the best place—'

'From what I understand, the physician in residence bled Princess Charlotte for months and starved her instead of feeding her up stout. Then he left her to labor for days without so much as ergot to hurry things along.'

As a physician, he could not contradict what she said. She did not argue from ignorance on the subject. She had explored the techniques of both physician and midwife. He had been trained in only one and taught to ignore the other as inferior.

'And the baby was breech. If the lady's hips are small it is like trying to force a melon through a keyhole.'

There a genteel squeak from one of the more impressionable ladies and a soft moan from Lord Thorne.

'He did not use the forceps when he had the chance,' she finished.

'I thought you did not believe in such things,' Sam supplied helpfully and waited for the fun to continue.

'She should not even know what they are,' St Aldric announced, trying to regain control of the conversation.

Evie ignored him. 'I said they were used too often. Not that they were totally useless,' she said. 'Although if you are skilled, it is possible to turn the child without them.'

'Is she in the habit of discussing such things with you?' St Aldric demanded of Sam, going a bit white around the mouth. Sam wondered if he was still so eager to have a doctor in the family. He suspected that, when they had a chance to speak in private, he would be called to task for leading Evelyn astray.

He took a sip of his wine. 'I have not been in the country for years, your Grace. But Lady Evelyn has questioned me at length on the subject of medicine, since I have been home.' Let the man think what he would of that. If he did not understand the risk of another man spending so much time with his future wife, then he deserved to lose her.

'Is that what you talk about?' St Aldric seemed honestly surprised at this. Had he expected the worst? And if so, why did he do nothing to prevent it?

'We talk of other things as well, Michael,' Evelyn said dismissively, totally ignorant of the duke's jealousy.

'You should not be talking of this under any circumstances,' the bishop announced, no longer able to contain himself. 'Nor should you doubt the superiority of men in all things, or worry overlong about alleviating the suffering of the childbed. It is woman's lot, since the fall of Eve.'

'But men are not superior in all things at all times,' Evelyn said with a smile. 'And my sympathies to my biblical namesake, but do you seriously believe that the Lord made women to suffer and then invented opiates to taunt us with the possibility of relief? I believe the Bible also says something about being stewards to the land. I assume that means that we are to make use of such natural palliatives when we find them.'

Now her father was holding his head, as though he were experiencing a megrim. The lady at his side gave a little shriek of outrage. But the matron opposite Lord Thorne responded with a solemn nod of approval.

'Evelyn.' There was the faintest touch of warning in the duke's tone, as though he thought that he could manage the sort of unspoken communication that one sometimes saw in couples whose hearts were beating in time.

'Yes, Michael?' Evie responded with a sweetness that would have had a smart man diving under the table for protection.

'Do you think it is proper to disagree with a gentleman who is our guest?'

Evie blinked back at him, all innocence again. 'Only on such subjects where I am sure he is wrong.'

The bishop tossed his napkin aside and pushed away

from the table. 'You must excuse me, your Grace. But this is simply too much.' He stood and stormed from the room.

St Aldric's ability to maintain decorum was dependent on a certain level of respect and the polite co-operation of all present. But Sam could have warned him that, with Evie involved, he would never see it again. Now the normally composed duke was trapped on the horns of a dilemma. Did he discipline his betrothed at the dinner table? Mollify his guests? Pronounce her opinions charming and pretend that nothing had happened?

After a moment's cogitation, he muttered, 'Bloody hell', and threw his napkin aside as well. Then he rose with a smile, added, 'Ladies and gentlemen, if you will excuse me for a moment', and disappeared after the clergyman.

At his rising, the people around the table dutifully came to their feet and settled back into their chairs when it was clear that he would not stay long enough to notice.

A nervous silence fell over the remaining guests, who began to eat quickly, as though hoping for an excuse to end the evening early. Sam savoured the remaining courses in his own good time. He could not remember a better meal.

'Evelyn, may I speak to you in the library for a moment?'

'Of course, Michael.' The other guests had already

departed and her father paused nervously in the doorway, his hat in his hand.

The duke gave him a reassuring smile. 'You needn't
wait, Lord Thorne. If you wish, you might return home
and send the carriage back for Evelyn. She will be perfectly safe here for an hour or so.'

Her father gave a relieved nod and abandoned her
to her fate. Although Eve could not imagine that it
was anything too grim. She watched Michael closely
as he led her to the library and saw no reason to fear.
He was clearly annoyed, but not so angry as to frown.
A few kisses and a small amount of contrition on her
part, and life would continue as normal.

Or perhaps more than a few kisses. Now that they
were engaged, there was no reason that she could not
employ more drastic methods to distract him, should
he prove difficult. They would be alone for at least an
hour and some of that time might be spent in the first
real intimacy she had shared with Michael.

As he closed the door behind them, he looked at her
in surprise. 'You needn't be afraid, Evelyn. I am not
happy with what occurred at dinner, but I am not going
to be such an ogre as to deserve the look you are giving me.' He sat on the sofa by the fire and gestured to
the cushion at his side.

'What look?' She glanced at herself in the mirror
above the mantel. *Oh, dear.* It was one thing to appear
penitent and quite another to look like Joan of Arc on
the way to the stake. And she had not even been think-

ing about her behaviour. She had been thinking of being alone with Michael.

She turned back to him, quickly composing her expression to something more pleasant, and took her seat. 'I am sorry, Michael, for the Friday face and my behaviour earlier.'

'I am pleased to hear you say so,' he said. Perhaps that was all that was required of her.

'Of course, the conversation at dinner could not be helped,' she added, so that he might understand her better.

'On the contrary,' he said softly, 'I think it can.'

'I fail to see how,' she replied. 'It is not as if I can sit silent through the meal.'

But judging by the look Michael was giving her, that was precisely what he expected her to do. 'There will be situations in the future that require you to exercise restraint.'

'Even when the opinions are as wrong-headed as some that were expressed this evening?'

'Especially then,' he said with a nod.

'I fear that will be impossible,' she said, again. 'I have many strong opinions of my own.

'But when we are married, I expect you to have fewer of them,' he said. 'And at dinner, it would be better to limit yourself to discussion of the food, or the weather, or perhaps fashion.' He smiled as though the matter was now quite settled.

And then he kissed her.

The interlude that followed was frustrating. She did

not particularly want to be kissed until the discussion between them had been settled in her favour. She understood full well what he was doing, since she had considered using just such a technique to win him over. Her mouth was occupied. Therefore she could not argue with him. It was manipulation, pure and simple.

And it did not seem to be working. His lips were on her shoulder and his hands on her ribs. While she no longer felt like talking, she was far too clear headed for this to be going as he'd hoped. If it had been Sam, she would have been near to losing her senses by now.

And she would have been kissing him back. The half-hearted attempt she was making to show affection to Michael would be attributed to innocence, for a while at least. But what happened if her uninterest continued to the wedding night and after?

After a half an hour or so, Michael released her. It appeared that he was not bothered by her lack of enthusiasm. His breathing was fast, his skin flushed and his eyes more black than blue. 'For the sake of your reputation, I must stop now,' he said, brushing back a lock of her hair. 'But I will see you again, tomorrow. Your father wishes me to stay to dinner. And after...' He kissed her again, more ardently.

Or so she suspected. It felt no different to her.

Then he escorted her out into the hall and helped her with her wrap, seeing her safely to the waiting carriage.

The door has scarcely shut before she realised that

she was not alone. She peered into the darkness on the opposite bench. 'Sam?'

'So I am no longer Dr Hastings to you?'

She had spoken out of habit, forgetting her plan of the previous evening. 'Whatever I might call you, you owe me an explanation for this intrusion.'

He eased himself into the light from the carriage lamp and shrugged. 'I saw your carriage and asked Maddoc, the coachman, if he might drop me at the inn on your way home. There is nothing more than that.'

'The carriage has gone and come once already tonight. Why did you not ride with my father?'

He shrugged again. 'I prefer to ride with you.'

'And so you waited outside in the dark for the better part of an hour?'

He leaned forwards, hands on knees to look at her, his apathy dissipating under her scepticism. 'Very well, then. The truth. I wished to talk to you about the dinner.'

'The duke has already lectured me,' she said, 'If that's what you mean to do, you needn't bother.'

'He has kissed you as well,' Sam said. 'I suppose you do not wish me to do that, either.'

'Certainly not,' she said. 'And what makes you think such horrid things about me?'

'You find kissing him to be horrid?' he said, cheered. 'Then I shan't fear a comparison between us.'

'I do not,' she said. The recent interlude had been more forgettable than horrid. 'I mean, why must you assume that we kissed?'

'Because he had you all to himself for some time. A little dining-room drama would not prevent him from seizing the moment.' He smiled in a knowing way that made her body tingle. 'And because I know what you look like when you have been kissed.'

'Then you waylaid me to remind me of something I would prefer to forget.' She thought for a minute. 'And by that, I mean your kisses. Do not think to attempt it again, or I shall scream for the coachman.'

'That is what Lady Evelyn would do,' he said. 'But the woman I love would be more likely to hit me than cry for help.'

'Striking a gentleman is probably another thing that Michael would not approve of,' she said. 'If you are a gentleman, that is. Of late, you do not behave like one.'

He ignored the insult. 'So the Saint does not approve of you.'

'He said no such thing,' she replied. 'He merely wishes that I be more circumspect,' But that was not how it had seemed. Michael had tried to put a muzzle on her and then tried to kiss away the feelings of confinement.

Sam noticed her silence. 'For what it is worth, I saw nothing wrong with you speaking out. Your argument was well reasoned. The bishop's was not.' Then he turned serious. 'You are an intelligent woman, Evie. You have strong feelings about many things. Never be afraid to give voice to them. Those of us who truly love you do not want that to change.'

'Thank you,' she said. That, at least, had not altered

between them. He understood her, even if she did not understand her own feelings. But such understanding would be useless, if he withdrew from her life and let her husband take that place. It was as it should be. But that did not mean she could not grieve the loss.

'I was wrong to tell you to marry him,' Sam said, suddenly. 'You two do not suit.'

He was right, but she had known that when she'd made her promise to Michael. 'You are saying this to trick me into your arms.'

He shook his head. 'I am saying it because it is true. You will not make each other happy.'

'We will not make each other unhappy.' Not intentionally, at least.

'That is not enough,' he said. 'You deserve so much more.'

'Than to marry a saint?' she said.

'You deserve your freedom. And you will be forced to give that up, if you marry St Aldric.'

'You can't know that.' But, of course, he could. Wealth and power did not come without responsibilities. She had tricked herself into believing that St Aldric would be the one to shoulder those. But after tonight, it was clear that he meant her to carry her share.

'If you were mine, you would have an equal say in our future.' The idea was almost as seductive as his kisses.

She must not listen to it. 'You say that now. But you have changed your tune before.'

'Not about my chosen profession,' he said. 'Believe

what you like about my feelings for you. But when have you ever heard me lie about that? I am sorry to admit it, but I loved medicine long before I loved you. It is to me as St Aldric's title is to him: an unchangeable part of myself. If you marry me, you will have my head as well as my heart. And I will teach you anything you ask.'

And what would she use the knowledge for? At dinner, it had not just been St Aldric she'd upset. The people around her had been horrified. Her father had been ashamed. 'After tonight, I think we have both seen where my curiosity has got me. I am already dancing at the edge of polite society. And now you are come with an offer to make me worse.'

'I offer to let you be yourself,' he said. 'And that is something that St Aldric would never allow. When you are ready to admit the truth, Evie, come to me. I will be waiting.'

The horses were slowing. Sam swung easily to his feet before they had stopped and was out the door with a thank you to the coachman, and not another word to her.

Chapter Twelve

'Doctor Hastings.' Whoever it was did not think the incessant knocking on his door would be enough. A ray of light from the hall struck Sam, rousing him halfway from sleep, and the sound of his name did the rest. But he could not seem to bring himself to full wakefulness. For a moment, he was back aboard ship and it was the cabin boy come for him. Only an emergency brought a visit at this hour.

'Ehh?'

Not a cabin boy this time. Tom the footman, who looked just as uncomfortable about waking him as he had in delivering Evie's letter, but this time he stood his ground without shifting and almost quivered with the need to act quickly.

'Evelyn?' Sam was fully awake now. A day had passed, and there had been no response to his offers in the carriage. But if she had decided to accept him, the hour did not matter.

'No, sir. It is the duke. He wishes to see you immediately.'

'Tell him to go to the devil.' Perhaps St Aldric could not read the hands on the clock. But the last thing Sam needed, at this hour, was another strained conversation with his new brother. 'Whatever it is, it can wait until morning.'

'That would not be wise, Mr Hastings. Doctor Hastings,' Tom corrected. 'He said it was a professional matter and of some importance. He called me to his room, but would not allow me to enter. He said I must not wake any but you and that I must bring you immediately.'

And much as he might wish to, there was no way to avoid the call, if it was truly a medical matter. He was bound by oath to go to the man. 'If this is but a bit of sleeplessness caused by overindulgence, I shall not be happy about it.' But what right did he have to take it out on this scared rabbit of a footman? Tom had even less choice than he when faced with such a summons.

'He seemed most distressed,' Tom said weakly. 'Please, sir.'

'Give me a moment, then, to gather my bag and pull on some clothes. And leave the candle.'

'Yes, Doctor.' The footman put his taper on the table and closed the door again.

Sam put on breeches, dragged a coat over his nightshirt and pulled on some boots. If it truly was an emergency, he could not waste the time for more. Then he blew out the light and fumbled his way to the hall and the waiting servant.

Tom led him down to the street and the Thorne carriage, helping him to a seat.

'Is the duke visiting, then?'

'Yes, sir. He came to dinner, but could not finish it. He did not feel well enough to return home. We put him in the blue room.' Tom closed the door and hopped on the back as the driver set off at a smart pace for Evelyn's home.

When they arrived, Sam was taken to the back entrance and through the kitchen, so that his arrival would disturb as little of the household as possible. Once on the servants' steps, he needed no guidance to find the guest suite. Things had not changed here since he was a boy.

He rapped once, quietly, on the door of the duke's room and waited, listening.

'Enter,' the voice that answered rasped, but whether it was from illness or an effort to keep quiet, Sam was not sure. He pushed through the unlocked door, holding his candle above his head to cast light on the patient.

St Aldric was sitting on the edge of his bed, legs dangling and head hung, as though it was almost too great an effort to hold it on his shoulders. 'I am sorry to wake you. But something is very wrong with me,' he croaked.

The symptoms developing were so obvious that Sam could guess the disease without stepping into the room. If the diagnosis he suspected was accurate, the situation was likely to get worse before it got better. 'You were right to call me and not to alarm the house. May I have your permission to examine you, your Grace?'

The duke gave a shallow laugh. 'At your service, Doctor.'

Sam lit the other candles in the room and stirred the fire, for the duke shivered, even though the room was warm. Then he set the candle he had brought in the holder on the bedside table and laid a hand across the duke's forehead.

Feverish. And how long had this been coming? He'd been in high colour almost two days ago, after the ball. Had his hand been warm that day, when it had touched him? Probably not, for Sam had noticed nothing at dinner the previous evening.

He pulled the little tube from his bag and explained, 'This is a recent invention. I will use it to listen to your heart and lungs.'

'Dead handy thing,' the duke said, showing a weak interest. 'It is good to know that you are an innovator.'

Sam pulled the duke's nightshirt aside and listened. His heart seemed rather fast, though his lungs were not congested. The tempo was probably due to nerves. But the swellings at the jaw line were plainly beginning. The duke's normally handsome face looked like a squirrel in fall with nut-packed cheeks. Sam ran a practised hand over the duke's glands and felt him flinch.

'Tender?' he asked. 'From here, towards the ears?'

'Yes.' The response could not disguise the pain.

'How about your belly?' Sam gave a few quick prods in the area by the pancreas and saw the duke flinch again. The infection was taking to his organs? This was not good. Not good at all.

He raised the hem of the nightshirt and looked lower. 'Pain in the testes?'

'Some,' the duke admitted.

How to explain this, so that the man was not overly alarmed? Sam gave his most sage, calming nod.

The duke looked at him as many patients did, as though hoping they would be told that it was nothing, and that they should stop being a ninny and go back to bed. 'You know what it is?'

And so did he, most likely. He merely wished for a different answer. 'A contagious inflammation of the glands, normally found in children. More serious in adults, however.' Particularly in men. But the duke was likely to know that, soon enough.

'Fatal?' the duke asked, after a slight hesitation.

'Hardly,' Sam said with what he hoped was a reassuring smile. 'Uncomfortable, of course. We must keep you isolated, both for your own sake and to keep you from transmitting the disease to others.'

'I cannot. Parliament…' The duke made to rise from the bed.

Sam put a firm hand on the middle of his chest and pushed him back. 'It will be quite beyond you for some weeks.'

'Evelyn…' the duke said, as though remembering that he must also be concerned for her. She would never have been second in his mind, had St Aldric truly loved her.

'She has already had this disease. In childhood, when it was less severe.' Sam could remember it distinctly, for he had been sick at the same time. 'Since she is immune, she will be able to visit you, if you wish it. But others had best keep their distance.'

'I notice you are not afraid for your health.'

'A physician is hardly useful, if he fears the diseases he treats,' Sam said. 'And I have a particularly strong constitution.'

'You must get it from your mother, then,' St Aldric said, with another groan. 'Our father was taken with all manner of illnesses. And now, look at me.'

'One disease is hardly a sign of a weak constitution,' Sam reminded him, 'and this is a common one. I am surprised you have not had it before.'

'You would know better than I,' St Aldric said. 'All I was sure of is that I needed a doctor.' He looked hopefully at Sam. 'I know you have refused my offers of a place in my household. But would you be willing to treat me now?'

'Of course,' Sam said, surprised that the question would even arise. 'You are in need of me.'

'So it is the position I offered that you disliked and not me specifically,' the duke said, his eyes narrowing in the puffy face. 'I had begun to suspect it was otherwise.'

'My feelings and the reasons behind them are not of importance at the moment,' Sam said briskly, fumbling in his bag to be sure that he was well stocked in the necessary medications. 'Do not trouble yourself about them. To me, you are no different than any other patient.' He removed the tinctures of opium and belladonna and set them on the bedside table. 'Right now, we must work to get you well and to prevent the spread of the disease to others in the household. Might you have any idea where you acquired the malady? How long have you been feeling poorly?'

'Several days, at least,' the duke muttered. 'And I did visit the sick ward in the foundling hospital where I am a patron. Some of the children there were ill.'

Sam all but snorted in disgust. If he had been called out of bed to treat any other duke, he would have found that the man had lain with a poxy whore, or was troubled by gout. But the Saint had got mumps from caring for orphaned children. It seemed that Sam could have no scrap of moral superiority, even in the privacy of his own mind.

He took care not to be sarcastic when he answered. 'That is the likely source. I can use the date to guess at the duration of the contagion. With luck, most of the household has already suffered through this. But to be safe, we will empty this floor and keep visits from servants to a minimum.'

The duke touched his own cheek, feeling the lumps on either side. 'I would just as soon stay out of sight, so as not to cause alarm.'

Sam searched his swollen face for any sign of vanity, then concluded that the truth was no different from the words. The man did not want to cause fuss or bother by infecting others or frightening the maids. Humble as well as charitable. St Aldric was infinitely tedious in his virtue.

'Think of it less as an absence of bother and more as a quarantine,' Sam said firmly, reaching for the glass at the bedside and measuring drops of medicine from the two bottles into the water. 'When Lord Thorne awakes I shall have him inform the rest of the house. And I will give you an opiate to help you sleep. I am sorry to say that the discomfort is likely to increase before it abates. But the belladonna should help with that. Meals for the next few days will be soft and rather bland.'

The duke sighed. 'The way I feel, I do not think I will care to eat them, so it will suit me well.' He took the cup and drained it in one gulp and settled back into the pillows. 'Send my apologies to Evelyn and to Lord Thorne for the inconvenience.'

As if Thorne would care, as long as the duke was alive. He would deem it an honour to have the man under his roof for a fortnight, whatever his condition. 'Of course, your Grace. I will visit you again in the morning.' Unable to stop himself, he gave a respectful bow of his head, took up his candle again and then withdrew to leave the patient to sleep.

Standing in the hall, Sam weighed his options. If it had been a normal patient, he'd have woken the housekeeper and left her the medicine and instructions to find him should conditions change. There was really little to do, other than to watch the man suffer through it and help him to deal with any consequences that the disease left behind.

But this was no mere mortal. He was treating a duke. Even if it had not been the Saint, Sam would have insisted on staying in the house, so that he might meet the man's every need. It would be a waste of his time. But it would be expected by all involved.

And it was not just any duke. It was his own brother. As family, he was probably expected to worry. Sam could manage no feelings beyond concern that St Aldric would be in the same house as Evelyn for at least a fortnight. He would be in no mood for romance.

But with her interest in medicine, Evie would be a dutiful nurse and very sympathetic. She would station herself at the bedside and treat him like an invalid. By the time St Aldric had healed, there would be no parting the two of them.

It was no decision at all, really. Doctor Hastings must stay in residence, until the patient improved.

Chapter Thirteen

On her way down to breakfast, Eve paused to listen at the door of her father's study. It was unusual to have him up and working at such an hour. And even more strange that there was a visitor involving him in heated conversation. It was stranger still that the visitor would be Sam.

They were arguing. *Please, do not let it be about me.* The situation was difficult enough without dragging Father into it. She had not been able to stop thinking about Sam's words in the carriage. Perhaps she did wish to continue her education after marriage. Her curiosity would not be so easy to kill as Michael thought. He would adjust in time to her ways. At least, she hoped he would. But either way, it did not mean that she wished to run away with Sam.

It might, of course. But she wouldn't want him bothering Father about it, until she had given the matter more thought. And with St Aldric still asleep in the guest room, they dare not try to settle anything today.

She leaned close to the panel and caught snatches of conversation.

'I simply think that it would be better to find another man for the job.' Her father was reasonable, but cross.

'I imagine you would. It makes you that uncomfortable, does it, to have me back in the house?' Sam was truly angry and more sarcastic than she'd ever heard him.

'Of course not,' her father replied in a voice best described as uncomfortable.

'Well, it should. Everything you told me was a lie. If you have any conscience at all, I hope it is bothering you.'

'At the time, it seemed the easiest course.'

'Easy?' Sam was not just angry. He was irate. 'You deserve to suffer some small bit of the torment I've known for the last six years. That you would allow me to believe—'

No matter the current difficulties between them all, he had no right to speak to her father in such a way. Unable to contain herself, Eve burst through the door. 'Sam!' She was angry at herself as well, for ever wanting to return to him. He had known of his true parentage for less than a week and the man she thought she'd known had become a spiteful, ungrateful whelp to the man who'd raised him. 'Cease this arguing immediately. It can be heard in the hall.'

'What? What have you heard?' Her father went white.

She turned to Sam, who was clearly the one at fault.

'I am shocked, Dr Hastings, that you would come here, before we have even breakfasted, to make a row about things that happened years ago.'

The two men glanced at each other in silence. Then Sam said, in a more moderate tone, 'I did not come here of my own volition. I was summoned.'

'By whom?' She laughed. 'I did not call you, if that is what you have been claiming.'

Her father stood and came around the desk to take her by the hand. 'It was the duke, Evelyn. His condition has worsened. He did not want to wake us and sent for the doctor.'

'Ill?' A hundred possibilities flashed through her mind. And the most unworthy one shouted the loudest. *If he dies, I will not have to choose.*

It was horrid of her. The choice had already been made and she was happy with it. Michael was a wonderful man. A saint. What sort of woman was she, to even consider his death?

'You needn't worry,' Sam said. 'He will recover.' His voice was soothing. It was his doctor voice, she was sure, meant to keep the family from worry.

'If there is anything I can do, any medicine I can send for, other physicians who specialise...' Her father was not calmed at all by it.

'As I told you before, Lord Thorne, I am quite capable of dealing with a case of mumps in my own brother.' So this was what had upset Sam. Her father had questioned his skill. But at least he had acknowledged that the duke was kin.

'It will be fine, Father,' Eve said. But she felt not so much calm, as numb. 'Sam is right. He can handle this easily. And Michael asked specifically for him.' That was a good sign, wasn't it? At least the two of them were not at odds.

'Very well, then,' Thorne responded, still sounding frosty. 'You are here in my house again at the request of the duke and there is nothing I can do about it. What do you prescribe, Dr Hastings?'

'Keep the curtains drawn and the staff away from him. There is no one on that floor of the house, is there?'

'We have no other guests,' said her father.

'Then send Tom to the inn for my chest and some fresh linen. I will occupy one of the empty rooms, since I have no fear of contagion. But I recommend you keep your distance, Lord Thorne, just as you did when Evelyn and I suffered through this as children. If you cannot specifically remember having this illness as a child, you must not come in contact with the infected.'

'But surely, a duke…' Her father was shaking his head in amazement, as though he believed that there was something about a peerage that should render one impervious to the ills of lesser men.

'Sam is right. You needn't worry, Father. I will stay with the pair of them, night and day, to make sure their needs are met.' Both men started at her offer, as though she was not capable of helping.

'That will hardly be necessary,' Thorne said.

'I agree with your father,' Sam said hurriedly.

'There is no risk to me, Sam,' she reminded him. 'As you just reminded Father, I had the disease as a child, same as you. And, Father, I would do the same for any other guest that fell ill under our roof.'

'But, Evie,' Sam said, using the calm voice again, 'your presence will not heal him any faster.'

'He is my betrothed,' Eve said, using the same calming tones that he was using on her. 'And he needs me.' After their last conversation, she was sure Sam did not want to hear that. But it was the truth. Even if it might change in the future, she would not argue it out in front of her father. Nor could she abandon Michael as he lay ill.

Thorne was looking at Sam now, leaving the decision to him. He was clearly against the idea, but did not want to be the one responsible for refusing her.

And Sam just looked tired. Of course, he had been up in the middle of the night to care for Michael. Perhaps it had nothing to do with her. 'She will take no harm in staying with him. And it is better than having a series of maids trailing in and out of the room, cutting up the peace. Having her at his side might steady him and alleviate some of the discomfort.'

'But it is hardly proper,' her father argued.

'Oh, please, Father. Michael is in no condition to compromise me.' It occurred to her that Sam was another matter entirely. But surely he would not trouble her in her own home with her future husband just down the hall. She put her doubts aside. 'You know I will be a help, for this is hardly different from what I accomplish when we are in the country.'

'That is with women and children,' her father said, aghast. 'St Aldric is a grown man.'

Sam cleared his throat to indicate the delicacy of the subject. 'I will tend the more personal needs of the patient myself. There is no dishonour in tending the ill.'

'Very well, then,' Thorne said with a sigh. 'You have my permission, Evelyn.'

As if his permission had been what she was requesting. She would do it with or without their consent. But if it made him feel better to think he could control her, so be it.

'She will be of aid to me,' Sam affirmed. 'And we will limit his contact with other, more susceptible members of the household, by caring for him ourselves. We will also limit gossip, for I doubt he will wish to be seen by others in his current condition.'

'This is true,' her father said, obviously encouraged. 'It is better to keep such things in the family and away from prying eyes.'

'Then it is settled,' Evelyn said with a smile. 'I shall tell Mrs Abbott to close off the third floor until such time as Sam deems it safe. Meals may be brought to the head of the stairs and I will see to it that they are eaten. A maid can come in once a day to change the linen and that will be that.'

Now her father was nodding along with the scheme, as though he had thought of it himself. And perhaps, at the end of it, she would have proved to Michael that her use in a sick room was far more important a pastime than remaining quiet in the dining room.

Once Evie had gone to make arrangements for the sick ward, Sam had no desire to continue the conversation he'd been having with Lord Thorne. His efforts to remain calm while notifying the man of his sick guest had quickly degenerated into a shouting match. It had been all he could do to be polite before he'd learned the truth of his parentage, but now he could not stand the man. If Evie had arrived a moment later, she'd have heard him bring forth every sordid detail of his parting, for he'd meant to confront Thorne with the effects of his casual lies and make him see what they had done to his daughter's happiness. With a warning glare to let the man know their business was not finished, he left to pay another visit to his patient.

St Aldric's condition had worsened since the previous evening. The swelling of the jaw was more pronounced as the duke stirred in his sleep in obvious discomfort. In his mind Sam ticked through the more extreme complications and prayed that he would not see them. Deafness and sterility were not uncommon. And despite what he had told the Thornes, rare cases turned fatal. Although he had no desire to be personal physician to the man, neither did he want to be the one responsible for the death of a peer.

But some things were inevitable.

He examined the thought, rejected it and examined it again. Nature would have its way, no matter what he attempted. But if he helped it along? No one would be the wiser. He had already dispensed with the witnesses who might question him, in the name of quarantine. An incorrect dosage of many of the medicines in his bag would be more weakening than strengthening. A bleeding, taken too far, was no different than a war wound. A knick in an artery would have the life of the patient drained away before the flow could be staunched.

If the duke died, Evie was no longer betrothed. After a period of mourning, she would be free to do as she wished. Thorne could not stop them. The only reason he'd found to separate them had been revealed as a lie. If he tried to find another objection, Sam would counter it. Or he could threaten to reveal the truth. What would the man do to keep Evie from learning that the father she worshipped and adored would stoop so low?

Murder and blackmail both. He sat in the chair at the side of the bed, horrified at his own thoughts. He had thought for ages that his love for Evie was some sort of spiritual disease. But it had been innocent, compared to his current state of mind.

Perhaps he was the one who needed treatment. Or perhaps this was what true temptation felt like, when one had the means at hand to do true evil. He had but to disregard the oath he had taken to do no intentional harm and take a life.

It was beneath unworthy. He looked again at the prone figure, the swollen jaw and the shadows under eyes. The man was suffering already and would likely suffer more. It was his job to help. And as he had argued in Thorne's office, this was not merely a peer, this man was his brother.

His blood. He stared at the sleeping face and the strange similarities to his own. Suppose it had been he lying there and St Aldric holding the poison bottle. He'd have nothing to fear. The man was a saint.

Or so it appeared. In his darkest hour, no living man was capable of the purity ascribed to St Aldric. But his ability to behave admirably, in words and actions, was the very opposite of Thorne. His pretended father had been willing to stoop to unimagined depths when provoked. If Sam was to be forced into a different family, there was comfort in knowing that it might be one where truth and honour had value.

But to accept the bond was to accept the duty. To be worthy of it, he should not meet honesty with deceit. Not today, perhaps. But when the patient was recovered, there would be a difficult but necessary discussion about the future of Lady Evelyn Thorne. 'Pax,' he whispered, laying a hand on St Aldric's forehead.

Still hot. Perhaps a cool drink should accompany the next round of laudanum.

In response, the duke stirred and opened his eyes. He winced as though the light hurt him and touched his cheek with his hand, only to pull back in pain. When on a sickbed, a peer looked like any other patient. He was frightened and alone, though he did a decent job of hiding the fact. Stripped to his nightshirt and flat on his back, he looked smaller than he had in the study. Sam did his best to ignore the fact. It was no consolation to be the taller man, if this was the only way it could be achieved.

'I hoped it had been a dream,' St Aldric said, in a scratchy voice.

'I am sorry, but, no.'

'Is there anything more that can be done?' He was not irritable. He was stoic in the face of the illness, neither blaming God nor the doctor, as some of his patients had been prone to do.

'Ice for the fever,' Sam said simply. 'A poultice for the swelling, or perhaps a good bleeding.'

The duke winced again.

'Laudanum and belladonna for the pain. You would not want a bolus, I assure you. Your throat will be too raw to take it easily. No strong spirits without my permission. Later, I will allow a draught of negus. For the most part, this is a thing to be borne and not cured. It will pass. In a week you will be better. But you will be in bed for two.'

The duke settled back into the pillows. 'There will be no lasting effects?'

And here was the question Sam did not want to answer. It was far too soon to tell. He turned back the sheet and looked down to examine the swelling, which was not yet great, but would grow worse.

The duke gave a gasp, half-pain and half-alarm, and tried to sit up.

Sam raised the sheet and pushed him back down on the bed. 'You would do better not to look. It will only upset you and will do nothing to speed recovery. But I expect you hurt, do you not?'

'Yes.' Now the duke's voice was small and childlike, near to a whimper.

'It is part of the disease. And one that you would not have had to bear, had you taken this infection as a child. I cannot tell you how bad it might become. But I will do everything in my power to minimise the problem.'

Although there was damn little he could do, now that it had begun. He measured a few drops of opiate into a large glass of spirits and pressed it into the duke's hand. 'Here. Drink.'

The duke took a sip. 'Vile stuff to have at breakfast,' he said, making a face.

'It is good that you stayed ashore, then,' Sam said, with a grim smile. 'I would not say that I cured everything with rum while on board the *Matilda*, but it seldom made the situation any worse.'

'If that is all that there is to it, then any man might be a physician.'

'You should be glad that it is all you need. It took only one battle to prove me handy with a saw and a needle. You will escape with all your limbs intact.'

'All save one,' the duke reminded him and took another drink.

He knew, then. And had already begun to fear. 'We cannot be sure of that problem for quite some time, your Grace.'

'Do not coddle me,' the duke barked, then added more quietly, 'And do not tell Evelyn.'

It was quite possible that Evie knew already. If she did not, it would not be long before she looked it up in one of the texts she claimed to have and learned that a union with St Aldric might well be childless. 'I will say nothing, your Grace.'

The duke sighed again. 'My name is Michael.'

Sam froze for a moment, then busied himself with his instruments, pretending that he had not heard.

'I request that you use it. Under the circumstances, it seems rather ridiculous to hear the title from you. You are family, after all.'

Family.

There was that word again. Sam had spent his life alternately assuming the Thornes were his family and praying that they were not. When he had returned to London, he would have chosen anyone in the world but the man in front of him to claim as kin. His plan had been to dislike St Aldric quite thoroughly.

Yet on talking to the man, he could not have wanted a better brother. Other than proposing to Evie, *Michael* had given him no reason for hatred. 'You would not prefer to be called Saint?'

The duke tried to laugh, winced again and gave him a feeble smile. His eyes were losing their brightness. The medicine was taking effect. 'Do you think it will keep me from blasphemy to remind me of that?'

'Having dealt with men in pain, I doubt it. Michael,' he added, trying not to feel uncomfortable. 'You may curse all you like, if you think it will help.'

'And might I call you Samuel?'

Sam would rather he not. It was too personal. And too soon. But if it was the only comfort he could offer, then it was cruel to deny it. He nodded. 'Or Sam, as Lady Evelyn does.'

'The fair Lady Evelyn.' The duke settled back into his pillows with a contented smile, intending to dream of Evie as he drifted towards narcotic slumber. It was only natural for a man to think of his fiancée at such a time.

Sam knew exactly the dreams in the duke's mind, for he'd had them himself. Each night, he had lain in his bunk, cursing himself for imagining her soft, white shoulders pressed to his chest, her lips on his skin and her sighs as she slept beside him. He needn't have bothered with self-recrimination. It had been a harmless diversion, after all.

Sam reached to take the half-empty medicine cup from the duke's sagging hand. As he did so, St Aldric opened his eyes again, pulled it back and raised it in a toast to Sam. 'And to my brother, Dr Sam Hastings, who could as easily poison me with the stuff in his bag as cure me. Arsenic. Mercury. Opium. No one would know the difference.'

His unguarded words startled Sam. But had he not told himself just the same? 'I would never... I have taken an oath, you know.'

'But I bet you wish you hadn't.' The duke toasted him again and their eyes met over the rim. Then he very deliberately drained the glass to the dregs.

That was true as well. A few moments ago, he had

stood over his patient and contemplated murder. And, worse yet, the duke knew it. That had been what the curious look on his face had meant just now. It was one-part trust that a brother would not kill a brother. And one-part dare to remind him that, should it happen just such a way, the Saint would understand.

Peer or no, the man was either mad or as fearless as any of the marines on board ship. And now his eyes were truly closing, his head drooping on the pillow. Sam took the glass away and walked quietly from the room to see how Evie had got on in her preparations.

She was standing at the top of the stairs. Her father was still beside her, shifting nervously from foot to foot, afraid to abandon his daughter in a sick ward. They watched him approach. By their worried looks, his conflicting emotions were still plain on his face. They could read death there. And they feared that his moment of weakness was a reflection on the gravity of the duke's disease.

He took a moment to pull his mind out of the dark place it was lurking, and carefully masked his true feelings as he might for the family of any patient.

'How is he?' Evelyn asked.

'Sleeping again,' Sam said, back in command. If a doctor could do nothing else, he must at least appear to be in control of the situation. Especially if it was one that was likely to inflict harm or cure itself, no matter what he might do. 'But he was concerned that you would be frightened by the extent of his illness.'

Evie made a huffing noise, as though diminishing

the duke's concern. 'He should not waste the energy. You will care for him and he will be fine.'

At least for the moment, she had forgotten that she was angry with Sam. She needed his help. And she was looking at him with the worshipful confidence she had held when he was her hero and she a troublesome little pest.

If he had acted on his base desires to do away with St Aldric, she would discover it. She would look once into his eyes and would know, and she would never look at him like this again. If he also shared Thorne's duplicity, that man would lose her trust as well. The punishment was deserved. But some things were too cruel to be just.

He gave her a solemn nod. 'He will be fine.'

She cast a worried glance down the hall to the sick room. 'Would it help him, if I sat with him for a time?'

Sam shrugged. 'It would not hurt. If it gives you comfort to do so, then I have no objections.' Not as a physician, at least. He was properly envious of any man who awoke to an angel at his bedside. 'If he is asleep, do not wake him. If he wakes on his own, do not allow him to become excited.'

She turned from him and hurried towards the room that held her betrothed, eager to tend him. Her father cast a worried glance after her.

'She will be fine,' he assured Thorne again. 'But you must keep your distance. If you feel any symptoms of the illness, or notice them in others, notify me immediately and segregate the effected persons to this floor of the house.'

'Is it really so serious a sickness, then?' Thorne was worried for his daughter's future and the possible end to his carefully constructed plans.

'Bad enough so that I would not wish it on an otherwise healthy man. Chances are excellent that he will recover.'

'But a full recovery…' Thorne gave him another worried look. 'I have heard of men who have had this difficulty. And they lived, of course, but there were consequences.'

Sam nodded, for he could not lie when confronted with a fact. But for now, their differences were moot compared to the reassurance he owed this man on the health of his guest. 'We will not know of problems until much later. It is why I insist on the quarantine and not upsetting the patient. He is already brooding on the possible outcome. And he should not, until he is stronger.'

Thorne nodded in agreement. 'You are right in this. Better that we let Evie keep his spirits up than to have a ring of worried faces around the bedside.'

'Very good. Now go,' Sam said, as gently as possible. 'We will send word if there is a change. But it will do him no good if you sicken as well. Trust us.' *Trust me.* 'He shall have the best possible care.'

'And about before…?' Thorne gave him another worried look.

'Now is not the time to continue that particular discussion,' Sam said, fighting the rage and disgust that still boiled beneath his professional calm.

'If you are alone with Evelyn and she should learn...' Thorne was hardening again, trying to regain control. His tone was both warning and threat. Although what he had left to threaten with, Sam was not sure.

'At the moment, the past is the last thing I wish to speak of. I have a patient, sir, and you have a guest who is ill. We must do what is best for him. There is nothing more between us than that.'

'And Evelyn?' he said again. 'Do you want what is best for her as well?'

'I fear we disagree on what that might be,' Sam said. 'For I would not lie to her, as you did to me. But neither will I dredge up the past, to win her. I will not speak on it.'

Still Thorne hovered, as though he expected Sam's betrayal before he could reach the second-floor landing.

'You have my word,' Sam added, his jaw clenching, 'as the son of the late Duke of St Aldric.' The oath was foreign to him. But he felt the weight of it as it left his lips. Family honour. How strange to have found it, after all this time. 'Now go.'

Without another word, Thorne turned and went down the stairs.

Chapter Fourteen

St Aldric looked terrible.

Eve could see why he had wanted to protect her from the truth. She had dealt with the disease in children, but in a grown man it looked far worse. If she had been the sort of weak woman he expected, she would have been shocked by the extent of the swelling and burst into sympathetic tears. She would have upset herself and made things more difficult for everyone involved.

Instead, she sat in the chair at the bedside and gathered his limp hand into her own.

He slept on, unaware of her presence.

Oh, Michael, what am I going to do with you? Although she had not wanted to admit it, this engagement was a mistake. She should never have yielded to Father's insistence. She should have found another way.

But it was quite possible that choosing Sam instead would be exchanging a bad mistake for a worse one. In some ways, he was just as she remembered. But the calm assurance she felt around him had faded. He was erratic: calm one moment, shouting the next, hating her father while he claimed to love her, offering no explanation as to why he had gone and why he found her suddenly irresistible once she belonged to another.

She needed time to think and it appeared that she would have at least a week trapped with the pair of them to sort her feelings.

She gave Michael's hand a squeeze, but he barely stirred. For good measure, she sponged his hot forehead with water from the basin, adjusted his covers and put her head to his chest to listen to his breathing, which was deep and regular. Sam had been right. There was nothing she could do right now.

She left the room and went out into the hall, glancing down it to the open door at the back of the house. It was a bedroom with an attached parlour that would be a logical place for the pair of them to sit while waiting for the duke to awake.

She gave an involuntary shiver at the thought. She had been eager to be alone with Sam a week ago, but now she was not sure how she felt. Still eager, apparently, for the shiver had been one of excitement. But she felt guilty as well. Poor Michael had no one but the two of them. And he was ill. It was very bad to be thinking of her own wants and needs, while he suffered.

Sam was sitting at a table by the fireplace, his medical bag at his feet, reviewing a text, and looking like the competent healer he was. Despite the strange way he acted towards her, he was a good man as well.

She did not wish to interrupt him in his work. But

really, how much study would he need to handle something so common? And was such intent concentration necessary? 'Are you trying to avoid talking to me?' she asked.

He smiled into his book at being caught. 'I have been reading the same page over and over for an hour, waiting for you to return. How is the patient?'

'Still asleep.'

'Very good. I will look in on him later.' He closed the book and set it aside, then looked at her expectantly.

What did he want her to say? 'Thank you for this,' she said, in a sombre voice.

'For doing my job?' he asked.

'For doing this particular job. I am sure it must be hard for you.'

'The duke requested me,' Sam said, deliberately misunderstanding her. 'After making the initial visit, it makes no sense to turn the case over to another.'

'I mean because of me,' she said.

'On the contrary—' he was smiling again '—I am quite at ease in your presence, Lady Evelyn. I think it is you who are uncomfortable.'

It was true, of course. But he was being deliberately provoking in pointing it out. 'I will manage,' she said, not allowing herself to be baited. 'And you can leave off calling me Lady Evelyn. Things are difficult enough without that.'

His lips twitched. 'Very well, Evie.'

'It is good that we are all here together.' She gave a firm nod. 'It will give you a chance to know your brother better.' And show some sign of love for him, so that she did not feel quite so foolish at insisting they know the truth. 'I am sure, once you have spent time with him...'

'That the same problem will exist between us,' Sam finished. 'He is engaged to the woman I love.'

'You are most free with that word of late,' she said.

'Better late than never.'

He was treating this newfound love as if it were a joke. 'But still, it is quite different from the six years of silence and the lust you claimed on your return.'

'Anything I said, was said because I wanted what was best for you,' he replied.

'And you have changed, now that I am engaged to another?'

'I have changed because I recently discovered that what was best for you was to be married to me.' He sounded very calm and very sure of himself, but it was really no answer at all.

'If you mean because of the business at dinner the other night, I do not believe you. You started speaking words of love a full day before that.'

He shook his head. 'I came to the conclusion before then. Dinner simply confirmed it.'

'Are you implying that Michael did something to render himself less than a suitable match for me?'

Sam laughed. 'No. The brother you found for me continues to be perfect. He is just not perfect for you.'

'And you are?' She had thought so herself, until very recently.

'No man is perfect,' he said. 'But I would try to be, for your sake.'

'That is not very different from the promises that Michael made when he was courting me,' Eve said. But his words had never made her heart flutter, as Sam's did.

'And how is that working so far?' Sam asked innocently. 'Since he is already deemed a saint, it does not seem likely he will have to alter much. But you, Evie?' He smiled again. 'You are most delightfully flawed. And I would not change a bit of you.'

It was just as she had thought, on the day he arrived. He was more honest than flattering. But there was so much love for her behind his words that she would rather hear criticisms from him than compliments from another.

'And while we are on the subject of your deficiencies,' he said with a smile, 'there was one I should have corrected when we spoke in the garden. You are quite wrong about our first kiss.'

'I was not.' If she was sure of nothing else, it was the moment that changed her life.

'Our first kiss was about a week before the time you remember. You were standing in the library, by the big windows, trying to reach a book on the top shelf without using the ladder. I came upon you suddenly, with the sunlight outlining your body, and for a moment I did not know you at all. I saw nothing but a beautiful young woman: an angel in a nimbus of light.'

'I do not remember any of this,' she said, shaking her head.

He gave a small snort. 'Of course you would not. You cared for nothing but getting the book.' Then he sighed, lost in a pleasant memory. 'But my eyes were opened to the promise of manhood. Then you turned your head and were my little Evie again, demanding that I help you.'

'And did you?' she asked, honestly curious.

He gave a small bow. 'Ever your servant, Lady Evelyn. I got you the book. You rewarded me with a kiss on the lips. Then you ran off as if nothing had happened. You might as well have ripped the heart out of my chest and taken it as well. I have not been the master of it, from that moment.'

'But the time in the garden?' For she was sure that she remembered it quite clearly.

'Was the first time I kissed you,' he answered. 'I planned for a full week, trying to find a way to ask if you might ever feel for me what I had come to feel for you. But my words failed me, each time. So I let my actions speak. And I had my answer.'

The kiss had made her feel just as she was feeling now. It was as if she was seeing Sam truly for the first time. He loved her. She loved him. And it had been so for ages. Why had she not seen it before?

She had. It was he who had been denying it. 'You said you did not remember.'

'I lied.'

'How very convenient,' she said, still not sure.

'I've told you many lies, since I returned.' But he did not seem the least bit ashamed by his admissions. 'Here, I will prove it to you. Would you like me to recite for you? I know the contents of your letters as well as any poem.'

He had heard her, as she poured out her heart to him for six lonely years. He had not answered, but at least he had listened. 'You read them?'

'Every word.' He smiled. 'They gave such comfort. You have no idea. When one went astray, or arrived out of order, I sat in a fog of despair, until the next came to cheer me again. You begged me over and over to answer. You grew angry with my silence and, at least once a year, you told me I was horrible and swore that I would hear no more from you.'

His smile disappeared. 'I dreaded those letters. Suppose, this time, you were sincere? Suppose my negligence had finally cost me my Evie?' He relaxed. 'But in a week, or perhaps two, you wrote again.' And tensed at another bad memory. 'In November of 'sixteen you were silent the whole month. But December brought another letter and a muffler so hideous I must assume you were the one who made it.'

Unable to stop herself, she gave a small joyful laugh, for he was finally saying what she had longed to hear. 'You have come back to me, after all?'

'I never left,' he whispered. 'I tried, but I could not.'

She had meant only to talk. To consider rationally, take her time and make the best decisions possible. Then she would have to break with one man or the other. But she would do it so gently that they might all be friends.

Instead, she seized Sam Hastings by the shirt front and kissed him.

It took no further encouragement for him to kiss her back. These were the kisses she had been waiting a lifetime for. More passionate than the sweet kiss of youth and more tender than the eager grappling of the last few days. Quick pecks on her face and throat, and slow forays into her mouth. His tongue thrust. It circled. It remained perfectly still, resting against her lips. And through it all he smiled. His breath came in deep, satisfied sighs and silent laughs of relief.

His arms were about her, neither too tight nor too loose. But she clung to his, afraid that he would escape. Sam was home. Not the strange imposter that had walked in the door. This was *her* Sam. And she would never let him get away.

He was pulling her back towards the door to the bedroom. And each step was like waltzing, if that dance could be done with bodies held so indecently close. She rubbed herself against him, pressing her breasts to his chest. He kissed her shoulder and cupped her bottom so that their hips bumped together.

For a moment, they both paused in shock. The brief contact was too good not to repeat. He brought their hips together again and they pressed into each other. Her knees buckled at the thought of them, joined.

He supported her, still holding her tight as he backed into the bedroom and shut the door. Then he shrugged out of his coat, stepping on it, and over, as it fell to the floor. She kicked out of her slippers, leaving them behind as well. And suddenly they were a frenzy of hands undoing buttons, untucking shirts and dropping garments as they came free of them. By the time they reached the bed, she was in shift and stockings, and he was shirtless and kicking free of his boots.

He had a manly chest. She had known he must look somewhat like the paintings she had seen of naked men. But pictures did not teach her the feel, or the taste, or the way he would laugh as she ran her fingers over his ribs and he caught at her hands to kiss them.

Then he rolled, pulling her with him, pushing her down on her back as his hands went to his buttons. He kissed her mouth again, pulling down his breeches and lying naked on top of her, heavy and hard between her legs.

The curtains were drawn and the room was gloomy, but hardly dark. If she wished, she could see him and watch as he loved her. Why was she closing her eyes when there was so much to learn? She opened them wide, so that she would not miss a thing.

He seemed to sense this, pulling away and laughing again, flicking her nose with his finger before kneeling above her as he untied her garters and rolled her stockings down her legs.

'You are not like the illustrations in the medical books,' she said, amazed.

'I am like them in all the ways that matter,' he said, in a voice that was deliberately lecherous. 'You are not like the books, either. You are the most beautiful woman I have ever seen.' He pulled her shift over her head. 'But that is exactly as I imagined you'd be. Do not be afraid,' he whispered.

She laughed at him. For when had she ever been frightened of Sam?

He growled and lay on top of her again, sliding down, holding a breast in each hand and taking the nipples into his mouth. If he meant to punish her for laughing, he was doing it wrong. This was only making her more excited, even when he bit her. She would not mind if they stayed like this for ever.

He stopped. He kissed her navel. And then he hooked his arms around her legs, spread them and kissed.

This was different. It tickled. But it was a new sort of ticklishness that seemed to travel over her whole body. She giggled. Then she laughed. She forced her fist into her mouth, trying to keep back the screaming, gasping, silent gales of laughter. She hooked one leg over his shoulder, trying to hold him still, and pounded her fists into the mattress and panted, trying to get control of herself. His kisses were unrelenting. If he did not stop, she was not sure what would happen.

And then, it did. Suddenly, everything changed. She could breathe again, but she did not want to. She just wanted to lie perfectly still and feel like this for ever.

He did not seem the least bit surprised at what had happened. He pulled away from her and grabbed a pillow from the bed, lifting her hips and sliding it under her. Then he bent her knees so that her feet were close to her body. 'This will make it easier,' he said.

She could not manage to say anything at all. His fingers were where his mouth had been, spreading the wetness and slipping inside, stretching her.

She did not want his fingers, she wanted more. She held out her arms and reached down until her fingers brushed his manhood. She steeled her nerve and explored, running a finger down the length and cupping his testicles.

His fingers froze, then pushed deeper as he leaned forwards, muttering, 'Damn! I meant to teach you to love me. Did you learn that from an anatomy book? Never mind. I do not care. Oh God, woman, do not stop.'

She ran her hands over him again. 'I want this.'

'A moment more.' He sighed, letting her caress him. Then he withdrew his fingers and took her hands, placing them between her legs and encouraging her to touch herself. It felt good.

The next moment, he was hovering over her and there was a slow push. She tightened her body, and could feel him inside of it. They were finally together. Her body twitched under her fingers, and tightened again, as he moved.

His body began to shake. There were a few hurried thrusts and he shuddered a second time, swearing, trembling and collapsing in her arms as she felt the rush of his seed inside her.

He lay still for a time, holding her, as weak and spent

as she was. Then he rolled without leaving her body, pulling her with him so she was half-sprawled on top of him. He fumbled a blanket up to cover them. Then he kissed her shoulder. 'The next time will be different.'

She pushed against him. 'I should hope not. I liked this.'

He was laughing now, so hard that his body was trembling again. 'Show some decorum, Lady Evelyn. You are far too eager for a girl who was a virgin only a few moments ago.'

'Well, I was,' she said, with a frown. 'And it is most rude of you to imply otherwise.'

'Darling, I know,' he said, still laughing.

'How...?'

'I am a doctor. I would not be much of one if I could not tell that.'

'I am sorry if I did not respond according to your assumptions,' she said a little tartly.

'You exceeded expectations,' he assured her.

'As did you,' she said, trying to sound more knowledgeable than she was.

'Then you did not expect much of me,' he said, still laughing. 'That was over before it was begun. In the future, I shall try harder to please you.'

The future. They would have a future and it would be full of this. How wonderful that would be.

'Of course, today, we did not have long. When we do this again, I will take my time.'

He stood, leaving her on the bed, and fumbled his way back into his clothes.

She held out a hand to draw him back. 'Where are you going?'

'I must check on my patient. He is most likely still asleep, for the dose I gave him was strong. But still, one must never assume.'

She sat straight up in the bed and felt the blanket fall away from her. She gathered it hastily around her. It was ludicrous to be embarrassed now, after what they had done. But she was.

She had forgotten Michael.

But, clearly, her lover had not.

Chapter Fifteen

Once Sam had gone, she gathered up her clothing, washed and dressed herself. Then she sat down on the edge of the bed and waited.

Sam returned to the room shortly, and dropped his bag on the floor near the door. 'The swelling increases, but that is to be expected. I gave him one more dose of laudanum, so that he will sleep through the worst of it. Later this afternoon, he will wake and we will treat more aggressively.'

He stopped in the doorway, finally noticing her expression.

'You are thinking of the engagement, aren't you?'

Of course she was. And it was too late to be doing so. Her personal sense of honour should have reminded her of it an hour ago. 'I betrayed Michael.'

'You have not married as yet.' Sam was so matter of fact about it. It was as if he was describing some easily cured disease.

'But I promised.'

'Then break it.' Sam sat down beside her and put an arm about her shoulder. 'You must tell him that you have made a mistake. Or would you prefer that I did? I did mean to speak to him on the subject, when he was better.' His face clouded for a moment. 'But then I had not expected things to move so quickly. Perhaps, when he wakes, I should—'

'No,' she interrupted. 'It must be me.' She was so tired of being presented with a *fait accompli*. She would not be rushed into the decision to part from Michael, as she had with the one to accept him. 'But it will not be today. He must be fully awake and healthy enough to understand.'

'Very well,' Sam said cautiously. Then he stroked her shoulders. 'But let it be soon, Evie. I love you. And I know that you love me. Now that you have felt how it can be between us, do not deny those feelings.'

'There will be a scandal,' she said. Worse than that, her father would be heartbroken.

'But we do not have to stay in London to see it. Run away with me.' The arm about her shoulder pulled her closer so he could whisper in her ear. 'Anywhere you wish to go. Scotland? Italy? The Americas? Name the place and I will take you there.'

'Would you marry me, then?' For now that they had done the deed, he did not speak of a wedding.

'Of course,' he scoffed as though he expected her to know. But how could she?

'I must say, your story has changed, since the night you told me to accept St Aldric. You swore then that you would never marry me.' She stared straight ahead, afraid of what his face might reveal.

His hand stilled on hers, and then dropped away. 'Many things have changed since that night.'

She did not want change. She wanted the constant love that she had shown to him. 'And how do I know that they will not change again, once I have broken with the duke?'

'Because I have always been yours,' he said. 'From the first, I have loved you.'

'Then why did you call it lust? And why did you refuse me, when I was free to offer you my heart?' She turned to stare at him now and waited for some clue that would reveal the truth.

His face darkened. 'At the time, I thought it was for the best. For both of us.'

'You thought for me, did you? And was I not to be consulted in my own future?' It seemed, just as her father had with St Aldric, that Sam did not think her capable of making reasoned decisions. But if she was married to the duke, he would treat her the same way.

'The situation was...' He seemed at a loss for words. 'The problem was delicate. You were promised to another man when I arrived. I did not want to interfere.'

'It is not interference if help is requested,' she said, exasperated. 'If I was promised, it was by someone else. I had nothing to do with the decision. You must have known how conflicted I was. I all but threw myself at your feet and begged you to love me.'

'Well…yes.' This seemed to make him more uncomfortable than ardent.

'I waited for years, between heaven and hell, knowing you would come back for me and fearing you would not. Can you not offer me any explanation, other than that you thought it was for the best?' Despite what had just happened, an act which should have answered all her questions, she was still angry at him. He had distracted her with sweet words and seduced her into breaking her promise. But it had changed nothing. He had left her without explanation.

She had smothered the anger she felt, wrapping it in prayers for his safety and fantasies that he would return for her. But she remembered the letters as well as he, for she had written them. She had begged him for explanations. She had called him out on his cruelty. And, for six years, he had said nothing.

He pulled her close again, his arms about her shoulders and his lips on her throat, teasing the nerves until she shuddered. 'I suffered as well,' he whispered. 'There was no heaven for me. Only the hell of being without you. But now, everything has changed.'

She fought free of him and slid down the mattress to put distance between their bodies. 'How has it changed? What is so very different today from a few days ago?' But she feared she knew.

'I…I…I…'

Sam, who was never at a loss for words when he was refusing her, could not manage to speak.

'Is it because I am engaged to your brother?'

'He is not my brother,' Sam snapped.

'You of all people should not deny the biology of this. You share a father.'

'But we are nothing alike.' Yet he sounded confused, as though he did not know who he was any more.

'That is a shame,' she said. 'St Aldric is a wonderful man.'

'And thank you for reminding me of that now.' He was petty and sarcastic again, and not the patient loving man he had been before he'd bedded her.

'Why does Michael's presence in my life suddenly bother you?' For it was past the point where that was easy to change. 'You approved of him when you met him.'

'I had no reason not to. He has no flaws, damn the man.'

'Jealousy is unworthy of you,' Eve reminded him.

'But it is well deserved,' Sam said. 'What chance do I have to be his equal?'

'You do not need to be. You are fine, just as you are.' Was that all this had been about?

'Oh, really?' he said, with a cynical smile. 'Because you cannot seem to stop talking about him. And obviously there must be something wrong with me, because, I find, after all this time, that my father did not wish to acknowledge my existence.'

'But you must have known...' For how else did one end up in a foundling home?

'I am a nameless nobody. And he is a duke. What

could I ever do to compete? What do I have that he does not?'

'Other than my maidenhead?' she asked, her stomach feeling sick and strange. 'You have that now. And my husband never shall.'

He realised what he had said and his face seemed to crumple. 'That is not what I meant. Not at all.'

'But it is true, is it not?' It seemed quite obvious, now that she thought of it. The moment he had learned the truth about himself, everything had changed.

'Evie, it is not as you think. I have longed to lie with you, of course. Dreamed of it, my whole life.'

'In lust,' she reminded him. For had he not admitted it before?

'Love,' he insisted, now that it was too late. 'I have always loved you. When it comes to you I am unchangeable,' he said. 'I thought I was not worthy. And I tried, all my life to avoid this moment. And I failed.'

It had been the most wonderful thing to have ever happened to her and yet he had fought against it. But once they were in bed, he had known just what to do to render her senseless with desire. So senseless that she had forgotten her duty to Michael. Those lessons had not been in the medical books. 'In this time you were fighting your love for me, were you innocent as well?'

'What?' The question seemed to confuse him.

'Like a monk,' she supplied. 'Celibate. Waiting in chastity for that time we might be together.'

'Of course not.' She saw his lips twitch. He had almost laughed at her question. 'That is quite a different thing.'

'Because you are a man.'

'And because I thought that I could never have you.'

For him it must have been an easy decision. He could not have her, but he must have someone. Now that the thought was in her head, she could not help but imagine him with others, doing what they had done. And, worse yet, he had done it even as he claimed to have loved only her the whole of his life.

'So you consoled yourself with others, until the very hour that I gave up waiting. At your suggestion... No. At your demand, I publicly accepted another man,' she reminded him. 'And then, suddenly, you rediscovered your love and seduced me.'

'Evie. Evie, no.' He was shaking his head, as though he could not believe the words she was saying. 'That is not how it happened at all.'

'Then tell me, Sam. Why now?' If he had a better reason, he must tell her.

But he offered no defence.

'If you have nothing to say for yourself, then I must assume I have guessed the truth.'

He shook his head again, as though trying to turn from something unpleasant. 'I cannot tell you. I simply cannot. You must trust me when I say that it was a horrible misunderstanding on my part.'

'I must trust you?' She stood and backed away from the bed. Even now, after all she had learned, she was not sure that she could resist him if he kissed her again.

'I trusted you before, when you said that it was never to be. And look where that has got me. I am dishonouring myself and betraying a man who needs me, who wants me and who, as you have pointed out, has never given me a reason to do this. Worse yet, he is ill. Conveniently unconscious because of the drugs you are giving him, so that we would not be interrupted. I am the one who has made the mistake, Sam.'

'Evie.' He spoke it as if he thought a name from childhood was a dispensation. 'At least do not doubt my treatment. Look in your books. You will see I mean him no harm.'

'Enough.' Perhaps he was right about that one thing. But it proved only that he could answer an insult to his profession more easily than his assault on her honour. 'I am sorry. But I do not think it is for leaving you, Sam. It is for listening to you in the first place.' And with that, she went back down the hall to sit at the side of her unconscious fiancé.

Chapter Sixteen

When Sam next returned to the patient's room, it was mid-afternoon. The duke was waking. And his nurse had not left his side since leaving Sam's. She'd held his hand, mopped his fevered brow. When Sam had listened at the open door, she was talking to the sleeping man in the low tones of a lover.

Now that St Aldric was conscious, she supported his head and gave him sips of iced water, tempted him with bites of custard and tried in all ways short of full confession to make up for laying with another man.

In response, St Aldric was looking up at her with the devotion of a hound, albeit a hound that had stuck his face in a beehive.

The swelling was still bad. But there was a brightness in the duke's eyes that came from returning strength instead of fever. The worst was not over, but it was clear he would fight off the illness.

Sam had been pacing the hall for hours, trying to come up with some explanation that might mollify his lover and explain his sudden change of heart. She thought him a jealous swine who had seduced her to spoil the happiness of his brother. He was not sure, from minute to minute, how he felt about her darling Michael. But Sam was certain that man's eventual happiness had nothing to do with what had happened in the bed down the hall.

He could offer nothing, other than the truth. *Your father is a liar. He never cared for me as I thought. He was old St Aldric's toady, and he is willing to put your happiness aside to gain the favour of the Saint.*

Her father had but to deny it, as any sane man would. Then Sam would blurt the truth of what had happened and fall even lower in her estimation. She would see him either as a man low enough to lust after his own sister, or one who would make up a despicable lie, slandering her father to mask his own indifference.

He had sworn to Thorne that he would not speak. And he had done it on his true father's name. As if he could borrow that family's honour when it was convenient, and put it aside when it proved troublesome. Perhaps he was as fickle as she thought. That morning, he had been ready to make peace with St Aldric and, an hour later, he had cuckolded him while he slept. There was nothing to say that would explain any of it. He could hardly understand it himself.

He went into the sick room and stood by the bed. 'And how are you feeling after your rest, your Grace?'

From the opposite side, Evie stared at him, as protective as a lioness with a cub. 'He is doing much better, now that I am here to help,' she said, all but accusing him of doping the man insensible for his own nefarious purposes.

'I am sure he is.' It was what he'd have told any worried housewife, on visiting her husband's sick bed. Women did not like to be told that all illnesses could not be cured with love and herbs.

'It seems I have a ministering angel,' St Aldric croaked, managing a smile.

'You are most fortunate,' Sam agreed. 'But you must forgive me if I send her from the room so that I might examine you.'

'Can I not stay?' She asked it sweetly enough, but then she turned her face from St Aldric and looked daggers at him, as though she expected Sam to do away with his rival the moment she had cleared the door.

'Do not worry, my love. I am confident that my brother the physician will settle me in no time. And then, perhaps, you might come back and read to me.' The duke gave her a pale imitation of the smile he had worn at their engagement ball.

'Of course, darling.' She left reluctantly, pausing in the doorway to give him one last lingering glance, as though a quarter-hour examination would be an eternity. It was like trying to part turtle doves.

The little hypocrite.

As soon as the door was closed, Sam turned back to the patient, as eager to get this over with as they were to be rid of him. 'May I have permission to examine you, your Grace?'

The duke cocked his swollen head to the side, considering. 'Perhaps the drugs have clouded my mind, but I distinctly remember asking you to dispense with the formality of my title. There is no one to hear you, you know. You could call me anything you liked. You could even argue with me, should you have a reason to.'

Despite himself, the corners of Sam's mouth twitched in amusement. 'Do not tempt me, your Grace.'

Another sigh from the man on the bed. 'Very well, then. But please stop asking for my permission before you touch me. You know you have it. Just make me well.'

'I will do my best.' He lifted the sheet. Judging by the extent of the inflammation, it was likely that the duke would never be himself again. He carefully replaced the sheet and reached for his stethoscope.

'Doing your best,' the duke said grimly. 'That is no answer at all, is it?'

The patient's chest and heart were clear. And his ears seemed undamaged as well. The situation was far from hopeless, although he doubted the duke would see it that way. 'Do you wish me to lie?'

St Aldric managed a false smile. 'Perhaps I do, if it means that there is a way to prevent the discussion we must have.'

Sam smiled grudgingly as well. 'I doubt it will give you comfort. I am not a very good liar, you see. I find that I get in no end of trouble trying to conceal the truth.'

'With Evelyn?'

Sam started so much that he dropped his stethoscope.

'You are right,' the duke confirmed. 'You are not a very good liar at all.'

Damn him. And damn his understanding nature. Did he not see that the whole situation was more complicated than that? And, once again, Sam had a strange desire to have a brother much like this one: older and hopefully wiser. Someone in whom he might confide the truth.

Then he remembered that he was the physician and not the patient. He was supposed to be the font of wisdom and comfort, not the receiver of it. 'I have no idea what you are talking about.'

'Of course you don't,' replied the duke in an even tone. 'But I have got you sufficiently off guard that I might get the truth out of you on my condition. We will discuss one thing or the other. What is my prognosis, doctor?'

'You should make a nearly full recovery,' Sam said, still not wanting to be pinned to an untruth.

'Nearly,' St Aldric answered flatly. 'And what part of me is not to return from this? Do me the courtesy of saying it, please.'

'There is no guarantee, one way or the other,' Sam prefaced, still not sure he wanted to commit. 'But in some cases such as yours, there is a loss of potency, or a chance of sterility.'

'I see.' There was a sort of dangerous quiet in the room and St Aldric's easy manner disappeared.

For a moment, Sam feared what any man would fear upon delivering bad news to a powerful man. There was a tendency in these things to kill the messenger. Not literally, of course. But a rumor of misdiagnosis, or malpractice, from a man of this stature would be enough to ruin him.

But the storm, if there was to be one, did not break. The tension grew and Sam added, 'There is no guarantee.'

'That will be all, for now, Doctor.' The duke glanced towards the door.

'It will be weeks, perhaps months, or longer, before you know the truth. You need to regain your strength first.'

'Before I attempt congress with Evelyn?'

Sam brought his hand down hard on the bedside table, unable to control his sudden and violent reaction to the thought.

'I know you would delay that indefinitely, if you could. Why you waste as much time as you do trying to heal me, I do not understand.'

'You asked me to,' Sam said.

The duke gave an empty laugh. 'And they call me a Saint. Perhaps nobility runs in our family.'

'Our family has nothing to do with this,' Sam said stubbornly. 'I helped you because you needed it. And now I am telling you what I would tell any man in your condition. Do not give up hope without a reason. It may take some time before we know if you are yourself again.'

'And how will I know?' Michael asked.

'If you father a child,' Sam said, cursing his own inability to offer more. 'There are no tests beyond this.'

'And if I cannot father a child?'

'Then it might be the fault of illness. Or it might have been the truth before. Or it might be the fault of the woman you are with.' Sam resisted the urge to shrug, for that was hardly a gesture that inspired confidence. 'You might have a son by the New Year. Or not.'

'You are useless,' the duke said. 'Worse than useless. Get out.'

And now he would call for another doctor. Someone who would lie to him, or bring some odd tincture that offered hope. 'You want me gone because I will not tell you what you wish to hear? You asked for the truth. It is not my fault if you do not like it.'

'Get out.'

'No.' He was refusing a direct order from a peer. It was likely professional suicide. It was illogical as well. If he cared at all for a future with the woman he loved, it made no sense to encourage this man to bed her.

But damnation, the man was his brother.

And his brother was a duke. St Aldric's glare was icy, and superior, a reminded of the difference in their ranks. 'How dare you refuse me?'

Sam sat in the chair at the bedside that Evelyn had occupied. 'I dare because I am more than a doctor to you. You wanted family, did you? Well, I have little experience with it. But from what I hear, family does not abandon family at moments like this.'

'What can you do?'

'I can say that I am sorry.'

'And what does that help?'

'You did not let me finish. I could say I was sorry that my brother is such a great blockhead. You are worrying about a future that is not certain.'

St Aldric's eyes were wide and near to panic. 'But if it is the future, do you understand what it means?'

'That all flesh is grass? That the plans of men are not equal to the machinations of God or fate or random chance?' Sam glared down at the man in the bed. 'I have given worse news to better men than you. I have watched children die. And here you are, grieving for ones that are not even conceived. I suggest, Michael, that you accept the fact that there are things that a title will not protect you from. If you are only a saint when your faith is not tested, then you are no saint at all.'

The duke was shaking his head as though he could refuse the future he might face and have another. 'I never asked to be a saint.'

'But you have been doing a fine job up 'til now,' Sam replied. 'The only prescription I can offer you is this. You must not worry, Michael.' He put a steadying hand on the other man's shoulder. 'We will deal with other matters if they arise.'

The patient seemed somewhat mollified by his confidence that all problems could be solved with time. But that was because he could not see the confusion in Sam's heart. He had said *we*, as if he meant to be there.

And before that, he had called the duke by his given name. Was there some brotherly feeling, after all? Or perhaps Evelyn was not the only one who felt guilt.

Chapter Seventeen

'The duke will be fine. I will be fine. Everything will be fine.'

What a weak word that was and how unlikely to be true. When she had left Michael's room her father had been lurking at the head of the stairs, eager for any news she could give him.

She had told him what he wished to hear. The duke was healing nicely and in excellent spirits. He would soon make a full recovery. She had never felt closer to him.

She had not the heart to tell Father the truth. She was not even sure she knew what the truth was herself. Sam had been evasive, when it came to the final outcome of Michael's illness. Michael was distracted, smiling to put her at ease, but clearly worried. And she was torn between the two of them: wanting one, and promised to another.

Now she was feeling the strain of unending cheerfulness in the face of problems and bemoaning, once again, the weakness of the men around her that they needed women to be happy when there was no reason to be. It must give them comfort to know that, in any situation, their wives and daughters acted like dolls with cheerful faces and lips painted shut.

If she married Michael, she had best get used to it. It was what he wished from her. He needed a wife who would smile and nod, and be as amiable as he was. She had managed several hours of it, just now, as she had tended to him. Keeping his spirits up was much more tiring than actually treating him would have been.

For the most part, she had talked nonsense. She had described the weather to him, told him about a bonnet that she meant to purchase on her next outing to Bond Street and kept him well informed on the exploits of Diana the kitten, who had caught her first mouse and been unsure what to do with it.

He had closed his eyes and smiled through most of it, informing her in a hoarse voice that it made him feel better just hearing the sound of her voice. But there was a furrow in his brow that made her suspect he would as soon have been alone and in silence.

How would he have felt if she'd given him any inkling of what had happened between her and Sam only hours before? He was dispirited enough without her begging forgiveness for her betrayal and informing him of the need to break the engagement immediately.

And now Sam was alone in the room with him. Although she had asked him not to, it was possible that he was telling the duke everything, settling the matter of her future between them. If not that, then what did he have to do that she could not witness?

She returned to the sitting room and glanced at the medical book Sam had been reading. If he was not in any way worried about the outcome, then what need did he have to study? She had heard that it was more serious for adults. But how, exactly? Michael had looked miserable, but no worse than she had been when she'd had this. She sat down on the couch and took up the book from the cushion where it rested, opening it to the marked page and reading what he had read.

'Evie!' It was Sam again, back from his examination. And he was using the warning tone that hinted she was meddling in things she did not understand. But the information was quite clear, as were the likely repercussions.

She closed the book closed with a snap of the cover and stared at him, searching for any signs that he was treating this patient differently than any other. 'You have been underestimating the severity of the disease, Sam. Or have you merely understated it?'

'It does no good to alarm the patient overly on a thing that cannot be predicted or changed.' His expression was grave, but there was nothing in it that indicated another reason to avoid the truth.

'But you must understand how serious the matter is.'

'Of course,' he replied. 'A man's potency is always of great import.'

'I mean to Michael, specifically.'

'Because you were to marry him?'

After what had happened, it was right to speak of that in the past tense. But with this fresh piece of news, her conscience strained in a different direction. 'It is of concern to me, of course,' she said, cautiously. 'But for St Aldric? You might not see...'

'Because I am only a bastard,' Sam added.

'Do not speak so,' Evie snapped. 'It is unworthy of you. The man is your brother.'

'Half-brother,' Sam reminded her. It was a matter-of-fact correction. The anger that had been present in his voice before was gone.

'Then you should have, at least, half a filial sympathy for him,' she said. 'Michael has spoken to me frequently on the subject of his family. Or, more importantly, his lack of family. He is quite conscious of the fact that there are no other members of it, save for you. It is why, when I realised the truth, I insisted that Father tell you immediately.'

'For him,' Sam said, as though this were some damning bit of evidence and not common sense.

'And for you. You deserved to know as well.' Even if he was being an infant in worrying about the particulars, it had been cruel of Father to raise him in ignorance. 'Right now, I am explaining why it was important for *Michael*. And why he is so eager to know you better. He is very alone.'

'We are all alone,' Sam said, as though it did not matter.

'But if we need not be?' she said, hoping that a little encouragement might make him understand. 'Discovering he has a half-brother eased his mind. But it will not help him in his most important job. He needs, above all else, to produce an heir.'

'For him, or for you?' Sam asked, the jealousy she had longed to see two weeks ago in full flower. 'Because if you wish children, I would be happy to provide you with them.' He was looking at her hungrily now and she could not decide whether to be excited or appalled.

'He needs a son for the sake of the people he is responsible to,' she said, shaking her head in disgust. 'Think of something other than yourself for a moment. He has tenants, servants and a seat in Parliament. Who will take on the responsibility of these, if he has no son to follow him?'

'Such a problem is years in the future,' Sam said dismissively.

'But to him, it is no more than a day. He thinks of the future as a matter of course.'

'The great man is so far above us that he does not live minute to minute?' Sam gave her an incredulous smile.

'In short, yes. You cannot think that I did not give this thought as well, when I agreed to marry him.' Because she was to have been a duchess. She hoped that it did not sound like she longed for the power attached to the role, but it would be a lie to say that she had not contemplated the advantages as well as the disadvantages.

'All the more reason to handle this situation with delicacy, your Grace.' It seemed with each effort to explain he became more insecure and not less. 'Just now, I discussed the possible outcome with him. I sent you from the room, so as not to embarrass him. He would not want you to see him as less than a man.'

It was another cause for exasperation. Men acted as though their only value lay between their legs. She would never understand them. 'But he knows,' she said, dragging Sam back to the facts.

'Did you think I meant to withhold the information permanently?' He laughed. 'It is not as if I would tell him an untruth, in an effort to manipulate this situation.' His smile faded. 'That was exactly what you thought. And it was why you read the book. You did not trust me to do the right thing.'

'You have lied to me before,' she said. 'Why should I trust you to tell the truth to him?' And how could she trust him with their secret?

He sat down on the chair opposite, a blank expression on his face. 'The duke's illness, and the way I choose to treat him, has nothing to do with us. When I came home, I loved you, Evie. I had never stopped loving you. I wanted to tell you how I felt. But the time was not right for that. I had to lie. You would not have understood the truth.'

'And now things have changed,' she said. 'Tell me everything.'

He wavered for a moment. Then he said, 'You must trust me—whatever I did, I did with your happiness in mind. I mean to be truthful from now on. And I have not lied to St Aldric about the consequences of his illness.'

'But you said you would not discuss the future with St Aldric, if it impedes his recovery?'

'You are talking about our future, I suppose,' Sam said, a grim smile on his face.

'Things must remain as they are until he is on the road to recovery. Then, perhaps we will try to discuss what recent events mean to his future and to mine.'

'Perhaps?' His eyes widened. 'You don't mean to tell him what has happened between us?'

'Of course not,' she said, shocked that he would even suggest it. 'Not now, not ever. I will not tell him that I have already been unfaithful. It would crush him.'

'I seriously doubt that,' Sam said.

'If it was discovered, it would be the death of my reputation. No one can know of this, Sam. No one at all.'

'So you can have secrets, but I cannot?' He leaned back in his chair and folded his arms across his chest. 'Very well, then. Henceforth, I shall lie about nothing that you don't want me to lie about. But once we are married, this will no longer matter.'

Had he spoken of marriage today? He seemed to think that it was a foregone conclusion.

'We are getting married, Evie,' he said, filling the silence.

It should make her happy, for it was what she had always longed to hear. And making love with him had been wonderful. That, too, was everything she'd dreamed it would be. Then why could she not say yes with her whole heart? And why could he not explain his mutability?

Then she thought of Michael, who would be even more alone than ever when she left him.

'Evie?' Sam was looking at her, as if expecting that a little prodding on his part would gain him the answer he wanted to hear. He got up from his chair and joined her on the sofa. He pulled the medical book from her hands, for she had been hugging it tight as though it were a protective shield. He set it on the table and eased closer.

If he touched her, he would kiss her. And if he kissed her…

She stood up and paced to the centre of the room. 'I think, for the time being, that we had best not discuss the future, either. And as to what happened, earlier in the day?' She gave a little shake of her head, not wanting to call it for what it was. 'I think it is unwise to continue in such a manner, when things are still so unsettled.'

'We are unsettled again, are we?' He was unsmiling. 'Very well, then, Lady Evelyn. We will wait until St Aldric is recovering. But he is of a particularly strong constitution despite this illness. It will not be long. A day, perhaps. Maybe two. And then you must make a decision.'

Chapter Eighteen

'I brought you breakfast.' She smiled in at Michael, who was sitting up in bed, still dazed from sleep. When he understood that it was she, he arranged his bed-clothes as modestly as an old maid. Then he gestured that she come nearer.

The poor man. The response in her mind was involuntary and she hurried to quell it. The last thing he would want at this point was her pity. Especially if, as she suspected, he was gathering strength to minimise his discomfort, so as not to alarm her. His cheeks and neck were still grossly swollen, although somewhat better than they had been.

Sam was right, it would not be long and he would be well again. 'How are you feeling today?'

'Wretched,' he said, not even trying to smile.

'Well, I have brought you tea and milk toast. And there is a poultice for after.' She held out the bowl to him and readied the spoon.

He held out his hands for the tray. 'Really, Evelyn.

While I appreciate your help, I can still manage to feed myself.' His voice was rough from the swelling of his throat, the words somewhat muffled by the difficulty of forming them.

'I see.' She would not be hurt by his tone. After the news he had received yesterday, it was perfectly natural that he would be short tempered. When she had returned to him, after talking with Sam, he had pretended to be asleep rather than acknowledge her presence.

She'd sat by him, until his breathing had become more regular and the play-acted slumber had become real. Then she'd continued to sit with him, enjoying the peace. She did not have the energy to argue with Sam again, nor did she particularly wish to speak with Michael. It felt good to sit, as the room grew dark, thinking nothing at all.

After, she had crept off to her room, not stopping to talk with Sam. She had not even summoned her maid, but had pulled off her dress and crawled beneath the covers to fall into a deep and troubled sleep. She had been up again at dawn, to prepare herself for another day of nursing.

But it seemed, if the patient could not avoid her by closing his eyes, he meant to bark at her until she left. 'Of course you can feed yourself,' she said with a smile. 'But I do not wish you to tire yourself.'

'Tire myself?' There was a pause that she suspected would have been a smothered oath from a man less patient than the Duke of St Aldric. 'You realise, Evelyn, that I have little to do all day but lie in bed, waiting for this complaint to pass.'

'And there is nothing more enervating than doing nothing at all,' she said firmly, thinking of how exhausting it was to sit quietly at his side and not give offence.

'Well, the least you could do is read to me from *The Times*,' he said. 'When I am well again, it will save me time in catching up.'

She adjusted his covers and laid a hand on his swollen cheek. 'I do not wish to upset you. I will ask Sam if it is all right.'

'By all means, ask Dr Hastings.' For the first time since she'd met him, Michael used a tone which was positively venomous.

Evie had to restrain herself from fussing with his covers again, trying to make up for her guilty memories. 'He is your physician,' she said as patiently as she could. 'Who else would I consult about anything that might affect your recovery?'

The duke sighed. 'I am sorry for being cross with you. You have done nothing to deserve it. It is the illness talking. I do not like idleness.'

'Really?' She smiled into her hand. 'I had not noticed.'

'And it bothers me to be dependent on Hastings.'

'We could get another doctor, if that is a problem.' Her father would welcome a chance to get Sam out of the house. And until she could find a way to break with

Michael, it might be for the best not to have temptation continually in her path.

The duke shook his head. 'I cannot very well send him away, after making such a show of asking specifically for his help. He has made it plain that he does not want to associate with me. I am sure he cannot like the position I have forced him into. Much as I would wish to know him better, this situation is not making it easier on either of us.' But he looked quite morose at the thought of giving him up.

'He is a very independent man.'

'It is a family trait,' St Aldric agreed.

And so was this sense of noble self-sacrifice. Stubbornness as well, although she could not tell that to either man. 'Given time, you will overcome his resistance. I am sure that he is pleased to have found his roots, after all this time.' Secretly pleased, perhaps. He had not said any such thing to her. It felt strange that she could not be sure of his feelings. Though they had shared every secret in their young lives, he was hiding things from her now. It did not bode well for their future.

'I must trust your judgement, I suppose,' Michael said, with another sigh. 'You know him better than I.'

Now she was blushing. And she suspected he had noticed it. 'Do you wish anything more?' She reached for the covers again, then stopped herself. There was a limit to the time she could spend smoothing a single sheet. 'Should I build up the fire?'

'Let it die down,' he said. 'It is too warm in here

already. I am not chilled and you are becoming quite flushed.' His voice was all sympathy, providing this easy lie to cover her reactions.

It was just like him, worrying about another. It made her wish that she felt anything more than a wave of fondness to be treated so. 'Very well, then. As long as you are comfortable. Please, enjoy your breakfast.' How much pleasure he could get from it, she did not know. It was as bland and flavourless as her love for him, but he seemed to like that well enough.

'You needn't remain, if you don't wish to,' he added, picking up the spoon and managing a small bite. But she thought he looked rather depressed at the thought of being alone again.

For a moment, she almost forgot her resolve of the previous evening and blurted the truth. *I cannot stay. I am not worthy of your affection. And I do not love you back.*

But with his recovery just beginning, she did not want to do anything that might upset or weaken him. 'It is all right,' she said. 'I will stay as long as you need me.'

He looked up at her and smiled. 'Whatever would I do without you?'

And though her heart felt nothing but a combination of guilt and grim determination, she smiled back. Then she opened the book she had brought to entertain him and started to read.

When he began to doze, she marked the place and set the book at the bedside for later, then sat staring down at the sleeping man. Even with a swollen jaw, he was handsome. And today was the first time she'd heard a cross word from him. Considering the circumstances, it was not surprising. Even a saint might be cross, when ill and faced with the news that Sam had given him.

The Saint. His nickname suited him. He was not just a duke, he was a good man. He did not deserve this illness, or the possible consequences from it. Nor did he deserve to be shunned by his brother. At least, if she were here, he might never be alone again.

What would he do without her?

It was just one more thing that he never need find out.

Chapter Nineteen

When Evie returned from the duke's room it was nearly lunchtime. Sam considered a second examination, but as if she could read his mind, Evie gave a single shake of her head.

'He is sleeping again. And he did not need the drugs for it. His forehead feels cooler and the swelling is coming down. He was able to manage his breakfast and nearly cleared the tray. All he needs right now is rest.'

Sam nodded. 'Your diagnosis is as good as mine, I suppose. If the symptoms are abating, I doubt I will need to bleed him. We will see what the day brings.'

He risked an encouraging smile. If St Aldric was on the mend, they might soon settle things between them. Although he dare not risk taking her back to bed, they might talk quietly for a while. He had not seen her since their argument yesterday. She would forgive him, if they could only be together. They had known each other for a lifetime and had loved almost that long. A week of disagreement would not separate them.

But now she paused in the doorway, neither advancing nor retreating. She just stood and watched him, without returning his smile.

He gestured to the chair opposite him. 'There is no reason why you cannot rest as well. He will be fine without you for a few hours. And you must take a bit of lunch. Your breakfast tray was untouched when Abbott came for it.'

'I was not hungry,' she said, still not moving.

'You are not taking ill, I hope,' he said, half-joking. 'If we are not careful, I will have to treat you as well.'

'No!' Her reaction was extreme and unexpected. She sounded almost as if she feared his touch.

He remembered how it had been for him, when he had wanted her and known it was impossible. The sight of her was agony and a touch was a cruel promise of a thing he would never have. 'I take it you have been thinking about what you must tell St Aldric.'

'I do not wish him to suffer more than he already has.'

'St Aldric, suffer?' Sam could not help the laugh. 'He is already healing. Two or three days of discomfort does not equate to suffering. If he thinks it so, then he does not know the meaning of the word.'

'You are being unfair to him,' Evie said.

She seemed to think he was cruel and not stating an obvious fact. 'You said yourself that he is better today.'

'But we will not know for some time if he will fully recover,' she said, still keeping her distance from him.

'Do you plan to remain silent until then? And I suppose that I am just to wait.' Sam gave an incredulous laugh. 'I wish you showed the same concern for my suffering as for his.'

'Six years passed with barely a word from you,' she said, shaking her head. 'And now, any delay is a trial?'

'Yes,' he said, for it was quite true. 'I am sorry that things were as they were. But that is past. We have waited long enough to be together.'

'We waited too long, I think. Now there is no future for us. I don't think there can be.' The playful and clever girl he remembered was gone. The woman standing before him was sadder and wiser than he'd ever wanted her to become. And he did not want to be the fault of it.

'What we have shared means nothing to you?'

'Of course it means something,' she said urgently. 'But meaning is not the same thing as promise. If you stay, we will go on as we have been. I cannot give myself fully to you because of my feelings for Michael. And you cannot give yourself completely to me, if you will not tell me the whole truth. We are at an impasse.'

Oath be damned. His mouth was already framing the truth, when he stopped himself. Just now, she claimed to have feelings for the duke. She had made her decision before speaking. What good would it do him to tell the truth, if she still did not want him?

If he told her everything, she would not thank him for his honesty. It would destroy her faith in her father. She would see him as a sad wreck of a man, grasping at straws as she pushed him out of her life. And he would be throwing aside his promise to Thorne, as if his good name meant nothing to him.

He had thought he was a fiend who lusted for his sister. Instead, he had become the sort of monster who would seduce his brother's betrothed, destroy her family and promise anything to have his way.

The truth would hurt the woman he loved. He had sworn he would never do that. And if he broke that promise there was no point in living after.

'You are right, Evie,' he said, sad that the way forwards, now he'd found it, was so very empty. 'There is nothing to be done.'

'You must learn to call me Evelyn,' she reminded him. 'As everyone else does. We are grown now, you know. There is no place left for childish nicknames.'

'Of course, Evelyn.' *Evie*, his mind insisted. She would never be Evelyn to him, no matter what his lips might say.

'It is for the best, you know.' Now that the moment was here, she was not angry. Nor did she seem relieved to be rid of him. There was only sorrow, as though she were mourning a death.

And he was still waiting for her to change her mind, like a prisoner hoping for reprieve. Had that been how she had felt, waiting for him to come home and not understanding the reason for his rejection? She had called to him, over and over, and he had refused her. But she had never given up trying to save him from himself.

Until now.

Really, what did he have to offer her? One hardly

needed to be rescued from the fate that awaited her. In fact, he was recuing her now, just by leaving.

'We will see each other, of course, from time to time,' she allowed, offering a sop. 'It cannot be avoided. He is your only family, after all.'

You are my only family. And a few words of truth would destroy hers.

'You know that we will not,' he said, as gently as possible. 'I will go, if that is really what you wish. But do not tell yourself that there will be any contact between us. I will not return. I could not bear to. And you must stop writing to me. This time, I will not read your letters.'

If the total and permanent loss of him bothered her, she did not say so. 'I have promised Father,' she said, insistently. 'And St Aldric, of course. I cannot go back on my word.'

But she could. They could run, right now, somewhere far away, where there would be no one to question them. 'They would understand.' In an instant, he imagined a whole life with her. And another. And another. And then he put them all aside as hopeless. Any choice required her co-operation. He had tried to win it and failed.

'It is you who must understand,' she said. 'I promised myself to a good man. He needs me. You know it is true. Set me free.'

His pain had no effect on her, now that she was resolved. She was as cold as he'd ever wanted to be, when he longed for her. Perhaps her affection was never more than a fleeting thing. But when they had lain together, it had seemed real enough.

'I know what is needed. I know what is required. And I know what people expect. But what do you want, Evie? What do *you* want?' For a moment, her eyes clouded and he was convinced that he could win her with reason.

'Was all your education for naught?' he said. 'You claimed an interest in medicine. There will be no place for it in the life you are choosing.'

And then he lost her again. 'Perhaps not. But, I will be able to accomplish much, as Duchess of St Aldric.'

'You want to do good?' he asked. 'You might help me in my work. We would do good together.' He imagined her, working at his side. He had thought it foolish at first. But now he could not imagine a better future.

She shook her head. 'It was a wonderful dream, Sam. But it was nothing more than that. It is time that I learned more conventional ways of helping others.'

'Without having to bloody your hands,' he said bitterly. 'I will not bother you again, Lady Evelyn. Not with my heart. Not with my work. And you can settle for your tepid marriage and your distant benevolence. I wish you well of it.'

'Next you will speak nonsense about differences in your ranks, or your not being good enough or rich enough for me.' Evie gave an exasperated sigh. 'In the end, the truth is this: St Aldric is honourable. He is truthful with me. You are not.'

And that was the rub. The one point he could not

refute. St Aldric was a saint and above reproach. For all his arguments about the nobility of his love, Sam had bedded her the moment they were alone. And he could never, ever tell her the truth about the past. He would not change and she would not forgive.

He had lost. He had been so sure that, now he was free to marry her, it would all fall easily into place. He had forgotten to consider her feelings, her needs and her sense of justice, which was as strong as any man's. So much about her was strong. And it was all lost to him.

His skin went cold and the world had a distant, cotton-wrapped quality, as his brain tried to deny what he was hearing. Shock, he thought. The prescription was brandy and lots of it. But that would be later, when he was away from her and not trying to salvage his pride. 'Very well, then,' he said. 'You must do as you promised, to St Aldric and to your father. Marry him. Be happy. Truly, that is what I wish for you. And that is a thing I cannot give.'

Chapter Twenty

Sam neglected the afternoon examination of the patient, instead sending Evie, telling her to do whatever she felt was necessary to help her betrothed. She had returned to Michael, shortly after their conversation, taking her lunch with her so that she might share a meal with him.

Sam had eaten alone, in silence, wondering how long it would be until he could make a graceful exit from the house and the lives of the happy couple.

When he next saw the duke, it was well past supper. The man's condition all but answered the question.

'Doctor Hastings,' St Aldric said with a smile, sitting up further in the bed so they might talk eye to eye. 'How long do you mean to keep me here, now that I am recovering?' His voice was stronger and his colour better.

'Another week, at most,' Sam said. 'We must be sure that the last trace of illness is gone before you resume your regular duties.'

'I think I shall go mad, with another seven days of inactivity.'

'You shall have Lady Evelyn to keep you company,' Sam said, managing an ironic smile. 'But if you mean to descend into mania, I will leave the name of another physician who might help. A school friend of mine is now keeper at Bedlam. I am sure he will be glad of the change.'

'You will leave?' The duke raised his eyebrows. 'Are you trying to escape me again? I did not presume that this illness would convince you to accept my offer. But there is no need to run off to avoid me.'

'I am returning to sea,' Sam said. He was not yet sure if it was true. But neither did he care. His future did not really matter, now that he knew he would not share it with Evie.

'Don't be an idiot.' The duke was grinning at him now, as if his life plans were all some enormous joke.

Sam kept his voice level. 'I understand the difference in our rank, your Grace—but I will not allow you to address me in that way.'

The smile disappeared. 'Devil take the difference in our rank, Sam. For just a moment, do me the kindness of remembering that we share a father, and that I am your elder by several months, and leave it at that. And I say you are an idiot if you stir from this place.'

Sam sighed and settled back in the chair at the bedside. 'If it will prevent you from agitating yourself, then very well, Michael.' The name felt odd on his tongue, but he forced it out. 'Say your piece.'

'We both know the reason you are leaving. It is Evelyn, is it not?' And now the duke pinned him to the spot with a glare. He had not seen the man use his rank in such a way. It was quite effective.

Sam weighed the possibility of lying, but only briefly. It seemed the Duke of St Aldric would not stand for prevarication. And if they were truly brothers, there ought to be some truth between them. 'Yes,' he said. 'It is because of Evelyn.'

'The solution is simple, then. I will retract my offer.'

'The hell you will.' He hoped that the new St Aldric liked the change in his demeanour. At the moment, he did not care that one must not dictate to a duke. 'Are you overcome with the idea that you can claim me as family? Biology does not give you a right to order my life for me. Or are you merely so caught up in your own rank that you think you can move people about like furniture? The honour of a lady is at stake and you will do nothing to compromise it.'

St Aldric laughed. 'I do not think the usual rules apply in this case. By giving her up, I would be doing her a service. She is staying with me out of pity. If there was the slightest chance of her heart breaking, you would be there to pick of the pieces, quick enough.'

'She would not have me.' Saying the words was like plunging into an ice bath. It was a brutal counter-shock to the numbness he had been feeling all afternoon. But it took some of the guilt away, so he continued, 'I tried. Heaven help me. I tried to take her from you. But she will not go. The breach between us is too great. I waited too long. And I have lost her trust.'

'I am sorry.' St Aldric settled back into the pillows again, looking as though he were the physician and Sam the patient.

'Don't be. She will forget me, once I am gone.'

'She belongs with you,' the duke reminded him, his voice patient and low.

'But she is better off with you.' Sam squared his shoulders and fiddled with the instruments on the table at his side, dropping them one by one into the bag on the floor. 'She will be a good wife, an excellent duchess. I wish you well. But you must understand if I do not stay for the wedding.'

'And this is how it must end, with all three of us being unhappy?'

'You? Unhappy?' Sam laughed, bitterly. 'The least you could do is take pleasure in your victory over me.'

'It was never my goal to be anyone's rival,' St Aldric said, with a shake of his head. 'I will do nothing to make Evelyn unhappy, for she is a sweet girl, and we could have done well together. But to find that I have family, only to lose it again?' He sighed. 'I cannot break with her and be an honourable man. And I cannot manage to keep you both.'

'That is the gist of it,' Sam agreed. 'At least, when you were at your weakest, I did not kill you. The thought crossed my mind. But I expect you know that.'

'I suppose I am glad that you resisted,' St Aldric replied. 'Although it might have been more of a mercy to finish me. If I am not to have an heir, there is little point in continuing.'

'Do not talk nonsense,' Sam said firmly, a doctor again. 'You have many years ahead of you. And I make no guarantees either for or against your chances of siring children.' Considering the extent of the illness, he was not optimistic. But anything was possible.

The duke was giving him a sympathetic smile again, as though he was the one to be offering comfort. 'You do not understand. I do not expect you to.' He lifted the sheet and glanced down at his still-swollen body. Then he winced and dropped it again.

'It is better than it was yesterday,' Sam reminded him. 'You are healing. And it could have been worse,' he said, as encouragingly as possible. 'Men have died from this. Or been deafened. Or disfigured.'

'And I have been rendered impotent,' the duke snapped.

'We cannot be sure.'

'Until I have tried for years without success?' he said, sounding every bit as bitter as Sam felt. 'As everyone continues to remind me, I am a young man, with a long life ahead.'

'You are,' the doctor agreed.

'To what purpose is this long life I am to have? Am I to work for a lifetime, caring for my people and my land, only to leave it to no one? When I die, it will all fall to ruin.'

'You cannot know that.'

'The not knowing is likely to drive me mad,' his

brother said, raking his hair with his hand. 'I will live. But St Aldric is as good as dead. And I must watch all that my family has built, in the end of its days.'

'Our family,' Sam said, feeling the fleeting sense of kinship again.

'But in this you cannot help me,' St Aldric said, staring at the wall across the room. 'I am alone.'

'You have Evelyn.' Sam did his best to make his voice encouraging.

'God help her. This cannot be what she wished for.'

'You are a duke,' Sam reminded him.

'And less of a man than you.' Michael stared back at him. 'She loves you. Would you want to know that your wife will spend every moment of your marriage dreaming of another man?'

It was Sam's turn to look away.

'Do not bother to lie about it. If this is a day for difficult truths, what is one more? Will you have the courtesy to admit it?'

'What I want does not matter,' Sam said firmly. 'It is what she wants that matters. I never should have forgotten that. I handled things badly. Now, she has made her decision. She chose you.'

'Does she know the extent of my illness?'

'She read the medical books herself. It is the reason she will stay with you. She would not have you be alone.' Apparently, it did not matter how lonely Sam might be. 'If you break her heart over this, or disgrace her in any way, I will come back and take the life I have just saved.'

'Then God help us all,' St Aldric said, collapsing back on to the pillows.

'If this is an example of His mercy, I would prefer to do without it,' Sam said, dropping the last of the tools into his bag and closing it. 'And now, Michael, if you will excuse me? I think I shall go down to the port and wait for a high tide and a fresh wind.'

Chapter Twenty-One

Sam was gone.

Eve had watched as he'd left the duke's room and walked past the sitting room without stopping. Shortly thereafter, she'd heard the slam of the door to the servants' stairway. And then she had seen no more of him.

She'd found a letter on the table, clearly outlining instructions for the duke's care, and what she should do if his condition changed for the worse. There were the names of several prominent physicians she might contact with problems. She could also contact them if St Aldric persisted in his desire for a personal doctor. If his condition devolved into sterility, as he feared, there might be some treatment for it that Sam had not learned. Other opinions might be sought.

It was everything she'd have hoped for from a truly dedicated doctor. And it was nice to know it came from Sam. Now that the decision had been made, he showed no jealousy and no desire for revenge. He wanted, above all, what was best for the patient. It seemed, in some things at least, he was exactly the man she'd have wished him to be.

But there was no word to her at all. Had she really expected a personal message, in a place where any might read it? An apology, perhaps. Or one last entreaty to change her mind and come to him. If he loved her, as he claimed, did she not deserve to know where he was going and what he was likely to do when he got there?

It was even worse than when he'd left the last time. Then she could at least write to him, even if he did not answer. This time, she had told him she did not care. And he had removed the temptation to change her mind, by making it impossible to do so.

It was just as well. When it came to Sam, she was no better than the Biblical Eve. She resisted now. But at some point, all her noble plans to be loyal to the duke would fail her. She would weaken and run back to Sam. But if she was married, they could not allow it to. He had severed the link between them with surgical precision.

It had been the right thing to do. Michael was her choice. Given the way things had turned out, he was the only choice she ever should have made. Their love might be a pale imitation of the kind she had hoped for, but he needed her in a way that Sam never had.

Sam was gone and she was alone. But that meant that the responsibility for the care of the duke fell to her. So she did as Sam would have done and made sure that the patient was settled for the night, offering medications that were refused as no longer necessary and refilling the glass at bedside with fresh, cool water. Then she had left him in peace until morning.

Tonight, she did not return to her room. Instead, she slept uneasily in the bed that she had shared with Sam. One of the housemaids had been deemed immune, having suffered through the mumps a year or two before, and was allowed limited access to the third floor, to provide the necessary cleaning. She must have visited here, for the sheets had been changed and the bed made up properly. There was no trace of what they had done there in anything but Eve's memory.

The next morning, before ringing for breakfast, she washed and dressed herself, taking special care with her appearance, so that she might be a pleasant sight for her betrothed. Then she went to the end of the hall to receive the tray from Abbott, approving the contents. They were hardly a proper English breakfast, but were they were much less bland than the day before.

Then she knocked once and entered the duke's room with a serene smile, sure that no trace of her heavy heart would be apparent to him. 'Good morning, Michael. I have brought you your porridge.' She set the tray down where he could reach it. 'There is the cream for it. Honey as well. And a nice cup of coffee.' She fell silent, reminding herself that, since the illness had not rendered him a blind, deaf, idiot, she did not need to recite the menu.

'Evelyn.' He sounded tired and she put her hand on his, willing strength into him.

'You are doing much better today. I can see the difference.' The illness was abating. The swelling had reduced much from the previous day. But he looked grey, as though he had not slept well. She hoped that this was not a sign of relapse, but merely proof that fighting the infection had tired him.

'That is good to know,' he said. 'But where is my brother physician, so that I may thank him for it?' There was a kind of dryness in the statement, as though there might be some irony in offering those thanks.

'He…is gone.' She swallowed, unsure of what to say. 'I shall be both doctor and nurse to you now.' She gave another artificially bright smile, hoping that this would be sufficient for an explanation.

'Why this sudden change in plans?' Michael asked, still expressionless. 'I assumed he would stay with us through the wedding, at least.'

'He does not like to stay too long in any one place.' It might even be the truth. She had not known the adult Sam long enough to ask his opinion. 'I believe his intention was to go back to the navy.'

'Then he is a fool.' St Aldric offered no other explanation for this.

'You need not worry. He assured me, before he left, that you were all but mended and that I would have no trouble tending you from this point.'

'Did he?'

'Yes.' She nodded eagerly. Too eagerly perhaps, for he was staring at her with the same ironic expression he had used at the news of his doctor's departure.

He was focused on her now. And for a moment, she felt that she was truly in the presence of a duke and not some handsome but powerful friend. 'And did he inform you of the likely result from this illness? He assured me you knew, but I would like to hear it from your lips as well.'

'That you might be unable to father children?' She put off the smile and made sure that she did not stammer over the words, for it would only make them worse. She must be as stoic as Sam would have been, when sharing an unfavourable diagnosis. 'Yes, I am aware. But we cannot know for sure until we have tried.'

'You mean, when we have married,' he said patiently.

'Of course.' That was what she should have said. Now he might think she knew far too much about the process. She should be innocent, and ignorant, if she was to carry on with this farce.

And it was wrong of her to think of her impending marriage to the Duke of St Aldric as a farce. It was an honour. All the more so because he needed her.

The silence between them had carried on far too long. What was she to say next? Or should she pretend that it was a comfortable thing between two people who would be so close as not to be bothered by a little quiet?

'And you are all right with this?' The duke chose not to notice the awkward moment. 'It means you might never have children. I should have thought, with your interest in midwifing, that you would want to be a mother.'

'Of course,' she said. 'But I am also aware that we do not always get what we might want in life.' Right now, she must not be thinking of Sam.

'And next you will tell me that Man proposes, but God disposes.' He waved a hand. 'Pray, do not bother.' Was it her ears, or did he actually sound cynical? He had been ill, of course. And at the moment, he was under much stress. But it was still most unlike him.

'That has ever been the case,' she said. 'It was thus, even before you became ill. We might never have had children. Though we are young and strong, we have no guarantee of longevity. There is simply no knowing the future.'

'*Carpe diem,*' he muttered, pushing his untouched breakfast aside. 'But that does not change my need for an heir. In fact, it increases it. If I die tomorrow, my life would have had no meaning.'

'Of course it would,' Eve said, patting his hand.

She was patting his hand again. She must stop it, or he would think she could manage nothing more than the platonic affection she might shower on any invalid. 'You are a great man, Michael. And no matter what happens, people will remember you as such.'

'They would remember me as the last St Aldric,' he reminded her. 'And I would have failed my family in the one thing that should have been simple.' He gave her another sharp look. 'If you had given me your answer when I'd first asked for it, we'd have been married by now. This might never have been a concern.'

Now, he would turn his unhappiness on her. She

wanted to argue that it was hardly her fault. There was no way she might have known the future and the results of her decisions. But it was true. She had hesitated when he needed her to be decisive. And it must never happen again. 'I'm sorry,' she replied.

'Sorry does not change the fact that I need an heir.' At one time, he had said that he needed a wife. But that had never been what he'd meant. Circumstances were forcing the truth from him. But she had told Sam she wanted the truth, even if it was unpleasant. She had no right to complain when she received it.

'There is a way that we might be sure of progeny,' the duke said, slowly and carefully. 'But it would require a sacrifice on your part.'

'Of course,' she said, giving his hand an encouraging squeeze. She owed him her loyalty now, if only to make up for the times that she had wavered.

'I must have a son. A legitimate heir. And that might be quite beyond me.'

He was staring at her as though she would be the key to it. But there was nothing she could do to alter the course of his illness. He must mean something quite different. 'Are you suggesting we perpetrate a ruse of some kind?'

'In a way,' he said cautiously. 'I did not sleep last night, trying to find another way. But I could think of none but this: you must appear to be pregnant with my child.'

'If we went away for a time, and returned with an infant…'

He shook his head. 'People would wonder. But if they saw that you were carrying a child, and if I acknowledged it as mine, they would not dare to question us. They would announce us fortunate. All gossip would be silenced.'

'But how…?' The answer was simple, of course. But he could not possibly be suggesting it.

'If you were to lie with a man not unlike me in appearance. Someone as alike as a brother…'

She already had. And she had promised herself that it would never happen again. 'I will not be unfaithful to you,' she said, setting the temptation as far from herself as she could.

'It is not infidelity if it is agreed upon by both parties.' He was looking at her without emotion, as though she was worth nothing more to him than the child she might produce.

'And our marriage vows mean nothing to you?'

'I will fulfil my part in them,' he said solemnly. 'But as I remember your part, you would be called to obedience.'

Sit quietly. Have no opinion other than the weather. Play with your kitten and do not think too hard, or speak too loudly. And now, this. 'What you are suggesting is horrible.' She dropped his hand. 'I will not hear it.'

'Not this year, perhaps.' His face was positively grim. 'But as time passes, and we do not have a son, you might feel differently. And I? I would insist.'

'You would require me to do something so repellent?'

'As to make you seduce the man you have loved for years?' Now he laughed and the cynicism was obvious. 'My half-brother would be the perfect candidate. I suspect, after a few more years at sea, he would be all too willing to bed you, should you tell him tales of your unhappiness with me. I have seen the two of you together and the way you look at each other, when you think no one might notice. He was a fool for not taking you from me, when he had the chance.'

'You knew?' It was pointless to lie, now that it was too late to matter.

He nodded. 'I knew from the first day that I would never have all of your heart. But it was not your heart that was required. I would have had no objection to a dalliance, once your obligation to me was fulfilled. But this solution will work just as well.'

She had thought him good, almost beyond belief. And she had berated herself for betraying him. But now she could hardly bare to look at him. 'How could you?'

'Easily, I assure you. Because it needs to be done. Think of it as one more duty that you will face if you truly wish to marry me. For you see, my dear, being a duchess is sometimes quite different than being a lady.'

'But when you offered, I thought…'

'That I loved you?' His smile, which had seemed to be benevolent, was really no better than patronising. 'At any time, have I attempted to mislead you? I did not make my offer out of love, nor did I flatter myself in believing that you accepted it for that reason. We are fond of each other. But it would be a lie to claim that it is more than that. The marriage was expedient for both of us. And expediency might demand the situation that I describe to you now. While I appreciate your willingness to stand by me in the face of adversity, this marriage is likely to require more from you than pity. Do you still wish to stay?'

'No.' Tears were slipping down her nose, and she wiped them away with the back of her hand. She should be strong enough to do this. Or she should at least have stopped to think through her answer. But there was no other answer she could make. 'I am sorry. If this is our future, I cannot marry you.'

Now he was patting her hand with the same sort of benign sympathy that she had offered him. 'I thought not. It is a shame, for I am sure we would have been a great success.'

'You are not angry?' He seemed almost relieved. Since she was as well, she could not bring herself to feel insulted.

'I am angry about many things, my dear. But not at you. You love my brother. He loves you. Go to him. Be happy.' St Aldric was giving her an exhausted attempt at a smile, as though he had completed some onerous but necessary task. 'And now, if you will forgive me, I wish to rest.' He turned away from her, face to the wall and sighed.

She reached out a hand and touched his hair, then she withdrew. She had no right. It was over between them.

If it gave him comfort, as it seemed to, then let the duke think that she was going to Sam. But she could not manage that, either. Her freedom did not remove the sting of knowing that he had waited too long to declare. Would he still want her, now that Michael did not? If this sudden love for her was anything more than jealousy towards his brother, he should have told her so when she'd asked.

If there was another motive for avoiding her and spurning her offers, and the sudden, convenient return of his love, he had said nothing about it. While she did not wish to believe the worst, she could find nothing else that made sense.

Chapter Twenty-Two

Walking to the study was like going from the sick room to a funeral. That would be what it would seem to her father, who viewed her impending marriage almost as though it were a live thing. And she had not just witnessed the death of it, she had been instrumental in bringing it about.

She had murdered her one chance at a title and a life of ease. No one would want a girl who jilted the most eligible bachelor in London. How picky must she be, if even a saint was not good enough for her?

Yet she felt almost happy to be free of it. She had parted from him as a friend. She would not have to lie to St Aldric about her feelings, since he understood them already. She would not have to stifle herself and conform to his ideals for a perfect wife. She could go on much as she'd been living it, lonely, but with time to study and to help the women in the villages around their country home.

But it would take all of her charm to persuade Father

that this was for the best. She would kiss his temples and assure him that there would be no problem with the duke. They would still be welcome in his home and he in theirs. Their household was well managed now. But it would continue to be so if she remained as a spinster in his house. She could care for him in his dotage.

The future, while it was not rosy, was solid and comfortable. Once he was over his disappointment, he would see the advantages of her staying. She would run the house for him, as she had. And she would always be his loving and devoted daughter.

Even if she could not have Sam it was better to live this way. She might be alone, but at least she was not living under the misapprehension that love would come to her. The past was dead. Memories were illusions. And even saints had feet of clay.

Now that she had arrived at it, she hesitated in the open door of the study. She felt like a very small girl again, wanting to see her parent, but afraid to interrupt his important business.

And, just as he always had, he looked up and smiled at her, as though she was the light of his life. 'Evelyn. Come.' He put up a hand, curling a coaxing finger. 'Doctor Hastings has finally freed you from your duties, so that you might visit me?'

'Father.' Her tongue was all but sticking in her mouth. *I have done a horrible thing.* She had not, really. She had done the only thing possible. But how to explain it?

He saw her distress and held out his arms to her, and

she went into them without question, drawing strength from his embrace.

'Does something upset you?' He held her away from him.

'Sam has gone,' she said. And for the first time that day she felt like crying.

'You knew he would,' her father said, unaffected. 'At best, he might have stayed through the wedding. But he has not been a constant friend, has he? He all but disappeared from your life for years. Now that he is back in London, I am surprised that he stayed as long as he did. But I suspect that was caused by nothing more than the duke's illness.'

'Father!' Now of all times, he seemed full of his old grudge against a man who could do him no real harm. 'Sam's going is neither here nor there. He can do as he wishes, for he is a free man.'

'Then what is troubling you, my dear? It is not St Aldric, is it? Hastings assured me that the man would make a recovery. Not complete, perhaps. But it has turned out as well as can be expected.'

'He is fine,' she agreed, after a steadying breath. 'As fine as one could hope to be, after a severe illness. He grows stronger by the hour. But he is in low spirits.'

'Ahh. Yes.' Her father took an equally steadying breath. He was obviously aware of what this particular illness might mean, but did not want to talk about such a sensitive matter with his daughter. 'Well, there is nothing to be done about the past and no predicting the future.'

'I tried to tell him so. But he would not listen.'

'He will come around in time,' her father insisted.

'Perhaps,' she agreed. 'But he was saying things today that could not be forgiven or forgotten. And it is quite clear that he never loved me.'

Her father laughed dismissively. 'That is hardly a problem, I am sure. He is a good man. He is fond of you. That is enough.'

'Not to me,' she said. 'At one time, I thought so. But truly, it is not. And I told him so.'

'I beg your pardon. But I could not have heard you correctly.' Her father put his hand to his ear, feigning deafness to give her time to correct her last statement. 'You do not argue with a duke, Evelyn, no matter how *outré* his behaviour becomes.'

'His behaviour was not *outré*,' she said, equally incredulous that her father would support the opposite side in any argument she might have. 'The things he said…' How much did she want to tell him of the suggestions made? 'Let me simply say that they could not be attributed to eccentricity. He proposed that we have a marriage so far outside the bounds of propriety that I told him I wanted no part in it. I asked for my freedom. He gave it to me. We have agreed to end our engagement.'

Her father was slack jawed in amazement, before sputtering, 'Wh-wh-whatever you said to him to cause this separation, you must go back immediately and unsay it,'

As though there would be any going back. 'Certainly

not. I am sorry, Father, but our conversation resulted from something he said to me. I had done nothing to provoke him.'

'Then perhaps it was a result of his illness,' her father said, voicing one last hope. 'He will be better in a week. When he is, he will apologise to you. All will be well again.'

'It was not the illness talking,' she said patiently. 'He is very nearly healed. But the possible repercussions gave us reason to discuss the future. We simply agreed that the proposed union would make neither of us happy and dissolved it. We are still on good terms. But we will not marry.'

'And what are you to do now?' her father moaned, his head in his hands. 'And do not tell me that it is a disagreement over Hastings. If he is gone again, he will not be able to interfere.'

'No, Father, I can honestly say that it is not. The difficulty lies between Michael and myself. I cannot tell you more than that.' She came around to the other side of the desk and hugged him, to prove that her love for him had not changed at all.

His arm came up to pat her on the shoulder as well. 'All the same, you might well have ruined your only chance at happiness. Who will have you, now?'

'You needn't worry,' she said, smiling now to show him that her heart was not the least bit broken. 'Not about anything at all. I am going to stay here with you. I am sure you would have missed me terribly, had I left you. But now I shall be here always, to care for you.'

'I am not yet so old that I need a nurse,' her father said sharply and withdrew his arm.

'I know that, Father,' she said. 'But you must admit, my housekeeping skills have been useful thus far. I still cannot sew a straight seam, of course. But I manage the servants well enough, don't I? Your home is as you like it. I will see that it remains so.'

Then he cleared his throat, as though preparing to broach some awkward news. 'The truth is, my dear, I had plans of a matrimonial nature myself. There is a widow that I am quite fond of. But now that you plan to remain...'

She had been prepared for anger. Perhaps some threat of punishment that she would easily avoid. But this reaction was totally unexpected. Her own father did not want her to stay. In fact, he had been in the process of disposing of her, to make way for another, and she had spoiled everything. She sat down with a thump on the chair by the desk, momentarily unable to support her own weight.

'Do not worry, my dear,' he said with the same reassuring smile she had planned to use on him. 'I am sure, if we make an effort, we will think of someone to take you. And we must look on the bright side. You may have lost the duke. But at least Hastings is gone again. We are most fortunate to be rid of him.'

Here again was his strange dislike for Sam, who had been as close to him as a son, almost since birth.

'But I doubt his family will see him, either,' she said. 'He refused the position that St Aldric offered him. And at the time of his parting, they were still no closer to behaving as brothers should.'

'You are too soft hearted by half, Evelyn,' he said, smiling at her with some of the fatherly warmth she had expected. 'In the end, they will both be better off if he returns to sea.'

'I hope he does not,' she said. No matter what had happened, she did not wish him ill. 'It is far too dangerous. I have told him so, but I do not think he listened.'

'Not so dangerous as it might have been, had he remained ashore.' Her father glanced at the door, as though wanting to make sure that there was no one in the hall who might hear. 'I have known, my dear, of your affection for him. It simply would not do. Some day you will see the wisdom of it and accept that it was not meant to be. If you ever wish to marry well, Samuel Hastings must not hang over the union like a cloud.'

'He would do nothing to hurt me,' she said. He had hurt her already. But no one would know about that.

'He would not be able to help himself,' her father said, with a sad shake of his head. 'He would always be searching for some sign of dissatisfaction between you and your husband.'

It was almost as St Aldric had described it, with Sam waiting in the wings for her first sign of weakness. But hadn't that been exactly what had happened already? She would not be sure for several weeks that she had not made a horrible mistake that might leave her running back to the duke and agreeing to his original plan of providing an heir in any way possible. 'Well,

I am not to marry St Aldric now, so that hardly seems a problem.'

'It is even worse, my dear,' her father said, almost wringing his hands with agitation. 'If you do not find another suitor, there will be nothing left to curb his acting on the impulse to offer comfort that you would not need.'

'He needed no curbing in the past. He left easily enough, the first time, and we have hardly seen him for six years.' This time, he'd been old enough to satisfy his lust. Once that had been done he'd left again, without so much as a thought to the possibility of issue.

'That was a different thing entirely,' her father said, with a resolute nod, as though the past was settled. 'It took considerable effort on my part to get him away from you.'

She could not have heard it right. Sam had said nothing of her father, in any of this. If he was not at fault, then why had he not said so? 'You were the reason for his departure,' she said, hoping that he would correct himself.

Her father looked embarrassed. 'It was well past time that you were separated. He had been too long in your company and had grown overfond of you.'

'He loved me,' she said, half-believing it.

'But not as he should have,' her father corrected. 'Not as I intended.'

'You intended that we love each other?' she said, still confused.

'As brother and sister. But certainly nothing more

than that.' And now her father looked incensed. 'The foolish boy actually came to me, ready to offer for you before you were out. He seemed to hope that, by making his intentions clear, you could be encouraged to wait for him. I told him it was impossible, of course.'

It had not been impossible. Not at all. She had waited as long as she could, even without his offer. 'You refused him and then he left,' she said. Sam had mentioned nothing of the offer, probably unwilling to admit to his early weakness at taking whatever bribe her father had offered.

'Not at first. He was just as stubborn as he is now. It might be an admirable quality, when one is without family and must make one's own way in the world. But not when it set his sights on something that he could never have.' Her father gave a little shake of the head and a rueful smile. 'Imagine, my dear, being married to someone with no name to call his own and in trade.'

'He is a physician,' she corrected. 'It is not so very poor a choice, if a gentleman must take employment. And it certainly would not matter, had there been love between us.'

'Of course it would have mattered,' her father said with exasperation. 'There would be no rank, less money and a house not so fine as the one you live in now. And certainly no bevy of servants bowing and scraping and calling you "your Grace."'

'I never asked for any of those things,' she said quietly, wondering if that was what Sam had thought when he'd first gone.

'But you deserve them, all the same,' he said. 'You are my only daughter, my one dear child. And I will have nothing less for you than a titled husband and a life free from worry. Sam Hastings could not offer that. Thus it was necessary for him to leave.'

'So Sam thought me too far above him?'

'On the contrary. He insisted that it would spur him to even greater success, to keep you in luxury. He would find a way to provide for you, no matter the risk.'

'And yet he went away.' And proved that it was all nothing but talk.

'Not easily,' her father replied. 'No matter my arguments, he would not be dissuaded. I threatened to cut him off without a cent. He did not care. I offered him money to leave. He would not hear of it.'

Eve's heart grew full at the thought of the young Sam arguing ardently for her hand. He'd claimed to love her. And it must have been true. What reason could her father have to lie about such things, when it was clear that he held Sam in contempt? 'And what happened then?'

'He threatened to put the idea to you. If I did not agree, the two of you would run off and be married in Scotland. Would it not be more respectable to bind you to him in betrothal? Then the pair of you would wait until he had established himself in business before seeking marriage.' Her father gave a huff of disgust. 'It was blackmail, pure and simple. He was toying with your reputation. I could not let it stand.'

But Sam's argument sounded quite reasonable to

her. It had been what she wanted. Even if her father had denied it, Sam should have put the suggestion to her. 'Why did he not run off with me, as he promised?'

'He would have, had I not offered an argument he could not refute.' Her father took a breath, then froze up, as if realising that he had spoken too much. 'And the rest is nothing for delicate ears to hear, my dear.'

Even after six years, Sam must have felt the same, for he would not speak, even if she thought ill of him. Whatever had been said clearly involved her, yet no one would do her the courtesy of sharing the secret that had altered the course of her whole life. She dropped her argument and smiled knowingly. 'You needn't bother to protect me, Father. He told me everything before he left.'

'He told you!' Her father's voice was thunderous and he rose and slammed his fist down on the desk for emphasis. 'That was between him and me and should have passed no further. He is a bounder and a cad. A viper in the bosom of this family. And if he would tell you such a thing, it proves everything I suspected about him. Blood will tell, Evelyn. Blood will tell.'

'His father was a duke,' she said softly.

'And his mother was a…seamstress,' he finished, as though narrowly avoiding yet another word that was not suitable for her ears. 'His revelation was nothing more than an attempt to turn you against me.'

'And that is why you must tell me your side of it,' she said, coaxing a little bit more of the truth. 'So that I might understand the whole.'

'I had promised to protect him,' her father said, 'and raise him as my own. But there are limits to what a man will do for a friend, even when that friend is a duke. I had never promised that he should marry my daughter. I am sure old St Aldric would not have expected that from me.'

Now old St Aldric's opinion counted above hers. Were dead men allowed to make up her mind for her as well? 'He could not have known what would happen,' she said, leaving the door open for more information.

'I could not tell him his father's name.' Her father could hardly meet her eyes. 'But that did not mean that I could not tell him that there was a good reason I had raised him. And that his parentage would require that the two of you never marry.'

'What difference could his true father have made in that?' But he had not known about the duke until just recently. Before that, he must have assumed he knew his origins and that they prevented him from marrying. It was only when he learned the truth that he was free to come to her.

A horrible thought occurred to her. *Oh, please, let it not be so.* 'What did you tell him, Father?' She took him by the arm and shook it, as if she could rattle the information from him, praying all the while that it was not as she suspected. 'What did you say?'

'I told him that he had mistaken the natural affinity of a brother and sister for something different. That the bond between you was an affection arising from blood and kinship. His confusion was unfortunate, but that he must see a marriage between the two of you would be against the laws of God and man.'

'You told him...' The truth surged in her stomach, so suddenly that she felt unwell.

'I told him that I had raised him like a son because that was what he was.' Her father looked embarrassed. 'And really, he was as much a son as I would ever have. It was not a complete lie. Merely an exaggeration.'

'And he left because he thought...' She gave a shudder of distaste and remembered his reactions in his rooms, and in the garden. His frenzied kisses, revulsion at his own weakness and his vow that there could never be anything between them.

The night of her engagement, the impediment had been lifted. And he had come to her immediately, a changed man.

Her father was still speaking. 'It was the only way I could think of to part the two of you. You had been as thick as thieves, for years. He had all but worshipped you, since the moment of your birth. But you must see that it could not have been...' The words were rushing out of him, as though a complete explanation would make them sound less heartless.

My poor dear Sam... It all made sense, now. His obvious attraction to her. His sudden disappearance. And his insistence that he felt nothing honourable. And now that he was free, she had chosen another and forced him away.

She rose from the chair and took a staggering step away from her father. It was like backing away from the life she had always thought was hers. She had never doubted his love. But she saw her own life, clearly, for the first time. He had kept her, like a plant in a sunless room, not noticing as her dreams had withered. He had thought he was protecting her, but instead he had been protecting his plans for her.

'I had to do it.' Her father held out a hand to her, as though trying to draw her back to his side. 'Do you not understand?'

'It is over now, Father.'

'Because he is gone.'

She shook her head. 'Because you cannot lie to us, ever again. If you love me as you say, then it must be the truth between us, always and for ever. Or you will lose me, just as you have lost Sam.'

But this time, she had been the one to lose Sam. She had sent him away. He had left without a word and she had no idea where to seek him. She turned, looking wildly around her, but knowing that there would be no clue. She looked to her father, who could no longer be trusted, even if help was offered. Then she thought of the one person who she could trust, though no sane person would dare to ask him for help in such a matter.

'Evelyn, wait!'

But the voice was already behind her and becoming fainter as she ran down the hall. She had not a moment to lose. She had waited too long already. She ran to the stairs and up the next two flights, chest tight from the mix of exertion and anxiety. She took only a moment to compose herself, before bursting into the sick room.

St Aldric looked up at her entrance with a benign smile. He was sitting up in bed and the morning papers were spread about him on the bedclothes.

The thought flitted through her mind that she should scold him for overexerting himself, then she remembered that she had no right to do so, especially not after the discussion they'd had only moments ago. If she was no longer welcome in the room, her advice would be even less so. Unsure how to begin, her knees bent, her head bowed and she whispered a breathless, 'Your Grace...'

'Don't talk rot, Evelyn.' He pushed the paper aside and gestured to the chair at his bedside.

She took it. 'I was afraid, that you would not wish to see me, after...'

'Your perfectly reasonable request that we dissolve our engagement?' If the parting bothered him, there was very little evidence of it. The slightly strained look at the corners of his eyes, perhaps. Or the faint crease in his brow. Vanity would demand her to be hurt by his indifference. But Eve could not manage to be other than relieved.

'I need your help,' she blurted. 'I have made a mistake.'

'Only one?' He was still smiling. 'Of course I shall help you. Unless you mean to come back to me, Evelyn. I am afraid I will not take you.'

That was almost insulting, yet she still did not care. She smiled back at him. 'I need to find Sam.'

Now the duke beamed at her. 'I was hoping you would say such. His plan is to return to the sea.'

'He promised me he would not.' She had been praying it would be Scotland. Or some other landlocked place that he might easily be retrieved from. But suppose he had gone with the morning tide?

'He promised you?' The duke gave a short laugh. 'He would break that promise, then, as quickly as he was able.'

'Why...?'

'When a man loses all he values, Evelyn, he is likely to do the most foolish and self-destructive thing he can imagine. You were the reason he went to sea before. And you are the reason he will return to it.'

It was so clear now. So simple. Why had she not understood? 'But how will I find him?' Three-quarters of the globe was water. And he sought to be lost.

The duke plucked a page off the bed sheets and thrust it at her. It was the shipping news, with a neat schedule of tides, arrivals and departures. He pointed. 'That one.'

'How can you be sure?'

'It is bound for Jamaica. Distant, dangerous and deficient in English women. That is the one he will choose. Africa would be better, of course. But it is damnable weather to go 'round the horn at this time of year. Most ships' captains are not nearly so suicidal as our Samuel is likely to be.'

'Suicidal?' She had imagined him to be adventurous, not fatalistic.

'It is why you must waste no time in retrieving him.' He handed her a note, pencilled in a shaky but legible hand on the flyleaf of the book she had been reading him. 'Give this to my groom and say that you must borrow my carriage. The crest on the door is very handy for moving crowds and loosening tongues.' Then he turned from her again, gathering up the papers to read.

Chapter Twenty-Three

Sam sat at breakfast in the public room of his inn, trying not to think about the past, though everything seemed to remind him of it. The chops and ale in front of him were a solid replacement for the shirred eggs, toast and kippers that he had eaten yesterday. The food at the Thorne town house had been as good as he remembered.

He did not want to remember.

He stared fixedly at the food in front of him.

Beer for breakfast had an unapologetically masculine feel to it. It was fortifying, as was the chop. It settled the liquor, which still sloshed in his stomach, after a drunken evening. If he meant to walk the docks searching for an outbound ship, he would need energy. He finished the last of the meat on his plate and paid the innkeeper for the meal and another day's lodging. And then he went to seek his fortune.

The Port of London was full of merchantmen. Stevedores hauled bales and barrels up and down the gangplanks and up the dock towards warehouses. Nearby, he could smell tobacco and salted fish. There would be cotton as well, and wool woven and ready for export.

The bustle of commerce was interesting. But life on such a ship would not be. And what need would any of these captains have for a doctor? While he could not say he wished for Napoleon to escape again, a lasting peace would render him unnecessary.

Unwanted. Extraneous. Unloved. There were so many words to describe him now. It had been a point of pride that, if nothing else, he was useful member of society. But the previous two weeks had left him feeling spent. He had nothing left to give. At least, he had nothing that anyone wanted.

The docks of the East India Trading Company were more compelling. They still stank of fish and sailors, but the undercurrent of spice and tea stirred his lethargic spirit. Perhaps he would not bother with doctoring. He could be an adventurer. If he liked Asia, he could settle there. There would be no shortage of disease in a tropical climate.

But perhaps the Dutch merchantman moored ahead would be better. Sugar cane and rum in the Caribbean. It might be less expensive to stay drunk when the supply was so near. And treating lepers was so selfless that he might compete with dear Michael for his sainthood.

One thought of his brother brought all the memories of Evie rushing back. He had told her he would not go to sea. It frightened her. Surely the events that had followed would exempt him from any promises made.

And if he went to Edinburgh, he might see something about St Aldric and his duchess in the papers from time to time. He would lack the strength to ignore it and would tear the old wounds open again thinking of her.

'Sam!'

He was thinking of her now, when he had promised himself he would not. The memories were so vivid that he could almost hear her voice. But these waking dreams were tame compared to what he saw whenever he closed his eyes. Perhaps he could find a way to do without sleep. Or else he would lie down some night to dream of her and never wake up again.

'Sam Hastings!'

That was not a dream. That was a real voice. But what would Evelyn Thorne be doing on the docks? He turned to look in the direction of the sound and saw the St Aldric carriage parked, in all its gleaming glory, and a liveried footman reaching to open the door.

Sam stumbled backwards into a passing navvy who swore and pushed him aside, but he hardly noticed. He could not see her. Not now. Not when he was so close to escape. And certainly not when she was rigged out as the damned Duchess of blasted St Aldric.

He had an insane desire to laugh. It seemed that, the closer he got to sea, the more his manners deteriorated. And it also seemed that he might have to jump from the dock and swim for India if he meant to get away from Evelyn Thorne. She was on the ground and running towards him, blocking his escape. It hardly mattered. The sight of her had frozen him to the spot like a statue.

'Ev-hhhh.' Her body hit his with no small force, knocking the air from his lungs. He tried desperately to catch his breath, but the mouth that covered his made it all the more difficult. His gasp brought her tongue into his mouth, and the need to trap it there and keep it for ever superseded anything so common and mortal as respiration.

He was breathless and lightheaded. If he could not manage to fill his lungs, he would black out and fall into the river. But he was being kissed by Evie and nothing else mattered. Her hands were around his waist, stroking his back to ease the tightness in his chest. And with each breath she took, she gave life back to him. She was air, and water, and sunshine. She was food and drink. She was everything he needed to survive.

He held her to him, so tightly that heaven and earth could not part them. She fit so perfectly in his arms, as if she was designed to complement him. No other woman had ever felt like this. No one ever would. No one but his Evie.

She leaned away for a moment and stared up at him, blue eyes wide and full of mischief. He ought to tell her that it was disquieting to have her kiss with her eyes open. But there was no changing Evelyn Thorne, once she had an idea in her head. He had best get used to it.

'I have found you,' she said proudly.

'You have,' he agreed. But why had she found him? Was this just another attempt to argue with him? Would it lead to another goodbye? He doubted his heart could stand that.

'I worried that I had lost you, when you were not at the inn. But the footman said your chest was there and I did not think you would leave without it.'

'True,' he said, hoping that this was not a prelude to another rejection.

She sniffed. 'You smell like beer.'

'Breakfast,' he said.

'And medicine.' She put her nose to his lapel. 'We must have this coat cleaned immediately, so that you make a better impression on patients.'

We? That sounded wonderfully possessive. But he must take nothing for granted. 'Evelyn?' He pushed her away so that he could think clearly enough to speak an entire sentence. 'Why are you here?'

'I came for you.'

What a beautiful sound that was. Almost as good as *I love you*. But it could have other meanings than the one he wanted to give to it. 'There is nothing wrong with the duke, I trust?' he asked cautiously and braced himself for the worst.

'Other than that I do not love him and he does not love me?' She smiled. 'No. There is nothing wrong with him at all.' She gave him another small kiss on the corner of his mouth.

For a moment he could not breathe again. And then he sighed like the lovesick fool he was.

She was staring at his lips, as though admiring the shape of them, and touched the lower one with the tip of her finger. 'The engagement is over. I parted on good terms with St Aldric. We are still friends. He loaned me his carriage and told me how to find you. And you must promise to be his friend as well. He needs friends, you see.'

'Yes, Evelyn.' He hardly cared what he was promising, so entrancing was the thought of that fingertip, just out of reach. He moved his mouth to catch it, nipping it lightly, sucking it into his mouth.

They were kissing on a dock and he could hear the distant jeers of passing seamen. The suggestions they were making were crude and vulgar. And, praise heaven, for the first time in his life, some of them were in the realm of possibility. He needed to get her away from here, to get her alone. And to get her undressed. And he needed it soon.

She pulled her finger away and gave him the lightest slap on the cheek to punish him, then let her palm rest there and dropped her head to his chest. 'Afterwards, I talked to Father.' There was no playfulness in her voice now. She sounded hesitant, and as shaken as he did when thinking of his conversations with Thorne.

He sobered. 'I see.' She had not been spared, after all. His hope was evaporating again, just as it had so many times in the past.

'He told me everything. I know what he said to you that made you leave.'

Sam closed his eyes, put his chin on her shoulder and let the world pass them by. It was a rude, coarse and unkind place—all the things that their love was not. But perhaps it suited him. Her father was right in one thing: he was unworthy of such a woman. 'I am sorry,' he said.

'You needn't be. I am sorry. I was the one who doubted. But never again.' She nestled against his chest and he imagined what it would be like, when they had exhausted themselves making love, to sleep with her just like this.

'Never again,' he agreed. 'My darling Evelyn.'

She lifted her head and kissed him on the corner of the mouth. 'And you may call me Evie, again, by the way. Or Evelyn. Or Eve. Anything you like, really.'

Anything I like. These swooping highs and lows of emotion could not be good for his blood pressure. But the possibilities in the word *anything* made him dizzy. 'More than anything, I think I should like to call you Mrs Hastings,' he said and waited for her to contradict him.

'I should like that as well.' She smiled and kissed him again, tugging his arm to move him towards the carriage. 'Perhaps we could get the special licence from Michael. Then we might be married tomorrow.'

'Not without your father's consent,' he reminded her. 'You have another month until you are of age.' When Thorne learned of their plans, there would be hell to pay. But it would be worth the price.

'I do not mean to wait that long,' she said.

'Neither do I.' He imagined the deep cushions and well-upholstered squabs that waited, just behind the carriage door.

'We will have to go to Scotland. But not Gretna Green. You must show me Edinburgh.'

It was a very long ride to Edinburgh. Several days. And the whole of it would be spent alone with Evie. Perhaps brother Michael did not mean to be so generous with his equipage as that. But the matter could be settled when they returned.

'Oh, Lady Evelyn, I think you are right,' he said, taking control and pulling her after him, up into the carriage, and into his lap. He imagined what would happen when his Evie met his teachers, his colleagues and perhaps his students. 'I must show you Edinburgh. And we shall see what it makes of you.' He grinned. It would be far more dangerous than going to sea. But it would never be dull.

* * * * *

The Fall of a Saint

To George Bloczynski,
who gave me my sense of humour.

Chapter One

'I am Mrs Samuel Hastings, but you may call me Evelyn.'

Maddie Cranston looked at the woman in front of her with suspicion. Mrs Hastings was smiling in a sympathetic, comforting way. But it had been her husband who had come to Maddie on that night in Dover with apologies and lame excuses, as though any amount of money could make up for what had happened. It was possible that Evelyn Hastings was just another toady to the Duke of St Aldric and therefore not to be trusted.

The duke had said she was a midwife. It would be a relief to speak to a woman on the subject, especially one familiar with the complaints of pregnancy. Sometimes Maddie felt so wretched that she feared what was happening to her body could not quite be normal. If anyone deserved punishment for that night, it was St Aldric. But if that was true, why did God leave her to do the suffering?

This stranger insisting on familiarity of address did not look at all the way one expected a midwife would. She was not particularly old and was far too lovely to have a job of any kind, looking instead like the sort of pampered lady who would hire nurses and governess to care for her offspring, rather than seeing to them herself. What could she know of the birthing and raising of children?

When one was surrounded by enemies, it was better to appear aloof rather than terrified. Life had proven that weakness was easily exploited. She would not show it now. She would not be lulled to security by a soothing voice and a pretty face. 'How do you do, Mrs Hastings. I am Miss Madeline Cranston.' Maddie offered a hand to the supposed midwife, but did not return her smile.

Mrs Hastings ignored her coldness, responding with even more warmth and, if possible, a softer and more comforting tone. 'I assume, since St Aldric sent for me, that you are with child?'

Maddie nodded, suddenly unable to trust her own voice when faced with the enormity of what she had done in coming here. She was having a bastard. There could be no comfort in that, only a finding of the best solution. She had been a fool to confront a duke, especially considering their last meeting. Suppose he had been angry enough to solve the problem with violence and not money? While she did not wish to believe that a peer would be so despicable, neither had she seen any reason to think otherwise of this one.

'And you are experiencing nausea?' the other woman asked, glancing at the water carafe on the table.

Maddie nodded again.

'I will ring for some tea with ginger. It will settle your stomach.' She summoned a servant, relayed the instructions and returned to her questioning. 'Tenderness of the breasts? No courses for the past month?'

Maddie nodded and whispered, 'Two months.' She had known from the first what must have happened but had not wanted to admit it, not even to herself.

'And you are unmarried.' Mrs Hastings stared into her face, as though it could be read like tea leaves. 'You did not attempt to put an end to this, when you realised what was happening?'

That was a possibility, even now. What future was there for her or the child if St Aldric turned her away? She would be a bastard with a bastard.

She stiffened her spine and ignored the doubts. If her own mother had taken the trouble to have her, she owed nothing less to her own child. The woman who bore her was conspicuously absent, now that wise counsel was needed. She did not wish to leave her baby without friend or family, to be raised by strangers as she had been. But what choice did she have? Her own presence in the child's life would make things more difficult, for it could not be easy to have a mother who was little better than a whore in the eyes of society.

An unmarried but powerful father was another

matter entirely. St Aldric had created this problem. Now he would be made to face the consequences of his actions. She returned her attentions to the midwife. 'No. I made no attempt to rid myself of the baby.'

'I see.' Mrs Hastings coloured slightly and changed the subject. 'And you are experiencing changes in mood, as though your mind and body are no longer your own?'

Now this was a question that could not be answered with a shake of the head, for it struck at the heart of her fears. She stared up at Mrs Hastings for a moment, then surrendered her courage and whispered the truth. 'I cannot seem to keep my temper from one minute to the next. First laughter, then tears. I have vivid dreams when I sleep. And waking I have the most outlandish ideas.' This trip was but an example. 'Sometimes I fear that I am going mad.'

The midwife smiled and relaxed into her chair as though pleased that they had found a topic she fully understood. 'That is all quite normal. It is nothing more than the upset of humours involved in the growing of a new life. You are not headed for the madhouse, my dear. You are simply having a baby.' As if there was anything simple about this, even from the first. The tea arrived, along with some flavourless biscuits. Maddie sipped and nibbled hesitantly, but was surprised to find she felt marginally better for the nourishment.

'It is a wonder that anyone does it at all,' Maddie

declared, taking another sip of tea. 'Much less allowing it to happen more than once.'

Mrs Hastings seemed to think this was amusing, for she made no effort to hide her laugh. 'You have nothing to fear from this point on. I will be here to take care of you.'

The woman could not possibly know what she was offering. But everything about her, from her soft-spoken words to the no-nonsense set of her body, was an assurance. Maddie risked relaxing into the cushions of the divan, if only for a moment. 'Thank you.'

'Before the onset of these symptoms, you had sexual congress with a man,' Mrs Hastings reminded her gently. 'Surely you understood what the ramifications of this behaviour might be?'

'It was not of my choice,' Maddie said, keeping her voice calm and level.

Mrs Hastings gave a small gasp of shock, but her smile remained as comforting as ever. 'Do you know the identity of the man who is responsible?'

This woman was different from her husband. Perhaps she could actually help with something more than ginger tea and kindness. Maddie decided to risk the truth. 'It was the Duke of St Aldric.' There. She had said it out loud. Even to admit it to one other person made the burden of the knowledge lighter. 'I was in an inn in Dover. In the night, he came into my room without invitation, and…' She was past crying about it. But to tell the story aloud to a complete stranger had not been part of her plan.

Evelyn Hastings's eyes opened wide again and her gentle smile turned incredulous. 'The Saint forced his way into your room and…'

'St Aldric,' Maddie corrected. 'He was inebriated. Afterwards, he claimed to have wandered into the wrong room.' But how was she to know if that had been true? Perhaps he said the same to every woman he casually dishonoured. In Maddie's experience, a title and a handsome face were not always an indication of good character.

Mrs Hastings seemed to think otherwise, for she was still staring in disbelief. 'You are sure about this?'

'Ask him yourself. He does not deny it. Or speak to Dr Hastings. He was there to witness it.'

Evelyn drew a breath, hissing it between her teeth. 'Oh, yes. I will most certainly ask my husband what he knows of this.' Her eyes were angry, but Maddie had no reason to think that anger was directed at her. It was more akin to righteous indignation for a fellow member of their sex. 'And you have no family to help you in this? No one to stand at your side?'

Maddie shook her head. 'I am alone.' There was no chance that the school that had raised her would take her back, after seeing what she had done with the training and education that should have got her a respectable position.

'Then you shall have me,' Evelyn said firmly, with a matronly nod of her head that hardly suited her. She rose from her chair as majestically as a queen. 'If you will excuse me, I must speak to my husband over this. And to the duke. It will all be settled once I am through with them.' Mrs Hastings drew herself up even taller, looking quite formidable, not just royal, but a warrior queen heading to battle. Then she disappeared into the hall, closing the door behind her with a resolute click.

Maddie smiled and settled back into the luxurious velvet cushions of the divan, sipping her tea. Perhaps Boadicea had arrived too late to fight for her honour. But she appeared more than able to gain reparation for the loss of it. Maddie need do nothing but wait.

Michael Poole, Duke of St Aldric, stood in the hallway of his London town house, one ear to his brother and the other tuned to the conversation taking place in the salon. He could not very well open the door again and demand that the ladies inside speak louder so that he might eavesdrop on them. But he had to know the truth, and the sooner the better. If there was to be a child, perhaps a son?

It changed everything.

'She found you?' His half-brother, Sam Hastings, was focused almost as intently on the closed door, staring hard enough to burn through it.

'She found me.' Michael had expected it, but not that it would come as such a relief. In each crowd he'd passed, he had wondered if he would see a pair of accusing eyes that should be familiar but were not. Now, at least, he had a name and a face to attach to that night, which had been but a blurry memory.

'I am sorry,' Sam said, as though he had anything to regret in this.

'You are sorry?' Michael laughed. 'What did you have to do with any of it?'

'It should not have happened this way. I should not have let her escape. The matter could have been properly settled in Dover. When I spoke to her that night, she claimed she wanted no contact with you, then, or in the future. I promised to respect her wishes. But I could have done more.'

'We had no right to keep her prisoner and force her to accept help,' Michael reminded him. The evening had been enough of a disaster. She'd have thought even worse of him if they had locked her door and demanded she stay until a proper settlement could be arranged.

'God knows, I tried without success to find her.' Sam was practically wringing his hands over the matter. 'England is a very large country and there are many unfortunate young women in it.'

An unfortunate young woman. Michael had never thought that his name would be connected to one who could be described thus.

'The fault is mine, not yours,' Michael replied. 'If I had drunk myself to unconsciousness that night, then I would not have caused her harm and you would not have had to bother to clean up my mess.'

'Or perhaps you could have remained sober,' Sam said as mildly as possible. 'No matter what you chose to do, we could not have foreseen the outcome.'

Had watching his father taught him nothing of the need for good behaviour at all times? 'I should have known better,' Michael insisted.

Sam gave no answer to this, which was probably proof that he agreed. Then he relented. 'You would never have sunk to this,' Sam reminded him, 'had you not experienced a shock from your illness.'

'I was upended by a sickness that would hardly bother a child.'

'The effects of the illness are not the same when the body has an immature reproductive system.'

'What a gentle way you put it, Dr Hastings.' Michael had lain for three days with a raging fever and balls swollen so that he could hardly bear to look at them, much less touch them. Then the disease had left him. But not as it had found him.

Or so he had thought.

Now, for the first time in six months, he had reason to hope. 'Miss Cranston has found me out and not because she is dissatisfied with your payment. She claims to be with child.' He paused to allow the doctor to conceal his surprise. 'Is that even possible?'

'Of course it is possible,' Sam said. 'I told you, from the beginning, that the negative consequences of the mumps on an adult male are not guaranteed. Yet you insisted on blundering through the countryside, inebriated and trying to prove your virility.'

'A bastard would have proven it well enough.' It had been what Michael had hoped for. The fear that a simple fever had destroyed the St Aldric line had turned to obsession. And from thus had come the hope that an accident with a member of the muslin set would assure him a fruitful marriage.

To announce such a thing to his own illegitimate brother showed how far he had fallen. Now that he was sober, the plan seemed foolish and cowardly. *Like father, like son.* It had been Michael's life goal to disprove the adage. He had failed.

'If you wanted a by-blow, it seems you will have one now,' Sam said, with a sad shake of his head. 'What do you mean to do about it?'

Michael was amazed that his half-brother did not see what was quite obvious. 'This current situation is much better than I'd hoped for.'

'You hoped to deflower a governess?' Sam realised how loudly he'd been speaking and dropped his voice to a whisper. 'And without her consent? Are you mad?'

'No. Certainly not.' Yet he had done just that. 'I never meant to enter that room. I lost my way.'

'Because you were too drunk to know better,' his brother reminded him.

He deserved the rebuke. His father had, at least, entertained himself with the willing wives of friends. But he had done worse than that. 'The woman I was seeking that night was hardly an innocent. Had there been consequences, she'd have been paid handsomely. I'd even have acknowledged the child.'

'As I assume you mean to do with this one.' Sam was offering the faintest warning that Michael must remember his obligations when dealing with the girl and her problem.

Sam had no reason to worry. After years of exemplary behaviour, Michael had made enough mistakes in the past few months to show him the ugliness of false pride and the lengths he must go to atone. There was no question in his mind as to what had to happen next.

The trick would be convincing the governess of it. 'If Miss Cranston is truly carrying my child, it need not be as an acknowledged bastard,' he said, cautiously watching for Sam's reaction. 'If I marry her and legitimise the heir...'

'Marry her?' Now Sam was staring at him with an ironic smile. 'Now I do not know whether to laugh or send you to Bedlam.'

'Why should I not wed her? Is there anything about the girl that appears she will be less than suitable? She is a governess and therefore educated. She is healthy.' And not unattractive. He was obligated to her. After what had happened, he owed her more than money. He should restore her honour.

'She probably hates you,' Sam said.

'She has good reason to.' He had seen the look in her eyes as she had confronted him with the truth. He would not have given a second thought to the woman standing in the street before his house. She was tidy to the point of primness, simply dressed in dark blue, and hair bound painfully tight, as though she feared it would do her an injury if a single curl escaped from

the pins. The lips that should have been soft and kiss-
able had been set in a determined frown and her brow
had furrowed above her large brown eyes as she'd recognised him. Everything about her had announced her
as just what she was: a disapproving schoolteacher.

She'd stepped in front of him, blocking his path as
no one else in London would dare to do, and said quietly, 'I wish to speak to you about the consequences
of your recent trip to Dover.'

The coldness in her voice still lingered with the
memory of the words. But none of that mattered now.
'I will give her reason not to hate me. A hundred reasons. A thousand. I will give her everything I have. If
the succession is to continue, I must have a wife and a
child, Sam. There may be no better chance than this.'

The door beside them opened suddenly and Sam's
wife, Evelyn, stepped between them, hands on hips.
'Explain yourselves, the pair of you. Tell me what that
poor girl is claiming has no basis in fact.' She turned
to her husband, growing even angrier. 'And that you
had no part in this shameful business.'

Sam held up a hand as though to deflect his wife's
wrath. 'I went with Michael to Dover, but only in
hopes of talking some sense into him. As the Duke
of St Aldric's personal physician, it is my job to keep
him in good health, is it not?'

His wife responded with a frosty nod.

'He was showing signs of what I feared was chronic
inebriation and had been—' Sam gave a delicate

clearing of the throat '—doing things that I do not wish to discuss in mixed company.'

'Consorting with whores,' Evelyn said, refusing to be shocked. Then she stared at Michael. 'That does not excuse what happened to Miss Cranston.'

'It was all a mistake, I swear. I was on my way to visit someone else and took a wrong turning. It was dark....' That was hardly an excuse. He should have been able to tell the difference between the buxom barmaid he'd been seeking and the diminutive Miss Cranston, even without a light. But he could have sworn, as he had come into her bed, that she was willing and expecting him....

'When I realised that he was missing above stairs, I searched Michael out and heard cries of alarm,' Sam finished. 'By the time I found him, it was too late.'

Evelyn gave a noise of disgust.

'It grows worse,' Sam admitted. 'Miss Cranston, who, as I understand it, was a governess, was visiting the inn to meet with a future employer. The man arrived two steps behind me and witnessed the whole thing. She was sacked without references before she could even begin.'

Michael winced. He had but the vaguest memories of the last half of that evening. What he'd thought had been a thoroughly delightful interlude had ended in shocked cries, tears and shouting. And he had stood swaying on his feet in the midst of it wearing nothing but a shirt, with Sam looking at him much as he was now, in disappointment.

'I have been sober since that moment,' he reminded Evelyn. 'And I would have settled with Miss Cranston the following morning had she not fled the inn before we could speak to her again.'

'It is too late to concern yourself with what might have been,' Evelyn said with a shake of her head. 'It is what you mean to do now that matters.'

'Is what she says true?' Michael asked, not daring to hope. 'Is she with child?'

'To the best of my knowledge, yes,' Evelyn answered.

Michael took care to school his face to neutrality. It was wrong of him to be excited at the thought. Even worse, he was glad of it. To have a child.... Better yet, to have a son....

When he was gone, there would be a new St Aldric to care for the people and the land. And this boy would be raised differently from the way he had been. It was as if, despite his reprehensible behaviour, a curse had been lifted from his house.

'I said, what do you mean to do about it?' Apparently, in his distraction he had been ignoring his sister-in-law.

So he explained his plan.

Chapter Two

The muffled conversation in the hall droned on. Though she knew they were talking about her, Maddie felt oddly detached from the situation. In the time before Dover, she had avoided behaviours that might incite gossip. Her expectations were modest and her future predictable. She would teach the children of strangers until they grew too old to need her. Then she would find another family in want of a governess. At the end of it, she would have a small amount of savings to retire on, or stay on in a household so fond of dear, old Miss Cranston that they kept her beyond her usefulness.

But that seemed a lifetime ago. No decent family would have her after the scandal. It had been foolish of her to suggest that particular inn, but when her new employer had suggested meeting her stage in Dover, the temptation had been too great. She'd returned to the place several times as years had passed, knowing that, in her dreams at least, she would be young and free of the responsibilities of her oh, so ordinary life. She had gone to bed thinking of nothing but Richard and their last night together in the very same room.

The man who had come to her this time was no dream lover. It had begun sweetly enough, but it had ended in a waking nightmare. The drunken stranger had been hauled from her bed, while Mr Barker stood, framed in the doorway, shouting that no such woman should be in a decent inn, much less allowed near innocent children. The argument had moved into the hallway and she had slammed the door, thrown on her clothes and run as soon as she was sure of her safety. But not before hearing the name of her attacker, as he demanded, in a slurred voice, that this other common fellow stop raising a fuss over strapping a barmaid.

After two months of unemployment, she'd run through most of her tiny savings. Then there had come the growing realisation that she would share her future with another: one too small and helpless to understand the predicament they were in. So she had taken the last of the money and bought a ticket for London.

Now she was visiting the house of a peer. She glanced around her. While the decoration was as elegant as she might have expected, her presence here was beyond the limits of her imagination. Even in the parlours of the families that had employed her, she had not dared to relax. There were always children to watch and to remove to the nursery when their behaviour grew tedious.

The same strangers were once again settling her

fate in a public hallway, while she drank tea. Now that she had heard the truth, there was no sign that this Mrs Hastings would be easily silenced. There was a sharp sound of exclamation from her, as though one of the men had said something particularly shocking. Their muttered explanations sounded weak in comparison.

When a settlement was offered, Evelyn Hastings might serve as a mediator. She would know that decent people did not raise a child in secret and on a few pounds a year. A bastard of a duke deserved a decent education and a chance for advancement.

Maddie thought of her own childhood. The family that had taken her in had not let her forget that her origins were clouded. And the proper schools where she was boarded made no secret that she was there at the behest of an unnamed benefactor. There had been raised eyebrows, of course, but the money provided had been sufficient to silence speculation and the education had been respectable enough to set her on the path towards a career.

Surely St Aldric could do better than that for his by-blow. There could be excellent schools, and a Season and a proper marriage for a daughter, or business connections and a respectable trade for a son. If the duke claimed his offspring, it would not be without family. One parent was better than none. Once she was sure the child's future was secure, she might quietly disappear, change her name and begin her life anew. No one need ever know of this unfortunate incident. She might be spared the snubs and gossip of decent women and the offers of supposed gentlemen convinced that, if she had fallen once, she might give herself again to any who asked.

It was for the best, she reminded herself, fighting down the pangs of guilt. The world would forgive St Aldric, and by association the child, but such charity would not extend to her. The door opened and Doctor and Mrs Hastings entered, followed by the duke, who shut it behind them.

Dear lord, but he was handsome. Maddie did her best to smother what should have been a perfectly natural response to the presence of him, for what woman, when confronted with a man like St Aldric, did not feel the pull of his charms? Apparently, God had decided it was not enough to give such wealth and power to a single human. He had made a masterpiece. St Aldric was tall but not thin, and muscular without seeming stocky. The hose and breeches that he wore all but caressed muscles hardened by riding and sport. Blue was too common a word to describe the eyes that stared past her. Turquoise, aquamarine, cerulean... She could search a paintbox for ever and still not find a colour to do them justice. The blonde hair above his noble brow caught the last of the afternoon sun and the hand that would brush the waves of it from his eyes was long fingered and graceful. But the clean-shaven jaw was not the least bit feminine. The cleft chin was resolute without appearing stubborn. And his mouth...

She remembered his mouth. And his arms bare of his coat, the fine linen of his shirt brushing her skin as they folded around her. And his body…

Her stomach gave another nervous jump. She remembered things that no decent woman should. And what she did remember should have not pleasure for her. That night had been her undoing.

Mrs Hastings saw her start and came quickly to her side, sharing the sofa and taking her hand. She was glaring at her husband, and at the duke as well, utterly fearless of retribution. 'Well, Sam, what do you have to say for yourself?'

A dark look passed between the couple, as though to prove an argument still in progress. But the doctor turned to her with the same sympathetic look he had given her in the inn as he'd led his friend away. 'Miss Cranston, we both owe you more apologies than can be offered in this lifetime. And once again, let me assure you that you are in no danger.'

But Maddie noticed the blocked door and lack of other exits. And the nearness of the fireplace poker, should Mrs Hastings prove unable to help her.

The duke saw her glance to it and made a careful, calming gesture with his hands. 'Miss Cranston,' he said, searching for words, 'you have nothing to fear.'

'Nothing more,' she reminded him.

'Nothing more,' he agreed. 'The night we met—' he began.

She stopped him. 'You mean, the night you entered my room uninvited, and—'

'I was very drunk,' he interrupted, as though afraid of what she might say in front of his friends. 'Too drunk to find my own room, much less that of another. I swear, I thought you were someone else.'

And her own arms had betrayed her, reaching out to him, even though an innocent governess could not have been expecting a lover.

'You called me Polly,' she said, almost as angry at herself as she was at him.

'I had an assignation. With the barmaid. And I was drunk,' he repeated. 'I had been drunk for several months at that point. What was one more day?' For a moment, he sounded almost as bitter as she felt, shaking his head in disgust at his own behaviour. 'And in that time, I did some terrible things. But I have never forced myself on a woman.'

'Other than me?' she reminded him. It was unfair of her. There had been no force.

But he must have seen it as such and counted her an innocent, for he looked truly pained by the memory. 'When I realised my mistake, it was too late. The damage had been done.' He took a deep breath. 'The night in question was an unfortunate aberration.'

'Very unfortunate,' she agreed, giving no quarter. But why should she? It was a lame excuse.

'Never before that,' he said. 'And never again. Since that day, I have moderated my behaviour. That night taught me the depths that one might fall to, the harm that one might do, when one is sunk in self-pity and concerned with nothing more than personal pleasure.' He was looking at her with the earnest expression she sometimes saw on boys in the nursery, swearing that they would not repeat misdeeds that occurred as regularly as a chiming clock.

She returned the same governess glare she might have used on them. 'That night taught *me* not to trust a door lock in a busy inn.' She needn't have bothered with the poker. The words and tone were enough to cow him.

'If there was a way, I would erase it so that you had never met me. But now I will make sure it stays in the past. Your reputation will be restored. You will never feel lack. Never suffer doubt. Everything you need shall be yours.'

Success! He was offering even more than she wanted. She would have a new life and another chance. 'For the child, as well?' she asked. For this could not all be about her alone.

'Of course.' He was smiling at her, as though there could be no possibility.

'We are in agreement, then? There will be a settlement?' She gave a grateful smile to Mrs Hastings, who had done miracles in just a brief conversation.

'The child will want for nothing. Neither will you. You need not concern yourself with a twenty-pound-a-year position in someone else's household. You shall be the one to hire a governess. You shall have a house, as well. Or houses, if you wish.' She did not need houses. He was becoming too agitated over a thing that could be settled simply. Perhaps there was madness in his family, as well as drunkenness.

Doctor Hastings saw her expression and responded in a more calming tone, 'You will be taken care of. As will the child. If the suggestions offered here tonight are not to your liking, you will have our help in refusing them.'

Evelyn Hastings nodded in agreement and squeezed her hands.

'Enough!' St Aldric cut through the apology with a firmness that seemed to stun both doctor and wife.

It did not shock Maddie. What could be more shocking than what had already occurred between them? The man was an admitted wastrel. It would not surprise her if he changed his mind suddenly and refused to pay, though it was quite obvious he had the funds. She raised her chin and stared at the duke, willing herself to be brave enough to see this through. Her mute accusation would be enough to break any resistance he might feel to help his own blood.

His blue eyes sparkled as he spoke, but not from madness; the light in them was as strong as blue steel. 'There will be no question of my acknowledging my offspring, Miss Cranston. There has been too much secrecy in my family thus far and it has caused no end of trouble. You have my word. The child you carry is mine and will have all the advantages I can offer him.'

'Thank you.' She had succeeded after all. Could it really be this easy?

'But…' he added.

Apparently not. What conditions would he manage to put on what should be simple?

'There is a complication,' he said.

Not as far as she was concerned. 'I will not speak of the beginning, to the child or anyone else,' she said, 'as long as you admit to its existence.'

'It is more than that,' the duke said, distracted again and pacing the rug before the fire. 'Six months ago. I took ill. The mumps. Had I been a child, it would have been nothing....'

'I am well aware of that, having helped several of my charges through it,' she snapped. 'But what would that have to do with our business?'

He continued, unaffected by her temper. 'As a result of the illness, I had reason to doubt that I would be able to produce issue.'

Now he was denying what had happened between them or questioning his part in the child he had given her. It was too much to bear. She used the last of her strength to draw herself up out of the velvet cushions to the unimpressive five foot four inches that she carried and stepped before him to stop his perambulation. Facing this man and being forced to look up into his face made her feel small, unimportant, weak. But she dare not appear that way, even for a moment. 'Do you doubt the truth of my accusations?'

He held up a hand. 'Not at all. I was surprised, of course. I spent the four months between recovery and our meeting in desperate and shameful attempts to prove to my own potency. It was on one such trip that

I found you while looking for a barmaid who was to meet me in a room just above yours.'

So he was a drunken reprobate, willing to lie with any woman to prove his manhood. It did not surprise her in the least. She folded her arms and waited.

'I do not claim to be proud of it,' he said, unperturbed by her disapproval. 'I merely wish you to know the truth. In six months, no other woman has come to me with the demands you are setting. I would have welcomed her, if she had. By the time I found you, I was quite beyond hope of that. I feared for the succession. Suppose I could not father a son? What would become of the title? The dukedom might return to the crown. What would become of my land and the people on it? They depend on me for their safety and livelihood. And if I could not do this one, simple thing...' He shrugged. 'I am the last legitimate member of my family, you see.'

She narrowed her eyes at the distinction. In her opinion, some people were too proud of their own conception, as if anyone had a choice in that matter.

'It is no excuse for what happened,' she said.

'I did not say it was. I merely wish to explain. That night, I'd expected to find a woman used to the risks of such casual encounters. But you are a governess, are you not?'

'I was,' she corrected. 'That is quite impossible now.'

'I understand that,' he said again. The sympathy in his voice sounded almost sincere. 'I do not mean to send you away with a few coins and a promise to take the child, as if you were some whore claiming to carry my bastard.' He took a step nearer to her and, unable to help herself, she backed away from him. Her legs hit the cushion behind her and she sat again.

Suddenly, he dropped to one knee at her feet. If it was an attempt to equalise their heights and put her at ease, it was not working. He was still too close. And though she had wished to bring the great man to his knees, it had been but a metaphor. The sight of a peer in the flesh and kneeling before her was ridiculous.

'You deserve better than that,' he said seriously. They were the words of a lover and her heart gave an irrational flutter. 'I meant to give you more and would have done had you but stayed in the inn until morning. I would have seen to it that no more harm came to you.' His voice was soft, stroking her jangling nerves. 'I never would have left you in a position where you might have to come to me and demand justice. But you ran before we could talk.'

She fought to free herself of the romantic haze he was creating. Did he expect her to take some of the blame for this situation? She would not. How could she explain the feelings of that night? She hardly understood them herself. Anger, fear, guilt and, dare she admit it, shame? Lying with another man was a betrayal of what she had shared with her darling Richard. That had been done in love. And she would never regret it.

But Richard was long gone, lost in the war. In his

honour, she had meant to keep the memory of that time pure. Now she could not manage to think of it without remembering St Aldric. 'I could not stand to be under the same roof with you a moment longer than was necessary.'

I ran. It had been foolish of her. But what reason had she to believe he would have treated her better than he had that night?

Of course, the man before her now did not seem as imposing as she had expected. He might actually want to help her. He was no less guilty, of course. But there was a worried line in his brow that had not been there when she had arrived. 'I understand why you did not want further dealings with me in Dover. I had given you reason to doubt me. But now I wish to make amends. You deserve more help than you received. So does the child you carry. I will not deny you, or him.' He was smiling at her. Had she not known better, she would have smiled back.

He continued. 'And to be the acknowledged bastard of a duke would open many doors. But...'

There was the hesitation again, proof that she was right not to trust him. She braced herself for whatever might come after.

'But would it not be better to be my heir?'

She could not help the single, unladylike bark of laughter at the idea. Then she composed herself again and gave him a sarcastic smile, pretending to ponder. 'Would it be better to be a duke than a bastard son?

Next you will be asking me if it is better to be a duchess than a governess.'

The room fell silent. Mrs Hastings stood and went to join her husband. The pair of them looked uncomfortable.

Now the duke was smiling in relief. 'That is precisely what I am asking.'

There was another long, awkward pause as she digested the words, repeating the conversation in her head and trying to find the point where it slipped from reality into fantasy.

'You cannot mean it,' she said at last. He was toying with her, waiting until the last of her courage failed, and then...the Lord knew what would happen. She would leave him this instant, running as she had before.

But her body understood what her mind could not and it refused to obey her. She tried to stand, but her legs could not seem to work properly. She made it partway to her feet, then sank back into the cushions of the couch.

St Aldric was unmoved from the place where he knelt before her. He waited until her weak struggle to escape had ended. Then he resumed. 'There would be many advantages, would there not? You would not need to fear disgrace or discomfort.' He was as handsome as Lucifer when he smiled, blue eyed and wonderful. His voice was low, almost seductive in its offer to remove all care. For a moment, she remembered how it had felt when he was on top of her, when it had still been a pleasant dream.

Before she'd known that what was happening was nothing more than lust.

'I would fear you,' she said bluntly and saw him flinch in response. The reaction, though very small, gave her a feeling of power and she smiled.

He continued, unsmiling and earnest. 'I swear I will give you no further reason to fear. Our son would have the best of everything: education, status and, in time, my seat in Parliament and all the holdings attached to it.'

'At this time, there is barely a child of any kind, much less a son,' she said. Duke or no, the man was clearly deluded. 'I am just as likely to produce a daughter.' In fact, she would pray for a girl, out of spite.

He shook his head. 'It was unlikely that you would have any child at all from me. I am sure this one must be a sign. It will be as it was for my father and his father before that, back very nearly to the first duke. In my family, the first child is always a male. If I have sired a child, it will be a son. And he will learn from me, as I learned, to cherish his holdings and be a better man than his father.'

That, at least, she could agree on. 'And to take care not to lose his way when frequenting inns,' she said.

The doctor and his wife both flinched at this, but St Aldric merely nodded. 'The next duke will be noble in title and character. He is far too precious to slight, even during the first months of his gestation. I want no question, no stain, no rumour about him, or his mother.'

He had added her, her disgrace and her reputation, almost as an afterthought to his mad plan. 'Am I to have no say in his future or my own?' She heard the Hastingses shifting nervously, clearly in sympathy with her, but she could not manage to look away from those very blue eyes.

The duke thought for a moment. 'You can refuse me, I suppose. But I will only ask again.' He reached out for her hand and she snatched it from his grasp. 'I need the child you carry.'

'Then take it and raise it after it is born,' she said firmly, sliding down the couch and looking away to break the hold he had on her. 'Give this child the advantages of your wealth and rank. But I will not be part of the bargain. I did not wish for this. I did not seek you out in that inn. It was you who came to me.' She could see by the shadowed look in his eyes that the truth of that still troubled him, and she took a dark, unholy pleasure in reminding him of it.

She looked up and saw the disapproving looks of both Doctor and Mrs Hastings, but their censure was not directed at her. If she refused the duke, his friends would side with her, just as they had promised. They had made the offer of help because they had tried and failed to dissuade him.

'No,' she said. 'The child is yours and I will not keep you from it. But you do not own me.' This time, it would be he who was alone to face an uncertain future.

'A son without a wife is no use to me,' he said, almost to himself. 'I do not need a natural child to be held apart from his birthright, as my father did to my brother.' He cast a glance in the direction of Dr Hastings, and Maddie noticed the resemblance between them that should have been obvious to her before.

The duke looked back to her. 'I need an heir. And I cannot marry another in good conscience after what I have done to you.' He reached out a hand to her again. 'Miss Cranston, you are not some common barmaid or London lightskirt. You were raised as a lady and are carrying my child. How could I offer less than marriage and still think myself a gentleman, much less St Aldric?'

He said it as if St Aldric were some superior being far above common manners and not simply the title he had been born with. She'd seen nothing saintly about him when they met. But suppose it had been a mistake? Perhaps he meant to do right by her after all. She felt a moment of relief, then counted it as weakness and batted the hand away. She must never forget who it was that offered and how long it had taken for him to find such remorse. This was not the time to be swayed by blue eyes and soft touches.

His hand dropped to his side, then rose again in supplication. 'I would ask nothing more from you than I have already taken. There would not be any intimacy between us. Once the child is born, you could leave if you wished. I would not stop you. I would not seek you out or force you to return to me.' He was still smiling. But there was a tightness in his face that made her think he would almost prefer it this way, so that he need never be reminded of how they had met. 'Let me give you the reparation I should have when we were still in Dover. I'd have married you then, had you but remained. Only when your honour is restored to you can this matter be settled.'

Since she had not stayed to talk with him, there was no telling if his words were true, or only a convenient afterthought that supported his current offer. But if he told the truth now, a single affirmative and she would be rich beyond care and she need do nothing more than she had already done. Her child would be safe and she would regain her reputation.

It was more than she had hoped for. And the offer was based on his assumptions that she had virtue to save other than the tissue of lies that her innocence had been, when he'd come to her. But she did not owe him details of something that had happened long before they'd met.

He noticed her hesitation and renewed his offer. 'I know I have no right to ask for it, but in exchange for your help, I would give you everything. Money. Jewels. Gowns. My name and title, and all the freedom that comes with it. If you wish it, it shall be yours.' His head dipped slightly, like a knight waiting to receive his lady's favour.

When she had set out for London, had she not

wanted to see him humbled? In one day, she had achieved her goal. But her victory had come too easy. The duke might appear to be a penitent, but he was still one of the most powerful men in England.

His modesty was an illusion, meant to put her at ease and win her cooperation. In a moment of carelessness, he had changed the course of her life. Now he thought that, in casually changing it again, he was doing her a service. But her true past would be lost to her: her job, her honour…and her Richard. This duke, handsome and kind as he might seem now, had ruined everything.

And no matter what she chose, his precious reputation remained untarnished. As he reminded her, even if he deserved punishment for his swinish behaviour, he was the legitimate son of a duke. The law could not touch him. Beside his power, the wishes of a governess who had been born on the wrong side of the blanket were as nothing.

But at least if she married him, he would not escape the past. She could be a continual reminder of his mistake. It was an appealing idea. And now he was offering her *everything*.

It was almost enough.

But suppose he found reason to change his mind? 'And what will happen if the child is not a boy?' she asked.

'It must be,' he muttered. 'Daughters in my family are few and far between. Why should it be different for me?'

Perhaps because he did not deserve such luck. He had done nothing to earn it. 'Enough of your problems and what you need,' she said. 'What if I bear you a daughter? Will you force your way into my room, as you did the last time?'

He flinched as if she had raised a whip to him and taken a strip of flesh from his back. Was it the reminder of their meeting? Or the possibility that she might carry a girl? Was the female sex completely valueless to him? His past actions certainly made it appear so.

He composed himself and raised his head to look at her. Then he continued. 'If you bear me a daughter, my promise would stand. All I ask is that you marry me. I can expect no more of you beyond that. In the event that the child is a girl—' he paused as though offering a prayer that it would not be '—I will explain all to the Regent and beg that he allows the title to pass through my daughter to her son. But I will not demand an act from you that you must certainly find abhorrent.' He was staring deep into her soul, willing her to give in.

If trust of strangers had come easy to her, she would have trusted this one. With eyes like that, so clear and blue, was it even possible to lie? And with the trust came the niggling desire to forgive him, to sympathise with him and to forget that she was the one who had been wronged. She could marry him and see that beautiful face each day for the rest of her life, those eyes gazing at her as though he cared.

Was she really so weak as that? He did not care. It was an illusion. 'You are banking on a male heir from a daughter who is not even born? That event, at a minimum, might be some twenty years hence. What guarantee do you have that you would be alive to see it? Or that the Regent will agree to any of this?'

'I will live,' he said. 'I will live because I must. I will have a son, or a grandson. I will not pass until I see the line established and know that there will be another St Aldric to take up the responsibilities of the holdings and the people who depend upon him.' With shoulders squared and jaw set in a way that displayed his noble profile, he stared past her as though looking into the future.

Was the title really so important to him? A man with such an extreme sense of his own importance might do anything to see success, even if it required him to destroy those around him.

It was a danger for her. But in him, it would be a weakness that might be exploited. 'You would not touch me,' she said cautiously, still searching for the trap in the words. 'And in exchange, you would give me…everything.'

'Anything you desire,' he said. He was holding his breath, waiting for her answer.

His friends looked alarmed. Perhaps they could see further than he did and realise the power he was giving her over his life. But Dr Hastings stepped forward and spoke. 'I can speak for my wife in this, I am certain. What he says is the truth, for though he might be guilty of other things, I have never known St Aldric to lie. If you feel, now or in the future, that he cannot hold to this bargain, we will take you in and I myself will call him out and defend your honour.'

The man was trying to make amends. And he was right in that it would be easier for the child, and for her as well, if they married.

But then she thought of Richard. She had loved, once in her life. It was a week that must last for ever, now that he was gone. She had long ago reconciled herself to the fact that there would be no children, no husband, no love for another until she found him again.

Was she willing to give herself, if not in body, then at least in law, to another man for the sake of convenience? It would render the past meaningless.

And here was the man who had put her plans for ever out of reach. She had not thought herself particularly spiteful. At least, not until she'd met St Aldric. Now he was giving her unlimited wealth and the power to set friend against friend. For a change, she held all the cards, to play or discard at leisure. Revenge was hers if she wished to take it.

But did she wish it?

The duke's hand still hovered before her and she reached out to clasp it. Had she expected the smell of brimstone when she touched him? A burn? A chill? This was nothing more than flesh and bone. He might be as handsome as Lucifer, but he was a mere mortal. And perhaps he was a fool.

His palm was warm and dry. As he rose and helped her to her feet, his strength made her feel safer than she'd felt since… She stopped the thought incomplete, for this man had nothing in common with Richard. She must never forget that, though the Duke of St Aldric might seem like a gallant rescuer, he was the cause of her current problems, not the solution. She forced a smile, imagining that she was strong enough to be his equal and not just a governess who had run out of options. 'Very well, then. I will marry you.'

And I will make you pay for what you have done.

Chapter Three

Was he sorry he'd asked? Not really, Michael reminded himself. If there was even the remotest chance that he might gain a son from it, he was content to be married. The identity of the bride hardly mattered.

Of course, it had not mattered before. Evelyn had been suitable and he had liked her well enough. But he did not think that what he'd felt for her could be called love. He was not even sure he'd have recognised that feeling, had it come to him.

He was quite sure, however, that he did not feel that particular emotion for Madeline Cranston. But marriage to her was the right thing to do. He could not choose another woman, knowing that this one existed and he had been the ruin of her.

He had made his bed with the unmaking of hers.

Of course, she had not asked for this situation either. She had looked horrified when he'd first suggested the plan. It proved she was not some empty-headed fortune hunter. But she was a lady and in this predicament because of him. He owed her. He must content himself with the fact that she was educated and not unattractive.

In fact, she was quite fetching when he could admire her unnoticed. She was more delicate than the women he normally favoured. The locks of chestnut hair that were not concealed by her bonnet formed lazy spirals, as though begging to entwine a man's finger. The brown eyes and gentle smile were just as lovely as he'd have hoped to see from a woman waiting for him at the altar.

It was only when she looked at him that the softness in her eyes became stony and the warmth of her smile turned glacial. It worried him that in the two weeks that he'd known her, the mother of his child had made no effort to be likeable.

A fortnight was no time at all. Soon she would see that he was not the beast she thought him. And then they might forge some truce for the sake of their child.

But suppose she did not mean to forgive him? To be tied to a woman who hated him for an indefinite future was as final as a trip to Tyburn. Worse yet, it was a repetition of his parents' marriage and the path he had vowed to avoid.

Even to the last steps, in the courtyard of St George's, Sam was questioning his plan. 'Are you sure, Michael, that there is no other way?'

'Are you suggesting again that I buy her off?' He stared steadily back at his brother, hoping that it would silence him.

'Of course not. The incident in Dover was badly handled by both of us. And now that you have found her again, you are not attempting to shirk responsibility. But she did not ask for marriage, Michael. Only that you care for the child. A settlement would have been sufficient.'

Damn Sam for offering such a reasonable solution. He could have given her what she sought, adequate funds to keep herself and raise his natural child. They'd never need see each other again.

Then he imagined his firstborn separated from him by a barrier of illegitimacy. His error might stand between the boy and his birthright. How naive he had been three months ago to think that a bastard would be nothing more than a demonstration of his virility with his half-brother as proof of how much trouble that might cause.

If there was to be a child, he could not imagine it anywhere but under his own roof. 'There is no other way that I wish to go,' he said, knowing it for the truth. 'I mean to marry the girl and protect the child.'

If his own childhood had taught him nothing, then Miss Madeline Cranston, soon to be her Grace the Duchess of St Aldric, would stand as a fresh reminder to him of what happened to those who strayed too far from the path of virtue. One might end up in a church, exchanging cursory vows with a stranger. But it was also a chance to start fresh. He would find a way to make peace with his wife. He would have the son he hoped for. The boy would be raised in an environment that was as far from his own childhood as humanly possible. That thought lightened his spirit as nothing else could.

Sam did not share his grand vision. His concerns were firmly grounded in the present. 'Was it really necessary to make such a public display of the wedding?' he asked. 'Pomp and circumstance will create more problems than they solve. Too many people have come to me already, asking about the woman and how you met her. How am I to answer them?'

'Ignore them. Soon there will be another scandal to attract the attention of the *ton* gossips and this will be quite forgotten.' Or so he hoped. When he'd offered for Miss Cranston, he'd imagined a quick ceremony in the family chapel would suit, and had pulled strings to get the special licence in record time. But that did not please his betrothed. Only the best church would do. And new wedding clothes, along with a full trousseau.

When he had reminded her that such things took time to arrange, she had responded, without a smile, that what was needed was money. She'd smoothed a hand over her still-flat belly and reminded him that time was of the essence. And since he had promised her whatever she wanted...

It had taken bribes, bonuses and additional fees all around. But the wedding and the pomp surrounding it had been ready within a week.

It was the first step towards a brighter future, he reminded himself, and fixed his face in the distant smile that would block even his only blood relation from prying further. 'If others ask about the circumstances of our meeting, our marriage or our future, you may tell them that it is none of their business. If they do not respect that, then tell them to come to me with their questions.'

'They wouldn't dare,' said Sam with a shake of his head.

'Exactly.' His brother was still too new to the family to understand how best to use the power of name and rank. 'The matter is closed.'

As long as they did not go to the duchess for the story. She might reveal the truth out of spite. She was waiting for him at the altar, watching him with a smile and a gracious nod.

Hypocrite, he wanted to shout. The loathing looks she gave him when they were alone were nothing like this one, which would seem to a bystander to be quite innocent.

In turn, he smiled back at her, playing the part of the eager bridegroom that society expected to see. He continued to smile as the bishop droned on about the sanctity of marriage and the need to procreate. The man had no idea what he was talking about. In Michael's experience, there was nothing particularly sacred about the unions he had seen. If his father had been a faithful man, he would not have left Sam as an unacknowledged, bastard son. Mother might have been quite different, as well. Michael had often imagined what it would be like to have an actual brother. But considering the chill silence that separated his parents when they were forced into company with each other, the lack of a sibling was not so very surprising.

Did his new bride have family? He had not thought to enquire. They were not here, at any rate. Nor were there friends. Perhaps she was as alone as he, the poor thing.

His mood softened. Then she turned slightly to look up at him. From a distance, the lavender gown she wore and the flowers in her hands reminded him of a *petit four*: small and sweet. But as he looked closer, the image faded. Though the colour suited her, the eyes staring up into his were dark, bottomless and intimidating.

She must have been a fine governess, he thought, for she was using her quelling stare upon him. He was far too old for that trick to work. The fierceness of her was an interesting counterpoint to her delicacy. He normally favoured fair women, but this one might have changed his mind. For all her dark looks, she had a sweet face and eyes that would melt him if she tried entreaty instead of demand. The child would not be unattractive, but possibly not tall. She was slight, fine boned and, thankfully, still slim. No one would suspect a pregnancy.

For a while. He felt another possessive thrill at the thought. It would not do to advertise her condition just yet. With Parliament out of session, they could retire to the country, finishing out the term of gestation in privacy. He had no desire to visit Aldric House, for the place held nothing but bad memories. Perhaps the future there could be different. The thought of the months ahead and the reward at the end of it had him feeling as giddy as a child waiting for Christmas.

'Your Grace.' The bishop's whisper hissed through the quiet of the church.

The vows. He had not been listening. Madeline glared all the more, as though he were the stupidest child in the nursery.

He smiled apologetically. 'If you would repeat the question, your Eminence?'

The bishop did as requested and Michael turned his attention to the business at hand, answering and repeating as charged with what he hoped was a confident voice.

Madeline Rosemary Cranston's voice was quieter, but no less steady.

Rosemary. Another omitted detail about his new wife. He would pay attention from now on. She might not enjoy his company, but he would give her no reason to fault it. When the bishop called for it, he offered the ring of braided gold that his mother had worn, watched as it was blessed, then took it back, slipped it onto her finger and promised to endow her with all his worldly goods.

There. The job was done, the knot was tied. They knelt and were prayed over.

Maddie seethed. He was the one who had wanted this wedding and he had not even been listening to the vows. To fumble over a simple 'I do' was a slight almost too great to bear. It was proof that he did not care about her at all. The marriage was just one more step that stood between him and his precious heir.

She calmed herself again, for it could not be good for the baby to always be so angry. The child had given her no reason for such bitterness. Its father had. But she would not blame an innocent.

The bishop was going on and on about fruitfulness and praying that God would endow her with a large family.

Her stomach twisted. One child with this man was more than she wanted. She had accepted that she was to live and die alone. The love she'd saved for the family she would not have with Richard would be doled out, a little at a time, to the charges she educated, for there would be no children of her own.

It seemed the baby she'd wanted would come after all, in a sham marriage to the stranger who had ruined her. *It is not too late to stop this.* The bishop had not finished the ceremony. Doctor Hastings had sworn to help her. He and Evelyn were there as witnesses. She had but to announce that she could not go on and they would take her in.

But what good would it do her to be alone to raise a bastard? The duke had made his feelings clear. He would persist until she surrendered and legitimised the child.

Now the bishop was speaking of submission, which was even worse than children. If St Aldric's goal was to have a woman in his bed, who had promised at an altar that she would not refuse, then she had played right into his hands.

A promise given under duress was no promise at all, she reminded herself. But all the same, her thoughts wandered back to that night, to awakening with a stranger.

She had been asleep and dreaming. It had been her favourite sort of dream. Richard had returned to her, just as he had said he would so long ago. Everything would be right at last. There was no job ahead of her, no more difficult children to teach. No more sour-faced parents expecting Miss Cranston to tend to the education of offspring that they could not be bothered to spend time with. After years without hope, she would be a bride.

And yet she had hesitated. 'I thought you dead,' she had whispered to him. 'In the Battle of New Orleans. There was no word of you after.'

'I am not dead,' he assured her. 'Just sleeping, as you are now. I am coming back to you. We will marry, just as I always promised. But tonight, it will be as it was before I left.'

She smiled and let her phantom lover ease her back onto the mattress. There was no pain, as there had been that first time. She was ready for him. She had been waiting for so long, for the long, slow glide of his body in hers. He was lying on top of her, his warmth taking the last of the chill from the winter air.

She wrapped her arms around him, feeling the

warm solidness of a man, whole and undamaged by battle. Two arms held her. Two legs tangled with hers. The lips on her throat were full and hot, the tongue tracing designs to the open neck of her nightshirt until it found her breast. If only for a little while, she was young again and happy. She sighed in relief as he entered her. She had been so lonely for so long....

She had given herself freely to him, returned his kisses and stroked his body, encouraging him to do as he would with her. She had climaxed with him, even as she realised that the voice crying out in triumph with hers was unfamiliar.

Then she had opened her eyes.

She was shaking again, with shame and self-disgust. She could pretend that the fault was all his, but that was not the whole truth. She had lain with a stranger. Worse yet, she had enjoyed it. She was everything she feared, a woman of no virtue and loose morals, no better than her mother had been.

Not now. She was in a church in London. Dover was as much a dream as Richard had been. She ordered her body to be still, but it would not obey, any more than it had on the night she had met the duke. She had been a fool to search out St Aldric and an even greater fool in marrying to spite him. If she was not careful, she would fall into his bed again, though there was no real feeling between them.

This could not go on. There must be some way to turn back the clock and return to the life she'd had. It had not been happy, but at least it had been predictable. She had but to open her mouth now, before the bishop pronounced the final words, and tell them it had all been a terrible mistake. But she could not bring herself to speak. She was trembling so hard she was surprised that the whole church did not see it.

Now she was swaying on her knees, very close to a full swoon. She gripped the communion rail before her, watching her knuckles go white with strain. Her vision narrowed as though she was at the end of a tunnel, looking down at the finger wearing the heavy gold ring.

The man at her side had noticed. He reached out and laid a hand over hers, as though he sought to comfort her.

She froze. If she put a stop to this, all of London would hear of the mad girl who had left St Aldric at the altar. She would be left with a bastard and a reputation not just tattered, but notorious. And he would grow in estimation to a tragic figure, undeserving of such horrible treatment. Beside her, St Aldric smiled and withdrew his hand. He thought he had quelled the shaking with his reassurance.

The man was insufferable. He had despoiled her memories of Richard and made her doubt her own heart. Then he'd left her in a delicate condition. He had trampled her life into dust. And now, though he cared less about her than he did the baby she carried, he thought all could be made right between them with a sham ceremony and a pat on the hand.

No matter what might lie in her future, she would

waste no more time in fear and trembling over the likes of St Aldric. And in marrying him, she would teach him the lesson he should have learned in the schoolroom: to do unto others as you would have others do to you.

Chapter Four

Michael stared into the glass before him, wishing that it held gin instead of champagne. It was far too early, in both the day and the marriage, to seek alcoholic remedy to the problems before him. If his current surroundings were a reflection of his future with Madeline, a strong drink at breakfast might not go amiss.

A church ceremony had cured the creeping sense of guilt he'd felt since the night in Dover. He had thought the worst was finally over and his life could return to normality.

But when Michael glanced out over the decoration of the feast she had arranged to celebrate their nuptials, he could find nothing normal in it. He must thank God for her good taste, he supposed. It could have been worse, had the surroundings been ugly. Of course, the level of excess was totally inappropriate for a wedding breakfast, which, in his opinion, should be small, tasteful and over quickly.

This had all the trappings of a masquerade ball. She had thrown wide the doors and cleared half the rooms in his town house to hold the crowd she had invited. Then she'd had the servants set every table in the place for guests. Every surface was decked with mountains of flowers, tropical orchids drooping on long stems from the midst of profusions of greenery. The walls were hung with ribbons and gold cages containing pairs of annoying, but beautiful, parrots.

Everywhere he turned little red faces looked down at him with beady black eyes. And whistled and chirped.

'Could we not have had doves?' he blurted, unable to contain his annoyance. Then, at least, the sounds would have been soothing.

'But, darling, doves are so common.' She gave him a pout worthy of a courtesan. 'And you said I could have anything. The guests are quite envious of it.'

The females, perhaps. All around him he heard awed whispers.

Lovebirds.... Very rare.... Straight from Abyssinia.... She bought every one on the boat....

The males looked as he felt, as though they were longing for a stiff drink to dull the effects of the squawking on their nerves. At least they did not have to pay for the damn things.

'It is a pity there was not time to teach them to speak,' she said.

He hid the flinch. With the evil smile she wore, he could imagine what she wished them to say. She wanted choruses of high-pitched voices accusing him of actions he could not defend. And doing it in front of what seemed to be half of London.

'A pity,' he agreed through clenched teeth. He could not shake the feeling, when he looked into his wife's triumphant eyes, that he was serving sentence for the crime. She must understand that this union was for the best. She was a duchess and not a gaoler. She had lost her position but gained a life of ease and a rank so august that no one would dare question her past.

Their lives would not be ordinary, especially not while they contained this many parrots. But they would be as far beyond reproach as any in England. That was all he had ever wanted for himself, and he had assumed by the way she lamented her lost reputation that it was what she wanted, as well.

He had meant to do little more than glance in her direction, to acknowledge her comment and prove that he was not bothered by it. But he had held the gaze too long, turning it into a battle of wills. For a moment, her confidence faltered and she looked as lost as he sometimes felt when under the scrutiny of this supposedly civilised society. Then she rallied and raised her guard again, looking as aloof as any lady of the *ton*.

Good for her. It had been rude of him to stare. Few men in London would have had the nerve to return such a look from a duke. But the little governess he had married weathered it well. None here would have guessed that, scant weeks earlier, she might have been a servant in their homes. She had best maintain that hauteur and let people think her proud. The more distant her treatment of society, the more desperate it would become to befriend her. If she was granted the gift of old age, she would be like those horribly intimidating dowagers that ran Almack's, casting fear into the hearts of all, lest some mistake on their part result in a fall from grace.

For now she was young and her antics, no matter how outrageous they might seem to him, would be copied as the latest fashion. It was beginning already. This morning, Hyde Park was empty, Bond Street was quiet and ladies who would be barely out of bed had dressed and forced unfortunate husbands, sons and brothers to dress and celebrate the marriage of St Aldric.

'It is good to see that you have found sufficient guests to share the day,' he remarked, trying not to think of the birds just above him that seemed to be following their conversation as though they understood each word. 'Are these people friends of yours?'

'No, darling,' she said with another false smile. 'I have no family. No acquaintances in town. No one to stand by me in my time of need.' She sighed theatrically.

It was another reminder of how low she had been when he had come to her. Despite the lack of money, family and position, Michael was beginning to suspect that he had never met a less helpless woman in his life.

She waved a hand to the assembly. 'These are your friends. I got the names from your housekeeper.'

He was tempted to sack Mrs Card for her help in this charade. She must have gathered every guest list in the house and combined them. Although he could recite their names from memory, he barely knew half the people attending. Which meant that along with the birds, he was paying to feed total strangers.

But the woman who sat beside him at a wedding breakfast fit for royalty was picking at her food as though it was so much garbage heaped on her plate.

'Do you not like it?' he asked, trying to mask his annoyance.

'You know I cannot eat,' she said, taking a small sip of wine.

And you know why.

She would not say it aloud, but she meant to dangle the truth in front of him like this, as though, at any moment, she might choose to announce to the whole of London how they had really met.

Was it just the circumstances of their meeting that had caused this vicious streak in her nature? Or had she been like this before, sour and disagreeable? His experiences with governesses in his own youth made him suspect the latter, for those he'd had had been a mirthless bunch. If so, she was not the sort of woman he'd have wanted to share his life and bear his child. If she hated the father, she would have no reason to love the son.

It was all the more reason to win her over, if it took

him a lifetime. He would do better than his parents had, in all ways. Madeline might have all the parrots she wished and gowns to match each feather. But he would abandon no son, as their father had done to Sam. Nor would he allow his home to degenerate into what his parents' had been, a battleground full of traps for the unwary.

If he failed? He glanced at his wife, chin stubbornly set as though she feared the food on her plate might leap forward on its own and attempt to nourish her against her will.

If she would not be swayed, then he had the resources to protect their child from her disdain. But the women put in charge of the nursery would be warm, affectionate and nurturing.

He spared a thought for Evelyn, sitting beside his brother at the other end of the table. Had things been different, she'd have been his, and a fine mother she would have made. She adored everything about children, even after seeing the birthing of them. He had been too particular last Season, while waiting for Eve to come to a decision. He should have offered for the first doting virgin he saw and got a ring on her finger. It would have saved him no end of trouble.

Of course, if he'd married Eve, he'd have made her terribly unhappy, for she had never loved anyone but Sam. She was beaming at her husband as though thinking of her own wedding, still sitting under her own honeymoon.

He wondered if receiving such devotion could raise

a similar response in his own heart. He had expected to be an amiable companion to any woman he married. But with so little previous experience, romantic love was quite likely beyond his ken. Without someone to show him the way, how would he find it? He looked speculatively at the woman beside him and tried to imagine her as his loving wife.

She looked back at him with annoyance.

It proved what he had often expected. If one wanted undying devotion, it would be wiser to get a dog than a wife. Madeline wished to be anywhere but near him and, at the moment, he wished to oblige her. 'It is a pity you are not well enough to travel,' he suggested, sipping his wine. 'A honeymoon journey at this time would be unwise. But now that the war is ended, a trip to the Continent would be lovely. Italy, Spain, France…'

For a moment, her glittering eyes softened. 'I have never been from England,' she said wistfully.

Did she have a weakness for travel? That was easily remedied and solved several problems at once. 'What a shame. I took the Grand Tour, of course. Or as much of it as was possible with Napoleon on the loose. I am sure it would be quite safe now, should you wish to visit the Continent.'

For a second, she looked positively eager. Then her eyes narrowed, her gaze piercing him like a gimlet. 'Oh, but, your Grace, I cannot possibly think of leaving you so soon. And there will be the baby to care for, as well.'

'He shall have wet nurses,' he reminded her. 'And governesses.'

'Oh, but I could not want to leave the training of *her* to strangers.' She emphasised the female pronoun ever so slightly, to remind him of the possibility that he might fail. 'I will be quite capable of educating our child. *Amo, amas,* amaretto...'

'*Amat,*' he corrected, unable to stop himself.

'I beg your pardon?' She gave him an innocent look.

'*Amo, amas, amat.* I love, you love, he loves. Amaretto is Italian. It is a bitter almond liquor.' Was she seriously as ignorant as she pretended?

'It does not matter, I am sure,' she said, her eyes wide and innocent. 'Love and bitterness are not so very far apart.'

It was a game, then. Another attempt to test his patience. 'While I have no doubt that you were proficient enough for your previous job, I thought you would not be interested in the education of our child,' he said, shooting her a triumphant smile over the rim of his wine glass. 'You mentioned you wished to leave me soon after the birth, did you not?'

Apparently, there was something in what he'd said that upset her. For a moment, all pretence disappeared and her composure cracked. She looked confused and frightened. Worse yet, she looked ready to cry.

He held his breath and prayed the mood would pass. People around him were supposed to be happy and at ease. He made sure of it. He knew even less

about womanly tears than he did of love. Perhaps
Madeline sensed it and was resorting to tactics far
more upsetting than tropical birds and bungled Latin.

Then the moment passed and she made a little pity-
ing click with her tongue. 'You agreed that I could do
just as I pleased. If it pleases me to leave you, I shall.
But not because you are bribing me with trips abroad.
Suppose I wish to stay?' She gave a feminine shrug.
'Perhaps you could send me away against my will. I
know what you are capable of. I am sure your friends
would be interested in hearing it.'

At last he was on familiar ground. He smiled back
at her. 'Why, my dear, one might think that you married me for no other reason than to await a chance to
tell that story.' Let her deny it, or admit.

'It will be a nice change for you. When we met,
you seemed most eager to ruin your own reputation.
I simply mean to be the helpmate you deserve.'

It was a pity that her plan would not work. Men of
his rank would be better, were it possible to shame
them into good behaviour. He took a sip of wine.
'Then let me avail you of the sad truth, Madeline. You
are as ignorant of the *ton* as you pretend to be of Latin.
The reason for our marriage does not matter to them.
Not really. They will gossip for a time. But they would
not dare cast me off for my piggish behaviour. Men
and matrons will applaud me for marrying you and
not leaving you to your unfortunate fate. And women
of a certain, liberal-minded sort will find me danger-
ously appealing. Do your worst. Tell your story, here,

now, before the cake is cut and your audience departs. And then we will get on with our lives.'

He took another sip of wine, enjoying her shocked silence and waited for the farce to end.

When the door closed on the last of the guests, Maddie could not help the feeling of relief. It was foolish and spiteful of her to attempt to goad a reaction from St Aldric in full view of the *ton*. Other than the few tart remarks he'd made to her, he'd taken it all with amazing sangfroid, as though it were perfectly natural to have his house and his life turned upside down by a stranger.

She had almost got to him when she had bungled the Latin. He had been marched through conjugations and declinations by a governess at least as strict as she was and had been unable to keep from correcting her. But it went too far against her grain to perpetuate such deliberate ignorance.

Perhaps that was what had upset her so. The knowledge that the only child she was likely to have would be raised by others. It was the best thing for the baby, of course. St Aldric could provide more than legitimacy to the little one. But to know that there would finally be someone who she could honestly claim as family and love as her own, only to walk away....

It was too soon to think about any of this. Much could happen between now and the birth. Her head was not clear enough to imagine the future. The servants had begun to clear away the mess. As the orchids disappeared towards the kitchen, she could take her first free breath. The cloying perfume had very nearly sickened her at the table and she had managed only a few bites of ham and the thinnest slice of wedding cake. And her head still rang from the sound of the birds.

That had not worked either. He had ignored the chirping and whistling. But judging by the murmurs of the guests, the *ton* would declare this the event of the Season. By tomorrow, matrons all over London would be stalking the docks in search of imported birds.

She was the only one who had suffered by this day. As she always did on visits to the town house, she felt small, insignificant and very much alone.

It had been easier in the past week, staying with Evelyn and Dr Hastings. Their house was elegant, but nothing so large as this. She felt almost at home there, after she got used to the novelty of sleeping in a room decorated for a guest and not a servant. Evelyn was both wise and helpful, putting her mind at rest on the subject of pregnancy and delivery. Doctor Hastings was quite different from what she had expected him to be, after Dover. He'd made it clear that his home was at her disposal for as long as she might wish it.

She had dared to imagine, just for a moment, that they were her family. To be so welcome and not obligated to work for her place was a novelty. Nor did she think St Aldric had paid them for their hospitality to her, as her absent father did the family that raised her. They took her in willingly, expecting nothing in return.

Then Dr Hastings had hinted, very diplomatically, that if she had a change of heart about the marriage or anything else, she was to come to him and he would help her.

It made her uneasy. Did he think her not good enough for the duke? Was he hoping, in the guise of kindness, to dissuade her from marrying his brother? Or did he know facts that had not yet been revealed to her and meant this as a rescue? It could be that St Aldric was just as dangerous as she expected him to be and that marriage to him would be a fresh misery.

But it was too late to worry now. She had chosen to marry him. Despite what a villain her husband might be, she was a duchess and she meant to behave as capriciously as the worst of them.

When she had demanded that a modiste must drop everything and provide a wardrobe fit for the wife of a peer, St Aldric had hardly blinked. Instead, he'd added, 'You will need a maid, as well. Do you wish Mrs Card to arrange suitable candidates for you to interview?'

A devilish part of her had decided that enlisting the housekeeper was the way to cause the most difficulty. But it left her in the embarrassing position of interviewing servants, using a tone that had been used upon her scant months ago. In the end, she chose one of the housemaids who had some experience with dressing and hoped for the best.

That girl, as the others had, accepted her as her future mistress with eager enthusiasm. She seemed to think any woman that might suit his Grace was near to perfection.

How could they all be so wrong about him? Was he truly able to hide the darker side of his nature to all but her? The servants seemed to view him not so much as a saint but almost as a God, rushing to do his bidding as though it was an honour to serve here.

Such misguided loyalty chilled her blood. And with it went any desire to upset the household instead of the master. These poor unfortunate souls had done nothing to deserve her punishment. She knew from experience what it was like to have employers with no sympathy for the servants and the difficulty their outlandish requests might make. She could make their lives hell with unreasonable demands. Or she could set the whole house into chaos by her inaction.

But there was something in the steady, cold gaze St Aldric had given her when he had introduced her to the staff that made her doubt the effectiveness of such a trick. The house would run on without her, she was sure, just as it had before there was a duchess.

If she had a grievance with their master, it would not be solved by taking it out on others. So today, she politely thanked Mrs Card for the extra work necessary to arrange a feast on short notice, then announced that she would retire to her rooms.

She gave a brief, helpless look to the woman. 'Someone must show me the way.' If she had come to marry in a normal way, would she still be ignorant of the bedrooms on her wedding night? Certainly not if it had been Richard, as she had hoped. She doubted that the man she had wed would be so particular about preserving his lady's honour once she had agreed to a marriage.

It made her think of Dover and the deliciously familiar sensation of a man inside of her, followed by the shock of discovering a stranger.

The housekeeper noticed her nervousness and smiled, sympathetic and cheerful. 'Of course, your Grace.' But where Mrs Card saw the excitement of a new bride, Maddie struggled with feelings of embarrassment and guilt still mixed with the low, erotic hum inside her, the desire to give herself over to sin, just to be as alive as she had when she had been with Richard. She did not want to be alone.

But neither did she want to be trapped in a mockery of a marriage. And the smiling housekeeper only made her feel guilty. Did this poor woman not realise her true feelings for the duke?

Apparently not, for the trip to the bedrooms was peppered with congratulations and good wishes, and the hope that there would soon be a child at Aldricshire, for his Grace had been so hopeful of that....

'Of course,' Maddie answered with a smile that felt even more false than usual, and continued up the stairs. They would realise, soon enough, the reason for the marriage. Rather than being shocked at her lack of chastity, they would probably applaud the coming of another little duke.

The housekeeper stopped at an open doorway with an expectant smile. 'Here, your Grace, are your rooms. They have not been used since the duke's mother was alive. But we have aired them and Peg is already unpacking your things.'

As though it would make her feel the least bit at home to think of St Aldric's mother, who probably had blood as blue as her son's eyes. 'Thank you, Mrs Card. I am sure I shall be fine now.'

With a bob the woman retreated, leaving Maddie alone. Or as alone as she was ever likely to be, for there was still a servant in the room. Her new maid was industriously filling drawers and searching for things that might need mending or pressing. As if that was even needed. The clothes were all new.

Too new. Though they belonged to her, Maddie felt no comfort in having them. She'd found the most expensive dressmaker on Bond Street and had nearly bought out the shop. The woman was frustrated by her lack of interest in the details and her instance with quantity over style. In the end, she'd had the same design made in multiple colours, so eager was she to get away from the swatches and the measurements and the assurances that this or that fashion would bring out the colour in her cheeks or accent her particularly fine figure.

The clothes were like the food at the feast today, beautiful, expensive and unpalatable. The room was overflowing with more clothing than she could ever have time to wear. St Aldric did not seem bothered, but the sight of the gowns made her feel guilty and wasteful.

She missed her old clothes. The dull and inoffensive wardrobe appropriate for a governess had been comfortable. Her maid, Peg, had set them aside with a sniff, and Maddie had not seen them since. She suspected, if she searched the shops frequented by the servants in this area, she would find that Peg had sold them.

Before they had gone, she'd managed to save a grey shawl, arguing that it was both soft and warm, despite the bland colour. She'd also salvaged a wrapper that she'd stitched herself out of dark blue flannel. Peg argued that it was not the least bit romantic. She much preferred the lacy pelisse that was meant to go with a nearly indecent gown. God forbid his Grace see the horrid blue thing; he would return to his rooms and not come back.

That was precisely what Maddie hoped. She reached for the shawl, rubbing it against her cheek for comfort as she examined her new room. It did not matter if it had been unused for years. It was a testament to quiet elegance, the green-striped silk on the walls and the cream satin of the coverlet, the gleaming brass of the candlesticks and the well-oiled wood of tables and cabinets. In comparison, her clothes were as garish as the parrots in the ballroom.

Peg did not seem bothered by them in the least. She

plucked the shawl from her mistress's hands and ran an admiring hand over the gowns in the cupboard. 'You have so many nice things, your Grace. So much nicer than the old ones. And the gown you are wearing now does not need a shawl.'

'The neck is too low,' Maddie muttered. Peg had declared it decent for church. But it still felt too low, too light and far too frivolous.

'It was no lower than the other ladies were wearing,' Peg said firmly. 'And much prettier. Though it is a pity that it will not fit for long.' She eyed Maddie's midsection speculatively.

'I don't know what you mean,' Maddie said bluntly.

The girl blushed. 'It's all right, your Grace. There is very little that a lady's maid does not notice and even less that she talks about.' She touched the gowns again. 'The dressmaker did not allow much in the seams, but I will have to let out the bodices soon enough.'

'I am only just married,' Maddie insisted.

'It's all right,' Peg repeated. 'You can hardly be blamed for getting an early start with a man like the duke.'

'Why is that?' There was little point in denying further what Peg would see with her own eyes each time she was dressed.

'He is a most handsome man,' the maid said with a giggle.

'Is he prone to...?' How best to ask this question? It was better to be prepared than to find out more unfortunate truths and be surprised by them. 'I do not know him well at all, really. People think so highly of him that it is hard to believe the truth of it. What sort of master has he been to the household?'

'The best one in London,' Peg said with a grin. 'In all of England, most likely. Kind, thoughtful and never has a sharp word for anyone.'

'There are so many in the peerage that abuse their power,' Maddie said as delicately as possible. 'They are given to all sorts of excesses. Drink, gambling, women…' She waited, hoping that the desire to gossip would prove too great to resist.

The girl gave her a wide-eyed look, as though she could not imagine such a person. 'Then we are doubly fortunate to be in this house.'

'Working for a man with no vices?' She had seen for herself that it was not true.

The girl paused for a moment, as though wondering how much she might admit to. 'There were some dark times, after the illness. Brooks, his Grace's valet, was quite worried. But his Grace is right as rain now.'

'And these dark times—were there events that I should know of? Problems with the household, perhaps?' The man had all but admitted his need to prove his virility. He must have started under his own roof.

To this, Peg's only response was an incredulous laugh. 'Oh, no, your Grace. Certainly not. He was far from home is all. And missing from Parliament, which was not like him. He is most diligent about that. And we are always glad to have him here, for it is a point of pride that we work for him. The duke is a perfect gentleman.' She leaned forward, as though she was afraid to be caught gossiping. 'He does not like it much, but the people here in town call him The Saint because he is so generous and good.'

'I would prefer not to hear that particular nickname in the house.' And there was the supposed saint, standing in the doorway that must connect their bedrooms.

The maid started at her master's voice and went hurriedly back to straightening the folds of the gowns she was hanging.

'I would not worry, for you will not hear it from me,' Maddie said, staring directly into his eyes in challenge.

'I did not think I would,' he said in a dry tone and glanced to the maid.

She curtsied, ready to leave the happy couple alone, and Maddie resisted the urge to grab for her arm and demand that she remain. She was not ready to be alone with the duke.

St Aldric stood his ground, leaning against the door frame, neither advancing, nor retreating. 'That's all right, Peg. You may stay.'

There was no logical reason for her to fear him, but her heart was in her throat to be in a bedroom with him again. It created a weird mixture of terror and excitement to remember his touch. He knew her as only one other man had. But unlike Richard, who she had loved with all her soul, St Aldric was still a stranger to her. He did not seem equally bothered. But he had known many women. What did he even remember of her, other than that she carried his child? And how much of that night did she remember clearly herself?

She did not want to remember it. It was over. They were together because of an accident, she reminded herself. A mistake. And the duke's weak character. And she would not allow it to happen again, for another night in his bed would mean that she was little better than a lustful animal.

She focused her mind on a battlefield far away, and a good man lying in an unmarked grave. Then she stared at the duke, safe and whole and undeserving. 'You wished something, your Grace?'

He smiled. It seemed normal and natural, and she heard the maid sigh at the sight, for the duke was even more handsome when he chose to smile. But Maddie could see it for what it was: a polite mask hiding whatever it was that he actually thought when he looked at her. 'I only came to suggest that you dress to go out. It is a fine afternoon and I thought we take advantage of the weather to purchase your wedding present.'

Chapter Five

A gift.

Maddie hardly knew what to say to that. Courtesy had the words *you needn't have bothered* rushing to her lips. She had taken so much already. The gowns…

A duchess cannot wear rags, she reminded herself. The breakfast…

A social success.

And the ring on her finger, heavier and more magnificent than anything she'd ever hoped to have.

And entailed, the voice in her head said firmly. If he wished to buy her something that was truly hers, then why should he not? It was a bribe to keep her silent and in good humour.

When he had retreated into his own room, Peg chose a smart walking dress of pale blue muslin and a bonnet trimmed in silk cornflowers. Admiring herself in the mirror, Maddie could not help but smile. While she did not feel like a duchess, in this simple gown she felt less like a governess in fancy dress.

Then she went downstairs to find St Aldric waiting in the hall wearing buff breeches, Hessians and a
wine-coloured coat, along with the same unflappable
smile he had been using in her bedroom. He was so
polite she might as well have been a stranger.

As he glanced up at her, it faltered, but not with
the annoyance she'd expected to see when she caught
him unawares. He was staring at her with admiration.

In response, she could feel herself colouring. The
most handsome man in London was looking at her
as though he was eager for her company. Lord help
her, she was smiling back. Her steps quickened on
the stairs, hurrying to his side.

Then she remembered her resolution in the bedroom less than an hour ago. She must not forget who
she was, who he was and what had brought them to
this. He remembered as well, for the look in his eyes
faded, the sincere smile faltered like a guttering candle and the false courtesy returned.

She nodded in acknowledgement, wiping the smile
from her own face, and allowed him to hand her up
into the seat of his high-perch phaeton.

If there was any trace of excitement in her, he could
attribute it to the carriage. The vehicle was as impressive as everything else about St Aldric: expensive and
elegant, it was so new that the paint was barely dry.
But the unsteadiness of it wore on her nerves. Suppose
they were overset? Was such a conveyance safe for
anyone, much less a woman in her delicate condition?

She considered fussing about it, or offering some

snide comment implying that he meant to kill her on the very first day of their marriage.

But he handled the ribbons himself and it might be unwise to upset him while he drove and create the accident she worried about. They were travelling at as spritely a pace as could be managed through the busy streets of London, but he navigated with confidence and took no foolish risks. As she watched him, so obviously skilled, she felt that creeping admiration of him that rose in her whenever she did not stop to remind herself what a complete bounder she had married.

'Where are you taking me?' She tried to sound petulant, but the words came out as curious and excited.

'Tattersall's. You cannot be a smart woman of the *ton* without a curricle of some sort, or at the very least a mare to ride in Rotten Row.' His smile was serene and distant, but she noticed the faintest smirk at the corner as he added, 'I expect it will be very expensive.'

That might have been the case. Perhaps this was a peace offering to her, formed in a way that saved face for the both of them. If she meant to spend his money, here was a chance.

Then he added, 'At breakfast, Rayland mentioned some fine stock he has up for auction today and I do not want to miss a chance at them.'

So that was it. He had been talking horseflesh on his wedding day when they were barely out of the church. He was making a public show of her wedding gift, so that anyone keeping a tally of correct marital behaviour would not be shocked that he had abandoned her at home to go to an auction.

Her feelings meant nothing to him. If he'd have asked her, she'd have announced quite truthfully that the thought of handling a carriage herself, or even parading on the back of some blood mare, was terrifying. She knew little of horses and even less of driving. To develop such skills while with child went against all common sense. If he'd wished to torture her, he could not have found a better way.

It grew even worse when they'd arrived at their destination. St Aldric handed the reins to his tiger and helped her down into a throng of men, hounds and horses. It was loud, dusty and intimidating. With the huge beasts stamping the dirt on all sides of her, she was near to panic.

And that was the only reason that she found herself clinging to his arm, as though his presence would be any kind of security at all. It was degrading. She hated having to ask him for help. Before they had met, she had made her way in the world alone, using good sense to avoid situations that were not safe for an unattached female. After Richard had left, she'd been scrupulous of her own safety and her honour. But if being the Duchess of St Aldric meant that she would be dragged into such places and forced to rely on her husband for security, then she was likely to dislike this marriage even more than she'd expected.

Even worse, her husband was patting her hand, as though her frailty was to be assumed. 'You needn't worry. The horse I have in mind for you will be far more easy than these brutes. We will find you a mare as gentle as a lamb.'

Of course he would. He would not wish to risk the safety of his child after all. The thought brought the bitter taste back to her mouth that she had not had since Evelyn began dosing her with ginger.

She took a deep breath and mastered it. 'Am I to have no say in the purchase?'

He looked down at her, surprised. 'I did not think you knew horseflesh. If you wish, you may decide what you are able to handle.'

It was a dare, she was sure. A society lady would show spirit and choose some impossible horse and he would laugh at her attempts to control it. He led her towards the auction, examining the mares that would come up for bid. They were big but gentle, with soft dark eyes and velvety muzzles, nuzzling gently at her to see if she'd brought them treats. They were not lambs, precisely. Rather like extremely large dogs.

She still did not like them. Nor did she like being so far from her element. But he was as content bartering for horses as he was when she'd turned his home into an aviary. It seemed he was at ease in any situation.

She would always be a step behind. A little lost. Struggling to catch up, even in situations she had orchestrated. At the wedding breakfast, he had greeted each person in the throng she had invited by name, deflected any congratulations that had seemed less than sincere with praise of his wife's taste and intelligence and even spoken knowledgeably when questioned about the lovebirds. He managed to be all things to all people.

Except to her, of course. She had seen the true man in Dover. What she was seeing now was nothing more than false coin. If everyone else was fooled, then London must be populated by idiots.

At the moment, the patron saint of the *ton* was too busy checking teeth and feeling withers to notice her annoyance. He led her down the row, pointing out a shoulder here, a fetlock there, pulling back lips and staring into eyes, giving no hint as to what was good or bad, treating her as though she might have some idea of what she was supposed to be looking at. He was making fun at her expense, waiting to see her prove her ignorance.

She let him carry on with it, refusing to take the bait and speak. Then she glanced past him, outside the gates.

In sad mimicry to the auction here, which was made up of the finest horseflesh in London, a group of farmers and drovers had gathered to make their own trades. Although there were probably some solid plough horses in the bunch, even she could see that many of the animals were as poor as their owners. One or two of the men moving through that crowd were bidding often and buying so many beasts that she suspected their purchases would be nothing more than hooves, hide and glue by the end of the week.

St Aldric took no notice of that sale. He was too preoccupied by the thrill of the chase on his side of the fence, gauging his competition and readying his bids for horses worthy to carry his new wife.

She sniffed. Horse mad, just like the rest of his set. He was likely to fritter away more money than she could imagine for the right to own more animals than he could possibly need. More proof that she had been a fool to try to shock him with her gowns.

She wandered away, in the direction of the drovers' auction. Her husband did not notice at all, but the groom, seeing her depart, hurried after. It was nice to know that someone truly cared for her safety.

Seeing the horses here was almost comforting. They were no smaller, of course. In some cases, they were truly massive. They needed the height and weight to pull ploughs and wagons. But at least they were calm.

It was the calmness of animals resigned to their fate that drew her. They stood between the traces, plodding forward at the pull of the reins. At the end of the journey, they did not come to a green pasture like the fancy horseflesh that her new husband admired. These animals, with their rheumy eyes and drooping heads, were headed towards the knackers. She thought of her own life in service and how it might have ended, too old to be useful and full of employers rather than friends. She turned in sympathy to pat the nearest horse.

It was the most flea-bitten, spavined nag she had ever seen. Its owner hung back from the crowd, obviously dreading the likely response when it was brought up for bids. When the poor thing was led to the front, there were snickers and catcalls of 'too thin for dog meat' and 'not fit for glue'.

She felt sorry for the owner, who looked even more dejected at the prospect of being unable to sell it. Bidding began, with the auctioneer's suggested forty pounds greeted with resounding silence. He followed it with thirty, then twenty, then ten. His voice grew more desperate with each suggestion. Still, the prospective buyers said nothing. The farmer who held the harness looked near to tears, at least, what she could see of him. As usual, she was small and short, and losing sight of the action with each shift of a head in front of her.

Finally, she could stand it no longer. 'Fifty!'

There was a gasp from the men around her and heads turned to find the source of the bid. This resulted in much muttering and rustling in the crowd, and bodies pressing in on her, making it even harder for her to see. She pushed forward, darting under armpits and working her way to the front.

'I am not sure I heard?' the auctioneer called. 'Did someone bid?'

'Sixty!' she cried again, louder so that her voice might carry over the laughter of the mob.

Someone shouted something about a madwoman in the back and she pushed hard against the man ahead of her, moving forward another few inches. 'Seventy!' She was at the front now, staring at the auctioneer as the nag puffed steamy breath into her hair.

'Excuse me, miss,' the auctioneer said with a toothy grin. 'It seems you have wandered into the wrong place. The proper auction is through the gate, yonder. And just past is the Jockey Club, if you are looking for a rider.'

Judging by the laughter around her, the comment was as rude as it sounded. She ignored it. 'I want a horse. This horse. And I am willing to pay eighty pounds for him.'

'Her.' She spun to attack the yokel behind her who dared to point out her ignorance and found herself staring directly into the chest of her new husband. 'The animal in question is a mare.'

She doubted the men around her knew who was in their midst, but she could tell from the hushed silence that they recognised rank and quality.

'Begging your pardon, my lord,' the auctioneer murmured, 'but the lady... I do not think she understands the principal of an auction, or the worth of the animal.'

'One hundred!' she said to the auctioneer. She turned back to St Aldric, staring up at him and daring him to correct her. 'You said I could make the decision.'

'So I did,' he said, with the slightest of sighs. He turned to the owner. 'How much do you wish for

this…horse?' He seemed almost unwilling to acknowledge the sex of the animal before him.

'It is an auction, not a sale. And I bid one hundred,'
she reminded him.

'The beast you have chosen is not worth half of
that.'

The farmer was too shocked to speak for himself,
but Maddie held her ground, unwilling to be forced
into a reasonable price. 'Fifty? That is far too little
for a beauty like this.' She stroked the animal's nose
and it responded with a sort of confused gratitude,
as though unsure of just why a human would touch
it so gently. But it submitted, fearful of arousing ire.

She smiled at St Aldric again, who looked as
though he was embarrassed to be seen standing next
to such a pathetic animal. That was enough to decide
her. She gave him an empty-headed, society smile
and gushed, 'I simply must have her.' She turned the
horse's head so that the mare could display a mouthful
of worn, yellow teeth. Perhaps this was what he had
been trying to show her in the others, for surely this
horse stood as the bad example by which she could
measure the others.

'This is a cart horse,' the duke said patiently. 'I
wished to buy you a decent mount. Or perhaps some
carriage horses. I have no idea what you mean to do
with this.'

'I shall name her Buttercup,' Maddie said, with
evil glee. If only for the colour of those horrible teeth.

The duke gave the same resigned sigh he'd made

after each of her outlandish requests and reached for his purse. 'One hundred pounds it is, then. If my wife wishes.' He glanced around at the crowd, who were leaning in as though expecting him to buy again. 'But this is the only purchase she will be making today.' Then he spoke to the farmer. 'If my groom gives you direction, can you bring the horse to my stables?' He glanced at Maddie and said, in an undertone, 'Or would you prefer that I carry her there on my back?'

It was another sign that he knew exactly want she was doing, but it was delivered in such a benign tone that it was clear no damage had been done to him. 'No, the delivery shall be enough, I am sure. Settle her in our stables, so that I might visit her at my leisure.' She stared at St Aldric, blinking innocently. 'Will she not look magnificent in Rotten Row, next to all the other fine horses of the nobility?'

'I am certain she will draw just the sort of attention you wish,' he replied.

'I shall want a carriage, as well,' she said, baiting him again.

'I am sure we can find a vehicle that will suit. A milk wagon, perhaps.' He turned and walked away and she had to hurry to keep up. For a moment she feared that he might abandon her here, surrounded by strangers and dangerous animals. And then he glanced back at her, offering his arm and proving that, once again, his perfect manners made him impossible to goad.

Chapter Six

Supper was a chilly affair in the main dining room. Michael debated taking it in his room, after making some lame excuse about the busy day and the need for rest. Even if that was true, it would appear that he was running from his wife. And she would think she had won.

Peers were supposed to be made of sterner stuff than that. If he could manage the interminable arguing of Parliament, he could learn to ignore the behaviour of the stranger he had married. With sufficient time and patience, perhaps she would learn to tolerate him, as well.

For now, she was picking at her food, even when there was nobody but him to see it. It made him suspect that, just perhaps, her apathy towards the delicacies of the breakfast was not feigned. When she chose, it was the things that were bland and easy to digest. The roast that had been prepared was going to waste. Her plate held poached fish and potatoes and she'd kept the soup bowl, which held thin broth. With the small breakfast, and the fact that he'd dragged her away from luncheon and tea to stare at horses, she'd eaten close to nothing.

No matter their differences, he could not stand by and watch her starve. But how to get her to eat? He turned to the footman waiting beside his chair. 'This is all delicious, of course. You can assure cook that I have no complaints. But I am feeling rather unsettled. Perhaps a baked egg or two would do the trick.' He glanced up as though it was an afterthought. 'Would you like one as well, my dear?'

She looked at him with relief. 'Thank you.'

The sincerity seemed to surprise them both. As the servant went to get the dish, they fell into silence again.

When the eggs arrived, she tasted one cautiously and set her fork aside.

He thought on it, for a moment. If heavy foods did not suit, and plain foods did not interest, what was left? He reached for the tureen of Wow-Wow sauce and ladled it liberally over his eggs, then offered some to her.

She sniffed suspiciously. 'What is this?'

'The latest thing. Cook says it is a recipe from a Dr Kitchiner. He seems to take a very scientific approach to cookery.'

'A doctor, you say?' She looked hopefully at the ladle.

'It is probably quite healthy,' he assured her. By the taste of it, it was a testament to the idea that what did not kill strengthened. But it was devilishly addictive and unlikely to make her feel any worse. He held his breath as she served herself and took the first bite of egg.

She smiled. She chewed. She swallowed. Then she reached for more. He watched with relief as she smothered her food in the stuff and ate with enthusiasm. Then she followed the main course with brown-bread ice cream and a shockingly powerful Stilton.

He felt a little of the tension within him relax. After breakfast, he'd wondered if she meant to starve herself just to spite him. It appeared that, once awakened, her digestion was like her will, made of cast iron.

He was enjoying his port when she pushed the last empty plate away, stifling a yawn.

He stood. 'It is late and you are, no doubt, tired. May I escort you to your room?'

Her eyes narrowed, suspicious, but she rose and nodded, preceding him from the room. She hesitated at the turn in the hall, and again at the head of the stairs, proving that his help had been necessary. She barely knew her way around the house without help. He made no effort to call attention to it, but did not leave her until they'd arrived at the door to her room, which he opened and held for her.

When she was through, he followed and shut it behind them.

She gasped and he held up a calming hand. 'I only

wish a moment alone to speak with you before you ring for the maid. Then I will be gone.'

'Very well, then,' she said, frowning. 'Speak.'

He ran the risk of undoing the good that had been done over dinner. But life would be easier if they aired their differences sooner, rather than later. 'I would like to know your intentions towards this marriage and to have an honest explanation for your behaviour.'

Surely she could not pretend ignorance. He gave her a pointed look. 'For example, are the antics of this morning likely to be repeated?'

'Antics?' she said, with her most wide-eyed, innocent stare.

'The elaborate and unnecessary gatherings?'

'You did not think it important to celebrate our marriage?'

'I am surprised that you did,' he said. 'We both know that you did not wish to marry me. This afternoon, the unfortunate horse…'

'You promised me freedom to do as I wished,' she reminded him.

'I did,' he agreed.

'I mean to do so.'

'I see.' He took a breath. 'And you may do as you like. But I do not understand it. Are these things truly what you want? Or are you attempting to bother me with them?'

She stared at him, unwilling or unable to answer the question.

'It matters not one way of the other,' he assured her.

'I doubt there is a punishment you could devise that I have not already wished upon myself. The man you met that night in the inn... It was not me.' It sounded ridiculous when he phrased it that way. But it was the truth as he saw it and he meant to repeat it until she believed him.

'You deny that you attacked me?'

'It was not an attack,' he said. Then he took a moment to calm himself, for he did not wish to appear angry with her for something that had been his fault alone. 'It was a mistake. It was me in body. I do not deny that. At the time...' He was pausing again. 'My behaviour was so out of character that I view the man who was so misguided as to enter your room as a virtual stranger to all I stand for, all I believe and all I hope to emulate.'

'But it was you all the same,' she responded, clearly unimpressed. 'Who you were, before or since, does not matter to me. It is who you were on that night that affected me.'

Of course that was true. It was naive to hope that they could put this behind them so quickly. Had his father not told him that it was a man's actions that stood after his words were forgotten? Old St Aldric had no right to lecture about character. Father had been guilty of a number of ignoble actions far worse than the night in Dover.

And that was the problem. There was much good his father had done in life. The other, older lords spoke of his speeches with respect and sometimes even awe.

But Michael could remember none of that when compared with the man he had seen in Aldricshire.

The same would not be said of him. He bowed his head to his wife, as a show of contrition. 'I am sorry beyond words. I would take it back in a heartbeat, if there was some way.'

'To keep me from distrusting you?' She stood, frozen on the doorstep, staring at the connecting door between the rooms.

'You will never need fear me,' he reminded her.

But she did. Her voice held none of the bravado he'd heard earlier. She had finally eaten, but she was still pale and so tired that she swayed on her feet.

'You have my word,' he promised again.

'I prefer more concrete examples. Is there a lock on my bedroom door?'

He gave a sigh of exasperation, wishing he'd had it pulled out years ago, as he'd done with the lock on his own door. 'There is one fitted there already.'

'To which you hold the keys,' she reminded him.

'We will change them, then,' he said. 'First thing in the morning. The door to the hall and the connecting door between our rooms, as well. I will have no key made for myself. Even the housekeeper shall be denied one, if that is what you wish.' It would be embarrassing. All in the household would know that he was denied access to a room where a husband ought to hold dominion.

The memory of being on the wrong side of a locked door was all too familiar.

'That is tomorrow. What of tonight?' she prodded, totally oblivious to his feelings. If one had nothing to hide, or nothing to contain, then one had no need to lock doors. And until this moment, his London home had been blissfully free of them.

The fact that he had no desire to enter her room did not matter. It was the appearance of the thing that was important to her. He reached into his pocket and removed the ring of keys that opened and closed her half of the master suite. 'Here. This is yours to hold, if it makes you feel more secure.'

She took the keys and he saw the furrow in her brow smooth. 'Thank you. And now, if you will excuse me?' She glanced towards the door.

'Of course.' He gave a small bow and exited through the hall door, turning to the left and entering his own room, only a few feet away.

Once he was safely alone in his room he took a second set of keys from his pocket and set it on the bureau. He stared at the ring for a moment before deciding that the keeping of it was not quite a lie. She had demanded the door keys and he had relinquished the duchess's set.

He smiled grimly. If she had thought to demand all keys, he would have relinquished the duplicate set meant for the duke. But she had not. He was in his right to stay silent.

And in his right to refuse her request. He had promised her complete freedom and what very nearly amounted to a pledge of obedience to her wishes. No matter the fact that she had earned it, it went against the natural order of things to be so womanly and submissive. He would be damned before he was locked out of even a single room in his house, for her or anyone else.

What she had really wanted was a promise from him not to enter. She could have taken his word on that. The demand for the key was a slap in the face of honour and never something he'd have expected from a wife. Did she want him to nail the door shut, to prove his intentions to avoid it?

Instead, it gave him the perverse desire to block it open, if only to prove that he was strong enough to stay on his side of the threshold.

But he did not wish to turn an uneasy truce into an argument. Nor did he have a reason to knock on the door and request further communication.

He had no reason to talk to his wife. That he should say such a thing on his wedding night was almost beyond his understanding. He turned back into his room to prepare for bed.

When he opened his eyes again, the room was still dark. Far too early to rise, especially after the trouble he'd had getting to sleep. He was annoyingly aware of the stranger sleeping in the next room. There was a presence where there had always been an absence. The occasional sounds of movement as Madeline prepared for bed. The muffled conversation with the maid and the close of the hall door as that servant departed. And then there had been nothing. Even the faint glow of candlelight at the crack under the door had dimmed.

It was not loud. But it was more activity than he was used to in this most silent part of the house, and he was not sure that he liked it. That was strange, for he had always hated the silence that came with total privacy. It was a reminder of the fact that he was alone.

Now he was not alone, and it had not been the magic cure to bring peace and an end to the insomnia that sometimes plagued him. Instead of feeling free to relax, he felt responsible for the source of the noise, worrying that she could not sleep either and wondering if there was something he might do to help. It was only when he was sure she was asleep and silence had come again that he had finally been able to close his eyes.

Something had awakened him. A sound of some sort, he suspected. Did she snore? It would be a nuisance, but he would adjust. Then he heard the sound again. It was not a snore, but he could not place it. Perhaps it was someone in the hall. Or maybe Madeline had summoned her maid. It was definitely a female voice, coming from the other side of the locked door. But he had not heard the hall door open. Nor was there an answering voice.

This was the sound of Madeline in conversation with herself.

She was an odd woman, was she not? Did she do

this often? Did she not realise that he could hear? The droning repetitiveness made him think that she was talking in a dream. She could hardly be blamed for that. He did not sleep easily in a strange place either.

Gradually, the one-sided discussion was becoming an argument, louder, faster and more agitated. Was he obligated to intervene in some way? If he rang for a servant, he would get his valet, who would then summon her maid. Half the house would be awake before she was. And in that time, the dream would continue to distress her, for she showed no signs of waking or easing back into sleep.

He threw aside the covers and padded barefoot to the dresser, rummaging around in a drawer for the key to the adjoining room. He had promised not to bother her. But perhaps, in this instance, it was better to do so than to leave her in distress. Once she was quiet, he would put the key away and they could both sleep in peace.

Through the door and into her bedroom, he found his way to her bedside without effort. He knew this room, as he did all the others, better than she ever would. But why she slept with the bed curtains pulled tightly shut, he could not decide. It must be stifling within, for the night was showing the first heaviness of summer air.

He pulled one back with the rattle of curtain rings and whispered, 'Madeline, are you well?'

'No,' she moaned. 'No. Stop.'

'Madeline.' He said her name louder, for she had

not heard him. 'You are dreaming. There is nothing to fear.'

'No,' she said again, although it was impossible to tell if she was speaking to him. 'Richard. Where are you? Come back to me.'

Who was that? She had not mentioned a brother, a cousin or anyone else by that name. 'Richard is not here,' he said patiently. 'It is only me.'

'No.' She tossed on the pillow, her head turning towards him, then away and then back again. 'Richard.'

She was getting louder. If he did not do something soon, the servants would come and find him standing over her bedside, watching her suffer. And she was suffering. Her lip trembled and her skin was pale, but beaded with perspiration. No matter the differences between them, it pained him to see her thus. In her sleep, she was distraught and even an enemy did not deserve that.

'Madeline.' He reached out and touched her shoulder.

She started. Her eyes were wide open now, still sleeping, and she was scrambling away, up the bed to wedge herself against the headboard, clinging to the curtain as though it was a shield. 'Not Polly,' she insisted. 'Not Polly. Who is she?'

It was him. In her nightmares, she was back in Dover. And she'd awakened to find him looming over her, just as she had that night.

He backed away. 'I'm sorry. So very sorry. I heard you cry out. I meant no harm.'

'Not Polly,' she gasped one more time, her eyes still sightless, trapped in a dream. 'It is me, Richard. Don't you remember?'

'You are having a nightmare,' he said, feeling more helpless than any other time in his life. 'You are safe here.' Safe from him. How odd that he should need to say it.

'Richard?' she said hopefully. Her eyes were closing again and there was the slightest hopeful smile on her face. 'You are not dead after all.'

'Yes, love. It is Richard. I am here.'

'Then take me away from here. So unhappy.'

He could give her everything but the one thing she truly wanted. He must remember that he was not the only one in this marriage who had known disappointment. Michael wet his lips and lied again. 'Of course, love. We will go back to where we were happiest.' Wherever that was. The words seemed to help. She settled back into the pillows with a sigh, her features relaxing.

He stared down at her for a moment, unable to look away. Had he never seen her happy before? He had known she was attractive, but he had not seen the beauty of her smile. So soft, so sweet and welcoming. And not for him at all. It was for a man who had not been there to protect her, when she'd needed it most.

Then he noticed the tears drying on her face. He had caused those. He ran the tip of a finger over her skin, smoothing them away.

She leaned her cheek into his hand, her lips grazing his fingertips in a kiss.

He froze, afraid to move. If she woke and caught him in her bedchamber, there would be no hope of gaining her trust. But dear God, it was sweet. Though he had more power, rank and money than any sane man might need, he envied this Richard, who once had the devotion of his little Madeline.

Very carefully, he pulled the covers back up and tucked them around her, gently wiping away a curl that was stuck to her damp face. 'Sleep well, darling. Everything is all right now.'

And it would be all right. He would see to it.

Maddie blinked awake to find the morning sunlight shining bright through the crack in the bed curtains. She had been dreaming again, she was sure. Her arms and legs felt heavy and tired as though, in her sleep, she had walked a great way.

At least she was not tangled in the sheets today. Some mornings she awoke paralysed in body as well as mind, so sad that she could hardly fight herself free of her own blankets.

Last night's dream, as she'd remembered it, had been different from what it had been in the past. She was at the inn in Dover, of course, but she had not lain with a stranger. There had been no shame. No embarrassment. Once again she had felt young, innocent and in love. It had been so real that she was sure she had been awake. To find a man standing over the bed should have frightened her, but strangely it did not. For though she could not see his face, she had been sure it was Richard. He spoke softly to her, calming her, and she'd wondered whether he'd finally returned, just as he had in the dream.

Then she noticed the change in him. She had kissed his hand, but he had not joined her on the bed. Instead, he'd stood over her for a moment, then arranged the blankets and eased her back to sleep as though she were a frightened child.

It was not the Richard she had known. It had been an angel. She could not see the wings, but she was sure they must have been present. Before he had gone, he'd promised to protect her and she'd believed him. He would always be here for her, guarding over her.

If dreams had meaning, this one said she must stop waiting. She was married now. Her true love was not coming home as anything but a sweet memory. It should have upset her, to have the last hope dashed. But he had told her, in the dream, that she had nothing to fear. She must trust him, just as she had when they were together. And with that knowledge, she had made peace with his absence and drifted deeper into sleep, waking refreshed.

It was odd that she should have the first restful night in so long while in the very house of the man whom she least wanted to see. But as he had promised, he had not bothered her in the night. There was the security of the locked door between them. Before she had climbed into bed, she had turned the key and set it aside. A few minutes later she had checked the door. And then she'd checked it again. Then, finally, she had crawled into bed, pulled the curtains and rolled away from it, vowing that she would not touch it again until morning.

It was foolish to doubt herself about such small things. Perhaps it was the life growing inside her, urging her to check and double-check each thing she did, as though testing her abilities to keep the young one safe. It was nonsense. The door was locked and the key was still on the dresser.

But who was to know if she assured herself that it was indeed locked, just as she'd left it? She climbed out of the bed and walked to it, took the knob in a firm grip and twisted slowly and silently, so as not to awake the duke. But instead of resisting, it turned easily, opening suddenly towards her because of the weight resting on the other side.

The Duke of St Aldric tumbled into the room.

She took a step back, clutching her wrapper in alarm and trying to disguise the ridiculously lacy nightgown that Peg had insisted she wear on her wedding night.

He was even more surprised than she. He looked up at her with sleep-dazed eyes, not quite sure of what he was doing on the floor.

'What is the meaning of this?' she demanded.

But the meaning was obvious, if still confusing. On his side of the door, a bench had been set to block the threshold and the duke had been using it as a bed.

He had been sleeping sitting up, leaning against the door. When she'd opened it, he'd fallen backwards.

'Bloody hell.' He was rubbing the back of his head now, glanced up at her and glanced hurriedly away as though not sure where he could politely look. He struggled to disentangle himself from the bench so that he could regain his footing.

She should have done the same. For while her modesty was mostly preserved, his was not. The expanse of his chest was bared where the dressing gown fell open. As the skirt of it flapped in his movement, lengths of naked leg were exposed, clear to the groin. Long, well-shaped legs, with firm calves and thighs.

Dear lord. A trail of gold hair, curling down the centre of his body, well past his navel, disappearing beneath the belt and leading to the tiny bit of his body still obscured by his robe—and the fabric that did nothing to hide the bulge of morning beneath it.

Then the moment had passed and the man was on his feet in the doorway, adjusting his clothing and properly covered.

They stood for a moment in silence. His eyes were unwavering, locked to hers, cool and gentlemanly.

It took all her strength not to look down again, to see if any trace of that glorious male body was still visible. Lust, pure and simple, was added to the many curious feelings that seemed to rise and fall in her like the tide now she was with child. Despite what had passed between them, she had to admit that her new husband was a beautiful specimen and worthy of admiration.

And one who looked as though, if he had less than perfect poise, he would have been shuffling and stammering at the awkwardness of this encounter. 'I heard you cry out in the night. You were clearly quite distressed.' He gave the belt of his robe another tug. 'When I had assured myself that there was no real danger, I returned to my room and remained there, against the door, in case the dream recurred.'

'You. Entered my room?' The angel that she had felt watching over her in the night was him? And then he'd returned to his side of the threshold to guard her as she'd slept.

'I meant no harm.'

It had not been Richard at all. It had been St Aldric again. She had grown used to finding him in her nightmares. But must he invade the happy dreams, as well? She could feel her cheeks growing red, not just from embarrassment, but anger. 'The door was locked.'

'There is a second key.'

'In your possession.' What point had there been in giving her her own key, other than to create a false sense of security in her?

'I will not be denied entrance to rooms in my own home,' he said, his demeanour cooling by the minute. 'You must trust, on my honour, that I will not use it but in the most dire emergencies.'

'And you discovered such an emergency on our very first night of marriage?'

'You were crying out loud enough to wake the household,' he said almost in a whisper. 'It was emergency enough for me.'

'It was only a dream.'

His eyes refused to meet hers, for they both knew what the cause of her nightmares had been. 'I will give you the key,' he said, reaching into his pocket.

'And how can I trust that there is not a third resting on your keychain?'

'You have my word.'

'Which you have already broken by hiding this from me. I demand that you move me to a different room immediately.' Preferably one on a different continent. Then perhaps she could escape the warring feelings of anger, confusion and guilt. At least if she were far away, she could free herself of the desire to look at his body again. She forced herself to focus on his face, just as he did for her.

As she watched, a variety of emotions moved across the perfect features like clouds over a clear sky. He was embarrassed, ashamed of what he had done at Dover and the lie he'd just told her. He considered something for a moment, rejected it, considered something else and seemed to settle on something. When his eyes lifted to hers again, they were dark, but far from unreadable. He was angry. As though he was being forced into something disreputable that he wanted no part of.

'It would be difficult to move you in this house, as the guest rooms, while lovely, would hardly suit the size of your wardrobe. But if we remove to Aldricshire, you will have the solitude you request. The lord's and lady's chambers there do not connect.'

How odd.

She'd very nearly said it. Or made some other foolish comment about the inconvenience that must cause. For while it was customary to have the nursery as far away from the adult rooms as it was possible to be, she had never heard of a husband and wife sleeping so obviously apart.

Until her own marriage, of course.

'That would be most suitable,' she said. It should be, for there was clearly something about the idea that upset him. That had been her object in marrying, had it not? To see to it that he was as miserable as she had been.

But why should sleeping apart from her make him unhappy? She'd made it clear from the first that there would be no communion between them. He was a fool if he expected he could change her mind by keeping her in London.

'I would like to leave as soon as possible,' she added, not wanting to tempt fate by the continued sight of him in the morning.

His mind calculated. 'After breakfast, then. The trip can be made in less than a day. We will travel lightly. Our luggage will be sent after.'

As though expecting her to offer some devilish

objection to this, he corrected, 'My trunks, of course, can follow. You are likely about to tell me that you cannot be expected to travel without a wardrobe. I will have Scott bring up the cases and instruct your maid to begin packing immediately.' He turned to the bell pull, ready to rearrange his life to suit her whims.

It seemed he was not inconvenienced in the least. He acted as if there was nothing in his schedule that could not be postponed or handled by another. It would be her fault if this trip broke her goodwill with the servants. After the work they'd put into the breakfast, the sudden move would create even more chaos.

If the servants had been surprised by this sudden upheaval, they had the grace not to show it. Footmen who had been pulling down the flowers in the ballroom were recommissioned to carry boxes from her room to one of two waiting carriages. They even smiled while lugging heavy trunks up and down the stairs. Apparently, if the duke requested something of one, it was treated as an honour to comply.

When she had enquired as to the need for two vehicles, she was informed that the second held her clothing. The first was for her and her maid.

And the duke?

Preferred, at least on this instance, to ride. As they set out, she saw him holding the bridle of a brute of an animal with eyes that flashed like the very devil. It was black and glossy, so different from the nag she had chosen on the previous day that one might even wonder if they shared a species.

St Aldric mounted without the help of a groom, swinging easily up into the saddle and then glancing to her where she sat in the carriage, so high that he had to look down to her, despite the height of the rig. Then he turned the horse and set off at an easy pace down the drive.

Though Peg seemed to think it an eternity, the trip was not to be particularly long. 'Nearly forty miles,' she breathed. 'I have never been so far from home in my life.'

Maddie hid her smile. Changes in position had forced her to criss-cross the country on several occasions. Before that, she'd not had a true home to miss. 'It is much easier this way than to travel in a mail coach,' she said. 'It is never nice to have one's schedule set by others and to be chased in and out of highway inns with barely time for refreshment.'

'If you need either, the duke says you must be sure to ask and we will stop immediately,' Peg replied.

Maddie frowned. He had said so, had he? Not to her. Although it seemed that he'd had no problem relaying that concern for her comfort to the maid.

When she mentioned that it might be nice to stop for lunch, the caravan drew immediately to a halt and one of the outriders produced a cloth for the ground and a basket of dainties that was more like a feast than a picnic. She dined on potted pheasant and champagne, a nice Stilton and strawberries that she was assured came from the vines that grew right in Aldricshire and were shipped each week to London. There was even a small pot of the medicinal sauce that the duke had offered her, and it seemed to make each food more appetising. She even tried a bit on one of the strawberries when she was sure no one was looking, and was surprised to find them sweeter than usual.

The only thing absent from luncheon was the duke himself. He had lagged far enough behind that she was assured he must have stopped at one of the inns they had passed.

Maddie frowned. Perhaps his fine black horse was not so fine after all. It could not even manage to keep up with the carriages. Or perhaps he was not satisfied with light wine and a bird. Despite his insistence that he no longer drank to excess, he might be bloating on ale, or washing a joint down with brandy to a degree that would render him unsteady in the saddle. She would laugh if that had happened, for it would prove that all his fine talk of sobriety was another lie.

Or perhaps, said a small voice at the back of her mind, *he does not wish to be with you.*

That should make her happy, just as the thought of his drunkenness did. If she was riding like a princess, and he was willing to forgo luxury after only two days of marriage to keep apart from her, then she was succeeding in her plan to make him unhappy.

She had never meant to be the sort of person that could not be abided by others. When one was a servant, one could not afford to be disagreeable. Her maid seemed to like her and chattered endlessly as they travelled about the sights they passed. The drivers, grooms and outriders treated her with kindness, as well. They all grinned, rushing over each other for the chance to serve the new duchess, plying her with treats and cushions as though she was fragile as a quail's egg, to be packed in cotton wool and not to be jostled. She had been kind and polite to all of them in return, apologising for any trouble she caused and showing appreciation for their extra efforts.

She'd offered none of that kindness to her husband, who had been willing to sleep in a chair to assure himself that her dreams remained sweet. Of course, her rest would be easier had she never met him....

Try as she might to remind herself that she was justified in her anger with him, she could feel those little moments of sympathy sneaking in, nibbling away like mice in the wainscoting. With comfort and condiments and kindness, he was trying to make amends for what he had done.

And she remembered the look on his face that morning, before he'd turned and ridden away. *I will not let it affect me in front of others. But see what you have forced me to do.*

Yesterday, he had requested her company for that ridiculous trip to Tattersall's and dinner, as well. Today, he did not seem to be bothered by holding apart from her. She had seen him smiling and chatting to the grooms before they'd set off. The few glimpses she'd got of him, when he'd been close enough to the carriage to see, he'd seemed quite content with both his method of transportation and the pace he'd set for himself.

It was only when he'd turned to her that a cloud had passed over his features. And that, only when there was no one else around who might see. As long as he kept away from her, he seemed his usual cheerful self.

It was possible that by tomorrow, she would not see him at all. He would settle her in his county seat and then disappear from her life. He would have all of the rest of England to be happy in. And she would have whatever ground she trod on to be bitter and miserable, even in the face of comfort that should have made a poor little governess jump for joy.

Without logic, the hurt she caused seemed to rebound on her. After she had lost Richard, she had understood that her chance for true happiness had passed. She would be alone until she died. To pass the years, she would keep busy and do good works. Her life would be solitary, but not empty. She had never imagined herself as abandoned, or avoided, until she had married the duke. But now she could picture her future as a very comfortable void.

They stopped again in midafternoon, in a spot just as green and beautiful as the place where she had taken lunch. At supper, they found an inn where she was rushed to a private sitting room, and offered the best that the humble place could offer. The innkeeper and his daughter were scraping and bowing, as though her presence was their greatest possible honour.

She thought to ask whether they had met the duke. Surely they must have, for it seemed this was a regular stop on the way to the manor and the most logical place to sup.

At mention of her husband, the man grinned as though it were possible to see such a great man as friend, pronouncing him kind, gallant and good-humoured.

His daughter produced what was quite obviously a virginal blush and sighed.

So he was a hero in Aldricshire, as well. It was only she who hated him and only she who had been treated with anything less than total respect.

Once again, there was that strange sensation in her stomach. It was probably just the upset of travel against the child forming in her. She had grown used to blaming any discomfort on the baby. But when she analysed the feelings, she was surprised to find that, after a single day of food and sleep, she felt worlds better than she had.

The troubles she was experiencing now were not digestive. They were emotional. Was it envy of the innkeeper and his daughter? Jealousy that they were so obviously happy with the duke? Was this sadness that she was not part of the happy throng surrounding him? He was uniformly kind to friends, servants and strangers, even from the first moment of their acquaintance. But her interactions with him were permanently tainted. And though he gave the same treatment to her, she knew it was given grudgingly.

She had brooded on this for a time, until eventually they arrived at the manor. It was very nearly full dark and the carriage lamps had been lit for some time. But in expectation of their arrival, servants had lit similar lanterns on posts at the sides of the long drive, so that they would know that they were at last home and welcome to be so.

Home. This massive edifice of grey stone was to be her home, for as long as she remained with the duke. Still, there was no sign of the master of the house.

The coachman helped her down and ordered the unloading of her chests. And, when he thought she would not notice, he stepped to the woman waiting at the doorstep and gave her a quick hug and a kiss. Then he was all business again and she was straightening her housekeeper's apron as though wishing to look pin perfect for the new lady of the house.

Maddie shot a quick, questioning look to her maid.

'They are brother and sister,' Peg whispered back. 'But they see each other so rarely, what with her bound to the house here and him being always in London.'

'Surely Blake drives his Grace when he comes home.' Even if he liked to ride, it made no sense that he would not at least send the carriage down as well when he came to Aldricshire.

'But his Grace does not—' Peg stopped as though

unsure how much it was her business to tell, then decided the news must be harmless. 'His Grace rarely stays in the country. He handles as much of the estate business as he can from London and leaves the rest to Mr Upton, who is his manager.'

'But when Parliament is not in session?' Maddie prompted.

'He stays in London.'

'Even in the heat of summer?'

'Sometimes he goes to Bath,' the maid said and then assured her, 'The rooms he has there are quite the finest ones on the Crescent. I am sure, should he take you, that the house he will choose will be even nicer.'

'And at Christmas?' Maddie glanced at the house, imagining it decked with greens and ablaze with lights.

'He is at some house party or other,' the maid said. 'His friends fight for the chance to host him, for he is most diverting company. Many of them have unattached daughters…' The maid realised that she had spoken too freely, to hint to a new bride what a catch her husband had been. 'He always says it would be quite unfair to Mrs Harker to force her to plan entertainments in a house that has no lady, no matter how eager she is to show the dandies from London what true hospitality might look like.' The maid brightened. 'But that will all be changed now you are here.'

Because she was here. Peg was imagining exotic decorations, laughter, music and full guest rooms. For a moment, Maddie was struck by true terror of the change in her position. Arranging for the bridal breakfast had been a lark and she had taken pleasure in planning the most extreme party imaginable.

But it had created an expectation amongst the *ton*. She would be expected to take the reins of a manor and to dress it lavishly, but in good taste. In six months, she would be great with child, or a new mother, and the house would be stacked to the rafters with friends of St Aldric, all expecting her to be the woman who had charmed a duke with her wit and novelty.

If her husband could be forced into her company at all. Which she was beginning to expect he could not.

Then she heard the distant hoofbeats and the trembling in the earth from an approaching horse coming hell for leather up the drive. The black beast seemed to materialise out of the darkness, covering the last yards at a full gallop, only to be brought to a sudden stop in a scattering of stone chips, just in front of the door.

St Aldric came out of the saddle as easily as he had taken it, as though a day's ride ending in a mad dash had been nothing at all to him. As he came forward, he looked at her in the same disapproving, accusatory way he had been doing before turning to look towards the house.

Then she saw the true reason for his displeasure. This time, his expression did not change to his usual benign smile. He glared up at Aldric House—at turrets and wings, at the majestic stone griffons that flanked the entrance and at the perfection of windows, glittering like oil in the darkness about them—and mere disapproval became loathing.

Perhaps it was a trick of the lantern light. When he stepped closer to the butler, the housekeeper and the rest of the waiting servants, his usual grin returned. It seemed so sincere most times. But it was nothing more than a role he was used to playing. He seemed truly to enjoy the company of his servants, enquiring after their health and their children and agreeing that it was, indeed, a very long time since he had seen them all. When he chanced to look away from their faces and at the house he was to enter, there was a tightness to his smile and a darkness in his blue eyes.

He might like the people and hold a diplomatic dislike for her. But was she the only one to see the truth? He hated every last stone of his family home.

Chapter Seven

He was home.

Or so the servants thought, at least. Michael was in no mood to enjoy their eager greetings and their good humour about the visit. He had been forced into this. It was yet another punishment for the mistake in Dover and for underestimating the damage he had done to the woman at his side.

Perhaps he deserved to suffer. But it was too much to expect him to enjoy it. When they were through the doors, Madeline was given the briefest possible introduction to the assembled staff. Then he announced that they were 'ready to retire'.

He saw her glancing around at the inlaid marble floor of the entry, the paintings, the mirrors and the width and length of corridors that led off to an impressive number of well-appointed receiving rooms. When she saw the extent of her new home, she would gawk at it like a housemaid on a tour of Chatsworth. If he was kind to her, he'd admit that it was a common response. Even the most jaded aristocrats could not manage to be blasé about Aldric House.

Only one who had lived here could learn to hate it.

The worst was yet to come. He turned to the housekeeper. 'I trust the rooms above are prepared for us?'

She smiled sympathetically back at him. 'They have been opened and aired, but are just as they were left, your Grace.'

'I see.' He had done nothing with the floor above since his parents had died. The memories were too painful. In marrying Evelyn or someone like her, he'd hoped that he might have found a woman capable of taking on the job of renovation. But the wife he had chosen, though she seemed to enjoy spending his money, would likely think the arrangement a fitting punishment and refuse to touch a thing.

He stared down at her, not bothering to disguise his feelings for her, or the situation she had landed him in. 'It is late. Please allow me to show you to your chambers.' Then he set out for the first floor, not bothering to see if she followed.

The last thing he wished was to give further evidence of the man who dragged his heels on these trips and avoided his bed, drinking too long in the library and sleeping before the fire then staggering to his bed only when he was too tired to care. She would confuse weakness for debauchery and think it further evidence of his base character.

He had dodged the trip in a closed carriage, the awkward questions, and even more awkward silences.

He had dawdled along the way and been forced to gallop the last miles to avoid arriving so very much later than the new duchess. In truth, the burst of speed at the end had made it easier. The feeling of the wind in his face was like a cold slap, temporarily banishing imagined demons.

Now he continued the speed and heard her laboured breathing. Judging by the cadence of her heels, she had to take two steps for each one of his. 'You do not have to bother, if you do not wish to,' she said, scampering on the mahogany steps as she hurried to catch up. But he refused to slow for her.

'You were the one who was not content in London.' They had reached the upper hall and he wheeled on her, causing her to draw up short and run into his body. Without thinking, he reached to steady her, then damned himself for his weakness and damned himself again for punishing the mother of his child, who must be tired from the ride. Whatever their differences, his feelings for this place were not her fault. Even without her complaints about the town house, he'd have taken her here eventually. One could not avoid one's family seat for ever.

He smiled down at her, hoping that she could feel the irony of it. 'I had thought you would be interested in your new home. It is quite the grandest you are likely to see in all of England, short of the Colton House and the Grand Pavilion.' After her behaviour in London, he expected her to covet it. To put a price tag on it and think of how many gowns the disposal of it might bring her. But there was no disposing of the prime symbol of his dukedom. If it had been possible, he'd have sold the place years ago.

'Of course I am interested,' she said, her voice small. 'But surely the housekeeper might have helped me to my room. You needn't have bothered,' she repeated. Her eyes were large and round in her white face, as though she feared him again and feared being alone above stairs.

He could understand that, at least, even if he could raise no sympathy. 'The housekeeper does not know it as well as I do.' It was only a house to her. Yet each room held a memory to him, especially the suites. 'She may show you the downstairs tomorrow and give you a formal tour of the grounds. But tonight I will show you your sleeping quarters.'

As he watched, she retreated from him, as though she was expecting a cell with a staple for manacles. Did she think this was some sort of prison?

If so, it was not for her.

He gestured to the left wing as they reached the top of the stairs. 'My rooms. You have made it quite clear that you have no interest in them, so a tour is hardly necessary.'

Then he gestured before him to the darkened alcove at the head of the stairs. 'Behind that door is the nursery wing. There is a schoolroom, a playroom, rooms for children and bedrooms for nurse and governess or tutor. I doubt they have been aired. We will not bother with them tonight.'

He had no doubt that the rooms were not just aired, but immaculate. His staff would allow nothing less. If there was a rumour that the new duchess might be *enceinte*, there would be fresh flowers, fires laid and candles lit tonight, so that the young couple could dote on the future.

The thought made him sick. Better to bring a child up in his bachelor's quarters in Bath than to keep the poor thing here. He tested the door to make sure it was properly locked.

He turned from it and gave a casual gesture to his right. 'These are your rooms. Lest you fear otherwise, this is the last time I will pass through this door.' The hall was not precisely gloomy, but it was long enough that the ensconced candles had to struggle to fight back the darkness.

She peered down the corridor as though afraid to advance.

'Which ones?'

'Why, all of them, of course.' It gave him a small, bitter feeling of satisfaction to see the shock on her face. 'If you wished to sleep apart from me, then your wish is granted.' He pushed open doors as he passed them, barely looking at the interiors. 'Rooms for your maids here and here. There is another closer to the bedroom, so that there will be no delay should you wish to summon her at night.'

'Maids?' The plural surprised her. Very good. The shock was satisfying. Let her see what it truly meant to be the Duchess of St Aldric.

She was staring into the tiny rooms as though any one of them would content her.

'The first guest room.' Far from the duchess, his mother had reserved that as a sort of punishment for those swains who had fallen out of favour.

'The box room for the trunks that will hold your wardrobe, when you travel. It saves the time of the servants hauling the things down from the attic whenever you take a whim to go to London.' It had been another guest room, at one time, before his parents had ceased entertaining in a normal way. He could see Madeline wondering at it. Let the question answer itself. They had reached the end of the main hall and he pushed open doors on either side. 'The guest suites, here, here and here. Each has a dressing room with space for a servant's cot, should they wish to keep valets handy.'

'Or maids,' she added, naive creature that she was.

He led her through the guest room on the left, opening a door on the far wall. 'And here is your salon.'

She was staring into the room, slack jawed with amazement. It had been long enough since he'd seen the room that he felt much the same. While the guest rooms had been similar in design to the elegant rooms of his town house, the salon walls were hung with Oriental silks. A large fireplace warmed it. The crystal chandeliers and sconces were fully lit and sparkling. A dining table and chairs took the middle of the room. At the end, there were armchairs, and in a place of honour, a *chaise longue*, covered in the same decadent fabric as the walls. He pushed through another door behind it to show her the dressing rooms and the maid's cot. 'And here is the corridor that leads to your bedroom.'

If the salon had surprised her, the bedroom left her mute with shock. The exotic decor carried into the bedchamber, with thick rugs from Persia and a floor and bed strewn with cushions. Michael had often thanked God that, as a child, he had been barred from the wing. It saved him the pain of imagining his mother in residence here.

Instead, he glanced down at his petite wife and wondered if she understood the meaning of what she was seeing. 'Do you find this sufficiently remote?'

'It's huge.' She could not manage anything else.

'It is yours,' he said, in blunt response to her amazement. 'There are any number of doors between your room and mine. Each one has a lock, with only a single set of keys. You may open or close doors between the guest rooms and yours as you choose and entertain without fear of interruption. Do with it as you will. Take chocolate, or breakfast in bed. Have suppers in the salon. Entertain here any guests you choose, male or female. It does not matter to the staff, any more than it would to me. This is your sanctum: your refuge from the obviously onerous task of being my wife. It is fully equipped so that you needn't come downstairs at all. Now, if you will excuse me...'

He did not wait for an answer. Instead, he exited through the door on the far wall, which led him into another embarrassingly convenient guest suite, and eventually back into the main hall.

Then he went back towards the master wing, disgusted with his own behaviour. It had given him a sort of sick pleasure to see Madeline stunned to silence by the opulence of her surroundings. But in this house, what other kind of pleasure could there ever be but an unhealthy one? With her trunks full of satins, and her horrible screeching birds and sad wastes of horseflesh, she had thought it possible that he could be shamed, or shocked, or even annoyed. What a silly little girl she was.

It was a pity she had not met his mother. The woman had been a master of that game even before little Madeline was born. And that, too, had been in response to a husband who had earned his punishment.

As he passed the nursery wing, his steps dragged a little. Was it still so cold there, as he remembered it? Now was not the time to investigate, if he wanted an untroubled night's sleep. It would be difficult enough to get any rest here without brandy as an anaesthetic.

Crossing the threshold on his side of the house was almost as difficult as coming to the house in the first place. Card rooms, billiards and a smoking room, all quite nice, if a bit gaudy. But they belonged on the ground floor and not tucked in amongst the bedrooms. Then there were the guest rooms. The staff had not bothered with the candles there, knowing how he detested the sight of their tasteless design. He had seen brothels in London with less of a sense of debauchery than the red-velvet hangings and excessive mirrors of his father's guest chambers.

At least his father had not bothered with the labyrinth of connecting rooms. While his mother had pretended to have favourites, his father had felt no embarrassment for the comings and goings from his bed. In fact, he often kept his door open to incite jealousy amongst the ladies who visited him. If one wanted his attention while he was occupied with another, she had but to enter the room and join in the fun.

Michael paused at the last door before his room, remembering the sly smiles of the women he'd seen leaving this wing, the sudden raucous laughter, smothered whispers and the cries of delight. It had been a stark contrast to the dead silence of his mother's side of the house and the equally silent nursery wing.

When he had been old enough to understand, he'd sworn that his life would never come to this. His behaviour would be exemplary. His marriage would be one of mutual respect. His family would be large and happy.

He had failed. For all the trying to be otherwise, he was his father's son. He went into his father's room, slammed the door and rang for brandy.

Chapter Eight

'But, your Grace, it is so lovely that it would be a shame not to try it.'

Maddie glanced at herself in the mirror, shocked at her appearance. Perhaps there was something in the air of this building that changed one to suit the surroundings. If so, they must open the windows and clear the miasma away. She had gone to sleep in a bedroom suited to a harem. Now her maid was trying to force her into a day dress suitable for a sultan's captive.

'Surely there must be something more practical that would serve.' The ladies she had seen in dishabille at the houses where she'd worked had been far more sensible in their dress. And likely they had been warmer. They'd had the sense to keep their bosoms covered. This confection of ruffles and muslin barely covered hers.

'But it is so very French, your Grace. And you look lovely in it.'

'It does not fit,' she argued. Had it been so terribly low when she'd tried it at the modiste's? Or was it just the pregnancy that had increased what the bodice was supposed to hide? Her breasts seemed to float on a tide of lace, ready to bob to the surface at any moment.

'Do not tug on it, your Grace. You will tear the trim. That is how it is meant to look.'

'I seriously doubt so.' In the mirror, she could see the tops of her nipples peeking over the edge of the neckline. The fabric under it was so sheer that even with lining it hid nothing. But to put on stays and petticoat rather defeated the purpose of dressing for morning comfort.

'Perhaps just a touch of rouge,' the maid suggested, glancing at her décolletage.

Maddie did not need rouge to create a flush in her nipples or anywhere else. The idea was completely scandalous and the blush it created was natural.

'It is only to take chocolate in the salon,' her maid prompted. 'No one need ever see.'

She wanted to argue that that alone was reason not to bother with it. But the sumptuousness of her surroundings seemed to call for such behaviour. The memory of the satin coverlet against her cheek and the ridiculously large bed that practically screamed to be sported in...

This was the true danger of her long-ago fall from grace. She knew too much about such things. Although the memory of Richard grew dimmer with each passing day, the sight of her husband's bare flank was etched for ever in memory. She could imagine running her hand along that flesh, the way he might respond to it and the feelings of pleasure that would arise in her to see him aroused.

The room felt unaccountably hot as she thought of it.

The past two weeks had been spent in a panicked rush towards the performance of wedding and breakfast. This morning would be the first uninterrupted quiet she'd had in ages. But that did not mean that she must sit barely dressed on a satin cushion, thinking scandalous thoughts about St Aldric's legs. It would have been more in character to find a book and a quiet spot to enjoy it in.

But that would have required roaming this museum of a house for a library. If the ground floor was anything like the bedrooms, there was no telling what disasters might await her. With its maze of connected rooms, her wing seemed designed to separate her from the rest of the world. Was she to be a prisoner here? Was it a punishment? Or did he truly think that such total privacy was either necessary or welcome?

It was quite beyond comprehension until after some sort of breakfast. She gave up with an exasperated sigh. 'Very well, then. I shall wear the gown. But no rouge,' she said hurriedly. 'And I will keep my wrapper handy, should I take a chill. Bring chocolate and some toast. And an egg or two.' She thought again. 'And some of the condiment that St Aldric recommended.' If nothing else, she must thank the man for the return of her appetite.

'Hallo,' a feminine voice called from the next room. 'Is her Grace receiving?'

'Evelyn?' She reached for her robe, but it was too late. The midwife had already entered.

'So this is where you are hiding.' Mrs Hastings poked her smiling head through the connecting doorway of the first guest suite. 'I am unannounced. And for that, I am sorry. Sam is talking with Michael on the opposite side of the house. But they deemed it inappropriate to entertain me in the duke's bedchamber. So I came to seek you out.'

'And I am deporting myself half-naked, like the Queen of Sheba,' Maddie said glumly.

'In this environment, one can hardly blame you,' Evelyn said with sympathy. 'If it helps you to know it, the downstairs is quite normal.'

'That is a relief. I had not seen it yet and feared the worst. When we arrived, St Aldric escorted me directly to this wing and abandoned me.'

Eve glanced around her at the opulent hangings. 'It is rather much, is it not? The dowager had passed long before my visit to Aldricshire. Michael took me no farther than the dower house and the receiving rooms downstairs. But if this room is any indication, his mother must have been quite colourful.'

'That is a charitable description at best.'

Evelyn admired her costume. 'And I must say that your current attire suits the room well. It is very...'

'Wanton?' Maddie asked, staring down at her own breasts.

'I was going to say feminine,' Evelyn supplied.

'I look like a Cyprian,' she said, tugging at her bodice again.

'I have seen more shocking sights in London, I am sure. It is a very pretty gown. In the privacy of your own home, it will do no harm. And Michael will find it most fetching.'

Michael again. Though Maddie could not manage it, Evelyn had no trouble calling the duke by his Christian name. Michael had brought Evelyn to Aldricshire. And apparently, it had been without her husband. It all sounded very cosy.

'I do not care if my husband appreciates the style,' Maddie said, annoyed. 'He will not find me on a recamier with my gown half falling off.'

Evelyn came to sit at her side and took her hand. 'I did not mean to tease you so. You may change if you like. But I think you are lovely, just as you are.'

'Thank you,' she said with relief. 'But the room is terrible, is it not? I think it is affecting my mood.'

Evelyn nodded in sympathy.

'And you say you have been here before?' She paused for a moment to give Eve a chance to correct her understanding, and added, 'With your husband, of course. He must know the estate well.'

Evelyn paused. 'Actually, he has never seen the place. Nor did he meet his father.' She paused again.

'How much has Michael told you of our history together?'

There was the name again. And the implication that this woman knew much more about her husband than she did herself. Did he mean to keep secrets from her? Or had he not thought it worth the effort to share them? 'Absolutely nothing,' Maddie admitted at last. Then she added, 'You know much more of my past than I do of yours.' Not that there was likely to be anything exceptionable about Evelyn. She seemed the epitome of social grace and decorum.

But Evelyn sighed as though relieved to unburden herself. 'It was not too many months ago that we all assumed I would be the Duchess of St Aldric. I was engaged to Michael. For less than a week,' she added hurriedly. 'But we courted for most of the Season and there was an expectation.'

How horrible. 'And then he...'

Evelyn laughed. 'No, darling. It had nothing to do with you at all.' She sobered and said, in a small voice, 'But I fear that I might have had some part in what occurred in Dover. It was after the broken engagement, you see, that Michael ran amok. It was the illness as well, of course. But it was also about that time that I chose his brother instead of him. And though he claimed that he was not bothered, I worried.'

'Because you had affection for him?'

'As a brother. Nothing more than that.' Evelyn looked relieved to be able to tell the story. 'There was never anyone for me but Sam. I have known him for as long as I can remember and loved him almost as long. But he was far from London and had never met Michael. And when I did...' She gave a helpless shrug and smiled. 'You must see the resemblance. I had to bring the two together. So I cultivated Michael's interest, persuaded Sam to return to London, the two of them were introduced and learned the truth....' She shrugged again. 'It was all a bit of a muddle, for a time. But things worked out for the best. We are quite happy now. And you will be, as well. Despite his behaviour when you met him, Michael truly is a saint amongst men, though he hates to admit. He will be a wonderful father and a husband, as well.'

'And now we are all in Aldricshire together,' Maddie added. Once again, she was the interloper, just as she had been in London.

'Sam is the duke's personal physician,' Eve explained. 'Not that his services are required, of course. Michael is as healthy as an ox. But we will admit to some curiosity about the house and grounds. Sam knows practically nothing of his father. And Michael rarely speaks of his childhood and visits the house even less so.' Evelyn smiled and laid a finger on the side of her nose. 'So I proclaimed it my professional opinion that you could not possibly manage without a midwife, so that we might use your strategic retreat to the country to investigate. I hope you do not mind.'

It was too late to object, even if she did. 'Of course not. But I know little about the place myself and I am not sure where best to put you.'

'It is all arranged,' Evelyn assured her. 'Michael suggested the dower house and it is quite suitable for our needs. It is small and utterly charming, tastefully decorated and far enough away so that you might have the privacy you need.'

Evelyn seemed to imagine a happy honeymoon already in progress. It was just another sign of the woman's optimism. 'We have too much privacy already. This whole wing is mine to command. The duke has space of his own on the opposite side of the house.'

By the worried look on Evelyn's face, the arrangement was as odd as it appeared. 'The estrangement between the last duke and duchess must have been more deep than Michael let on. Sam was born shortly after Michael. The duke never acknowledged him. The duchess was upset. This—' she waved a hand to encompass the house '—must have been the result.'

And now the new duke had married a near stranger who had requested a divide between them as deep or deeper than any his parents had known. The experience must be quite painful for him.

But had that not been the object all along? If she meant to hurt him, she had succeeded in making him come here. But strangely, there was no joy in it.

'It must have been difficult for him,' Maddie said cautiously. 'He does not seem to like the place at all. If mine are any indication, I cannot imagine what his rooms must look like.'

'So Michael is sequestered on the other side of the

house and you have not seen his rooms?' Eve raised her eyebrows.

'We have only just arrived,' Maddie said hurriedly, not wanting the situation to sound any more unusual than it already was.

'Well, I am aflame with curiosity. I will torment Sam mercilessly until he has uncovered every last detail. Then I shall share them with you.'

'Please, don't.' Even in war, there must be some rules. And if anything were hallowed ground, it should be childhood.

'It is all right, I am sure,' Evelyn announced, paying no attention. 'If he thought to marry me, he must have known that I would learn all his secrets.'

'As if I could manage to keep anything from you, Evelyn. You are a terrible nuisance and I am lucky to be rid of you.' The duke entered, his tone affectionate and his attention focused on his former fiancée.

Then he froze in the doorway, shocked to immobility. He was staring at Maddie, half-clothed and reclining, just as she had feared he would. His gaze was riveted to the neckline of her gown and the non-existent coverage it provided her modesty. His blue eyes were practically black. His breathing was slow, deep and, without thinking, hers slowed to match it. The air between them seemed to crackle with tension. Her nipples tightened as though presenting themselves to be kissed.

Deep inside, she felt a trembling, like the rush of water, and the growing desire to relax into it, lean back onto the chaise and show him that the skirt was as thin as the bodice. The muslin would caress her legs and reveal their curves to him. And he would smile and send Evelyn away.

Beside her, she heard Evelyn giggle. Then the duke broke his gaze and turned to speak to someone in the hall behind him.

Sam Hastings. Evelyn would not be laughing if her own husband entered the room to find her in this condition. The man was a physician. But that did not mean she wished to be displayed before him like an anatomy lesson. Maddie grabbed for the blue wool wrapper and shrugged into it, pulling it tight over breasts and thighs to hide her shame.

'And here you both are at last,' Evelyn said, ignoring her scramble for decency. 'Michael, you must take us all through the public rooms. The tour you gave me last year was most interesting. Maddie must be eager to see her new home.'

'I am sure she is,' St Aldric said. He was staring carefully into her eyes, as though the interlude a moment ago had never happened.

'Well, she must not set out without a guide,' Sam announced, entering the room, oblivious to what had just occurred. 'If the rest of the house is as confusing as this wing, we shan't see her again if we leave her to find her own way.'

'I am sure she will be fine. Now, come along, the pair of you.' Eve rose and took them both by the arms. 'Take me to the breakfast room, for I am simply famished. Maddie will meet us there directly, when she has dressed.'

As they left, Peg appeared with the forgotten eggs and toast.

Maddie waved it away. 'It seems we are breakfasting below, with the Hastings. Find me a gown I can wear without creating a scandal. Then, for God's sake, find me someone who can show me to the breakfast room.'

After they had eaten, Michael led the little group through the ground floor, reciting what he knew of art and architecture by rote and watching their reactions. They were properly impressed. Madeline, particularly, was in awe. Her soft lips parted in a continual 'oh' of surprise. It was a pity that she had changed the gown, for the thought of those perfect breasts rising and falling with each 'ooh' and 'aah' would have been a beautiful sight.

The appearance of her, careless of her beauty and displayed for him like an Aphrodite in that horrible salon, would cause him many restless nights, he was sure. Judging by the dress she had chosen to replace it, overly heavy, overly drab and covering her practically to the chin, there would be no repeat appearance of the goddess once the guests had gone. It was a pity. For all their difficulties, he could not deny that she was the most human thing in this mausoleum he had inherited and the most beautiful.

For now he contented himself with casting sidelong glances at her and watching her amazement at each new glory: inlaid floors, carpets as thick as fur upon them, white marble fireplaces scrubbed so clean they might never have held an ash, crystal, china and gold. At least there was something she admired about him. If she had meant to spend his purse to empty, she must see how impossible that would be. Mother had tried it upon Father, without success. Madeline would have no better luck with him.

The supper that cook prepared for them was a fitting ending to the day: the best food on the thinnest plates, with the heaviest knives and the whitest linen. And, as he had requested, a tureen of Wow-Wow sauce. Cook had been quietly horrified, thinking it was a reflection on her seasoning. Then he'd made it clear that it was for the duchess, whose digestion, of late, had been delicate. Cook had smiled knowingly and prepared the sauce.

There would be gossip below stairs. But for a change, it would be happy gossip.

Tonight, Evelyn was making enough conversation for the four of them. Michael sometimes found her outspoken nature more annoying than endearing. But it was better than the uneasy silence that he'd have had to endure, had he eaten alone with Madeline.

'I am sure Maddie particularly enjoyed the music room,' Evelyn announced.

'Of course,' he said, wondering if his wife had some talent in that area. He ventured a guess at what might have caught her fancy. 'The harp is particularly lovely. It has been in the family for three generations.'

'The school did not have a harp,' Eve informed him. 'But she is quite proficient on the pianoforte.'

Madeline remained silent.

Was this meant as some sort of hint as to her past? 'You taught it, at this school?' he offered.

'I took lessons,' Madeline replied, still looking down at her plate. 'When I was a student. Before taking work as a governess.'

The conversation was faltering and Evelyn rushed to rescue it. 'It is a shame that the Colvers could not come to the wedding breakfast. I am sure they would have been most proud to see you so well settled.'

Who were these people and how was he expected to know them? He had known his wife only a few weeks and had learned nothing about her past. But in that time, Eve seemed to have gathered a wealth of information.

'I did not think it necessary to inform them. I have not seen them in years,' Madeline said, still not looking up.

Perhaps she had thought he would not allow common folk in his house. If so, it was unfair of her. What difference would a few more guests have made to that bird-infested farce of a breakfast? 'If there was family that you wished to have, we could have arranged it,' he said as patiently as possible.

Madeline raised her eyes and gave him a pointed look. 'They were not my family. They were the people that my true parents paid to keep me until I was old enough to board. Then they washed their hands of me. If they should hear of my rise in station, they will likely appear. But I see no reason to seek them out.'

'Then you are...'

'A bastard,' she informed him.

Why had he even begun the sentence? It was beyond tactless to discuss her parentage at dinner. It displayed his total ignorance of Madeline's past and her feelings about it.

Eve was nodding in satisfaction, as though she had scored a point in a game. If they were playing, she could at least have shared the rules with the rest of them.

Sam seemed very busy with his roasted potatoes and oblivious of the conversation, but then he found it amusing to let his wife run wild and torment the rest of them. Michael ground his teeth and struggled to maintain his composure.

Now that Eve had finished with Madeline, she turned the conversation, indirectly, to Michael.

'As I was saying, the tour of the house was delightful. Especially the bedrooms. They are quite unique. But I based my opinion on the duchess's wing only.' She glanced at her husband. 'I take it Michael showed you his rooms, Sam?'

When addressed directly, Sam could not ignore her. So he nodded and took a large bite of meat, chewing slowly so that he could not answer.

'Well? What were they like?' Evelyn leaned forward to hear the answer.

The doctor swallowed. 'They were...' Sam glanced at Michael, as if wishing to spare him pain.

'As ghastly as the duchess wing?' Eve supplied.

'A bit much to take,' Sam said diplomatically.

'Details please, Dr Hastings,' she said with the impish smile that Michael had found rather irritating when he'd courted her. 'You are a man of science. Do not make diagnoses using such vague words. How did you find the duke's wing?'

'Evelyn.' Michael smothered the anger he was feeling and kept his tone low and cautionary.

Sam gave him another apologetic look, then replied. 'It was a cross between a gaming hell and a house of ill fame.'

'So it was a fitting contrast to the seraglio on the other side of the house.'

Michael threw his napkin aside. 'That is quite enough, the both of you. You come into my house and defame my family—'

'Our family,' Evelyn corrected.

'I beg your pardon?'

'We are in your house because you invited us here. You have encouraged us for some months to treat your properties as our own. Sam is your brother. I am your sister-in-law.' She glanced across the table. 'And Maddie is your wife. Soon, she will be the mother of your child. We are your family, Michael. If there is a burden to bear, who better than us to share it with you?'

'It is not a burden,' he insisted. But if it had not been, why did his heart feel easier now that others had seen it?

'It is an unnecessary secret to the people at this table,' Eve said. 'It is obvious changes will need to be made if you wish to reside here. You could have informed Madeline of the fact rather than dropping her into the middle of it.' Then she turned to Madeline. 'And you, Maddie, might have explained your past to Michael to prevent embarrassment later. Illegitimacy need not be a shameful thing. But openness between the two of you would have prevented the awkward exchange I orchestrated tonight.'

'We hardly know each other,' Madeline argued.

'But you will have a child between you. And while you might go your separate ways later, it is less shocking to claim ignorance of the present behaviour of a spouse than to know nothing of their past.'

Michael glared at her. 'I suppose you mean to give us no peace until you are sure every stone has been turned up and we have no privacy at all?'

Sam sighed, pushing aside his plate. 'I suspect that is true. The woman is relentless, your Grace. I have not had a moment's peace since I married her.'

'And you have never been happier,' Eve informed him.

'Yes, Evie,' he said, and shrugged in defeat. But Michael could tell by the glint in his eye that he was secretly amused. 'Now, if you will excuse us, Michael, I think we will forgo pudding and port and make our

way back to the dower house. It is a short walk, but
the weather appears to be changing and I do not wish
to be caught out in the rain.'

'Very well.' Michael stood and, with his wife, they
escorted their guests to the door.

When the other couple had departed, a moment of
silence fell between them, as he searched for words.
'I am sorry,' he said. 'For Evelyn.'

'Evelyn is—' Madeline smiled. 'Evelyn is Evelyn.
She cannot help but meddle, I think.'

'I am sorry for my own behaviour, as well,' he
added. 'I was rude and neglectful of you. I should
have asked after your family and your past.'

'There was very little time,' she said, staring out
the window over the dark grounds.

'I should have made the time.' Eve had been right.
Even if this was not a love match, there should be respect and courtesy on his part. 'There is another wing
to view, you know, other than the bedrooms.'

'The nursery?' If she was curious, it did not show.

'Come. We will tour it, then we can retire.' Behind
locked doors on opposite ends of the house. No matter how he tried, life here had not changed so very
much. But if it was necessary to share secrets with
one's wife, the last of them were there.

Chapter Nine

They mounted the stairs and he fished in his pocket for the key. The lock on the door to this wing was unusually heavy. Judging by the slight scratches in the wood and the shininess of the brass compared to the other doors, it was more recently installed. What could be here that needed to be so tightly contained?

'I keep my slaughtered brides in the last room, if that is what you are wondering,' he said with a sigh.

Despite herself, she started.

He sighed again. 'I am not actually Bluebeard, if that is what you suspect. It is just a nursery, as I said yesterday. I keep it locked because...I had no need of it.'

But the strange pause told her there was more to the story.

He had found the correct key, and it turned smoothly in the lock. It was well oiled, as were the hinges of the door. When he crossed the threshold, he shivered. 'It is good that you are dressed warmly.

There is sometimes a chill in this corridor. We will not linger long here.'

It was an odd statement. In a wool coat, he should be warmer than she. Yet she felt no change in temperature. He had taken a taper from the hall and lit candles as they went, opening doors and explaining the rooms and their purposes.

If he had sought her professional opinion as a woman who had seen more than the usual share of nurseries, this one was every bit as splendid as the ground-floor rooms had been. There was none of the ridiculous ostentation of the duchess wing, nor the maze of interconnected rooms. The nursery wing was laid out quite sensibly. The main room was more pleasant than any she had worked in. In daytime, light would shine through the mullioned windows. She was sure, when she opened them, she would feel a fresh breeze and hear the faint sound of the river a few miles away.

The room would serve as a sitting room for the children and their teacher. She could see the varying doors leading from it lead to a schoolroom, a suite of bedrooms for older children and a proper nursery with cradle for little ones. The last door she opened led to a bedroom and sitting room for the governess.

She could not help the little thrill of satisfaction she felt at the sight of it. It was well appointed and cheerful, and much nicer than anything she might have expected from her last posting. This was the sort of place that suited her, not the grand room of a duchess.

She fought to control the smile as she turned back to him. She was not brought here to tend the children. He would think her quite mad if she requested to move her things to this bedroom. No matter how preferable it might be, it was not meant for her.

The duke stood, his back to her, staring out the window into the darkness. Lightning flashed in the distance and the first streaks of rain marred the glass. 'As you can see, it is quite grim here. I would be obliged if you devoted some portion of your time to have it properly equipped for the child. You have some professional knowledge of such places after all.'

'Grim?' she said, surprised. That was the last word she'd have used for the shelves of books and the cupboard that must be full of playthings.

He nodded, still not turning. 'I have not been here in quite some time. I had hoped it had changed. But unfortunately, no. This room is exactly as I remember it. Strip it to the bare walls and start again.'

She had thought to spend his money like water out of spite. But every fibre in her resisted making changes to a setting so perfect for the raising of children. She imagined her own child here and felt the little stirrings of excitement in her heart at the thought of a baby of her own. It would be St Aldric's child, of course. And he would be possessive of the heir and the law was quite clear on his ownership.

But by nourishing it with her heart's blood, and keeping it safe in her belly, it was hers, as well. Despite what Eve had said in the dining room. It would be her first true family.

But this room called to hold a large and happy brood, not just the only baby they were to have together.

'So much space for one child.' She imagined the neat rows of beds in the school that had housed her. She'd had not a moment's peace until she'd left it. She had longed for privacy. But as the only child in this monstrous house, he would have been lonely. She felt an unbidden sympathy for the man.

He did not turn. 'There were nurses, of course. Teachers. A governess or two.'

'Did you enjoy their company?' The children she'd watched had grown quite fond of her.

'Father chose them and discarded them according to their education and my needs.' He described them as though they were so many possessions. But for a twist of fate, he might have thought the same of her.

She turned to the cupboard to see what it was that the young marquis had entertained himself with. The shelves were surprisingly empty. She had expected blocks, puzzles, balls and lead soldiers. Instead she saw row upon row of carefully aligned models. She took one up: a tiny sheep with real wool and four dark legs that were little more than twists of wire. Behind it was a fishing boat with full crew and nets made of thread full of tiny lead fish. After that came houses, farms, shops and mats of straw painted like water, crops and roads.

'This was yours?' It was surprising. Knowing children as she did, she'd never have trusted them with something so delicate and so obviously valuable.

'And my father's before me.' He had come to stand beside her, taking up a tiny farmer and turning it in his hands. 'Each little figure was modelled on an actual tenant. The houses you see here in miniature still stand on the roads.'

'You played with real people?' It was strange and barbaric to think of a little boy playing God over this tiny world.

'Of course not.' He shuddered again and placed the figure carefully on the shelf. 'I learned from them. I knew names, places, each brick in the road and each sheep in the field.'

'If they broke, were you punished for it?'

'They did not break,' he said. 'I saw to that. If they were damaged, I mended them. If they wanted paint, I took up the brush and did it myself. They are as clean and perfect as the day they were made.'

But he did not seem happy about it. His usual, somewhat artificial, smile had become something much more grim.

'Will your son play with them, as well?'

He hesitated. And since he rarely did, the pause was profound. 'It is an excellent way to learn one's holdings.'

'But it is a great responsibility for a small child.' She picked up the sheep again and touched one of the legs, giving it a gentle push with her fingertip, seeing the wire bend.

The man beside her was holding his breath. She was sure, if she went so far as to break the little animal, he would feel his own leg snap.

She released the pressure and set it gently back on the shelf. 'It is very interesting. But I see no reason to keep the wing locked. Or to have a lock on the door at all. Why did you bother to seal it up?'

'Why did I install a lock?' He laughed. 'My parents did that when I was still young to keep me from roaming the house.'

'Your parents locked you in.' The idea was unfathomable. She had been in strict households, of course. And dealt with undisciplined children. But never had there been the need to keep them prisoner. It was beyond imaging that the little boy who had cared for toy people as though they were real could cause enough trouble to need a lock on his door.

'I was too curious,' he said with a shrug. 'My parents had little time for me. I had the run of the house and grounds when they were in London. But when they were here, they retired to their wings with their friends and did not wish to be bothered.' He reached to straighten one of the toy buildings and returned the sheep she had examined to what must have been its proper place.

'Sam was concerned that his birth had caused the estrangement between them,' he said, 'but I am sure it was far deeper than that. It was my birth that gave them the excuse to lead separate lives. Once they had an heir, they did not need each other.'

Apparently they had not needed him either. 'It must have been very lonely for you to be shut up here, away from everything.'

'I thought so, at first,' he said. 'Until they locked the door, I would creep about the house at night, trying to discover what it was that so fascinated them.'

'And what did you find?' She could guess the answer.

'Not my parents, that is for certain. My mother kept her doors locked, long before they closed up the nursery. But my father's wing was open. And there was a woman there who offered to explain everything to me.' He shut the cupboard door, but did not look at her as he spoke. 'I suspect she was angry at having to share my father's attentions. Or perhaps she was jealous that her husband was with my mother. She said she would show me everything. So I followed her into one of the bedrooms and had my answer.'

'While you were still in the nursery?' Surely he would have gone away to school when he was old enough. But that meant he was... 'Just how old were you?'

'I don't remember,' he said firmly, as though he did not like to look too closely at the past. 'But not more than twelve. She said there would be cake after.' He smiled, as though it were a joke. 'I remember it was a deciding factor.' He paused. 'To this day, I cannot abide sweets. And I cannot stand this house. But perhaps now you understand how I came to be the sort of man who might attack governesses. For all I know, it is a family trait. Now, if you will excuse me, I am tired.' He fished in his pocket and handed her the keys to the nursery. 'Put out the candles and lock the door when you leave.'

Then he turned and left her in the most silent wing of the house.

Chapter Ten

The storm that had been just a threat during supper had finally broken and was hammering the windows. Maddie slid down under the covers, waiting for it to end. It was unusual that rain bothered her. When dealing with children, it had been her job to provide the comfort. But this house was so very strange. She had been too tired to notice it last night. But tonight, after talking to the duke, she felt it in her bones. To be the only person in a wing made her feel all the more isolated.

And to do that to a child...

Even with governesses and teachers and nurses, and the fact that the surroundings were far from appropriate, a child would want to see his parents. It sometimes seemed that the less interested the parents were, the more the little ones craved attention. They must have thought they were protecting him by keeping him isolated. It had come too late, of course. The story he'd told had been quite horrible. He had been far too young to understand what was happening to him.

When she had come to London, St Aldric had seemed so far beyond the reach of ordinary humans that she could hardly comprehend. The world bowed to his title and thought him a saint. And in her mind, he had been by parts a villain and a sham.

She had never expected to find him so human once all artifice had been stripped away. To see the house, and his reaction to it, she could imagine the frightened little boy he had been. His parents had not known what to do with him and had locked him away. And so he had retreated into his toy fiefdom to become the man his father had not been.

He had been wrong. The nursery had been warm enough. But the bed she was lying in was large and cold, and she hated it. If she stayed here, was she destined to become as his mother had been, entertaining favourites in secret and keeping her child behind a locked door? At one time, she might have thought it a fit punishment for St Aldric. But no matter the past, she would not stoop so low. Whatever else she might say of him, the duke did not want to turn his back on his offspring as his parents had done to him. Or as hers had done to her.

There was much that she did not understand about the Duke of St Aldric. But she was sure of one thing: he had been lonely here. Likely, he still was. A person with many true friends did not need to be as polite and guarded as he had become. At supper tonight, Evelyn had needed to remind him that he had any family at all. If this was how he behaved with those nearest and dearest to him, she doubted that anyone in England was acquainted with the real Michael Poole hiding behind the saintly title.

He had no one and neither did she.

If Madeline understood anything, it was loneliness. And tonight she did not want to be alone. Though they were joined in matrimony, they were separated by class, by circumstance and by the width of this enormous house. Perhaps they were too different to be one in spirit. But there was another, very physical way to ease the pain of isolation.

She had meant to keep apart from St Aldric, fearing him and her uncontrollable response to him in Dover. But why? She was no longer some shy governess protecting what was left of her reputation. She had survived ruin not just once but twice. And while chastity might be sensible for a spinster, in a married woman it was unnatural.

She could remember the way the duke had looked at her this morning when he had surprised her in the salon. He had wanted her. And her body had responded. The feeling was still there, and building in her. Her breasts were tender with it. Her body throbbed. Her mind was alert to the presence of him, lying alone somewhere on the other side of the house.

Lightning flashed again, with thunder following close upon it. It gave her a brief view of gold tassels and silk draperies, etched in sharp relief before the darkness came again. It was a crime to find such ugliness in a house that should be so beautiful. And judging by Sam's description, the duke's room was no better.

Perhaps St Aldric had told the truth when he said he had changed for the better. He seemed a different man from the one she had met in the inn. But he was different from the one she had married in London, as well. His quick wit and false smile failed him here. He was unhappy. He was vulnerable. And she was no longer afraid of him.

She pulled her nightgown over her head and dropped it, ignored her sensible robe and pulled the sheet from her bed, wrapping it around her body to keep away the chill.

Then she took the winding way through her suite to the main hall and the door at the end of it. A few more steps and she was standing at the door to his wing. It would not be locked, she was sure. He'd had enough of locked doors. She was right. The knob turned without resistance, and the hinges were as silent as the nursery door.

Beyond it, the hall was dark but for a pair of sconces at the end. It was a relief, for she was sure she did not want to see the details. It was enough to know that the rugs muffled her footsteps and the mirrors on the walls showed her the golden glow of candlelight on her own flesh. She reached out to trace her fingers along the wall and touched not paper, but velvet. Thick fabric curtains deadened sound and concealed

God knew what sins. There was a heaviness in the air, as well. Incense? Tobacco? Or was it opium? It made her feel light-headed. Perhaps that was just nerves.

Unlike her own wing, there was a door at the very end of this hall. It was the logical place for the master's room. Her hand paused on that doorknob for a moment, then turned it and pushed the door open. She went through, closing it behind her, and was plunged into immediate darkness.

But she did not need sight to know that she had found him. While the hall might smell of sin, this room smelled of him. Cologne and musk, brandy and tobacco. She had noticed it earlier as they'd stood together in the nursery. There it had been reassuring. Now her body gave an answering shudder as it sensed he was near.

The fire had died in the grate, but another flash of lightning showed her the figure on the bed. He was lying on his back, a hand across his eyes. The sheet that should have covered him was tossed aside, revealing his naked body to her for the first time. The light was gone again. But she did not need it to remember what she had seen. The strong limbs, the broad shoulders and chest tapering to a narrow waist and the powerful manhood that would wake to her touch.

She surrendered to her desire and climbed into his bed.

He woke with a start and tried to sit up.

She pushed him back down with a hand on the middle of his bare chest and he relaxed as he recognised her, waiting for her to speak. 'You said I could have what I wanted,' she said. 'And tonight, I want this.' Then she reached between his legs and stroked him once, from root to tip.

The body that had been sleeping came instantly alive and she felt another answering shudder inside of her as she coaxed him to full erection.

For a moment, he seemed too shocked to move. Then his hand closed over hers, stroking once with it before pulling it away to twine his fingers with hers. He pulled her forward onto his body so that she could lie atop him, chest to breast and leg over leg.

And when their lips met, she knew she had been right in coming here. The kiss was gentle, but only for a moment. Then it dissolved into a thing of mutual hunger, open mouthed and desperate. Had she forgotten so much? Or had she never been kissed like this? His lips were sweet and she could not get enough of them. His tongue delved deep and then swirled against her lips before he withdrew to suck and bite his way down her neck to her breast.

Nothing had ever felt this good. They had barely begun and she could already feel the first tremors of orgasm. But before she was finished, she wanted to touch every inch of him and feel him moving inside her.

She pulled away from him and he moaned at the loss, reaching for her to bring her close again. She laughed and batted his hands away, then dipped her fingers in the moisture pooling between her own legs and spread it on him. And then she rose up on her knees and teased herself with the tip of him, spreading herself, working him against the little nub there for a moment before sliding down to sheathe him with her body.

There was another bolt of lightning and she saw him smile. Perhaps it was the stark-white light that seemed to change his features, but the look on his face was different from his drawing room expression. He was staring up at her with pure, unguarded joy. Even if it only lasted for a moment, she was lying with the man and not the title. Her body responded with a shudder of delight.

The storm broke as they moved together, accompanied by the rumble of thunder. Flashes of brilliant white light gave her brief glimpses of his arched throat and his hands reaching for her, just before they settled between her legs. His fingers spanned the crease at the top of her thighs and his thumbs joined to rub circles against her.

As his tempo increased, her control slipped and she leaned forward, grasped his biceps and thrust against him, faster and faster, crying out as she felt him spend himself inside of her, letting it carry her over the edge.

She collapsed against him, exhausted. He pulled her close, burying his face in her hair and brushing the loose strands of it together with his hands. Neither of them spoke and she was glad of it. She did not want to explain to him why she was with him. She was not sure she had an answer for it. She only knew that it been good. The storm was passing. She was at peace now and he was beginning to doze, so she kissed him one last time upon the forehead and fumbled for the sheet. She wrapped it around her body and crept back down the hall to her own room and bed.

What had just happened?

Michael lay flat on the mattress just as she had left him, trying to analyse the situation. He was cold. His bed sheet was missing. It was proof that what he'd experienced was not just some erotic dream.

When he stumbled across the room to stoke the fire, he found the sheet she had been wearing when she'd come to him. It smelled of perfume and musk. He gathered it to his face and inhaled deeply before taking it back to bed.

The day had been full of unexpected events. The arrival of the Hastingses had given him the chance to explain some of the more embarrassing family history to Sam. His brother had taken the news as he took all surprises, with the calm measured response of a physician. It had put Michael at ease.

And then to find Madeline wearing that gown... Common sense should have made him insist that she cover herself in the presence of guests. Instead, his mouth had watered at the sight of her. Her breasts were full, ripe and barely covered. He had wanted nothing more in that moment than to send the guests away, lean her back on the chaise and bury his face in them. He had not wanted to acknowledge an attraction for her, but it was there. And it was growing stronger.

Had she known what his response would be? Did she come to him because she felt something, as well? Or was this meant as some new torture?

Perhaps he had married a succubus. She had taken something from him, and it was more than just a bed sheet. It felt as though some substantial part of him had gone missing after the brief exchange between them. If the soul had been a corporeal thing, something that he could lay hands upon and test for soundness, he'd have done it now. Had she stolen it?

He thought not. He was lighter, but in no way incomplete. He felt drained, but giddy. If he looked into the mirror, he would likely be smiling. If she was trying to hurt him, then she truly did not understand men. It had been the excitement of an anonymous encounter that had got him into this situation. And he had thought those days were behind him.

It had never occurred to him that one might find such bliss with one's own wife. They might not find common ground in daylight, but the occasional erotic encounter in the night would be most welcome. Sam had hinted that some women, when with child, were taken with hysteria that might manifest in this way. He had said that there was no real harm in it. But the advantages were obvious. The only disadvantage Michael could imagine was the chance that, once the child was born, this desire would be a distant memory to her and they would be strangers for the full four-and-twenty hours of the day.

He sobered suddenly. If his life had gone just a hair differently, if he had not taken sick, or at least remained sober in Dover, he might have found a companion for both days and nights.

Then he set the thought aside. He knew little of marriage and even less of love. He had seen successful examples of neither, other than through Sam and Evelyn. But he did understand physical satisfaction, and he had achieved that tonight. He closed his eyes, laid his cheek against the perfumed sheet and slept.

Chapter Eleven

Maddie awoke the next morning with a strange contentment. The bed, which had seemed large and intimidating the night before, was warm and cosy, even though it was empty. It was still too quiet, of course. She wished that the duke occupied a room in this wing so that she might hear the sounds of another human being waking nearby. There should be servants talking, doors opening and closing and perhaps a laugh or a cough.

She buried her face in the sheet she had taken from his room, catching a whiff of his scent. She was not alone. When she had set out on her adventure the previous night, she'd given no thought to what the morrow might bring. But what was she to do now?

Peg was laying out the same dress she'd chosen yesterday, still hoping that Maddie would agree to it. And part of her did. Today, if the duke came to her wing and saw her in it, things might be quite different.

But Sam and Evelyn might arrive again and embarrass her. She waved the gown away and requested something with a higher neck, but without the prudish modesty of the one she'd changed to yesterday. She had not thought herself vain, but she spent an unusual amount of time admiring it in the mirror before declaring it suitable. She wanted to be sure that the colour flattered her and that the bodice showed enough of her blossoming body to attract, but not so much as to give offence.

Only then did she allow Peg to begin upon her hair. In the past, a centre part and a few pins had been enough. But today, she wondered whether curls might not be needed to add softness around her face.

Was she stalling? Or did she seriously want to look her best before meeting the man whose bed she had shared last night?

Either way, Maddie's heart was pounding by the time she walked down to the breakfast room and came face-to-face with the duke.

He smiled as she entered the room, but he always did, even when he was not glad to see her. It was not last night's smile. This was the same sort that he gave to Evelyn. Not exactly insincere, but common. 'Eggs?' he asked. Without waiting for an answer, he took the dish and filled her plate, then pushed the sauce dish in her direction, as well.

'Thank you.' Her response was as empty as his offer. Did he have nothing to say other than to offer her food?

'You're most welcome.' Was that a hint of a real smile she saw on his face? But it was gone, replaced by the same detached look he often used when speaking to her. Perhaps he remained guarded because they would be denied privacy.

'Will we be seeing Doctor and Mrs Hastings for breakfast this morning?'

The duke shook his head. 'Eve sent a message stating that they would be visiting patients in the area and would not arrive until supper, if then.'

'They are very dedicated to their work,' Maddie said, thinking that perhaps it might have been better that they not be so. Their devotion to medicine meant she would be alone with the duke.

'Indeed they are. That was quite a storm we had last evening,' he added. It was another benign comment.

'I hadn't noticed,' she lied.

'It has been some time since I've visited here,' he added. 'But I do not remember the weather being so volatile.'

If he was referring to her behaviour in bed, he could at least say so directly. She did not wish to be hinted at or handled. She had rather liked the man last night who had been both figuratively and literally naked with her.

But that man was gone and the Duke of St Aldric had returned, bringing all of his empty courtesy with him.

'That is probably because you spent so much time

in the nursery,' she snapped. 'I expect the view was quite different from there.'

It was wrong of her to strike in so vulnerable a spot. But it was very effective. At the mention of the nursery, his smile disappeared, replaced by something much more like a grimace. 'I did not take you to that wing so you could admire the view,' he said. 'I had hoped you would use your expertise as a former governess to suggest improvements to it. Now that you have had a few hours to think about it, what are your recommendations?'

So he wanted her expertise as a governess, did he? If that was all he wanted, then it was all he would have from her in the future. She looked him squarely in the eye, using the expression she saved for naughty children. 'You wish me to do what I can to make this place less grim for your heir? Then I will open the door to the hall, but nail the cabinet shut with your little toy people inside, until such a time as the child is old enough to understand the responsibilities he is to inherit. And then I will purchase some normal playthings.'

Apparently he had been hoping that she might suggest a cheery paint colour or a new rug. The bluntness of her actual recommendation wiped all expression from the duke's face.

Before he could speak, she continued, 'You asked for my help. I gave it. While you might understand the care and cutting of each blade of grass in your little kingdom, the land I am used to ruling is much smaller.

I know of children and the proper care of them. And I tell you that your perfectly preserved miniatures are not a toy so much as a source of terror.'

'They are necessary to teach the value of the holdings,' the duke said firmly.

'But keeping them spotless and unbroken for generations is unnatural,' she said. 'No one can go from birth to death without a little damage. It is nothing to fear. Children often learn from mistakes. If they are never allowed to make them, they have problems later in life.'

'I have made mistakes,' he said. 'You know I have, for you never tire of pointing them out.' He rose and threw his napkin onto the table. Then he departed the room with a slam of the door.

That was not what I meant.

For once, she had not intended to call him to task over Dover. Her concern was for the future, not the past, and the very real fear that their child might be tasked with the same impossible mission of maintaining his father's sainthood.

St Aldric was not infallible, any more than she. And after last night, she much preferred the real man to the facade. She might even be able to make a future with him, if she ever saw him again after this morning's argument.

When she had finished her breakfast, she'd almost worked up the nerve to go to him to try to explain. But by then he had sequestered himself in the study with Upton, the estate manager, and a line of tenants was forming in the front hall, readying themselves for a long-delayed audience with the duke.

At some point, she might have to face the crowd, as well. They would want to meet the duchess and to gawk at her as though she was the bear caged in the Tower of London. With this marriage, she had become a curiosity to be displayed for the masses.

But she could not manage it today. Not when she could still remember the rows of tiny people locked away in the nursery and worry that she might meet someone who had a passing resemblance to one of them. The thought gave her chills.

She turned away from the study and the front of the house to the French doors leading into the back gardens. If the London town house had been impressive, Aldric House was magnificent and the grounds around it were a reflection of that perfection. Walkways of crushed white stone and boxwood hedges separated the rose garden from the kitchen garden. Last night's rain was drying on the grass and the air was full of the smells of summer.

Best of all, it was natural, wholesome and real. The flower beds might be carefully tended, but they lacked the fearsome design of the bedrooms, or the aloof dignity of the ground-floor rooms. The plants here were well established and growing together like welcoming old friends. She wandered down the rows between them, which led her to the back of the house, and the stables.

She would not linger there for long. She had not grown any fonder of horses in the few days that had passed since her visit to Tattersall's. But as she passed one of the paddocks, she saw the animal a groom was leading towards the freshest green grass in the field.

'Buttercup?'

The horse did not answer to a name it had only heard once. But the sound of Maddie's voice made the big head swing in her direction, as though the nag was trying to remember why that particular sound seemed familiar.

'Aye, your Grace,' the groom said with a bow. 'That is what his Grace calls it.' The man said *it* as though he felt the word *horse* might not be appropriate. 'It is a sad thing, to be sure. But his Grace seemed to think that it was important to have it—who am I to question him?'

If she had saved it from the knackers, then it made sense to keep it with the other cattle. But that did not explain its presences in Aldricshire. 'I know this horse was in London just a few days ago,' Maddie said. 'Surely she did not walk all the way here.' At the time of purchase, she would have doubted that the beast could manage the trip from the auction to St Aldric's London stables. Yet here she was, forty miles away and as close to healthy as she was likely to be.

'No, your Grace. His Grace thought that the country air would be better for her old lungs, but she was not strong enough to make the trip on her own. She rode here in a wagon.' The groom smiled. 'It was

quite a sight when they arrived. I think it was an af-
front to the dignity of the St Aldric cattle to have to
carry one of their own. But Buttercup took it placid
as a milk cow.'

'He brought her here,' Maddie said again, still
amazed.

'And gave special instructions for her care,' the
groom added. 'He has already been down to visit her
this morning with a sugar lump and a carrot for her
breakfast.' The groom grinned. 'I cannot tell why
he has her. But he seems to think she is worthy of a
peaceful retirement. And she is grateful for it, pricks
up her ears when she hears his voice and comes like
a faithful dog.'

When she had purchased the poor animal, Maddie had not thought further than causing a moment's
aggravation. But a thing as large as a horse did not
simply evaporate once the joke was over. Now she felt
proper guilt for her actions. She had thought Buttercup good for nothing more than dog meat and glue
and had paid an exorbitant sum, not caring what was
to become of her other than that she might be a vehicle for revenge.

But St Aldric could not be moved to anger over a
thing such as this. Instead, he had rescued the horse,
just as he had spent his youth repainting model farms
and tending cotton-wool sheep.

Maddie held a cautious hand to the mare, who re-
garded her sceptically.

'Oh, come on, then,' she said in a matter-of-fact

tone. 'The duke may have cared for you, but I was the one who bought you in the first place. I deserve some small credit for it, don't I?'

The horse gave her an experimental nuzzle and then pulled away when she noticed the absence of treats.

She plucked a handful of clover out of the grass at her feet and offered it to the horse, who took it gingerly. 'See? There is nothing to fear here.' And it was true, was it not? There had been no danger to her, even if she provoked him. There had been no threat at all since the moment she had accosted the duke in the street. Last night they had lain together, but she had been the aggressor.

Three weeks ago, she could not have imagined it possible.

Maddie patted the horse's nose. 'It is a strange old world, Buttercup, full of unexpected events.'

The horse mocked her with an understanding stare and a deep snort that blew spittle onto her hand.

Maddie wiped her fingers on the grass and took the horse by the nose again, staring into its eyes with her best governess look. 'The next time I come to you, I shall bring a carrot. You had best accept it gratefully, or I shall have the grooms put a saddle on you.'

The horse looked properly chastened by the idea of a ride and snuffled her hair with grudging affection.

She took her leave of the stables in a more pensive mood than when she had come to them. Even if she had done the poor mare some good, she had been stupid and spiteful to buy it, thinking only of herself and her needs. It was wrong of her and she was sorry for it.

It made her feel rather foolish to have lectured the duke about the need to allow a mistake now and then. She had made a rather large one with Buttercup, but he had been the one to deal with the consequences of it.

The path she had taken from the house continued downhill towards the river. At the foot of the gardens there was a small, round building made of rough stone and spattered with bird droppings. She approached quietly, not wanting to disturb the residents.

She had never worked in a house with a dovecote. But now, it seemed, she was mistress of one. She enjoyed the taste of the bird, but today it would be soothing to see the soft grey feathers of doves and pigeons, to hear the cooing and perhaps to scatter some grain for them and watch them feed.

But when she poked her head into the room, it was not pigeons that looked back at her. The matched pairs of beady black eyes that looked down on her from the majority of the nesting holes were set in bright red plumage and the whistles and chirps were the same that she had heard on her wedding day.

The man tending them gave her a sad look. 'Welcome, your Grace. And thank you for honouring me with a visit.' He stared up into the rafters. 'Although I am not usually quite so upended as this.'

'You are having difficulties with the birds?' she

said, feeling the same twinge of guilt as she had at the stables.

'These new ones are putting the pigeons out of sorts. I suspect they'd pack off their nests and move to Rayland's property if they could manage it. But if they go, what am I to do with a bunch of parrots?'

'Lovebirds,' Maddie said softly. 'Abyssinian love-birds.'

'Parrots are parrots,' the bird keeper said stubbornly. 'The brighter the bird, the more delicate their temper. Other than peacocks, of course. Those are just plain loud. But at least peafowl are big enough to roast.'

He was obviously unaccustomed to visitors, for he waxed to his subject. 'There is not much meat on these lovebirds at all. And if they be from Africa, then how will they winter? I shall have to set burners to keep them warm. But if I do not open a window, they will all die of the smoke. And they do live up to their names, it seems. I must gather the eggs each day, for they are paired up and cannot seem to leave each other alone. If I am not careful, we will be arse deep in parrots.' He snatched his hat off and bowed. 'Beggin' your pardon, your Grace.'

'You have my sympathy,' Maddie said, caught between amusement and horror at the thought of a waist-deep sea of birds. 'I will talk to his Grace about them. I am sure we can find homes for some of the pairs. They are all the rage in London.' She had been the cause of this problem, as well. But perhaps if she could get rid of the birds, she might be the solution.

But before she had even known there was a problem, St Aldric had dealt with it. Perhaps it was wrong to be thinking of the bible verse about knowing the fall of a single sparrow. But it seemed The Saint, much as he hated the nickname, had earned it by his behaviour. She thought again of the miniature sheep, the fishing nets of knotted string and the tiny farmers standing in front of each small house. There was no detail too small to be handled, no name forgotten, no hardship that could not be eased.

And then he had dishonoured a governess. How abhorrent that must have been to such a carefully ordered existence. She remembered his apologies and his insistence that this had never happened before or since. If it had not happened to her, she would have nothing but the rest of his life to judge him by.

And she would have given him absolution.

She thanked the bird keeper and turned back towards the house. As uncomfortable as it might be, she needed to talk with her husband and bury the past between them, once and for all.

Chapter Twelve

Children often learn from mistakes. If they are never allowed to make them, they often have problems later in life. Michael listened to the sound of his own steps on the mahogany floor of the hallway, as precise and modulated as ever. They were unvaried and he counted them without thinking. If someone had called upon him to recite the paces necessary to reach any room in the house, he'd have a number in his head before they could finish the question.

He had reached the door to his office. As an experiment, he broke step, letting his foot drag on the parquetry before continuing.

It felt wrong. His body struggled to be in step. As he crossed the threshold, it ought to be right, left, not left, right.

The only places he did not know by heart were the bedroom wings, where he had rarely been permitted. While his wife's part of the house might remain alien to him, he should at least take the time to learn his own domain. How else would he ever find comfort in it?

With a wife and child, he would be forced to spend time here. He could not raise a son in London and expect him to learn and understand his role as the next St Aldric. He'd had some half-formed thought that, when the time came, he would leave his wife here to deal with the house. But that had been when he'd thought to marry Evelyn. On their visit here, she had proclaimed the place quite charming. And he had made sure to show her only the main rooms, making up some lame excuse about the bedrooms not having been aired.

But he'd meant to dump her here and to let her sort out the details. Now, if he left, it would be Madeline and an impressionable child. He could not allow that until he could be sure that she would not use his absence to insert her own mad ideas in the place of his far more sensible ones.

He stopped. What knowledge of child-rearing did he have other than what his father had given him? As a boy, he had been miserably unhappy. And while he was mostly satisfied with his adulthood, behaviours that had seemed precise and orderly now seemed rigid. The care with which he'd kept the little animals in the nursery was not so much responsible as unnaturally fussy. They were but toys. He had not wished to make even the smallest error, knowing how costly it might be.

Once grown, he had refused to allow for the possibility that sickness or weakness might change the plans he'd set for himself. He had thought that his own body could be as easily controlled as a machine. When it failed him, he had been like a rudderless ship. And when he had strayed...

The fact that the root of his mistake needed to point out his flaws to him was all the more galling. When she was not hurrying to keep up with him, her gait was regular without being regimented. It was the step of a governess, a woman who brooked no nonsense, but was capable of changing course and altering plans when needed to keep ahead of her charges.

Last night, she had proven that she could be spontaneous, passionate and deliciously improper.

'Your Grace?' Upton was staring at him.

He had paused with one foot on either side of the threshold and was daydreaming about bedding his wife. He smiled at his estate manager and continued into the room, turning his mind to business.

After a brief meeting about the state of finances and projections for the seasonal profits, Upton went into the front hall and collected the first tenant in the line of those who had requested an audience with the duke. So many people to see him. Each one had a problem or a petition that would require careful thought and wise judgement.

He did not doubt his ability to deal with them fairly. It had simply become too easy to avoid these sessions by staying in London and allowing Upton to deal with the day-to-day running of the estate. But was it really fair to the people to do so?

The smiles on most of their faces assured him that it was not. Many came today to offer thanks rather than complaints, as though they were bringing tribute to an emperor. While he dared not admit it to the Regent, he expected it was similar to holding court and more than a little flattering.

He had missed his tenants, of course. But did he deserve this? He could feel the knowledge of the holdings that had been carefully drummed into him from birth slipping away from disuse. He glanced up at the man approaching the desk, searching for a name, and for a moment his mind was a total blank.

Then he saw the ham the man carried beneath his broad arm, which reminded him of pigs. But there was not a whiff of manure about this fellow, which meant butcher and not farmer.

'Old Joe?' He smiled at the man's start of recognition. 'Surely not, for it has been too long. Young Joe, then.'

'Not so young anymore, your Grace.' The man grinned back at him.

'But I see you have taken the shop in the village. Is your father still with us?'

The man nodded. 'And with enough teeth yet to test our wares and assure me that this was worthy of you.'

The ham. He remembered it well. Smoky, sweet, pink and cured, but not dry. Michael's mouth watered at the thought.

Joe noticed and produced a blade from his pocket, slicing expertly through the rind and offering a sliver of meat.

Michael took it and tasted with a sigh. 'Paradise. It is good to be home again.' And for a moment, the words were not a lie. There would be cheeses, ale and a loaf from Mrs Weaver. Strangely enough, Mrs Weaver was from a family of bakers, though the Bakers grew and spun flax. One by one, the names and faces were coming back to him with the flavour of the meat.

'Good to have you here, your Grace. And your bride.' Heads swivelled up and down the row, for many had brought gifts as an excuse to visit the manor, hoping to catch a glimpse of the new lady.

'I will relay your good wishes.' He tried not to let the thought of Madeline put a chill on his tone and passed the ham to his overseer for safekeeping, turning the conversation to thatching and glazing of cottage and shop, and the need to grade the road of the village before the rains of winter.

One by one, the people came and he greeted them, listened to their problems and accepted their gifts, asked about their children and their lives. While Upton took notes in his little leather journal, Michael filed the information carefully in that part of his mind reserved for important facts about the land.

The line was dwindling, but he sensed a change in the crowd, a murmuring at the back and an awed hush.

Madeline was lurking in the hall.

He cursed silently that her interest had turned to the house at such an inappropriate time. He'd given her no warning, no instructions on what might be expected of her, simply because he had not wanted another argument. Worse yet, there might be a veiled threat that she meant to embarrass him with more talk of his mistakes while he was surrounded by the tenants.

She had been improving of late. And after last night, he had hopes. Some things were obviously changing for the better. Their tryst had made him forget the nature of their marriage and the way she'd behaved in London. The temporary truce between them could end as quickly as it had begun.

But at breakfast, he had teased her until he'd managed to provoke an argument. Then he'd walked out on her and slammed the door. He had been foolish.

There was a growing murmur in the crowd beyond the office door as she moved through them. And the nearer she came to him, the more tense he felt. Perhaps appearances were deceiving. The only people they had seen recently were servants and Sam and Evelyn. Madeline thought too well of them to misbehave in front of them. She had been on her best behaviour and he had grown complacent. In any case, they knew him too well to give much credence to her bad opinion of him.

His people knew him, too, but not as well as they should. They were glad to have him back and they were full of hope that he might stay. Suppose she realised this and worked to widen the breach? She could set the whole region in an uproar with a few well-placed rumours. She would make him ashamed, both of his behaviour towards her and the woman he had chosen to be their duchess.

Embarrassing him in London was one thing. If she came between him and his people, he would grow to hate her. But it had not happened yet. He stood and smiled, ready to offer her the respect due to his duchess, whether or not she deserved it. Damn it to hell, he would greet her as a bridegroom if it killed him. 'Is that my wife I see, loitering at the back? Come here, my dear, and meet our tenants.'

She moved forward in a hesitant lockstep, her eyes wide. There was no sign she meant to make mischief. In fact, she looked intimidated, almost to the point of fear.

But frightened animals were often the most dangerous. He would be on his guard. He gestured her to his side and signalled Upton to bring a chair for her, but she wavered on her feet, unwilling to take it. Which meant that he could not sit either. Even a pleasant meeting day was tiring and he did not wish to stand through the last third of the petitioners.

The next family stepped forward. It was the Bakers, husband and wife and a girl of about fourteen, come to discuss the dry season and the possibility that the rent might be late. What did one have to weave when the flax had died? He nodded sympathetically while Madeline stood at his side in confused silence.

'But that does not mean we have nothing to offer,' Mr Baker said earnestly, despite his protestations that they need not worry. 'It is a trifle. A nothing, really. But our daughter is learning from her mother, as she should. And with the cloth we've made, she's hemmed a handkerchief. A wedding gift for your lady.' Cautiously, the girl held out the folded square of cloth, dropping her eyes and holding her breath as she waited for the reaction.

Michael's heart sank. If his wife wished to destroy the morning, she had been given the chance. She had but to take the thing and announce that it was nowhere near the quality on Bond Street. That while he might admire the St Aldric crest, he must see that the griffons were not quite equal, the monogram not quite centred. The cloth was not nearly fine enough for a lady's delicate skin. While it would be embarrassing for him, it would be crushing for the girl and humiliating for the Bakers, who had done nothing to deserve her enmity.

It was too late to order her away. One sly comment and the good feeling of the morning would be gone, the day ruined. It would be the sort of visit he'd feared and no amount of tumbling in the bed sheets would make him forgive her. He waited in silence for the inevitable.

'It is…' She reached for it. 'Is…' He could see her shoulders begin to shake, probably from derisive laughter. 'Oh, I am so sorry.' She crushed it to her face and stifled a wail. The linen was growing damp with her tears and the words seeping around the edges of it were barely coherent. 'So beautiful…touched… do not deserve…thank you…'

Mr Baker took a step back from the desk, obviously alarmed, but Mrs Baker shot a glance to her daughter and nudged the girl to a curtsey. 'You're welcome, your Grace. You honour us. We work in wool, as well. There is a fleece in our shop right now that could be made up into a wee blanket, soft as a cloud, just right for a babe's cheek.'

Madeline's watery eyes appeared over the top of the linen, soft and brown as a doe's despite the tears, and she gave the slightest nod.

Mrs Baker nudged her daughter again. The girl's mouth was as round as an egg as she dipped to curtsey a second time. Then the mother gave a triumphant smile at having happened on the best piece of gossip in the holding. She had not only given the first gift to the new duchess, she had found the real reason that his Grace had returned to the country after so long.

Maddie withdrew as soon as she was able to master her tears, and hurried to her room. But the garish decor made her feel worse and not better. Her cupboards were full of silk gowns and muslins in more colours than she could name. There was more here than she could need in a lifetime. And all of them were pulling tight across the bodice as her body expanded. They would not fit, even if she could find an excuse to wear them. Now they were hanging in this horrible bedroom, which was itself a mockery of extravagance. The dovecote was full of lovebirds. The pasture housed that pathetic nag that she had forced on St Aldric. None of it brought her any satisfaction.

She had thought St Aldric distant and insincere, but he had done everything he could to help her. The people who worked the land around them adored him. He knew them by name and watched over each and every one of them as though they were his own family.

Though they had never seen her before, they welcomed her with joy and with gifts, never suspecting that she came to them ready to do mischief at each turn.

She had been trying to make an enemy of her husband while telling herself that she had made a husband of an enemy. Soon she would bring an innocent baby into this horrible house and she had no idea how to go on.

The tears were coming again. This time she did not try to stop them. She felt small and alone. So she turned and fled the duchess's suite for a room where she could truly feel at home.

Some time later, the duke sauntered by the open door of the governess bedroom, as though trying to pretend that there was any excuse for his presence in the nursery wing other than searching for her. He hesitated on the doorstep, making no move to come closer to her. 'Forgive my asking, Madeline—but are you well? In the office just now, you were rather overset.'

She sobbed aloud again and held out a hand to him. Then she dropped it, not wanting to involve him in this pathetic display of emotion.

'Do you wish to return to your own room? I doubt this one has been aired.'

She shook her head.

'Do you wish me to summon your maid? Or Evelyn, perhaps?' He turned, ready to go.

'No!' She was not sure what she wanted, but it was not to be prodded with tea and company. The tears were coming faster now as the enormity of the changes in her life caught up with her. She was pregnant. And she had married a stranger. What had she been thinking? Had she seriously been planning to spend the rest of her life in anger? As a governess, she had been quite clear with the children she'd taught on the importance of living up to responsibility and not wasting time in petty squabbling. But who was to teach that to her?

And what to do with her new title, her new position and the obligations that came with it? And the fact that, last night, she had climbed into his bed and demanded to have her way with him?

'Oh, hell.' Apparently even a saint lost patience when confronted with illogical displays of emotion. But just as she was convinced that he was about to storm off and leave her to her tantrum, he came into the room and sat on the bed beside her. Then he put his arms around her and kissed her. His mouth sealed hers, trapping the escaping sob in her throat while his tongue stroked gently over hers.

For a moment, she was still unsure of what she wanted. Then she gave up and let him kiss her. It was nice, at least, until it became difficult to breathe through her stuffed nose. She pulled her mouth free, leaned into his body, put her face into his coat and wept.

She felt him stiffen. Did he despise her? She had been awful to him. And all along he had been trying to make amends. The thought made her weep all the harder.

A rational voice at the back of her head informed her that such thoughts were the madness of a pregnant woman. She'd had a logical reason to be angry. It did not make her horrible. But the same rational voice reminded her that it was her choice as well to decide that enough was enough, to forgive and to declare the matter closed.

She heard St Aldric sigh again. Exasperated, frustrated and ever so slightly affectionate. 'There, there.' His other hand came around her waist and he patted her on the back. 'It will be all right. Tell me what you need. Whatever it is. I will make it so.' And there was the sigh again, as though he was silently wondering if it was even possible to make her happy. 'What do you require of me? How can I help?'

It was so very *him* to say such a thing. He was thinking of her first, now that he'd found her in need. Had she ever seen him selfish in his desires? In Dover, of course. But last night, he had definitely been a generous lover.

'I saw the horse,' she whispered. 'And the birds.' She sobbed again. But this time she put her arms around his waist, clinging to him.

He sighed again, thoroughly confused, and hugged her in return, leaning back onto the bed, holding her to his side. He lay there awkwardly, his shoes upon the floor. She drew her legs up onto the mattress and curled against him, comforted.

He released her for a moment, fumbled in his coat to produce a handkerchief and offered it to her.

'Thank you,' she managed, 'but I have a handkerchief.' She held up the sodden lump that had been the carefully made gift.

He pressed his own linen into her hand and waited while she blew her nose in a most unladylike fashion.

'Better?' he asked. She could not see his face, but when she wiped her eyes and looked up, she saw he was smiling. It was not the tight, frustrated smile of vexation that she was used to. He was bemused.

'A little,' she admitted. 'I am sorry...to be so emotional,' she finished, still not sure that she wanted to apologise for anything at all.

'Sam assures me that such spells are common amongst increasing women,' he offered. 'You have nothing to fear from them.'

'Do you consult him in all matters pertaining to me?' she said, her tone drying along with her eyes.

'He is my brother,' St Aldric said, as though the explanation were a simple one. 'He assures me that his wife is more knowledgeable on the subject. But I go to him, since he has known of us from the first. He is also a physician.' There was a slight pause. 'And even if Evelyn is the authority, it would be deuced awkward to consult her on such a personal matter.'

'Because you were once betrothed?'

'Because she would torment me unrelentingly,' he said. 'And because she is female. For a gentleman to express curiosity about such things would be unnatural. Especially about such things as the previous evening.'

She gasped.

'Do not worry,' he said. 'I did not discuss the specifics. But I have ascertained that fluctuations in the humours, both pleasant and unpleasant, and an increase in certain appetites, strange cravings and preferences, can be blamed upon the fact that you are increasing. You will not be held responsible by me or anyone else.'

'Last night…' she said, not sure how to enter that into the conversation.

'Was an increase in appetite. I will not upbraid you with it. Nor will I mention it again,' he said, once again the most diplomatic of men.

'Then you did not like it?'

His head was resting again her hair and she could feel him laughing as his lips rubbed gently against the curls. 'Quite the contrary. It was incredible. But I will have no expectations that it will be repeated.

I mean to make no demands on you, just as I promised from the first.'

'I see.'

'However, should you wish to do it again, use me as you wish. I will humour you, because you are with child.' There was no artifice in the grin on his face.

The tears had stopped. And now she was laughing. 'How gracious of you.'

'As always, I am your humble servant.' But parts of her humble servant were pressed close to her and feeling somewhat less than humble. She squirmed against him, arranging herself so that she might be closer. It was wrong. It was the middle of the day and she was still in her walking dress. He had interrupted what he was doing to come and find her. For all she knew, half the village of Aldricshire was still in the receiving room, waiting for him to return.

'Madeline?' His voice was quiet enough, but she had never been so close to him that the sound of her own name vibrated against her skin.

'Hmm?' she said, putting an ear to his chest so that she might feel his next words as well as listen to them.

'I think, unless you want me to humour you immediately, that we should probably leave this bedchamber.'

'Because it has not been aired?' She made no move to let go of him. Instead, she rolled onto her side and adjusted her hips so that his growing erection was well placed between her legs.

'With each passing moment it becomes more difficult to go.'

'Harder, you mean?' She pressed her legs together, trying to trap him between her thighs.

'You are teasing me.' He did not seem annoyed by it. He was merely acknowledging the truth.

'And you are a very busy man,' she reminded him. 'You would have to be very quick about it, so as not to disrupt your schedule.' She cupped him from behind and squeezed.

He gave a single groan of frustration. Then his hand was on his breeches, tugging so hard she heard a button pop and the fabric tear. His mouth covered hers and his kisses were rough and hungry. His tongue filled her mouth as she bit and sucked in response. He was yanking up her skirt, leaving her uncovered, spreading her with a stroke of his fingers before sinking one of them deep inside her. 'Is this what you want, witch?'

It was delicious, this feeling glowing in her again as she clenched her muscles around it. But it was not enough. 'More,' she whispered. 'More.'

He withdrew his hand and entered her, hard and fast, his lips pressed to her ear. 'Minx.' He thrust hard as he whispered, 'Temptress.' He thrust again. 'You are driving me to madness.' And he was driving into her, relentless in his frustration, eager for satisfaction.

He was not the only one going mad. She was panting as she grabbed his cravat and yanked at the knot, opening his shirt so that she could ring his neck in kisses and then in bites. It was fast and wicked, and she could not seem to get enough of him. Her breasts were straining against the confinement of her stays. Her body was wet for him, and his size, the movement, his hands tearing at her hair, pulling her leg until her knee rested against his waist, so that he could go deeper, deeper....

She cried out as she broke, going limp against him, but he continued, his final thrusts stoking the fire in her to a low, hot glow. Then he stiffened and relaxed in her arms.

She drifted back to earth to face what had just happened.

His head lifted from where it had been nestling against her covered breasts. He was smiling. 'You look quite shocked, Madeline. Please do not tell me I misunderstood your intentions.'

Misunderstood the feeling of her hands on his bottom? What had made her do that, in broad daylight, when she'd been crying only moments before? 'No. You did not misunderstand. I am just surprised that I have such intentions. They come upon me rather suddenly, you see.'

'Then I am glad I did not miss them,' he said. He moved his hand from beneath her and rubbed idly at a muscle on his neck.

She looked at the spot he had touched. So he was not perfect, then. He had a blemish. A single scar, or rather a group of them. Three parallel lines running a few inches at the side of his throat. By day, his valet must use some skill to see that they were hidden by the cravat, lest they spoil the perfection that was St Aldric.

'What did you do there?' she said, curious at this single sign of vulnerability.

'This?' He smiled. 'I should think you would know the answer to that better than I.'

'I?' She leaned back, surprised.

He snatched her hand from his chest. The shock of it curled her fingers involuntarily into a claw. He dragged the tips of them lightly along the skin of his neck.

Each one marked the path of a scar.

'That night,' he said softly, 'when you realised what had happened, you scratched me. That was the moment I knew I'd made a mistake. When I awoke the next morning, the blood had dried on my shoulder. I should have taken better care. It is funny how quickly such a minor thing can go septic.'

'You were ill?' she said, surprised again.

'Hardly. A little redness. A week's bother, more or less. But they did not heal smoothly, as they should. Hence the scars.' The affected shoulder gave a small shrug. 'I did not deserve to leave that place without some mark of it. Now when I look in the mirror, knowing that the scars are there, just hidden by my linen, prevents further excesses.'

She had marked him. She felt an unnatural grief for having spoilt something so beautiful. 'I'm sorry,' she murmured.

He pressed her hand to his throat, covering it with his own. 'You have no reason to be. I am sorry for not being the man you wished for.'

But perhaps you are.

Wasn't this man what she had actually always wanted? Not because he was a duke, for she had never in her wildest dreams thought to want that. She had wanted someone to lie beside her, to share laughter, to make her feel safe and part of his life and family.

Someone to love.

His fingers covering hers were warm, gentle. Gentle man. That was what he was. They stayed just like that for several minutes, his body still rested in hers. But the place where their hands rested on his throat was a much more intimate joining. She could feel the pulse beneath her fingers. Each swallow. Each sigh. Slowly, she felt her own breathing, her own heartbeat, falling into synchronicity with his.

She had been so angry for so long. Not without reason, but it was so tiring to hold that anger. It had been like gripping an animal, always struggling to escape. If she loosed it, it might turn with fang and claw and devour her. But to hold it meant scratches, small, septic.

She closed her eyes and let it go.

Chapter Thirteen

It had been his first summer in Aldricshire in nearly five years. Although he still did not like the house, Michael had to admit that he had forgotten many of the pleasant advantages of spending the Season here. He smiled at the retreating back of the two last tenants, who, though they were not leaving as friends, had at least accepted his opinion on the boundary between their fields and would abide by it. Upton had set aside the heavy book of maps and was gathering up the ledger and the rent money.

The people here were happy. The land was prosperous and he enjoyed his long walks through it. His wife was healthy. There was a rosy glow about her that reminded him of the blooms in the garden: lush, sweet and intoxicating. If the servants thought it odd that he spent most nights with her in a small bedroom in the nursery wing, they said nothing to indicate the fact. Even the sanest man was allowed an eccentricity now and then. This would be his.

He could blame it on her, if he wished. It was simply the irregular mind of a pregnant woman and former governess nesting in a familiar place. She might even agree with him to save him embarrassment.

But it had been his idea. The mattress was better than the one in his room, possibly because of its more innocent past. The space was small and comfortable. There were no bad dreams in it. He slept each night like a babe, his arms wrapped around Madeline in the place where they had first made their peace.

Michael walked back to his study, shaking his head, still not sure what it was that had convinced her of his good intentions. Had it been something he'd said or done? If so, he'd have done it earlier. She had fallen to weeping and muttered something about horses and birds. Suddenly, the trouble had been over and she had been his.

She had always been desirable. He could not deny that he had admired her, even at the start. But he had concluded that his feelings towards her were no different from what he felt whenever he saw an attractive female. She was comely, therefore he wanted her. When she'd come to him that first time? A man would have to be a fool to refuse.

But in the past few months, she had grown into something more than a pretty girl. Her wavy brown hair had grown longer and the soft loops of it tickled his face when he kissed her. Her body was soft and full, like an extra pillow for his head as they slept together. Her huge brown eyes smiled more than they cried. But if she wept, she turned to him for comfort.

And when he had kissed her...

He felt the rush of emotion again. Affection, of course. But this was different. It was as though she was an extension of his own body. Perhaps it was the natural reaction that any man had when looking at the woman who carried his child.

Or was it love? Could it really be that easy to feel that emotion? He was still suspicious of it, for it had been a stranger to him until now. He had loved his mother, of course, but that had been quite different and seldom reciprocated. He had respected his father because he had been obligated to. Father had been St Aldric, therefore he deserved respect. But he had seen his parents so rarely that feelings of affection towards them were theoretical, not practical.

When he had first decided to marry, he had chosen Evelyn because he'd liked her. He had not loved her. He had not known her all that well if he'd thought that she could be moulded into a duchess. She was perfectly charming, and totally unchangeable. His brother was the only man who asserted any influence upon her at all, and he was welcome to her.

But being married to Madeline was different. He admired her quick mind. He did not dictate to her and she did not blindly obey. Yet they seemed to agree on many things, and managed well together. Each time she returned his kiss he felt something rush through him, as though he wanted nothing more in the world than to have the moment frozen in time for ever. Especially good were the nights they spent lying side by side on the small bed, talking softly of nothing in particular, whispering and joking until one or the other of them drifted off to sleep.

Was one supposed to be so happy and to have no reason for it? Compared to the quick and dispensable pleasures available to a single man, this joy seemed dangerous. What would become of him if it ended?

Here was his wife now, framed in the doorway, swaying slightly, and out of breath as though she had rushed to come here. It was not like her to be hurrying around the house in the middle of the day. He was on his feet and halfway to the door without a thought. 'Madeline?' Was something wrong?

She held up a hand, as though she could hear something he could not. She looked confused. 'I must talk to you,' she said, with a little gasp. 'In private.' She glanced at Upton in apology. 'If it is not too much trouble.'

'Of course not.' He gestured and the man exited with his ledger, shutting the door behind him. 'What is it? The baby?' It was far too soon for that. 'Is there something the matter? Should I summon Dr Hastings? Or Evelyn, perhaps?' He put a hand under her elbow, leading her forward into the room.

'No. No,' she said with a little laugh. 'There is nothing to be alarmed about. I do not need the doctor.'

'But if I can help you in some way...'

She smiled at him as though he had said something wonderful and took his hand, placing it on her abdomen.

There was a twitch. Then another. It was as though someone was running their hand against a curtain he was touching. And briefly, their hands had met.

Michael jumped in surprise and pulled away as quickly as if she'd had a wasp's nest hidden in her skirts. Then he placed it back where it had been and waited. It was happening again. The movement was slower this time, as though the other person had lost interest in the game and was settling back to nap.

It was the most miraculous thing he had ever felt. Life. Their child. He could see by the look on her face that she agreed. She was as excited for this as he was. Her face, her body, everything about her seemed to radiate happiness. And she was smiling at him.

'Well?' she said, for his hand was still on her belly and he had not said a word.

Though he was never at a loss for words, he was stunned to silence by the enormity of it. He had a wife—and he was going to have a child. In a place where he had never known anything but misery, he was happier than he'd ever been.

Because he was with her. And she was with child.

He shook his head and smiled.

She nudged him with her hand. 'Speak, St Aldric. Do you have nothing to say when presented with such an important piece of information? Your heir is healthy enough to be kicking me.'

Call me Michael.

It was the only thing he could think to say. But the fact that he had never heard her use his given name was not germane to the discussion. 'Amazing,' he said at last.

'It is, isn't it?' She smiled back at him. 'I should not be surprised by it. But still...'

'Nor should, I,' he agreed. 'But it is still amazing.' He kissed her quickly, because he could not resist the chance. Then he put both hands on her now-still belly, moving slowly over it, reaching up to touch her breasts.

'St Aldric,' she said breathlessly, taking his hands and moving them lower.

There was his title again, at a time when he had no desire to be so formal. 'Madeline?' he said in a response and pulled her towards the chair behind the desk.

'St Aldric,' she said a little more firmly. 'We are in a common room.'

'And no one would dare interrupt us,' he said.

'Do you not have work to do?' she reminded him. 'It is the middle of the day.'

'It can wait,' he said, kissing her throat. 'But I cannot. Let me touch you again.' He moved his hand lower so she could have no doubt as to what he meant.

'But in a chair?' She grabbed the arms and tried to stand. 'I am not quite so nimble as I once was, your Grace.'

'Still so formal with me, Madeline?' He dropped to his knees in front of her. 'Let us see what we can do to change that.' Then he pushed up her skirts and kissed her thigh.

Her breath caught and she murmured, 'It is broad daylight.'

'All the better to see you, my dear.' He kissed her again, running a finger under one of her garters to tease the flesh beneath.

'Suppose someone in the garden should pass by the window?'

'Then likely they will be very shocked to see this.' He pushed her legs apart and licked between them.

Her hands pushed against the arms of the chair, trying to rise, but it only brought her body closer to him. So he caught the lips of her and sucked them into his mouth and smoothed his hands down over her belly until she relaxed.

'Oh, my lord.' She released the wood and ran her fingers through his hair.

'That's better,' he whispered into her skin. 'Much better.' And yet still not quite right. He kissed her again, working moving his tongue slowly back and forth over her. Then he paused. 'Speak to me.'

'Darling.' She gave a convulsive shudder.

He kissed her again, harder, touching his tongue to her opening and dipping into it again and again.

'Oh, my sweet.' She was arching to meet him now, totally helpless to resist the pleasure.

'Totally yours,' he agreed, and went back to the little bud of pleasure.

'I love you,' she whispered.

The words caught him off guard. Was he expected to answer them? Instead, he responded with an unrelenting kiss that left her panting so hard it stopped all further speech. He tormented her for a moment longer until she was writhing in the chair. If she'd have said anything then, it would not have been proclamations of love. It would have been a plea for release. Then he sent her over the edge with a final flick of his tongue and laid his head against her thigh, waiting for her to calm.

When he looked up at her, she was breathless, silent and smiling.

He touched one of the dark curls in front of him and gave it a gentle tug.

'This was unexpected,' she admitted.

'We have done it before,' he reminded her.

'Not here.'

He nodded.

'But it was nice,' she admitted.

It had been more than nice. He had made sure of that. 'Thank you,' he said, matching her prim tone.

'You are not always so open to me in the middle of the day.'

But she was the one who would not call him by name. 'We have done this before,' he reminded her again.

She laughed then, in a way that he had not heard before. At least, not from her. It was the polite drawing room laugh he frequently heard in London, the sort that even Evelyn Hastings used on those rare times when she was trying to have manners. 'But even so, the Duke of St Aldric does not often go to his knees and pleasure me without a thought to what the household might say.' She straightened her skirts and stood, giving him a saucy wink. 'I am most grateful, your Grace. I will return the favour at a more decent hour, if you will meet me in the usual place at bedtime.'

'Your servant, madam,' he responded with the same false courtesy that she was using on him. They exchanged smiles and he blew her a kiss, and she was gone. The interlude had been enjoyable and he looked forward to the evening, for he was fortunate to have a most passionate and demonstrative wife.

But he could not shake the feeling that something had just gone very wrong.

Chapter Fourteen

Autumn was coming and life was good. But it bothered Maddie that she felt it necessary to remind herself of the fact so very often.

Judging by the kicks it had been giving her, in less than a month she would give birth to a healthy child. The fear that filled her when she thought of that was so different from what it had been, when this had begun. Then she'd wanted nothing more than to escape the inevitable. It would be a disaster for both her and the child she carried.

But now? She was still afraid, of course. What if the child was not healthy? What if she was not strong enough to bring it into the world? Or to mother it once it arrived? Suppose it was different from caring for the children of others? Suppose she did something wrong? With no one to teach her, how was she to manage?

It was silly to worry. Was she not a duchess? And would she not be one until the end of her life? Duchesses were not supposed to be afraid. She had wealth, status and at least one good friend, for Evelyn had become as close as a sister to her. She had even managed to get rid of all but two of the lovebirds. After the wedding, she'd received several pieces of polite correspondence from guests, enquiring about how to procure them. Each time, she had packed off a matched set, along with instructions for care.

The final pair she kept for herself, finding a gold wire cage and setting it in the corner of the duchess bedroom. Like it or not, the decoration suited them.

If she could manage that, she could manage one small child on her own. And she must remember that she was not alone. Despite what she had expected when she had agreed to the proposal, Maddie had found a husband who was totally devoted to her. He thought of nothing but her happiness and her comfort. Her life was safe, well ordered and happy during the day. At night she had a lover who played her body like a harp, knowing precisely what it took to arouse her, to bring her to climax and to calm her to sleep.

The only thing she did not have was his love. He cared for her as he did all of his other possessions, with total dedication. But there was a benevolent distance to him, as though he viewed her as a responsibility, albeit a pleasant one. St Aldric allotted her whatever portion of his heart was left, having already given the larger share of it to his lands and tenants. And beneath the title, there was still a thin layer of artifice that separated her from the true Michael Poole, on all but the rarest occasions. She suspected it would always be so. But it kept them from arguing about foolishness and prevented either of them from being hurt.

Eventually, she might learn to be satisfied with that. Devotion was nearly as good as love. She had learned from the loss of Richard that romantic love, while quite nice when you were in it, caused a great deal of pain when it left. She should be grateful, but it was difficult. The pain seeped around the edges occasionally, just as it had when she'd forgotten herself, announced her love for him and got no similar response.

She'd a mind to tell him that if he had not wanted her to fall in love with him, he could have done his part to prevent it. He could have been, in some small part, the man she had feared he was when she'd married him. He could have been the shallow, careless reprobate he had seemed on the night they'd met.

Instead, he had been lovable. In her weakened state, she had been happy to succumb.

But with practice, she was learning to be as he was, passionate at night, affectionate by day and unceasingly polite.

That was why she spent her mornings in the morning room and not lounging in the salon. She was prepared to receive company, even though she had no expectations of any. She visited the village, taking time to talk to the people there and learn their names and families. If she had married a saint, she must learn to be worthy of him.

The last thing she expected, when the butler finally came to announce that she had a guest, was that it would be someone from her own past. 'It is a Mr Colver, your Grace. He said you would know him.'

'Of course.' She rose, forgetting for a moment that she did not have to. After all this time, she had not expected a visit from the man who had taken her in as an infant. That he would seek her out now could not be good news. Joyous things came in letters and not surprise visits. She hoped he was not here to relay the loss of Mrs Colver. Though the pair of them had turned her out after they'd learned of her affair with Richard, she no longer felt bitterness towards them. It had worked out for the best.

Without thinking, she wiped her hands on her skirt to remove the nervous dampness from the palms and said, 'Bring him to me.' Then she sat again, trying to order her mind and use the tricks that she had learned from watching the duke. She put on the false but interested smile, rehearsed in her mind the correct questions about family and friends and the sympathetic speech she would give that might comfort the man on his probable loss, without displaying her own distress.

But the man who stood in the doorway was not the shopkeeper who had been a surrogate father for the first years of her life. It was the younger Mr Colver: the one person she had been sure was lost to her for ever.

'Richard!' She could not help the joyful exclamation or the way she ran into his arms. He was live and whole. There were no scars on his face and no limp when he walked. Despite all she feared, he had survived, right down to the curl in his black hair and the easy smile. This was the moment she'd waited for for so many years. Her love had returned to her just as she'd dreamed.

And it was too late.

He was trying to kiss her, just as he used to, with a smile on his face and a firm hand twined in her hair. But he could not hold her as he had because of the obstruction of her belly. And the shallowness of her breathing had more to do with the baby pressing against her ribs than it did a rising tide of desire.

It was her enthusiastic greeting that had led him on. Now she must put a stop to it. She worked to disentangle herself from his caress before he attempted to slip his tongue into her mouth and kiss her like a lover. He was acting as if nothing had changed between them, but if he had found her here, he must know it had. It was sad that she must be the one to break his heart, for she had never meant to. But their time was past.

'Richard,' she said again, taking a step away to establish some boundaries between them. 'I must apologise for the informality of my greeting, but you took me quite by surprise. And it is so good to know that you are well. Come. Sit. I will send for refreshment. I am sure we have much to talk about.'

The butler, who was normally polite and expressionless, was staring at the pair of them, shocked at the intimacy between her and this stranger. But he managed a stiff nod and said, 'Of course, your Grace.'

'Brandy, please,' Richard said to him with a smile. 'I am parched and we have much to talk about.'

Spirits in the morning. Maddie gave the butler a nod of permission and requested tea for herself, hoping that it would steady her nerves. Then she chose a chair by the window instead of the sofa she preferred, to be sure that there would be some space between them.

Of course, St Aldric would have managed mischief no matter where she sat. Just the thought of it made her hot.

Richard was beaming at her. 'You are looking well, my love. Is that blush on your cheek for me?'

'Women in my condition are prone to flushing,' she said hurriedly. She must not be annoyed with him for his bad timing, or his confusion about the change in her affections. Her marriage must have been nearly as great a shock to him as it had been to her.

'And I assume congratulations are in order?' he said with an ironic glance at her belly. 'I had not expected to find you thus when I finally returned. It has been nearly nine times nine months since last we saw each other.'

The footman was entering with the refreshment tray and she hissed at Richard to caution him. Until she could figure out what was to be done in such a situation, she had no wish to add to the gossip.

But Richard ignored her, blundering on as the footman retreated. 'When I left, I thought there was an expectation between us,' he said. He looked hurt. But after months with St Aldric, she was growing good at seeing behind false fronts. He might pretend to be upset about her perceived infidelity, but he was too pleased with the quality of his brandy to be convincing.

'I thought you dead,' she said flatly. 'The Horse Guard could tell me nothing of your whereabouts after the Battle of New Orleans. I spoke with your parents, and they knew nothing either.'

'Probably because I had not contacted them until just last month,' he said with a dismissive wave of his hand. 'You know my father had no patience for me when I refused to take over the shop from him. It was why I bought the commission.'

'He was upset because you took money from the till without asking,' she said as gently as possible. Richard had been stubborn then, as had his father. The fights had been horrible. 'And they did not approve of what happened between us. I was not welcome in the house after you left. But the school did not mind if I remained there during holidays.'

'Do you blame me for that now?' He looked indignant.

'Certainly not,' she said hurriedly. 'It did not matter so very much to me. But I did miss you, once you were gone. To hear not a word, even after the war had ended...' There was probably a logical explanation. Soon he would tell her of a wound followed by fever and a recovery in some distant sick ward. He would assure her that contact had been impossible. Then she could go back to feeling sorry for her betrayal instead of annoyed that he had waited so long to come to her.

He smiled in the same knowing way he had when he'd seen her. 'I was busy.' He glanced down again. 'Just as you were.'

Busy. She deserved more than that after all this time. Months had turned into years. Had he really been too busy to write to his true love? There was no point in resurrecting the exact reason for his disappearance. 'I am married now.' Any marriage, for any reason, meant a permanent parting from Richard.

'So I see.' Richard was still trying to look hurt.

'I waited,' she reminded him, lest he think her too changeable. 'I waited for years. And I did my best to make it easy for you to find me if you returned. I wrote your parents as well, with each change in position.'

'When I visited them, they gave me your last letter and informed me of your intent to move again,' Richard said with a smile. 'But when I went to find you, another governess worked in your place. And your employer told me a most interesting story. And then there was the announcement in *The Times* of the sudden marriage of the Duke of St Aldric.'

He knew. Perhaps not everything, but enough to guess what had happened.

'There was an embarrassing misunderstanding,'

she said, amazed that she was saying such a thing. 'For a time, it was all quite difficult. But we have settled things between us and are quite happy now.' Not as happy as she might have wished, but better than she had ever imagined.

'It is a comfort that you did so well from it and avoided any scandal.' There was a dangerous pause. 'Because of an accident in Dover, St Aldric made you a duchess.' He looked down again. 'I suppose that it is his child you carry?'

'Suppose?' This hurt even worse than his expression. 'Of course it is his. Who else's could it be?'

Richard shrugged. 'There was a rumour about that he was unable. And you must understand, after what we were to each other, that I of all people know that you are quite willing...'

'I loved you!' Surely he did not think her some common trollop.

She heard an approaching footstep in the hall, louder than usual, as though someone wished to be heard before he entered. A moment later, St Aldric stood in the doorway, smiling and gracious, pretending that he had heard nothing of the previous conversation. 'I was told you had company, my dear. A Mr Colver?' He was looking at Richard, as though weighing him with a glance. 'Am I to meet a member of your family at last?'

Maddie rose to encourage Richard to get to his feet. 'Your Grace, may I present Mr Richard Colver.' She would not stammer or flush. She was the Duchess of

St Aldric and should be more than able to handle such a temporary awkwardness as introducing her former lover to her husband. 'He is the eldest son of the family who raised me.'

Richard had the sense to bow, and St Aldric acknowledged him with a nod of his head and a smile that was several degrees cooler than normal. 'Mr Colver.' Michael put a slight emphasis on *Mr*. It was unusual, for he never felt the need to point out another's inferiority.

Perhaps there was some military rank she could use when addressing Richard to make a better impression. She chided herself for this sudden snobbery. Had a few months with the duke really changed her so much? At one time, she'd sworn that she did not need money or rank to wed Richard Colver. But neither did she enjoy her husband's insolent pleasure at the lack of them.

'Maddie and I are old friends, your Grace. Very old, very dear friends.' Why could not Richard manage to behave as a gentleman? He was a shopkeeper's son in the house of a peer. Their old friendship did not give him right to such a possessive smile and the deliberate use of a diminutive that St Aldric did not make use of himself.

'Of course,' the duke replied. 'She speaks of you often.'

'Does she really?' Richard was grinning in response, as though wondering about the truth of this. But he could not be as surprised as Maddie was. At times, St Aldric might be evasive. But she had never heard him speak total untruth.

'But I have not seen Richard in a very long time,' she reminded them both. 'Years, in fact.' She looked at Richard again. 'As I told you, I thought you dead. In the Battle of New Orleans.'

Richard responded with a puppet-like nod, as though he were only agreeing with a complete falsehood to keep the peace.

'He saw the announcement of our wedding and sought me out to offer congratulations,' she finished, for her husband's sake. It might not have been his reason for the visit, but it was the only one she was willing to accept. 'Now that you have done so, Mr Colver, you must be eager to continue on to visit your parents. They are in Norfolk,' she added, to assure St Aldric that this would not be a regular occurrence. 'That is quite a distance from here.'

'Then I expect you will want to rest before your travels,' the duke said with his usual false smile. 'If it has been years since you've talked, there is much you must wish to say, if you are indeed such old and dear friends.'

'I am sure that Mr Colver has other plans,' she said hurriedly.

'On the contrary, I am at liberty.' Richard smiled back at the duke, ignoring her attempts to put him off.

'Then you must stay with us as long as you like,'

the duke said, the picture of hospitality. 'In fact, I insist upon it. Should we put him in the red suite in the west wing? The view is lovely. It will be most convenient, I am sure.' The phrase was innocent enough, but she knew his meaning. The red suite was part of the discreet maze that connected to her bedchambers. He was asking if she meant to cuckold him. To carry on as his mother had, entertaining lovers while he was still in the house.

'That will not be necessary,' she said, firmly hoping that it would reassure him.

'That will be delightful.' Richard had talked over her objection, accepting before she could find a way to put him off.

'The blue rooms are much more suitable,' she insisted. 'They are larger and more convenient to the servants.' And less embarrassing, since they were nearer the head of the stairs and opened onto the main corridor of the wing. 'I will speak to the housekeeper immediately and arrange for them to be opened. If you gentlemen will excuse me?'

It was a risk, leaving the two of them together to compare stories. But she had other things to worry about. The staff must prepare a guest room in a house that was not fit for guests. And she must invite... No. She must demand the company of Sam and Evelyn at dinner. A few minutes alone with the two men had seemed an eternity. She did not think she could stand to take supper alone with them, as well.

But first and foremost she must find Peg and tell her to lock all doors in the duchess wing that were not the blue suite, especially any that connected to her own room.

Chapter Fifteen

So this was the man that his wife truly loved.

Michael could not help but be disappointed, for he'd thought that she had better taste. He supposed Richard Colver was handsome enough, with thick, dark hair and the devil in his eyes. If she'd known him all her life, Madeline might have been too young and naive to resist his charms when he'd first seduced her. But it did not explain what the man was doing in his house and why he had heard his wife protesting that she loved him.

Now that Madeline was gone and they were alone together, the lout had the gall to stare back at him with a smug smile upon his face, all but announcing his previous intimacy with Michael's wife.

The duke waited. And waited still longer, until nearly a minute had ticked by and the smile of the man at last began to fade. Then he walked to the sofa and arranged himself upon it, gesturing to the most uncomfortable chair in the room. 'Please, Mr Colver. Let us sit.'

The interloper took the offered chair and tried to find a comfortable position in it, then reached for his brandy.

Michael stared at the glass, making no comment about it one way or the other. But the intense gaze was a reminder of the fact that the man who paid for the liquor had the sense not to drink it before noon.

Colver set it aside again.

'So, Mr Colver—' he smiled '—I am always interested in meeting friends of my wife. Please, tell me about yourself.'

Colver's silence to this was telling. In Michael's experience, men who paused significantly when asked such a simple question were searching for the best lie to tell. 'I am an old friend of Maddie's.'

'So you said.'

'And a veteran of the war in the Americas,' Colver added.

'The Battle of New Orleans,' Michael reminded him. 'But that was several years ago, was it not? What has occupied you since?'

'That is of little importance,' Colver said.

Which likely meant drinking and gambling and whoring.

'When I discovered that Maddie had married, I was eager to renew our acquaintance and assure myself that she was happy.'

'She is.' He was unaccustomed to making such

blanket statements for her. But who better to do it than the man who shared her bed each night?

'We were quite close, your Grace.' Colver was smiling again, regaining his confidence. 'One might even say we were betrothed.'

'Either you were or you weren't,' Michael said bluntly. 'Which was it?'

And there was the pause again. 'We had an understanding,' Colver said. 'She agreed to wait for me while I made my fortune so that we could be married.'

'How unfortunate that you did not arrive sooner.'

'Unfortunate indeed, your Grace. I would have withdrawn from the situation had she not reached out to me, speaking of her unhappiness and her longing that we might be together again.'

It was obviously an untruth. She would never have said such a thing. At least not lately. He was sure of it.

'And when she told me of the unfortunate circumstances of your meeting, the uproar in the night when you were discovered....'

He knew about Dover. Who could have told him of that but Madeline? Had his wife's sudden change in manner towards him been nothing but a trick? Of late she had seemed aloof. And there was the continual use of his title.... What did he really know of women?

Most important, how well did he know Madeline?

Nothing would be served by ejecting the man from the house before he understood the extent of the problem. 'Whatever occurred has been settled between us for some time. She is married and with child.'

'I had not expected that she would marry another,' Colver argued. 'But the fact that she is with child is not so big a surprise. When one is in love, one is sometimes less than careful about such things.'

'She deserves none of the blame for this,' Michael said, conscious of his wife's honour. 'I was the one who was careless that night.' And she had not loved him when they had conceived.

'But we were very much in love,' Richard admitted.

Suddenly, Michael realised that they were talking at cross-purposes. He had been blurting awkward statements to a man whose meaning had been quite different.

He felt like a fool.

He had been sure of only one thing in the past nine months. Despite his fears, he had been able to father a child. But suppose Colver spoke the truth and Madeline had rushed to him with another man's baby?

No matter what had passed between them, this man had waited until he was sure Madeline had married well before coming to her aid. His behaviour was suspect and his answers to other questions had been evasive. There was no reason to believe him now.

But there was always the possibility that, in this, he spoke the truth. Michael's doubt was small. But if he was not careful, it could grow like a worm in an apple.

'So you were in love,' Michael said, dismissing something that had no part in the discussion. 'How fortunate for you. But I fail to see what your lost love has to do with my wife and my child.' No matter what the truth might be, and what he might feel for a woman who could not even call him by name, he was positive he hated Richard Colver.

'We will not argue about the parentage of the child, for that is beneath contempt.' But Colver smiled as he said it as though he had no doubt of the truth, but wished to humour his host. 'Maddie is another matter entirely. She claims she thought me dead. Accepting your offer was clearly an act of desperation.'

Then take her and be gone. It was the wounded cry of his heart. But since Michael was not even sure he had a heart, he ignored it. 'You assume, now that you have finally arrived, that she would prefer to go with you.'

'We would leave the baby with you, of course,' Colver said.

'How magnanimous of you,' Michael responded.

'But should that child be a girl, it would be quite awkward, would it not? Then you would have no heir and no wife.'

Or he could succumb to instinct and have Colver thrown into the street. Then he would lock the doors of the duchess wing with his wife inside and visit her nightly until they had a son. There would be no further nonsense about escaping from a life of luxury with an itinerant soldier.

Then he imagined Madeline tugging helplessly on an immovable door, just as he had done so long ago. Madeline, to whom he had promised everything, including her freedom, should she want it.

'Of course, we might handle this in another way,' Colver suggested to fill the silence. 'A simple settlement for the loss of her affections and I will take my broken heart and go.'

'You wish me to pay you to leave her?' Michael laughed. 'It did not take money to make you go away before.'

'But now I am concerned with her welfare. After what happened in Dover…' He shook his head in disgust. 'I could not part from her so easily,' he said.

'You wish me to buy you off.' Michael thought about this for a moment and laughed again.

'We were practically married,' Colver repeated.

Then Michael rose and advanced on the man. Colver was the taller by a tiny margin. One hoped a trained soldier would have skills to defend himself.

Colver raised his hands, ready to fight.

'Before you strike, remember who it is you hit. It is more than a simple crime to slap a peer. You will hang for it.' It was a pity, really, for Michael most wanted to punch the man. But it would not have been fair to provoke a fight just to see his opponent arrested.

'Then do not threaten me,' Colver said with a stammer.

'I am not threatening,' Michael said with a smile. 'It is more of a promise. If you go from here, it will not be because I paid you to do it. I might have the power to buy you off, but if I do, you will be back again when the money runs out. I have the power to make you disappear. A word from me and you will be in Newgate. Two words and you will hang.'

'You would not dare,' Colver said with no real conviction.

'I would not bother,' Michael said in response, 'unless Madeline requests it of me. My affection for her has kept me from interfering so far. Since you are such an old friend of hers, I would not deny her your company. If, once our child is born, she wishes to go with you, I will not stop her. I promised her anything. And I mean to give it to her, even if what she wishes is you.'

Michael stared at the man until he was sure that Colver understood what an unworthy choice he was, and then continued.

'But if Madeline grows tired of you, or you annoy her in any way, God help you. There is no telling what might happen. What with the pregnancy, she is in a most volatile frame of mind. I suggest, whatever she might decide to do with you, that you treat her well. For if you hurt her, I will end you.'

And then he excused himself from the room to give his wife's lover the privacy to run or stand his ground.

For the first time since he'd come back to Aldric House, Michael locked the door behind him before taking to his own wing. He did not like locked doors, even when he held the key to them. Tonight, however, the less he knew about what went on in the rest of the house, the better.

He had hoped that the problem might have solved itself after his terse conversation with Colver. But though the man was not particularly smart, he was persistent. He had moved into the room that Madeline had selected for him and would likely be there until someone put him out by force. Since Michael had no intention of intervening, it would be up to his wife to settle the matter.

Dinner had been a tense affair, even with Madeline's attempt to keep things civil by inviting the Hastingses. Colver had taken any chance to remark on his close association with Madeline, trying to turn the conversation to mutual friends and jokes that only they would understand. Madeline was clearly uncomfortable, looking the way he had felt in their early days together, when he expected any word from her mouth to be a snide reminder of the past.

But the tone had changed when Sam had found his own reason to dislike the newcomer. After the ladies retired to the parlour, Colver had mentioned his service in the army. The former navy doctor had turned the conversation to detailed analyses of every battle fought in the past fifteen years, while making sure that Colver's glass was never empty.

When the precious Richard had staggered from the room to relieve himself, Sam had announced, 'If that man is an officer and a gentleman, then I am Lord Nelson.' He went on to say that, while the man appeared to have served in the campaign he described, his knowledge of the battle was probably gained by watching it over his shoulder as he deserted his comrades.

Colver had returned to the room, Sam had opened another bottle and things had gone downhill from there. By the time Evelyn had collected her remarkably clear-headed husband for the walk back to the dower house, the servants had been forced to carry an unconscious Colver to his room. Michael was already feeling the effects of too much port and the folly of trying to keep pace while drinking with the military.

Now there was a knocking on the locked door, assuming the hammering was not just in his head. He glared at Brooks, the valet. 'See to that. And tell whoever it is that I am not in the mood for company.' Then he kicked off his own boots and stretched out upon the bed, waiting for death or morning.

But the valet did not return. When he opened his eyes a few moments later, Madeline was standing before him, hands on hips.

'Do not look at me in that way,' he said, too tired to pretend that he was not angry.

'And do not hide behind locks when I wish to speak to you. I told Brooks if he tried to prevent my entry, I would call the footman and have the door removed from its hinges.'

'Very well,' he said. He folded his hands behind his head and leaned back against the headboard, trying to maintain his calm. But for once he did not wish to settle things diplomatically. He wanted an argument. 'What do you wish of me?'

'I want to know what you intend to do about our guest.'

'Colver is your problem, not mine.'

'But you did not need to invite him to stay,' she said. 'Nor did I appreciate your attempt to place him next to my bedchamber.'

'Was that not what you wished?' he said. 'When I came upon you this morning, you were declaring your love for him.' It was a word, nothing more. And though he was uncomfortable when she said it to him, he hated to hear it applied to another.

'I did love him,' she said, refusing to deny it. 'But that was in the past. Did you expect me to lie about it, as you did when you said I told you of him?'

He laughed. 'What a curious omission that turned out to be, for I am sure it is an interesting story. I was not lying. You did not mean to tell me of him. But I learned of him all the same. You were weeping for him in your sleep on the night we married. Begging him to rescue you. From me.'

She looked shocked at this and he could not resist adding, 'You still call his name in your sleep sometimes when we are together.'

'We were to be married,' she snapped, as though that was explanation enough.

'And you believed that?' He laughed again, enjoying her discomfort. 'He never meant to marry you, you stupid girl. He tricked you out of your maidenhead. Then he left you. I wonder how many other fiancées he ran to the army to escape. And how many he has gained since returning.'

'That cannot be true.' Her voice was soft and trembling with rage.

'Did you imagine him remaining celibate for you, all the long years?' Perhaps tomorrow he would regret how much pleasure it gave him to hurt her with the reality of it, but tonight it was vindicating. He raised his arms to heaven and then dropped them. 'But I forget. You claimed you thought him dead. He looks whole enough now, does he not? I am sure, when next he tricks you out of your clothes, you will find his body unmarked.'

'How dare you?' She was white with rage, swaying on her feet, as though the burden of carrying both the truth and the baby was too much for her.

'How do I dare?' He touched his own breast with a forefinger. 'I am sorry if you do not wish to acknowledge the obvious. But what a surprise that now that you have married me, he's located his lost love. What could be so different?' He laid the finger on his chin, as though contemplating. 'I would guess he is after two things—to bed you and to be paid to go away after.'

When she spoke, her voice was as dead as her complexion. 'If you are so sure of this, then I ask again, why did you invite him to stay?'

She was standing so close to the bed that he could smell her perfume while she stared at him with those bottomless dark eyes. Something at the core of him was shouting that he should stop being an ass and admit his mistake. Then he could order the lout from the house and things could return to normal.

Instead, he spoke the truth.

'Because I could not resist the chance to acquaint myself with your tragic lost love. And to discover if it is true that, as you insist, you have not seen him in years.'

'Why should it not be true?' The fact that she could not guess his intent was proof of her innocence.

But he could not stop badgering her. 'Do you deny that you were intimate with this man?'

By the look on her face, he knew that he had uncovered the one secret she had wished to keep. 'On the night we met, I never claimed to be innocent. I didn't get the opportunity to.' Her voice was still quiet, but in shame, not anger.

'You let me assume it ever since,' he reminded her.

'Because you wished it to be true,' she said, shaking her head. 'But did you ever question, your Grace, how there come to be so many fallen women in this country for you to make sport with? Not everyone can afford to be as pure as you expect them to be. Nor are some of us so fortunate as to have married the first man we loved.'

'Fortunate?' he said with a smile. 'You think it would be fortunate to have married a deserting soldier instead of a duke?' Perhaps she did. If she loved Colver, she would have wanted to marry him.

She had claimed to love Michael, as well. It was another proof that words were cheap.

'On the night we met,' she said, 'I had chosen to meet my new employer in Dover for a reason. That was the inn where I had stayed with Richard the night we said goodbye. I prayed that he would come for me and give me children of my own. It was him I was hoping to see. You came to me instead.'

'So you say.' It explained the welcoming arms he remembered and the way she'd cried in her sleep. But there was another possibility. 'It does not explain how I came to be in the wrong room that night,' he said.

'You were drunk,' she reminded him.

'I had never been so drunk before that I could not find my way.'

'There is, as they say, a first time for everything.'

'Or you could have learned of my identity and tricked me into the wrong room. It would have been a most profitable way to explain an indiscretion that had already taken place.' It was a wild assertion, but it made as much sense as what had actually happened between them.

She gasped. 'You think that I was already with child?'

'It would have been extremely convenient for you to find a member of the peerage drunk enough to be gulled into taking on this mess.'

'How dare you?' He had forgotten the voice she had used upon him in those first days when she had hated him. 'It is one thing to doubt me. But to doubt your own child? That is beneath despicable, St Aldric. The baby is yours. Do not think to deny it now.'

'That is just it. I can't deny it. I have accepted you for all to see as my wife and the mother to my heir.' It was happening again, just as it had in Dover. He had drunk too much and gone too far. But this time he was hurting her with words, displaying every irrational fear without thinking of the consequences.

'Then let me assure you,' she said, stepping back out of reach of him. 'You may believe what you like. But I am willing to swear on the Bible, if there is one to be found in this den of iniquity, that the child I carry is yours. I had not seen Richard for years before this morning. When I parted with him, it was in the sincere belief that he would return for me and make me his bride.'

'Very well,' he said, wishing that a simple agreement could take back the horrible things he had already said.

'But what I do not understand is why it should matter to you who I love, or who I am with?'

'You are my wife,' he reminded her.

'And you promised me, from the first, that you wanted nothing more from me than the child.'

Of course he had. But had she forgotten what had happened these past months? 'I thought…'

'That there might be something more between us?' She smiled sadly. 'So did I. I even embarrassed myself by announcing my love for you. Since you did not answer in kind, I have come to assume that my feelings are not reciprocated. If that is true, you can hardly demand that I be faithful to you.'

'You are my wife,' he repeated.

'And you, St Aldric, are blind to your surroundings.' She glanced at the room around her. 'Your parents were married, were they not? Did they not teach you what it means to have a marriage in law and not spirit? You want someone to share your bed. I understand that, for it was what I wanted when I came to you that first time. And when we are in bed we suit well together. But I will not always be young and pretty. Some day you will tire of me, and that will be the end of it. You will take a lover and I will regret that I did not leave when you gave me the chance. Now, if you will excuse me, it has been a trying day. And, much as I might like to, I lack the energy to leave you tonight.'

Chapter Sixteen

To Maddie, the arrival of Richard Colver was proof that one did not necessarily want to have one's prayers answered. She had waited for this moment for so long, never thinking that it would be unwelcome or that Richard would turn out to be anything less than the handsome hero she remembered.

Last night at dinner, his easy smile had looked more like a leer. She could see traces of grey in his hair, the red in his eyes and the sallowness of his skin. The changes looked more like dissipation than age. And during what should have been a polite dinner, she had caught him admiring both her bosom and Evelyn's as though he expected them to be served for pudding. He had no trouble availing himself of his Grace's meat and wine, shovelling the food into himself as though he could not decide whether to eat or stuff his pockets and run.

Had he always been like this? Because it seemed that the duke had been right: the man to whom she'd given her innocence was a selfish, greedy swine. He had not loved her then any more than he did now. She could not imagine he was here for any reason but to make trouble.

And he had succeeded. It had led to the row she'd had with St Aldric before bed. If he had simply been jealous, she might have flattered herself that he cared for her more than he did. Judging by the smell in the room, he was as drunk as he'd been on the night in Dover. Though he might promise that the scratches on his shoulder were enough to keep him sober, they had failed to do any good yesterday. He'd questioned her honour and accused her of lying about something so important as to the paternity of their baby. His doubts hurt far worse than the absence of loving words.

It had been a miserable few minutes, but she had come away with a new understanding of several things. For one, she was sure that she wanted nothing to do with Richard Colver. She would not go so far as to call herself a fool for loving him. She had been an innocent, young girl and could not have known better, but only an idiot would go to him now.

Another less pleasant truth had come out, as well. She still loved St Aldric, even after the horrible things he had said. But he had made no similar declaration, nor did she suspect one was on the way. When confronted with difficult truths, he'd announced she was his wife, treating her like any other property. He had not cared enough to keep her safe from Richard. In fact, he'd gone out of the way to throw them together.

She would have no help from her husband in ridding herself of this nuisance, since he did not care enough about her to remove the man himself.

She doubted Michael would welcome her infidelity. In fact, he seemed to expect it, even though she'd given him no reason. Nor had he promised her that he would be faithful. When she had told him he'd grow tired of her, there was no vehement rejection of it. When given a chance to prove her wrong, he had not promised to cherish her for ever. He had simply stared at her, as though amazed that she had the nerve to point out his hypocrisy. It showed that he felt nothing at all for her other than hurt pride that she had not been a virgin when he had first lain with her.

If they were not careful, they were destined to follow the path of his parents. And, much as he claimed to hate the past, he was doing nothing to prevent the repetition of it.

She would leave before that happened. She did not want to see women sneaking into the duke's chambers, nor did she wish to flaunt lovers in front of him. In the past months, she had begun to imagine a future for them that was quite different from the original plan. They would share a life together. There would be a houseful of children. Even if St Aldric could not manage to love her, he would adore the children. Wasn't that what he'd wanted all along?

If not, she would have enough love for all. She absently touched her stomach, as though she could offer some reassurance to the baby resting so close to her heart.

But now she was back to the place she had started: in a loveless marriage and about to produce a single child.

This morning, when she came down to breakfast, there was no sign of St Aldric. Richard was sitting at the head of the table as though he belonged there, with heaped plate and an ironic smile.

Maddie made a mental note to invite Evelyn and Sam to every meal from now on, even if it was necessary to claim illness to get them to the house. 'Good morning, Mr Colver.'

'Good morning, your Grace.' He stood for a moment and bowed, then sat and went back to eating.

She enquired after the duke. The footman informed her, with a meaningful cough, that his Grace had elected to take meals in his room. She'd have called him a coward for refusing to meet a rival, but to force himself to stay in the duke's wing, a place he could hardly abide, was its own sort of punishment. After last night's excesses, she hoped his head ached, as well.

For herself, her appetite had fled with the argument and no amount of Wow-Wow sauce was likely to bring it back. She had slept poorly as well, for the baby would not allow her a moment's comfort.

But neither St Aldric's suffering nor her own rid her of the problem at hand. 'Well, Mr Colver,' she said again, unsure of how to start the conversation. 'it has been lovely seeing you again after all this time.'

He grinned at her, taking another swallow of coffee. 'And more than lovely to see you, my dear. It is good to find that you have fallen on your feet after the time we spent together.'

As opposed to falling on her back? she wondered. Many women in her situation had been forced into a far more dishonourable course of action after being abandoned by a lover. 'Now that you have assured yourself of my safety, you will most likely want to be moving on,' she suggested.

'I see no reason why I should. Your husband invited me to stay as long as I wished,' he reminded her.

'But that does not explain why you are here in the first place,' she said.

'I wanted to be sure that you are happy,' he said.

If he had two good hands but had not written her, then her happiness had not occurred to him in several years. 'Your concern for me is touching,' she said, 'but unwarranted. Now that I am married, I am quite secure.'

He sighed. 'It is a shame that we are not all so fortunate.'

He referred to himself, she supposed. But she was at a loss as to what he expected from her. She thought for a moment and put on an attitude of optimism and encouragement, just as she did when dealing with sulky children. 'It is true that life can be difficult. But

when one perseveres and applies oneself to betterment, there is no telling what can be accomplished.'

'A noble sentiment,' he agreed. 'Success is possible
when circumstances do not work against one. When
one is betrayed by a lost love, for instance. With marriage comes certain expectations, and the dissolution
of a betrothal ends them.'

True, she supposed, but how did it pertain to this
situation? 'Since I have married,' she assured him,
'no damage was done.'

'To you, perhaps.'

It took her a moment to realise that he was referring to himself, but his dejected look was spoiled by
the fact that his cheeks were bulging with St Aldric's
bacon. 'You cannot seriously claim breach of promise,' she said.

'You promised yourself to me. Then you abandoned me to marry St Aldric.' He had the nerve to
look injured.

'Because I thought you were dead,' she reminded
him, snorting in disgust. 'Next you will be saying that
I took your honour.' St Aldric was right. The man was
an ass. He had used her and abandoned her. Now he
was trying to find a way to use her again.

'I would not have made love to you had I not
thought you serious and constant in your affections,'
he said. 'In waiting for you, I have denied myself the
opportunity to marry well. Now I have nothing. Not
even you.'

The fact that she placed last in value told her everything she needed to know about his true feelings for her. 'And what do you expect me to do about your tragic circumstances?'

'Normally a settlement is in order.'

She smiled, for to this she could answer. 'Then you are talking to the wrong person, Richard. I have nothing to give you.'

'But you are a duchess,' he said, confused.

'With not a penny in my pocket,' she said, confident that it was the truth. 'I used the last of my savings before the wedding. I have not had reason to ask for a thing from St Aldric since.' She thought for a moment. 'Unless you are willing to take ladies' clothing, a pair of lovebirds or, perhaps, a horse. Go to the stables and tell them that I have given you Buttercup.'

'I do not need a horse,' he said firmly.

'It is just as well, for I do not wish to give her up. If it is money that you are after, then you will have to talk to the duke.'

'I have already spoken to him,' Richard said with confidence. 'And he leaves the decision to you.'

Damn the man. If she asked, St Aldric would give any sum she named to this interloper and he would be gone. But she suspected that whatever they had shared in the past months had been ruined by the fact that Richard had come here at all. She looked at him for a moment, wondering just what it was that she had seen in him, to hang so many dreams upon. And then she said, 'You wish my decision, Richard? Then here it is. If St Aldric thought you deserved money, you would have it already.'

'You mean to side with him, despite what he did to you in Dover?' Richard asked.

'I fail to see how my giving you a settlement would change the past,' she said as reasonably as possible. 'And since you made it clear just now that you would trade my love for gold, I am not inclined to give you either.'

'If I spoke in error,' he said, trying to look earnest, 'it was because I thought there was no other choice. You are more valuable to me than St Aldric's gold. It is only because I doubt you will leave him that I make the suggestion. St Aldric does not love you. If he did, he would not permit my presence in the house.'

Though she feared that half the words from Richard's mouth were lies, occasionally he found the truth.

'Not all marriages can be based on love,' she said, knowing that it was true. 'But we get on well enough together. That is more than many couples have.'

Richard was unimpressed. 'From what I hear from the people of this area, it should not be too difficult to get on well enough with St Aldric. I suspect it is his saintly nature that keeps him from reminding you of how oddly matched you are.'

'Perhaps so,' she retorted, 'but I notice that manners do not prevent you from mentioning it.'

Richard gave her a tired shake of his head. 'I merely wish you to remember what was obvious from the start. You are a governess, Maddie. And he is a duke. If not for the child you carry, he would not have looked twice at you. He would have chosen someone much more like Mrs Hastings. Someone from his social set.'

Perhaps it was true. But even though it would have been more appropriate, he had not married Evelyn.

Because she had turned him down.

Very well. Her husband did not love her. And perhaps they did not suit. She might have a future that held every material possession she might want. But it seemed strangely empty when she thought of the man who would share it—always polite, always solicitous, yet never truly hers. Maybe she would have to leave him. But not until she had placed the baby safe in his arms. Without thinking, she touched her belly again. *I do not want to leave you, as well,* she promised silently. *But we cannot always have what we want.*

Richard saw it and nodded. 'You are right to be thinking of the child. But it will be here soon, Maddie. And then what will you do?'

She did not know, so she could not answer.

Richard was looking at her as he had years ago, in the way that had made her believe in him. 'I know you do not want me here. And I know there will be no money. But I mean to stay until the baby is born. When it is come, if you wish it, I will see you safely away from here. I owe you that, at least, my dear. When you find that you can no longer bear to stay here, you need have nothing to fear. I will take care of you.' Then he pushed his plate aside, got up from his chair and came to her, kissing her once on the forehead before leaving her alone.

Chapter Seventeen

After the previous evening's activities, Michael did not expect to meet Richard Colver over breakfast. But it seemed that sleeping late after too much drink was not amongst the man's vices. When asked, Brooks relayed the information that Colver was already in the breakfast room with her Grace. Michael debated interrupting the pair of them and forcing his company upon them.

But then he remembered his fight with Madeline on the previous evening. If he had treated his wife with the kindness she deserved, there would be nothing to interrupt. She had told him she loved him. She had done it before, of course. But he had not wanted to hear it then. It was only when he thought he might not hear it again that he realised the value of those three little words.

She loved him. And he had refused to reciprocate.

Even now, he was still not sure that he could go to her and say the things she wanted to hear. He had made so many wild accusations that an apology was in order. But to follow it with the announcement that, he thought, perhaps, that he loved her? Even if he could deliver it with confidence, he doubted she would believe him. She would look at him as she sometimes did when she suspected that his thoughts did not match his words.

If nothing else, he did not wish to see Madeline in the company of Colver. Nor was he sure she'd want him under any circumstances. He would wait until after breakfast, and then he would find her and choose his words as carefully as an argument in the House of Lords. In the meantime, he would seek out his brother and get some of the familial advice that Eve thought was important. Sam knew more of love than he ever would. Surely he might be of some use on the subject.

When the servant showed him into the dower house, Sam was alone in the parlour. It was unusual, for he rarely saw the husband without the wife. Sam had explained that, after spending years separated from his true love, each moment with her was precious.

He had thought the devotion an admirable thing. But today it reminded him of his own wife and her supposed soulmate secluded in the breakfast room.

'Where is your wife this morning?' Michael said, trying not to scowl. 'After your excesses of last night, she has not run back to London without you, I trust?'

'Of course not.' Sam gave him the same knowing

smile he always wore, confident that, after years of waiting, Eve would have him drunk or sober. 'She is helping with a delivery in the village. But it is not too much longer that she will be helping at the main house. That is not why you are here, is it?'

To this, Michael could manage nothing more than a grunt.

'That is not the response I was expecting,' Sam said. 'You are the father-to-be. You have been badgering me with questions on the dreary details of human gestation for six months. But now that the race is almost run, you have lost interest?'

'I am not without interest,' Michael said. 'There are other things on my mind.'

'More important than the birth of your first child? Which, by my calculations, could occur at any moment?'

As a physician, Sam was not prone to exaggeration, but Michael suspected that, in this case, he might be guilty of it. Madeline had seemed fine on the previous evening, other than the fact that she had been furious with him.

'I am just as interested in the baby as I ever was,' he said. 'But at the moment, it is this Colver fellow that bothers me.'

'Then send him away,' Sam said with an incredulous shake of his head. 'You needn't be burdened with an uninvited guest at a time like this.'

'Madeline's guest,' Michael said.

'In your house,' Sam reminded him.

'But suppose she would rather that he stayed?'

Sam laughed. 'Has she told you this?'

'No,' Michael admitted.

Sam nodded. 'Then I assume you waited until Colver was dead drunk and we were gone, and had a terrific row about him. You said something supremely stupid to her, rather than sending him away when you had the chance. Now she is likely to cling to him out of spite to teach you the lesson you deserve.'

'Well, what am I to do about it?' Michael snapped. He did not like being read so easily.

'Apologise. Swear your love for her. Tell her that she must give up Colver or you will remove him yourself. And you can give her jewellery, I suppose. But I have never found that to be necessary when arguing with Evie.'

'Suppose I do not?' Michael asked.

'Do not what? Apologise? Then there is no hope for you. Whatever it was, it was likely your fault and you had best own up to it.'

'Suppose I do not love her?'

He could see by the shocked look on Sam's face that the possibility had not occurred to him. 'Then send the man away all the quicker. You do not want him in your house, and her feelings towards you, or him, do not matter.'

But even if he was not in love, he was sure her feelings did matter to him. 'When we married, I promised that she was to have her own way in all things.'

'I was there,' Sam reminded him. 'I thought it very foolish of you.'

'At the time, I was only concerned with getting her to agree to stay with me for the baby's sake. But now if she wants to go with Colver...'

'You wish to change your earlier agreement,' Sam said.

'I have grown used to her,' he admitted cautiously.

Sam snorted. 'You speak as though she were a hound or a pair of well-fitting boots.'

'It is more than that,' Michael said, trying to find the right words. 'She is pleasant company.'

'In what way?' Sam pressured. 'Do you think she makes an adequate partner at whist? Or do you simply enjoy lying with her?' Sam laughed again. 'Do not look so shocked at me. You are married to her after all. If you are intimate, it is as it should be.'

Michael was surprised. 'Is it so obvious?'

'To look at the pair of you, it is quite plain that yours has not been a marriage of convenience for some time,' Sam said. 'You dote on each other.'

'We do?' He tried to think of anything he might have done that would have lead to Sam's conclusion. 'While she is affectionate to me, it is nothing out of the bounds of propriety. I treat her with the courtesy that my wife deserves.'

'And when you are together, your eyes follow each other around the room. When you think we are not watching, you find any excuse to touch hands or stand too close to each other. If I linger too long over port after dinner, you begin yawning and making comments about the need for the duchess to get her rest.'

'She tires easily,' he insisted.

'She would need less sleep if you did not keep her up all night.'

Given a choice, he'd rather she take to afternoon naps than forgo their time together. 'You said that it was quite normal for breeding women to be affectionate,' Michael reminded him.

'Then you must be breeding, as well,' Sam concluded. 'I have not known you for long. But until recently, I have never seen you making calf's eyes at a woman, or staring at the door each time she leaves the room for a moment as though you cannot wait for her return.'

'I look at her no differently than I ever have,' Michael insisted.

'Not two days ago, I caught you feeding morsels to her from your plate and encouraging her to lick your fingers after each bite.'

'I worry when she does not eat,' he said, aware of how foolish it must sound.

'But that does not make it necessary to feed her by hand.' Sam shook his head. 'I would have stopped you had it not been so terribly amusing.'

'I doubt you will have source for such amusement in the future,' he said, remembering how they had parted. 'After the way I behaved last night, it would be safer to hand feed a tiger.'

'And if there was a tiger in the garden and she required you to feed it by hand, would you do it?'

Michael thought for a moment. 'If it made her smile, of course I would.'

'Then you have your answer as to your feelings for her,' Sam said with a nod. 'Now, take the advice of your personal physician. Go back to your wife and tell her of them. Nothing will cure your particular ailment of the heart but honesty in this one thing.' And with that, Sam dismissed him.

Michael walked back towards the house, still confused. While the doctor's simple instructions seemed like the right course of action, he could not help but think that there must be more to it. He had apologised to her before and could manage that without difficulty. If he remembered what Sam had said about his recent behaviour, he could announce his love for her with confidence.

But what if he told her to give up Colver and she refused? To put the man out of the house was to break his word—but to let him stay?

This was why he'd avoided love in the past. It led one to contemplate things that were intensely painful, like hand feeding tigers and entertaining one's wife's lover. Perhaps he had best go to the office and think about it for a while to find the right words. Or open the lock room and bring jewellery.

Or do neither. Madeline was waiting at the top of the stairs. Not for him, although it almost seemed that way. She was leaning against the wall, bending forward with her hands on her knees, as though she'd lost the strength to go farther.

He reached out to help her. 'Are you all right? Is it the baby?'

She looked at him strangely and shook off his offer of aid. 'Not all my problems are caused by the baby, you know.'

'Of course not.' Did she mean that he was a problem? Or was the problem that he seemed to care more about the child than the mother? 'I am sorry,' he said.

She closed her eyes and pulled herself up from the wall. 'I am just being difficult. I was winded after climbing the stairs. As you guessed, it was because of the baby. And I stopped to rest.'

'I am sorry for last night, as well,' he said. 'I said many things. And all of them were wrong.'

Now that the apology had passed, she was neither angry nor satisfied. She did not seem particularly interested in it either way.

'And I love you,' he added. Then he waited for the change that would make everything all right again.

She looked sorry for him, as though he'd tried his hardest and still could not learn the lesson she was teaching, but she said nothing in response. If this was how she'd felt when he had remained silent, he was beginning to understand the problem.

'About Colver,' he went on, meaning to get it all out at once before he lost his temper or his nerve.

'He means to stay until after the baby is born,' she

said, as though something had been settled without his knowledge. 'And I think that is probably for the best.'

What did she mean by that? If he was not the father, what use would Colver be? But to ask those questions would mean another argument. 'Sam said it could be very soon,' he said instead.

She nodded.

'He says you need your rest.' That had not been what he'd said at all. But it was probably true.

'I was going to lie down,' she agreed. 'I am not feeling well.'

Now that she mentioned it, she did not look well. But he did not mean to frighten her with it. 'It will all be over soon,' he said, hoping that it would comfort her.

Apparently it did not, for she was giving him the searching look she sometimes got when she was unsure of his meaning. Then she spoke. 'Before I go to my room, I have a question for you. If you could live life over again...'

It was the beginning of one of those rhetorical questions that women asked, which never seemed to end well. He braced himself for the worst.

'...would you have been happier marrying Evelyn?'

'Good God, no.' He had answered too quickly and too honestly. He corrected himself. 'She did not want me. She is in love with Sam.'

'But in all other ways, she would have been a better match,' Madeline informed him.

'Certainly not.'

'She would have been less trouble,' Madeline insisted. 'She knew your friends and they her. She would not have troubled you with lovebirds, or sad horses, or former lovers.'

'I love her dearly,' Michael said, embarrassed that the words came so easily when talking about someone other than his wife. 'But only as a sister. She'd have cheated on me with my own brother before the year was out. Not to mention that her manners are abominable and she refuses to change. In our one and only dinner together, she reduced one of the guests to apoplexy. And when I kissed her, I felt nothing.'

Madeline was smiling now. It was weak, but it was there. 'Apoplexy?'

He nodded. 'You have, on occasion, attempted to try my patience, but you are not nearly as successful as Evelyn can be. And she does it without even trying.'

The smile was gone and Madeline was looking strange again.

Perhaps he had misspoken again by criticising her friend. 'Would you like me to help you to your room?' he asked, for she was leaning against the wall again.

She shook her head again and turned down the hall of her wing with a vague wave of her hand, as though she could not be bothered with his help.

Apparently he was not needed. He did not like the feeling of being unnecessary in his own wife's life.

'Perhaps I shall see you at dinner,' he called after her. He would invite Sam and Evelyn as well, in case they were needed. Then he would go to the lock room and find some jewellery.

Chapter Eighteen

The bed in the duchess wing, for all its pillows and satin, was not conducive to restful sleep, but neither did Maddie want to open her eyes. She had dozed through the afternoon, but felt no better than she had when she'd lain down. The duke had sent up a pile of letters from prospective maids and nurses and nannies that she should be reading to prepare for the coming interviews. Apparently, when one was giving birth to the future Duke of St Aldric, a girl from the village would not do for even the simplest task.

Or perhaps it was just that St Aldric was still in a pet over Richard and trying to vex her with this. He had been most strange when she'd passed him in the hall earlier, apologising as he should have and talking no more nonsense about being tricked into marriage.

Then he'd announced, out of the blue, that he loved her, as if the only thing he'd got from the previous night's argument was that she expected to hear those particular words. But he had been wearing the same shallow smile that he used in the office and the drawing room, as though the event called for diplomacy and not passion.

The true Michael who hid behind her husband had not appeared until she'd asked him about Evelyn. For a moment or two, he had forgotten to be polite and seemed truly relieved that the engagement had failed. Then the courteous smile had returned and she had gone to her room.

And Richard, who she had longed to see for so long, would not go away. Did he not notice that she was near to bursting with another man's child? She'd have shouted the news to him before this, if the sweet little thing in her belly would allow her to take a breath. But his speech in the breakfast room that morning had been almost sincere once they had stopped talking about money. Perhaps he truly wanted nothing more than to help.

She had proven to her satisfaction that he had been wrong about Evelyn, of course. But there were so many things of which she was still unsure. Could she stand to live the whole of her life with a man who could not manage to feel for her?

Until she saw the baby, and its gender, and whether its birth would bring any real emotion to its father, she was not sure what she meant to do. By law, the child was his and her feelings for it did not matter. If she left, she must leave alone. That would mean leaving half her heart with the duke and the rest with her child. She would stay to be close to her son, even if it meant sacrificing her pride.

But suppose she had a daughter? There was no question that he would want a boy. But a girl might be little more than a disappointment to him, just as its mother seemed to be. She thought of her own childhood and the ever-present knowledge that, whatever it was her parents had wanted, she was not that thing.

No daughter of hers would feel unwanted, even for a moment. Perhaps St Aldric would let the two of them retire together from his life. The girl could be raised properly, with all the advantages of her birth and one parent who cherished her above all.

In either case, Maddie had no intention of welcoming the duke back to her bed without some indication of sincere feeling on his part. She would blame her past willingness on the vagaries of pregnancy and turn him out of the bedchamber. He had promised he would make no demands upon her. For the sake of her own breaking heart, she would hold him to his word.

It would not be too much longer before she had the answer. No matter the sex, the baby would come soon. Everyone kept telling her so. They had best be right, for Maddie could not stand much more of the physical misery that accompanied the emotional upheaval. If men did this to one, then they were more trouble than they were worth. She had long suspected it and now she was sure.

There was no comfort to be had in rising or sleeping. She was bloated and ugly. Today she did not feel well at all. And now there was a bumping in the walls, as if the largest rat in Aldricshire had located her bedroom with the intention of breaking up her peace. She had not noticed a similar problem in the nursery wing, thank goodness, but she would not risk bringing a child into a house full of vermin. If she could manage to get out of bed, she would go there with a broom and search. It would give her great pleasure to dispense any interlopers she found. Then she would take the broom to St Aldric for his foolishness in not allowing a terrier, or at least a cat, in the house to do the job for her. With all the little wire-and-wool animals in the nursery, there had been not a single one to be useful at a moment like this.

There was another thump and a rustle, and one of the hangings on the far wall rippled with the movement behind it. Maddie dragged herself to her feet, grabbed the only thing that came to hand, a bedroom slipper, and raised it over her head, advancing to strike.

Then the curtain pulled aside and a rather dusty Richard appeared, arms outstretched. 'My darling!'

'My God.' She yanked the fabric away to stare at the wood panel that had slipped to the side, revealing a narrow passageway behind the wall.

'I discovered the door pull in the wall of my chambers. Then I understood why you had been so insistent that I take that particular room.' He was smiling as if he'd found treasure and not just cobwebs. 'I knew if I but followed the passage that it would bring me to you.'

As if she'd have bothered with secret passages when she could have installed him next door for convenience. The thought of a more convenient Richard was almost as appalling as this sudden arrival in her room. It had been hard enough to breathe before, but the sudden shock of his appearance had taken the wind right out of her. 'What are you doing here?'

He looked at her as though it was the most obvious thing in the world. 'I have come to love you, my sweet.'

'I do not recall asking you to,' she said as reasonably as she could manage, pressing her hands to her stomach to settle the cramp. 'In fact, I have asked you to leave.'

'We agreed this morning that I was to stay until the baby was born,' he reminded her. 'I feared your feelings for me had cooled and you wanted nothing more than my friendship. But now that I discovered this?' He waved at the passageway behind him. 'It has all come clear to me.'

'Then you had best enlighten me,' she said, 'for I do not understand at all.'

'You wished for me to seek you out. To prove myself worthy of you.'

'You had years to find me,' she reminded him. 'I made it as easy as I could for you. Now you think that by crawling through a hole in my bedroom wall everything has changed?'

'But the time was not yet right to come for you,' he said with a smile. 'I had nothing to offer you.'

'Because you abandoned your commission and ran?' she said.

'I did not run.'

'Perhaps you walked, or rode,' she said, tired of the whole business. 'But if the Horse Guard thought you dead and you did not inform them otherwise, then I must assume you are a deserter.' She had thought his arrival in Aldricshire was an unpleasant shock. But it was nothing compared to this.

'You do not know what it was like,' he argued. 'Alone and friendless, so far from home.'

She laughed. 'Of all the arguments you might bring, my lack of sympathy for the lonely will do you the least good.'

For a moment, he did not look so sure of himself. Then the smile returned. 'But I have found my way back to you now.'

'You should have at least knocked,' she said. 'Or called out to explain yourself before entering my room.'

'At one time, you would not have minded,' he said. His sea-green eyes were as deep and beautiful as she remembered, but not as innocent.

'That was a long time ago,' she said. 'And I am married now.'

'But that is the wonder of it,' he said. 'Your husband has promised me that the decision is yours and he will deny you nothing. We can be together, even now.'

'If I wish it,' she reminded him.

'You do not have to tell him if you think it likely to upset him.' He pointed to the passageway again. 'We can love in secret, just as we used to.'

When they were young, he had assured her that secrecy was necessary to protect her honour. But now it was probably due to a very sensible fear of St Aldric. The duke's patience might wear thin once he discovered that there was a passage between the rooms.

She had a good mind to tell him of it.

'Love me now,' Richard insisted. 'Once the baby is born, you can be free of him. The child is all he wants from you. He told me so himself.'

Would St Aldric really say such a thing? Then the sudden pain she felt was her heart breaking.

Then she remembered that Richard was a terrible liar and she did not need to listen to him. The pain eased.

But Richard remained. 'Leave the baby with him,' he said. 'And come away with me as I suggested this morning. It will be as it was when we were first together.'

The idea that she would trade one moment with her own flesh and blood for a lifetime with Richard Colver took the last of her patience from her. Her body had no more space to contain the growing ire than it did to take a decent breath. 'This morning you spoke as my friend. Now you wish to be lovers. Before that, you wanted only my financial support because you claimed I had ruined your prospects.'

'And I will still need your help,' he admitted. 'But if you separate from your husband, he will not make you live without funds.'

'You wish me to leave him because when I do, he will support me and I will support the pair of us?'

'You make it sound so sordid, my dove.' He reached for her again.

'Because it is,' she said, tapping him lightly on the forehead with the slipper she had been holding. 'Have you no desire to supply for your own needs?'

He sighed. 'The life of a veteran is not a happy one. Many of us are begging in the street.'

'Those who are missing an arm or a leg, perhaps. Those who are unfit to work.' Had Richard ever spoken of a job? He'd had a nebulous plan to make his fortune while in the army. He had talked often enough of his father's unfairness. But even now she was sure that Mr Colver would take him back, should he decide to return to the family business.

He gave her a pitiable look. 'I will, of course, apply myself to some job or other. It is simply a matter of finding one that is suitable. Until that time, my sweet pigeon, I see no reason why we cannot begin our life together.'

'Oh, Richard,' she said, shaking her head, with a smile. 'There is one very good reason.'

'What is that, my little chicken?'

'Because while I might wish to leave my husband,

I do not wish to leave my baby. And I would not trade either of them for another moment with you. Now pack your things and go to…Norfolk. Or to Hades. Really, I do not care.' She did not feel up to having this discussion. In fact, she rather thought that it would be nice to crawl back into bed and die.

'But my dear duckling, my…'

And that was the last straw. Ducks waddled. Now so did she. She turned and grabbed the first handy thing, a bolster trimmed with gold tassels, and swung it at him. 'I am not your little duckling. I am not a bird of any kind and especially not a lovebird. Most important, I am not yours.'

Richard dodged the pillow and stepped farther into the room, towards the bed. 'You are speaking of the marriage to the duke? Do not be silly…angel.'

It was not a bird, but it still had wings. She grabbed a hairbrush from the vanity and threw it at his head.

'You were mine long before you were his.' He was circling the room, trying to get close to her again. 'And glad to be so, as I remember it.'

'Because I loved you,' she said. The words seemed to cramp inside her, as though the baby and everything else about her rebelled at the knowledge.

Richard, merely looked surprised. 'When I left you, you had no trouble forgetting me. You have tumbled into quite the downy nest, while I have not a feather to fly with.'

More feathers. She gave an inarticulate growl of disgust and looked for something else to throw.

He held out his arms to block her aim and took another step forward. 'You cannot mean to send me away so soon. To forget the love we shared. To separate yourself from your oldest and dearest friend?'

'We are no longer friends,' she said. Today she did not feel friendly to anyone, and even less so to Richard. 'Nor are we lovers.'

'But we can be again, can we not? We could start fresh.' He put down his hands and smiled at her as he used to, when she was young and trusting. Then he added, 'It would be quite safe to be so, for you are already with child.'

'St Aldric…'

'Is on the other side of the house and will not hear a thing,' he said, his smile changing to an evil grin. 'And you are more than enough woman to handle the two of us.'

If that comment was meant to reflect on her current size, there would be hell to pay. She grabbed another pillow and swung with all her might for his head. When it struck, the seam split in a burst of feathers, but the exertion left her short of breath and clasping her middle.

'Not that you are unattractive,' he said, sensing his misstep. 'You are the very bloom of health. Lovelier than you have ever been. Now, what say you to a tumble?' He made another lunge for her, sprawling on the bed.

She grabbed the first thing handy, the heavy brass

candlestick on the bedside table and swung it like a club, catching him in the shoulder.

'Out.'

'My… Ow.' Her next blow had taken him before he could find another avian endearment.

'Out,' she said, brandishing the candlestick. 'Now. From this room, from this house. Do not wait for your things. They will be sent after.'

'But I am willing to wait,' he said, hands on his heart. 'A lifetime, if necessary.'

She took another swing. Except for the pain in her stomach, it felt good. 'And that might not be so very long,' she said, waving her makeshift club in front of her. 'If you do not go now, you will end this day covered from head to toe in bruises. And do not think you will not.' She swung again, catching him another thump to the arm, which actually raised a look of alarm.

'I will not leave you,' he insisted, dodging the next blow. 'Call the servants if you must. It will be quite embarrassing when they find us in the middle of a lovers' spat.' But he did not look quite as sure as he had.

She shook her head and smiled as a mad idea occurred to her. 'Waiting for the servants would take too long. I am breeding, as you say. And my moods are…volatile.' She swung again and he actually rolled away onto the floor, scrambling to put the bed between them.

'Now, now, Maddie….'

She threw the candlestick and watched it bounce

off his shoulder before searching about for something else to pitch at him. 'You want my company, do you, Richard? After all this time? You returned from the war and did not rush to me while I was still young and sweet-tempered. Well, you have found me now—and how do you like me?' She sent a paperweight from the desk sailing past his head and into the cheval glass behind him. It hit with a resounding crack and half the mirror slid from the frame to shatter on the rug.

'For God's sake, Maddie! Have you lost your mind?' He turned to back towards the salon door, finding it locked and muttering, 'Damn.'

'Perhaps I had no mind to begin with,' she said, on fire with pain and evil glee. 'But I know you are right in one thing. I am more than enough woman for the pair of you.' The porcelain ornament she grabbed next caught him in the forehead, raising a trickle of blood before it bounced away.

'Ask the duke—he will tell you how much trouble I am. A tartar, a shrew, a fishwife. I have taken each opportunity I could find to make his life a misery. Your arrival here is just one example.' She grabbed the poker from the fireplace and hefted it in her hand. 'And the thing is, Richard, I am quite fond of him. One might even say that I love him. He did not dishonour and abandon me as you did.'

She brandished the poker like a sword. 'Oh, my first beloved—' she swung '—my duckling—' she swung again '—my fine proud cockerel.' She smiled, advancing on him. 'People keep telling me that I have an increased appetite. But I think it might be for violence. If you do not have the sense to leave me this instant, you will be a capon when I am finished with you. And the duke and all his servants will not lift a finger to help you.'

With that, her one true beloved turned and ran down the passage to his room and slammed the door behind him.

Chapter Nineteen

Maddie summoned Peg, who looked in horror at the destruction in the room. 'Throw it all away,' she said, waving her arms wide. 'And tear down the draperies, as well. Then tell a footman to nail the walls shut.'

'Beggin' your pardon, your Grace?' The maid looked at her as though she had made the sort of mad comment that one would expect from a tosser of pillows or a breaker of glass.

'And see to it that Mr Colver is removed from the house. Immediately.'

'Very good, your Grace.' This, at least, made some sense.

With the removal of Richard settled, Maddie staggered towards her husband's office before the next pain could come again.

'St Aldric! I demand to speak to you this instant!'

Seeing her expression, Upton immediately began gathering his notebooks to retreat. But the smile that the duke gave her was as neutral and unperturbed as ever, as though he did not wish to air their troubles in front of the staff. 'Yes, my love?'

'Do not mock me with endearments,' she said, grabbing the corner of the desk. She caught her breath and spoke again. 'This house is…unsatisfactory.'

'Really?' Now he was drawling. She had never known him to drawl, even on the days when he had been most impatient with her. 'Whatever is the problem, my dear? Would you like something larger? If I could convince the Regent to let us Carlton House—but it might not be big enough to hold your wardrobe.' He was teasing her and she was in no mood for it.

'This one will do nicely, once it has been gutted and redone,' she said, glaring at him. 'Do not give me that look as though you do not know the problems here, for it is plain that you do not like it either.'

'I will admit to no such thing,' he said, glancing at Upton as though to remind her of the need for manners. 'It is my boyhood home, you know.'

'And I do not wish to stay another night in it.'

'We will return to London in a week, or perhaps less,' he said as reasonably as possible. 'But I doubt Evelyn will encourage you to travel at this time. And you must remember that you have a guest.' He rolled his eyes upwards. Then he went white as a thought occurred to him. 'Or does he mean to take you away…?'

So the idea that she might leave with Richard had struck him dumb. She wished that she felt well enough to enjoy the fact, but now he was grabbing at her arm.

She was sure that if she tried to leave, he would restrain her.

Then another pain took her and she stood gasping for a moment, forcing out words in short, breathless sentences:

'I sent Richard away.'

'He came into my room.'

'Through a passage in the wall.'

Her discomfort went unnoticed, but the words caught his attention. While his expression did not really change, she saw the impassive mask drop away as he stared into her face. 'He what?' She could feel the muscles beneath his coat sleeve tensing as though he was preparing for a fight.

She caught her breath again. 'He entered my room without my permission. I do not even allow you to do so.'

The duke had always been a tall man, but he seemed to grow even taller with outrage at the offence to her. His arm was as taut as a bowstring, ready to let fly. 'And where is Colver now?' There was murder in his blue eyes and his smile was thin, angry and very, very real.

She would remember to be thrilled by the response, but later, when she was not so preoccupied. She could feel the next pain, waiting, only moments away. 'I do not know. The servants have probably removed him by now. But I dealt with him myself. Some things in my room were broken.'

'Things?'

'A paperweight, a mirror, some assorted crockery. I was upset,' she said, gasping as though she was about to be pulled underwater. 'It took some time to perfect my aim.'

His lips twitched. Then he said, very softly, 'I think I was very fortunate that the rooms in Dover were devoid of ornament. I deserved a thrashing that night.'

The pain took her again and her next words came out in a squeak. 'You deserve one now, for you are responsible for the miserable state I am in.'

'The state you are in?'

'You dolt.' This time, the pain was strong enough that she lost her breath and could barely mouth the words. 'If you ask Evelyn…she will tell you more than you want to know.… It has been nearly nine months and two weeks since Dover.'

'They said soon,' he agreed.

It was a shame that a man who was so beautiful could be so dense. The pressure had eased a little and she took a breath and spoke again. 'Two weeks too long. I have been ready for at least a month. But the baby waited until now.'

'Now?'

She clutched the desk as the pain subsided and her knees went weak. 'Now. But that does not mean that I will forget the inadequacies of this abomination of a house.'

'Now.' He seemed fixated on the one word. 'We must get you to your room immediately.'

'You are not listening to me,' she said, slapping

him on the biceps. 'I do not want to go to my room.'
She dug the nails of her other hand into the wood of
his desk, both for support and because she was afraid
he would send her away before she could finish what
she was saying. 'I hate my room. I will not go back
there. It is full of broken glass.'

'One of the guest rooms, then.' He reached for her
arm again, trying to guide her away from the matter at hand.

'The whole wing is ridiculous. Rooms upon rooms.
All leading to each other. Secret passages and lovers
like mice in the walls.' The pain took her again and
she started to double.

She got a brief look at Upton, who was still in the
room with them, caught between amazement and terror.

She balled her fists and pounded them against the
rigid muscles of her stomach, begging them to loosen.

But the duke's hand caught hers, pulling her back
into his chest, wrapping himself around her in a protective shell. 'Of course, darling. I am sorry that I
brought you here. Upton,' he said, in the proper duke's
voice that did not sound at all like the real Michael
who was holding her. 'Prepare a budget, find an archi-
tect and hire some carpenters. We will wish to begin
in a week, perhaps, two.'

'Immediately,' she insisted. 'It must be totally redone. We must have a main corridor as decent houses
do. And normal bedchambers beside each other. Yours
is extremely inconvenient.'

He was walking her slowly towards the door. 'Perhaps it is your room that is the inconvenient one. But now that you have ruined it by tossing crockery about, we will find you another place. Near to me.'

'Your wing is no better. You sleep in a brothel.' She caught her breath and freed her hands, making an expansive gesture towards the second floor. 'Atrocious decorating and the smell of tobacco smoke and liquor. And opium.'

'I agree,' he said, moving a little more quickly. In an aside to the overseer, he whispered, 'Get Dr Hastings and his wife. Quickly, man.' He turned back to her. 'I am sure the housekeeper would take exception to the statements about cleanliness. The rooms have been aired.'

'I am extremely sensitive,' she reminded him. 'And I know what went on there. It cannot be cleaned. It reeks of sin.' She pointed a dire finger in the direction of the back of the house. 'Only the nursery is bearable.'

'Then that is where I shall take you,' he said, kissing her hair.

'Not until you have removed the lock.'

'I will have the lock struck off at once, as soon as you are settled,' he agreed. 'But now we must get you to bed.'

She felt her abdomen begin to tighten and clung more tightly to his neck. 'There is no point in a door there at all. We will not cage this child like an animal, Michael.'

'Michael,' he murmured, as though he had never

heard his own name before. His hands were messaging her back, pressing deeply against knots of muscles that did not want to release.

'What if there was a fire? And we could not get to the baby....' She gave a small sob, for the thought frightened her and she hurt. 'And he was trapped there...with that silly little farm.'

'We will put it away,' he agreed.

She could not seem to stop the tears and the pain was still coming, even longer and harder than the last one. 'Blast and damn.'

He started at her exclamation.

'I have had care of boys, Michael. It is not as if I have never heard the words before.'

'I see.' He was smiling at her.

'And this hurts,' she reminded him.

'Of course, my love.' He stooped to get a hand behind her knees and scooped. Suddenly she was in his arms, being carried quickly towards the second floor.

'I can walk,' she said, kicking her feet.

'You have had care of boys, Madeline, but you have never had a baby. Let me help you.'

'Very well.' But she feared, before this was over, that the majority of the process would fall totally to her.

'Evelyn will be here soon and she will take care of the rest.'

'And we should have real pets for the children, not wood and wire. You may not think so, but they are both sanitary and good company for a child. You must procure a pup from the stables. And let one of the kittens from the kitchen be brought up to the bedroom to keep the rats out of the cradle.'

'I will get them at once, my dear. As soon as we have got you to bed.'

That would probably be for the best. The pain and the hurry were making things very confusing. Michael wasn't himself at all. Or perhaps he was very much himself. She was forgetting which was which. But at least he had listened to her complaints. When he put her down, it was in the governess's room in the now-doorless nursery wing. The sheets were clean and the coverlet was soft cotton, without the nonsense of satin and ribbons that would be hard to clean.

He sat her down on the edge of the mattress and helped her out of her clothing, then called for Peg to bring her a clean nightrail, slipping it over her head, and then sliding her into the bed.

He sat by her side, stroking her hand and wiping her brow until Evelyn came and chased him away so that they might get down to the serious business of having the next duke.

It seemed an eternity since Maddie had come into his office raving like a madwoman. But by Sam's watch it had been only twelve hours, which he claimed was neither too long nor too short.

Now they sat together on the top stair, waiting. Michael had waved away suggestions that they retire to the library and had refused the chairs that the servants offered to set for them in the corridor. It did not seem right that he should wait in comfort while she suffered for something he had caused to happen. But he wished that he had not succumbed to her demand to remove the nursery door. The extra layer of wood might have blocked some of his wife's cries.

It was small comfort that Colver was not here to get in the way. But damn them both. He would haul the blighter back, relinquish his bride and make the fellow marry her if it would ease her labour.

But she had called him Michael. And she had done it more than once. She had been in pain, and she had come to him for help, calling him by his given name.

The thought made him grin. He wanted to move heaven and earth for her. He would have to find a quiet place for mother and child to rest while the remodelling was done. Or he could simply demand that the workmen proceed in complete silence. Compared to housing a dozen tropical birds, how hard could it be to close up a few doors?

Maddie cried out again and the breath stopped in his throat as he waited for the shrinking silences between the pains. The uncomfortable, bony feeling of the mahogany beneath him was a small penance. And the baluster he gripped anchored him to the spot when he felt like fleeing for the brandy decanter.

'It will not be much longer,' Sam said. He was far too comfortable with the whole process, but the sounds of the cries were not ripping out his heart, because they did not come from his wife.

'How can you know how long it will take?'

'I have seen deliveries before.'

'Each one was the same, then?'

Sam paused. 'No. Each is unique. But you have nothing to fear with Evelyn there.'

'And this midwife wife of yours—' he released the newel post long enough to gesture towards the closed door '—has she been 100 per cent successful in her job?'

Sam paused. The silence was answer enough. The silence coming from the childbed was equally bad. The cries had been loud but regular. What did it mean that they had stopped?

'That's it. I am going to see her.'

'You must not.' Sam grabbed at his arm to pull him back down on the stair. 'There is no room for you there. Let Evelyn get on with her work. They will send for you when it is over.'

When it was over. What the devil did that mean? If he waited until it was over, there was a chance that he might have waited too long. He would lose her and she would never know how he felt. Sam hurried past him and stood in the doorway of the nursery, trying to prevent his entering. But blood did not give him the right to stand between a duke and what he wanted. Michael pushed past and through the door.

Maddie stared up at the crack in the ceiling and waited for the pain to stop. But the pain never seemed to stop now. It just rose and fell like waves, and the troughs were shallower and shallower. She was sure she had seen that crack in the plaster before, in happier times. But the laudanum made it hard to remember when.

'You cannot be here, your Grace. You will not wish to see.' Evelyn was using her firm and matronly voice. And she was trying to shoo a duke.

What a ludicrous idea. In Maddie's experience, dukes were very hard to shoo. Another contraction took her, and took her breath, locking her body in a vice, squeezing.

'Michael. Come away. This is no place for you.'

Sam was here, as well? Was everyone to witness this? Could she have no privacy at all? All she wished was to be alone. To crawl into the woods like an animal and wrap herself around this pain until it stopped.

'Bollocks. Get out of my way, the pair of you.' She heard the scrape of a chair, but could not manage to turn her head towards it. If she did, she was sure that the world would be on fire to match the pain she was feeling. Even now, the edges of her vision were red like blood, the crack in the plaster running like a river through a burning city. She shut her eyes to protect them from the flames.

'Madeline. Do not die!'

As if Michael could command even that. He was only a duke. She wanted to laugh, but she had not the breath for it.

But she knew he was with her, clutching her hand so hard that her fingers hurt. And for a moment, it was the only real point she could find, beyond the agony of the next contraction. She focused on it, letting it hold her to the earth.

'I am sorry. So very sorry for causing this. You need never go through it again.' A hand smoothed her forehead, wiping the hair back. 'Just the once. It will be over soon. I am here.'

How did he know? He was not a doctor. Nor was he a midwife. But what good had either of those been to her in the past few hours? She was alone, all alone with this.

Then she felt the squeeze of his hand again and she squeezed back. Or tried, at least. Another contraction took her and all the strength left her arm, directed elsewhere as though her entire body was a fist.

'Never again. You will be free if you wish. A life of luxury. Comfort. No pain, I swear. No more pain.'

How was that to be managed? she wondered. Death was the only end to pain. The idea was strangely appealing. Quiet. Dark. Silent. Painless.

'Madeline!' His voice dragged her back in time for another pain. Everything was red again, loud, sharp and hurtful. 'Do not leave me. Please. Not now. You may have your freedom tomorrow. But not until you are done with this.'

As though what she was doing was a small task. And he seemed so sure it would end. To her it felt like it would go on for ever.

'Maddie! Maddie! Stay with me. I love you.'

He could not have said it. It was a dream and the words were conjured from what she wanted to hear.

'I love you, Madeline. Damn it, woman. Do you hear me? I love you. And I will never stop telling you so. But you must come back to me so that you can hear me say it.'

'There!' Evelyn seemed pleased with something, God knew what, but the midwife had come to her other side and was leaning close, over her face.

'Maddie. Open your eyes. Just for a moment.'

She tried. Evelyn looked quite mad and nearly as dishevelled as she felt. When she turned her head, Michael looked even worse. The smile he gave her did not help at all.

'Push,' Evelyn said, low and urgent. 'When the next contraction comes, push with it. Let your body tell you what to do.'

Everything about her squeezed. But there was a pressing downward. She was making horrible animal noises.

It stopped. She gasped for breath. This was easier. She tried to speak, but there was no energy for it. She nodded to Michael, panting, unsure of what she was agreeing to. But a nod was all she could manage.

He smiled and nodded back, encouraging.

'Push.' Evelyn was nearly as commanding as a duke. And much easier to obey.

'Oh, my God.' Michael seemed shocked. But when she looked to him, he was smiling.

'It is perfectly normal, your Grace.' Evelyn, still

calm and in control. And then to her, 'We see the head, Maddie. A few more minutes. That is all we need from you. Then you can rest.'

Rest would be good. Another push came. Like the tide. She went with it. Evelyn was gone from her side, but Michael did not leave. He shot nervous glances to her belly and back to her face. Then he grinned. He looked very foolish and totally undignified.

'Again, your Grace. Again.'

'Do not call me that!' she managed to shout at Evelyn. There was nothing graceful about this. She pushed again.

There was a cry.

It was not hers.

And a shout of triumph from her husband as though he had done any of the work.

She fell back into the pillows. 'The baby?'

'Let me take her. Let me.'

Evelyn's laugh. 'Let me clean her first, Michael. Then she will go to her mother.'

Her?

But why was St Aldric so happy?

'We have a daughter,' Michael said, kissing her on the forehead. Once. Twice. Again. 'We have a daughter. And, save her mother, she is the most beautiful woman I have ever seen.'

There was a heavy weight in her arms. Warm. Soft. And it was moving.

She slept.

Chapter Twenty

When Maddie woke, her husband had not moved from her side. From somewhere, she heard a faint mewling and felt another squeeze of her hand. 'Michael?' She was hoarse from crying out. And if she looked the way she felt, hot and damp and worn out, then she must truly be a fright to behold. She should send the duke away and summon her maid to repair the damage. A mirror would surely tell her that she did not look like a duchess at all.

But he did not seem to mind. Without a word, he put an arm behind her back and held her, steadying a cup as she drank. He was cradling her close against him, just as she would hold an infant, and looking at her as though she were the most precious thing in the world.

'Where?' She leaned up, trying to see the baby. It felt strange. She was weak, but she felt weightless, as if she was floating in a pond.

'The nurse will bring her to you shortly. But you must rest.'

'Her?' He had said daughter. Then he'd called her beautiful.

He was smiling in a way she had not seen before, like a man utterly besotted. 'Could we, perhaps, name her Eleanor? It was my mother's name.'

And now, apparently, he was thinking fondly of his mother. God knew why, for they could not have been close. It was strange that he should ask, as though she was to be allowed an opinion. Strange that he should even care, after all the fuss he had made about an heir. 'You needed a son,' she reminded him. She looked eagerly towards the door. Right now, she wanted nothing more than to know that little Eleanor was healthy and safe. 'I will give you one next time. Now let me see my little girl.'

'You must not speak of a next time,' he said softly. 'This was too hard for you. I will not see you suffer again.'

'How else will we have a boy?' she said, still staring at the doorway to catch the first glimpse of her daughter.

'As I told you when I married you, I will find another way. But do not fear for Eleanor. She will be treated like a princess.'

'Of course she will,' Maddie agreed.

'And she shall have both a puppy and a kitten, just as you wished.'

She did not remember wishing for any such thing.

But her memory of the past day or so was cloudy. Except for one thing. 'You said you loved me?'

'I adore you,' he said, kissing her hair. 'You are my life. And that is why I will not risk you again. No more children, Maddie. I could not stand to go through this again.'

She waved the idea away. 'One child is not enough. Eleanor will want a playmate, or perhaps two or three.'

Michael looked doubtful and opened his mouth as if to refuse her again.

Maddie gave him a stern look. 'If it bothers you so, next time I will not let you watch. But I mean to do it again. Not today, of course. But in a year or two. It will be much less frightening now that we have done it once.'

'Shh.' He laid a hand against her shoulder, pushing her back onto the bed. 'Do not agitate yourself. You are still weak.'

She tried to sit up again. 'Not so weak that I will let you cast me off.'

'I am not casting you off,' he said patiently, then leaned in and kissed her forehead. 'I promised you your freedom from the very first. I will not hold you here and make you suffer just so that I might have an heir.'

There was no reasoning with the man. And so she grabbed his dishevelled cravat and dragged his face to hers for a kiss. For one who would forswear her company for her own good, he was not fighting very hard to resist her now. His mouth tasted salty, like sweat and tears, and he did not kiss at all like a proper duke. Instead, he responded with all the joy in his heart. She liked it very well. 'If you want no more children, we will not have the fun of making one,' she said when she was through with him.

'But you will be so busy with the renovations that you will hardly have time for me.'

'I will?' she said absently, touching his beautiful lips with her fingertip.

'You came into my office, raving about the need to tear down the walls and start afresh. It was after you turned out your precious Richard.'

'Richard was not the least bit precious,' she admitted. 'Richard was an ass. He took horrible advantage of me, then acted as though I owed him for the privilege. He was quite horrible and I wasted years of my life waiting for him.'

'And that is why I found you,' Michael said. 'So he was not totally without worth.'

'But I did not know what a devil he was until I married a saint.'

'I am not a saint,' he reminded her, still frustrated by the label.

'Of course not, Michael. You are as prone to mistakes as the rest of us. Because you are flesh and blood.' And what glorious flesh it was. Even the exhaustion of giving birth had not totally dulled her desire for the man leaning over her bed.

'And I was not raving when I came into your office,'

she added. 'I was merely expressing my opinions adamantly, because I was frustrated. And in pain.'

His expression softened immediately when she mentioned pain, and he rubbed his face against their clasped hands.

Who knew the man had such a weakness for her comfort? 'It was far more difficult for you to watch the pain than for me to experience it,' she said, and gave him a sympathetic look. 'And really, you shouldn't have been there. Men are too delicate for childbirth. It is why God has given the job to women.'

The idea shocked him to silence.

So she leaned forward and captured his lips, turning the contact into another delicious kiss. When she leaned back to look at his face, she was reminded yet again what a handsome man her husband was. And how lucky she was to have that Adonis wrapped around her little finger.

Then the nurse brought their daughter to them. And Michael had been right. She was the most beautiful girl that Maddie had ever seen, with deep blue eyes and a wisp of blonde hair. 'She looks like you,' Maddie whispered. 'And Eleanor is a lovely name. Now that I have her, my life is almost perfect.'

'Almost?' He pretended to sigh. 'How will I manage, now that I have two ladies to make unreasonable demands upon me?'

'You needn't worry about one of us, for your daughter will not even talk for a year or two.' Maddie smiled.

'But you did promise me that I could have whatever I wanted if I married you.'

'I did,' he agreed. 'And what do you command of me now, your Grace?'

'I want your heart, for the rest of my life.'

'You have it, my love.'

She ran her hand up his chest and let that finger slide beneath his neckcloth until she found a bit of bare skin to touch. 'And your body, as well.'

He swallowed nervously, but he nodded.

'And I want you to give me a house full of children, who all look like you.' Then she kissed him again to make him forget what an enormous house it was.

* * * * *

MILLS & BOON®
The Regency Collection – Part 1

MILLS & BOON®

Why shop at millsandboon.co.uk?

Each year, thousands of romance readers find their perfect read at millsandboon.co.uk. That's because we're passionate about bringing you the very best romantic fiction. Here are some of the advantages of shopping at www.millsandboon.co.uk:

* **Get new books first**—you'll be able to buy your favourite books one month before they hit the shops

* **Get exclusive discounts**—you'll also be able to buy our specially created monthly collections, with up to 50% off the RRP

* **Find your favourite authors**—latest news, interviews and new releases for all your favourite authors and series on our website, plus ideas for what to try next

* **Join in**—once you've bought your favourite books, don't forget to register with us to rate, review and join in the discussions

Visit **www.millsandboon.co.uk**
for all this and more today!